THE KINGDOMS OF SAVANNAH

THE KINGDOMS
OF SAVANNAH

GEORGE DAWES GREEN

THORNDIKE PRESS
A part of Gale, a Cengage Company

GALE
A Cengage Company

**LIBRARY OF CONGRESS CIP DATA ON FILE.
CATALOGUING IN PUBLICATION FOR THIS BOOK
IS AVAILABLE FROM THE LIBRARY OF CONGRESS.**

ISBN-13: 979-8-8857-8375-0 (hardcover alk. paper)

Published in 2022 by arrangement with Celadon Books.

Printed in Mexico
Print Number : 1   Print Year : 2023

Esther, this is the one passage in the book where I can't ask your help, can't get your insights and razor editing, and it's starting to sound a bit long-winded and unshaped, and I'm sure you'd cut this whole first sentence, wouldn't you? Anyway, I will love you always and this book is for you.

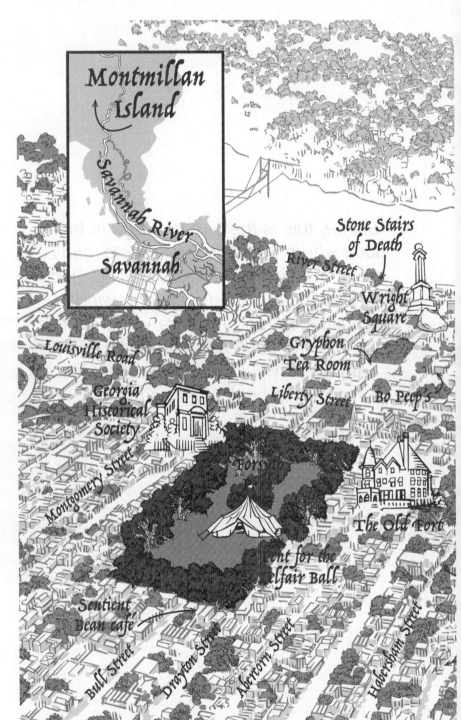

PROLOGUE:
WHY DIDN'T THE SKELETON
CROSS THE ROAD?

A soft spring night in Savannah. In an hour Luke will be murdered, stabbed to death, and Stony will be snatched off the streets and hurled into darkness, but for now it's just the two of them walking to their favorite bar for a nightcap. Luke's a white kid, early twenties; he has big-ass bones and hulks when he walks. Stony's Black, forty-three. A bit lame from a bum knee, which various websites have been telling her is a torn this or an inflamed that, or gout maybe or rheumatism. Her mother says rheumatism would be just deserts for sleeping in the woods all the time, out in the damp. "You're lucky you don't get no *fungus*. You're lucky you ain't been ate by no *wild pigs*." Her mother loves to mutter the names of dangerous things. Fungus, snakes, the police, that Nigerian prince tryin to catch her money. Stony misses her. She thinks maybe tomorrow she'll take the city bus down to the Ta-

11

temville neighborhood for a visit. But for now she and Luke make their way peacefully around Lafayette Square, past the fancy houses with their gas lamps and dark gardens. Stony can pick out the fragrances. The wisteria, the early tea roses, jessamine. She takes after her mother, and there's always any number of things eating at her, but tonight she's not brooding about anything. Tonight she loves Savannah, she loves Luke, her Kingdom is more or less safe. Tonight she's floating.

Then just as they're about to turn onto Drayton Street, Luke says, "Shh! Shh!" and stops. Stony hears it too. Whistling. The guy they call the Musician, who wanders around the city at night and whistles. First his tune comes low and caressing like a clarinet, then it swoops up an octave and it's a flute, as clear as ice. They can't see him. You never see the Musician when he's whistling, but the melody seems to come from all around, from the trees and the porches. When a mockingbird to their left starts singing, the Musician holds up a moment and then *replies* to that bird. Stony's in bliss.

But along comes a ghost tour to fuck up the moment.

Open hearse. Full of tourists. Rattling up Drayton Street, with the ghoul-guide on a

12

loudspeaker booming out: "OK, GUYS! WHY *DIDN'T* THE SKELETON CROSS THE ROAD?"

Wait for it.

"HE HAD *NO GUTS*! HA HA HA HA HA!"

As the hearse passes, one of the drunken tourists looks down and shouts: "YO, FRANKENSTEIN! YO, UGLY WITCH!"

Then it's gone. The Musician's gone too. Stony and Luke strain their ears, but nothing.

Ghost tours are a plague, she thinks. I live in a city whose principal industries are death and the production of bad puns about death, and no wonder we all get so gloomy. But when she looks over to Luke, she finds he's grinning. Actually quite pleased to have been cast as a mythical Savannah monster. He's bipolar and he's been on the upswing for some days, with money in his pocket from life-modeling for SCAD — the Savannah College of Art and Design — and now he brings forth his sweet childish laugh, which is surprising for a man so big, and Stony can't help but laugh with him. Ahead is the sign for their bar: Miss Bo Peep with her neon shepherd's crook and naughty pantaloons, watching over her neon sheep and also over the flock of inebriates lighting

13

up smokes on the sidewalk beneath her. Coming to Peep's always feels like coming home. Stony and Luke get a dozen fist bumps and high fives before they're even at the door. Rednecks, shrimp packers, teachers from SCAD, soldiers from the 3rd Infantry, old Billy Sugar with his long, grizzled whiskers. He's here most nights but never goes inside because he's always got his dog, Gracie, with him, and anyway has no money, and anyway prefers the night air. He drinks from a flask, which he shares with old, wizened Jane, who was a hooker back in the days when sailors in the big ships were allowed port leave (she must be eighty but insists she's only "semiretired"). Everyone likes to close their night at Peep's. Stony and Luke greet everyone and work their way inside. Some patrons are just leaving so they manage to grab stools at the horseshoe bar. Sinéad is playing on the jukebox. On the walls are a thousand photos of the original owner, a bootlegger known as Bo Peep, wearing a porkpie hat and posing with all his chums and cronies.

Right away the bartender brings them a margarita and a PBR.

This bartender's name is Jaq. She asks for no money, never does. Just sets out their drinks and goes back to work.

14

But Stony calls after her: "No, Jaq, tonight we're payin, we're flush! I found a Bolen Bevel arrowhead. Sweet one. Got good money." Not *great* money: eighty-five bucks. But Stony sets a twenty on the bar and insists, "Do *not* give me no change, bitch."

Jaq smiles and rings the tip bell and moves to the far side of the horseshoe bar, and Stony watches her.

Luke murmurs, "Hey, Stony."

"What?"

"Your crush is showing."

"Ha ha. Is it?"

Laughing it off, but he's right. It's a thorny one. Three nights a week, ever since Stony got back into town from the Kingdom, she's been coming in here to gaze at this girl. Jaq's twenty-three. She's Black with a fountain of box braids, and cuts such a sweet compact figure in her jeans and her little crop tee that when she stretches for a pour from the taps, all her admirers must suck in their breaths. And there are many of those, particularly now so close to closing: boys who linger at the horseshoe bar and give her hopeful looks because sometimes on a whim she *will* pick one out and go off with him. In the late-night rush she works fast and her braids fly and she's snappish with the clientele ("Stop waving your money

15

at me, asshole! You think I'm a *frog*? That I only see *movement*?") but she's often laughing and even when she's not her eyes have little darts of light, and she's always curious and questions everything. When she gets a break, she'll pick up her camera and furry microphone and make videos for her MFA application project, which she calls *Some Town Out of a Fable.*

"I will admit, though," says Luke, "you did just get a smile from her."

"Oh, yeah?" says Stony. "I'm sure she's really into crones."

"You're not a crone."

"Thank you, Luke."

"You're just so very fucking old."

They sip their drinks and listen to the jukebox and keep watching Jaq.

Till Stony feels a tap on her shoulder. She swings round on her stool and it's some guy, pale and clean-shaven and small, with a jacket that doesn't fit and a black polyester tie, like he's a Jehovah's Witness or something. He says, "Hey, you're Matilda Stone, right?"

She shrugs. Matilda is her name but her friends never use it.

He says, "You're like an archaeologist?"

A curt nod so as not to encourage him.

"Like, a professor?"

16

Actually, no, she's not a professor of anything. She's a *contract* archaeologist, though she hasn't been fully employed in a long time. She lives off the occasional arrowhead, or when the county's paving a new parking lot they bring her in to make sure it's not on a burial ground. Plus now she's got a "patron" who helps her out a bit. Though if this dude here wants to think she's a professor, let him.

She asks, "Do we know each other?"

"You don't remember me? Lloyd? From Statesboro?"

"Nope."

"We met at Wild Wings."

"I doubt that."

The guy has a friend who comes up now. Also clean-shaven and buzz cut, also with a tie and ill-fitting jacket. Stony wonders, is this some kind of JW *convention*?

But as soon as they get Jaq's attention they order shots of Jack Daniel's (so no, they're not JWs). And Lloyd buys Stony another margarita. Which is nice of him, but the price is, now he's bought the right to bore her. Which he does, in a cracker whine pitched right up there with the insects. Starting with a discussion of his work. He sells wholesale plumbing supplies out of Statesboro. Stony knows Statesboro, has

17

driven through it many times and always felt sorry for it, partly for its ugliness but mostly for the banality of that name, in a part of Georgia where towns have names like Enigma and Sunsweet and El Dorado.

Lloyd seems to notice that she's drifting, for he suddenly shifts to, "Hey, ain't them screamin eagles awesome?" For a moment her ears perk up. But turns out he's not talking about wild raptors. The Screaming Eagles, it seems, are a sports team. Back in Statesboro. Winner of last year's inter-subdivisional something or other. When all she wants to do is gaze at Jaq.

Then comes a little surprise. He brings his face close to hers and says, "Hey, you know you got yellow eyes — you know that?"

"Yeah?" she says. "Well my daddy was a jackal."

Little joke but he doesn't laugh. He keeps looking into her eyes.

Oh Jesus. It finally dawns on her. He's hitting on her.

What's this about?

Nobody's hit on her in quite a while. And I *could* use some cock, she thinks, and maybe he's got a perfectly nice one.

Though on second thought, no. Since it would come attached to the rest of him, to

18

the wholesale plumbing supplies and the Screaming Eagles. She says, "Hey, listen, I gotta talk to my friend about something so excuse me, OK, Floyd?" And swings her stool back to face the bar.

To find a camera staring at her.

Jaq, on her break, is recording her.

Shit. Stony's heart jumps in its cage.

"Stony," Jaq asks, "would you tell us about where you live?"

Cameras terrify Stony. She knows she's mentioned to Jaq, more than once, that lately she's been living in a Kingdom. But those were slips. She sometimes drinks too much. The whole Kingdom thing has to be kept quiet. "Jaq, not everyone wants to hear about that."

But Jaq's breath is so fresh and sweet and she pleads so tenderly. "Just a little bit for my doc? Before I have to start working again? Do you *really* live in a Kingdom?"

And Stony finds herself crumbling. "Well. I do."

"What's it like?"

"But I mean I just shouldn't —"

"Is it in Savannah?"

"Near."

"Who else lives there?"

"The King's soldiers."

"Who are they?"

19

Stony feels a pinch — Luke squeezing her thigh. *Shut up.*

Right. She knows. But maybe the margarita has gone to her head a bit because she's feeling kind of loose-tongued. She wants to say just one thing, and she does. "They're free people. OK? The King's soldiers are the only free people to ever live in the State of Georgia. They *live,* that's all. They're not on the Savannah Death Trip, they're not ghosts, they're not anybody's slaves. You can't fuck with 'em."

This all comes out scrappier than she intends. Jumps out, at a moment when there's nothing playing on the jukebox. The patrons of Bo Peep's are listening because they see Jaq recording her, and now Luke is squeezing her *hard.* She feels faint. She lowers her eyes and mumbles, "Hey, sorry. Talk to Luke, OK?"

Jaq obligingly pivots the camera away from her and says, "Luke! What's up?"

"Not too much," he says. Then he grins. "But you know who we just heard? Out there? The Musician."

"He's out tonight?" says Jaq.

"And whistling so gorgeous, and I swear to God he did a duet with a mockingbird." Giving that Luke laugh. The bar loves him, and Jaq loves him, while Stony's still sunk

20

in her sense of shame. A feeling of humiliation that verges on nausea. Luke is saying, "And them tourists on the ghost tour, you know what they shouted at us? *Yo, Frankenstein! Yo, Witch!* That's *us.* I mean we're the stars of Savannah, Jaq! Ha ha ha!"

Someone at the far side of the horseshoe insists: "Need a beer!"

Jaq calls back, "What you need is to chill the fuck out." And holds her camera on Luke.

Stony takes this moment to steal away. She goes outside and stands in the night air. Bums a smoke from Billy Sugar and says hello to his dog: "Hey there, Gracie." Giving her a scratch behind the ears. Then she leans against the big front window, under the light of Peep's peachy pantaloons, and asks herself, why did I say all that? Why did I feel I had to share my crazy shit with all of Peep's? Jesus. Poor homeless woman thinks she lives in a fairy Kingdom and commands an army of elves? How fucking pathetic. She feels sick now, swoony. Drank too much, clearly, but can't remember doing it. She shuts her eyes and feels like she's bouncing around in her own rib cage, bouncing and dropping but there's no bottom, no splash, just an ever-spreading feeling of unwellness and trouble.

21

Somebody speaks to her. Not Billy Sugar, some other guy. She hopes that whoever it is, whoever's standing here, will go away. But he keeps talking. "Hey, Matilda. I got a message for you. Hey, look at me, Matilda."

Oh God. It's Lloyd from Statesboro.

Matilda is officially her name, but no one ever uses it except employers and the police. And now this guy. She opens her eyes. "Do me a favor and get the fuck outta my face?"

"Matilda, listen. The boss sent me to get you."

"Huh?"

"You gotta save the Kingdom."

"Wait," she says. Trying to collect herself. Take this all in. Who is this guy? What does he know about the Kingdom? Does he really work for the boss?

"He needs you right now," says Lloyd. He hands her a note. She focuses.

Meet me now. Bad shit. Lloyd knows where.

She raises her eyes. "Where?"

"I can't say but I'll drive you there."

She shakes her head. "Uh-uh. I just met you."

"Awright. You got a car?"

She shakes her head.

22

He shrugs. "You wanna take an Uber? OK. Get an Uber and follow me."

"I can't get an Uber. I don't have a cell phone. Lemme get Luke."

"No, the boss just wants *you,* Matilda. Says it's top secret, says it's the King's treasure and all. Hey, what about a taxi? Why don't you call a taxi?"

She tries to laugh. "A *taxi?* Like, are there still taxis?"

He shrugs. "I don't know, Matilda. I just gotta get you to the boss."

And she's thinking, maybe she should trust him? He seems like a creep but likely he's just boring. He's kind of cracker-formal, a little awkward and gruff, but that doesn't make him dangerous. You shouldn't pigeonhole people, Stony. He's just trying to help out here. And abruptly she says, "OK. I'll go with you."

"Yeah?" he says. Very politely. "You sure you comfortable with that?"

"Uh-huh." She puts her hand on his arm. "Kinda drunk but yeah. Wait." She turns to old Billy Sugar and tries not to slur her words. "Hey, Billy? Tell Luke I had to run?"

Billy with his beard looks like someone from the Old Testament. The way he's scowling at Lloyd from Statesboro. "Stony? You sure?"

23

"I'm good, yeah," she says, and off she goes with Lloyd from Statesboro.

Actually she's not good at all, but for the Kingdom she'd go anywhere, with anyone. She lets him prop her up, and they cross Drayton and head toward the gloom of Madison Square. She asks, "But what *about* the Kingdom? What's the matter? What's this . . . crisis, tell me."

"I don't know," says Lloyd. "Boss says. That's all I know."

He keeps pulling her with him, hustling her along, and she's thinking, oh maybe I shouldn't. Be doing this. But she's really confused. Her thoughts are like moths and she can't corral them. She tries to take her arm back.

"Walk," he tells her.

He's not asking. Oh shit. And he's strong. So much stronger than she is. Mistake. Shouldn't be here.

But then a voice: "Hey, darlin, hold up."

She turns. It's Luke. Her gentle giant, come to rescue her.

"Stony, what's up?"

Lloyd from Statesboro replies for her. "My girlfriend, she's a little drunk."

Luke shakes his head. "Not your girl-friend."

"Tonight she is."

24

"Get your hands off her." Sounding resolute, which isn't Luke's usual manner. Stony gathers herself and steps toward him, struggling to keep her legs straight. When she falls, she manages to fall in his direction. He catches her and puts his arm around her, and turns her back toward the warm light of Bo Peep and her neon sheep.

"You OK, Stony?"

"Just. I might. That guy. That . . . something. In my drink."

"Try to walk," says Luke. "Let's get out of here."

Walk, she thinks. Walk is easy. Keep my eyes on Miss Peep, and lean on Luke, and head toward that light. And she does manage a few steps. Till that other guy — Lloyd's buddy — steps in front of them.

"Give her back," he says.

"Oh get fucked," says Luke, pushing past him. But some event takes place. It's too quick for Stony to follow but involves a gleam of metal. Luke groans. Blood wells on his T-shirt. He has such a look of helplessness. He's suffering because he can't rescue her. As he reaches for her, he sags, falls to his knees, and that breaks her heart. A man's hand covers her mouth. She bites at it but with no effect. A pickup truck stops beside them, and the men take Luke and

25

heave him into the pickup bed, and shove Stony into the cab. Lloyd from Statesboro slides in next to her and turns the key.

She keeps trying to cry out. No sound comes.

She sees the door handle. It's in the shadows and out of focus, but it's her last chance. Gotta do this, she thinks. Pull the handle, open the door, jump out. Shout. Run. Go now.

Nothing happens.

Get that handle, she thinks. Open the door, roll out.

Watching her hand from afar as it slowly gropes for the handle. Please, girl. Can't you go quicker?

But her hand moves as though through syrup. Lloyd, while driving, reaches over calmly and places her hand back in her lap. Then her mother shows up at the window. "You can't trust strangers, Matilda. Some of them are bad people."

"I see that, Mom."

"They'll drug you, darlin. They'll *hurt* you."

"I know, Mom. But you're not helping."

CHAPTER ONE:
SOME HIDEOUS COMPROMISE

Ransom Musgrove has been summoned to the house of his youth, the Romanesque revival mansion from the 1880s that everyone calls the "Old Fort" — on account of the parapet and the grand turret and the gargoyles and all the ivied brickwork. As he comes up the walk he gets flashes from his boyhood. Under that pecan, first kiss with Debbie Gannon. Under the crepe myrtle, third base with Lu Ann Farris. Up in the brown turkey fig tree, wasn't there some death match with his big brother, David? He has a vague memory of David taunting him, of getting so mad he went for David's throat and forgot to hold on to the limb. He doesn't recall what happened next.

Then at the front steps he has one more memory.

Thirteen years old. Standing out here awaiting the carpool to school and daydreaming, when his mother appeared on the

27

balcony. Although it was a bright, sunny morning, she was drunk. Clearly she'd been out partying the night before and hadn't been to bed yet. She began to disparage him in the third person, one of her favorite pastimes. She said, "While the kid dawdles there like an idiot, gathering wool, concocting his little fantasies about how the world *should* be, the *real* world keeps marching on, doesn't it? Clomp clomp clomp, crushing his little dreams. Does he even notice? No, he's too stupid. Is he going to be a hobo? Well yes, that's certain, unless he gets some ambition and starts kiting checks. Ha ha ha."

He hoped that the arrival of the carpool would shut her up. And it did, for a moment. Mrs. Tarkanian's big Suburban pulled up, and he squeezed into the second row with two other kids while Mother, up on that balcony, produced a silk handkerchief and waved it. Mrs. Tarkanian waved back. "Hey, Morgana." His mother said, in a loud tragic voice, "Hey, Laurel. Goodbye, Laurel. Goodbye, my son who is destined to be a vagabond." Her position when drunk was always: I'll speak the truth and the public be damned. As the carpool pulled away he felt his mortification in his jawbone and his spine, and silently begged for death. How-

28

ever, the other kids made no comment. Maybe they'd thought she was joking? Or they hadn't understood the word? However, years later a girl who'd been in that car told him she'd thought it was "romantic, scary but kind of romantic the way your mom stood up on that balcony that day telling the whole neighborhood how you were *destined to be a vagabond.*"

It's not lost on him that Morgana's prophecy has come true.

Up four steps to the porch, to the front door with the spiderweb fanlight and sidelight, and he hasn't even seen her yet but already he feels the bad juice in his veins, and has to remind himself that *she* summoned *him* (sending her accountant to find his tent under the Harry S Truman exit ramp), that he's still a free man, he's thirty-three years old and should she try to start anything, to flip any of his switches, he can just turn and walk away. Anytime he's so inclined. So he tells himself.

He turns the door crank. Here comes Betty the maid.

"*Raaan*-sum!"

Betty's a white woman in her late thirties. She grew up on a farm in Odom, Georgia, and wears a perpetually awestruck look, and dresses in baggy browns and grays, and always has a slow and languorous drawl even on the rare occasions when she isn't riding her magic carpet of downers. When she says, "Oh, your mama will be so glad!" the last words seem to roll on forever: *sooo glayyyy*-uddd.

She hugs his neck and then holds the door open for him.

He steps inside.

His eyes have to adjust. The foyer is always kept in the gloaming, with only a thin light slanting down from the oriel window. There's the pomp of the staircase, and the bronze sconces and the walnut secretary desk, and the still lifes and fantastical landscapes that Morgana loves. His forebears scowl down from their frames. He appreciates that none of them pretend to be happy.

However, Betty does pretend. When he asks how she's doing, she smiles and says, "So well, Ransom." *Raaan*-sum. He knows this to be false. A few weeks ago she went to the home of her ex-boyfriend's new flame and borrowed a cup of sugar from her. Then found her ex's Durango on the street, and emptied the sugar into the tank. Not coy about it. Bystanders took out their phones and recorded her. She posed with that cup the way Annie Oakley would pose with her

30

pistol. Then she returned the cup to the new girlfriend and thanked her. The videos became popular of course. Now she's in a great deal of trouble but keeps a brave face and says to Ransom, "It's such a lovely *dayyyy*, isn't it?" and leads him straight to his mother.

Morgana stands at the dining room table. She's plumping up an immense arrangement of flowers. "My beloved," she coos, raising her cheek for the requisite buss. "You look terribly thin. Are you eating dandelions and wild asparagus?"

"I'm eating fine, Mother."

And somewhat to his surprise, she drops it. Doesn't needle him at all. Doesn't accuse him of "assuming some pose of dereliction to which you are frankly *unentitled*," or charge him with "plunging a dagger into the heart of your family." She simply gestures for him to take a seat. With a quick smile, as she resumes her arranging.

She must truly need something.

She is wearing a mauve silk shirt and her honeycomb brooch, and looks quite formal. Not "imperial": her enemies call her that, but really she's too small and birdlike to fit that description — and, just now, too busy. She's laying in a base for her spray. Building a pedestal of ruscus and aspidistra and

31

stock and freesia (Ransom grew up amid her flowers and knows them all). She asks, "Would you care for iced tea?"

"Thanks, yes."

She nods; Betty goes off.

He watches his mother work. The snip-snip of the shears. After a moment though, she frowns and says, "Oh it's impossible."

"What is?"

"It's for my event tonight, the Spring Soiree for the Disabled. Every year the big spray is all anyone talks about, and every year it gets harder to assemble. Would you just look at *these*?" Holding up a few stems loaded with garish blooms. "They're called Papaya Popsicles. They're ludicrous yet must be given prominence, because they were grown by Rebecca Cressling, who donated sixty thousand dollars last year. What do you think?"

"Sort of blaring."

"Yet it gets worse."

She shows him a clutch of black blossoms with long white whiskers. "We must also give pride of place to *these*. Bat flowers. Have you ever seen the like? Grown by Jane Rundle with great care in her greenhouse. And why did she do this? No one can say. But she has bequeathed us one point five million dollars in her will, so we must not dishonor her little nightmares. I thought of cutting the stems long, that they might loom over the whole show like so many Grim Reapers — a metaphor for how Jane's death looms over *us*. Looms yet never quite *happens,* does it? But that would demote the Popsicles. You see my dilemma? I have to feature both Popsicles *and* bat flowers. I must create some hideous compromise."

"Mother?"

"Yes, dear."

"You asked to see me."

She turns to give him a full look.

"Right. Well. Yesterday Johnny Cooper came by."

Johnny Cooper manages Musgrove Investigations — one of the many little sidelines created by Ransom's father and still in Morgana's possession.

He says, "You still haven't sold that?"

"No, but I've rather neglected it. Of course, it's never brought me a dime in profit. But then it didn't for your father either. Frankly I believe profit wasn't the point for him. I believe he used it in his business dealings. To keep track of his rivals."

Ransom's gaze flicks away from her: he turns to the portraits, his scowling forebears. She catches the shift.

"Darling," she asks, "are you hiding a smile?"

"Why would I do that?"

"Because you think he was keeping track of *me*."

Just at that moment though, Betty reappears, with a pitcher of her lemony tea and two of the pineapple-crystal glasses inherited from Great-great-aunt Inez.

"And Betty," says Morgana, "do you suppose you could stop by Mooney's and collect those three hams?"

"Right away, ma'am."

"None but the long-cured. If he tries to pass off one of those honey-glazed tourist things, tell him to shove it back up from whence it came. You hear?"

"Uh-huh."

"And get Mr. Riley to check the oil on the beast."

"Yes ma'am, uh-huh, I will." Adding, as she withdraws: "Oh handsome Ransom, you need to come live here with us."

Haaaand-some *Raaaan*-som.

Then she's gone.

Morgana puts down the shears, and takes a seat.

The house is still but for the grandfather clock with the slight lisp and her sigh. "Well, maybe he *was* having me followed. I mean

34

I'd have deserved it. I wasn't a good wife. Not then anyway. I felt I had to live in a state of constant romantic excitement. I was reading too many eighteenth-century novels. I recall thinking, what's the point of living if you can't live in a swirl of scandal? I wonder if there *is* a file on me? I wonder if there are any good surveillance photos of me?"

She sips from the pineapple glass. She has a wistful look.

"At any rate," she says, "I know your father loved that business. He loved going with Johnny on stakeouts. And taking you along. You remember?"

"Yeah. I liked going. Dad would pick up a bucket of wings from Church's and we'd eat in the car. Then I'd fall asleep and Dad and Johnny would watch the Thunderbird Motel all night."

"And when you got home I'd always make you tell me everything. I'd say, Report, and you would. You recall that?"

He nods. But feels a bit impatient. "So, Mother. What did Johnny want?"

"Oh, well, it seems our little detective agency has been approached by a big client. Or rather the lawyer for a big client. The client himself is in jail."

"For what?"

"Arson. Also I'm told the state has reached

35

for a murder charge."

"Jesus. You're talking about Archie Guzman?"

"You know the case?"

"Everyone in Savannah knows the case. What's he want from you?"

"Well, naturally, an investigation. Why, does that seem strange? You think he should go to one of the bigger outfits? Such as that fetid place that does all the repossessions? What's that called again?"

"Screven."

She makes a face of disgust. "Yes yes, Screven Security. Honestly I was wondering myself: Why pick little us over them? So I called Burt Randolph — Guzman's lawyer — and put it to him. And you know what he told me? He said ours is an old and esteemed agency."

Ransom can't help but roll his eyes. "Old, for sure. You got a seventy-year-old gumshoe who needs a hip replacement. Plus your three wino part-timers, they're old, plus that rotting old office over the souvenir shop."

"But in fact he said *greatly* esteemed. Also he raised, unprompted, the question of a retainer."

"How much?"

"Oh they're being quite generous."

"How much?"

She sniffs. Waits a beat. "Two hundred thousand dollars."

Ransom gives a low whistle.

"Plus three hundred more," she goes on, "should we happen to uncover evidence leading to Guzman's exoneration."

"Good God. That's insane."

"It *is* rather a large —"

"No, I mean it's insane that Guzman thinks *anything* will lead to his exoneration. Have you read the papers?"

"A bit. I know he's somewhat unpopular —"

"Despised. By everyone. Rich and poor, young and old, it's unanimous. Everyone hates the Gooze. He bulldozes anything that's beautiful, he builds the ugliest crap imaginable and sues everyone for the right to do it, and he's the meanest slumlord in town. Treats his tenants like dogs. For himself he built that pig mansion out in Thunderbolt, you've seen it, it's a pile of crap. And now he's gone and burned a man alive."

She presents her mild face. "Well, he says he didn't do that."

It's this look particularly, the lamblike expression she sometimes employs to suggest she has no angles, that she's really *not* relentlessly seeking the hidden switches in

37

the psyches of everyone close to her, but only searching for *the truth:* this is what gets under his skin. He feels the poison rising. His voice comes out too loud. "Mother, they found the gas can in a dumpster. With his fingerprints all over it. The house was eaten up by termites and he'd lost his C. of O., and he'd been telling his workers he was gonna torch the thing. And he *knew* folks were camping on the second floor. He *let* them do that. If they were working for him, that was part of their pay. But this detail must have slipped his mind, in his eagerness to collect that insurance. So poor Luke Kitchens wakes up and the house beneath him is in flames and he can't get out. Doors were all chained up. Place was a deathtrap. The Gooze *knew* that. Tell me you're not taking him as a client."

She keeps the soft face. "Why, what's the problem?"

"What's the temptation?"

She thinks for a moment. "Well. Greed, I suppose."

She smiles. Admiring her own candor.

But she adds, "Also, my beloved, the man does maintain his innocence. Even if he is, as you say, universally loathed — a sort of modernday Deadeye Dick — we might at least examine him on the question."

"We?"

"You must accompany me to the jail."

"No."

"But you must. I need you."

"Still. No."

"You still have your license to practice law, I checked. Burt Randolph has attached you to the case. And we can go and have a nice privileged chat with Mr. Guzman, without his people there. Draw our own conclusions. You can drive. You know I *hate* driving on the Southside. Those awful strip malls, all that traffic. Which reminds me, your friend Moses Jones? The paraplegic? I know he likes to go to that café by Forsyth Park in his wheelchair, and I hate to think of him negotiating the traffic around there. I've been thinking the Society might set him up in a little carriage house just around the corner from the café. So there'd be no busy streets for him to cross. Don't you think?"

"Jesus. You trying to bribe me?"

"Of course. And extravagantly, I might add, since all I'm asking in return is a ride to the jailhouse. I'm not asking you to come back home. Or go through rehab. I'd just like you to sit in on one meeting."

"I told you, no. Get my brother."

"Don't be absurd. I need a curious mind

on this. Besides, Guzman has asked for you."

"Why?"

"That's a real *mystery,* isn't it?" she says, stretching the word with a playful drawl. Then she rises and returns to her flowers. Leaving him to his decision.

It is, he can't deny, an intriguing offer.

At his encampment under the Harry S Truman Parkway exit ramp there are at least a dozen folks who are homeless because of the Gooze. Owing to deformities in Georgia tenant law, landlords are not obliged to give thirty days' notice. With Guzman you're lucky to get twenty-four hours to hump your stuff out to the street. He'll put you out on Christmas at midnight if the whim strikes him, and you can sit on your couch on the sidewalk, in the freezing rain, while carolers stand before you and sing hymns of peace and loving-kindness. It would be a treat to see him in shackles.

Jaq comes down Waldburg Street on her bike to the big black skeleton of the house that Guzman torched. It's surrounded by a new chain-link fence, and she cruises past slowly, looking for a good camera angle. But nothing satisfies, so she loops round to the alley and comes at the house from behind.

40

Between a dumpster and a wildly overgrown Cherokee rose is somebody's back gate: she locks the bike there. Then crosses to the chain-link fence, scanning for a good spot to set up. But this still isn't the right vantage. There are too many live oaks dripping with too much Spanish moss: they block a clear view of the second floor, where the horror went down. She needs to be inside this fence.

One time in high school she and four classmates from the Treutlan School broke into a beach house on Tybee Island. But this is different, this time she's alone at a crime scene and she's not a teenager anymore, she's twenty-three, and if the police show up, they won't take this kindly.

But she has things she wants to say about this crime, on camera and in that yard. So she glances to either side and then jams a toe into the fence, and sticks her fingers in the diamond mesh and pulls herself up. Reaches high to grip the branch of a sycamore, swings her legs over the top of the fence, and drops into the yard.

Still the stench of the fire.

Stepping carefully so as not to place her foot upon any nail or cooked rat or shard of glass till she finds a spot with a good open view. She shrugs off her backpack. Takes

41

out the camera and tripod, and sets up with the camera aimed up toward the charred beams of the second floor. She stops down the aperture, then goes to stand in the frame.

"He was twenty-two," she says, "a year younger than me. He was a big guy. He had an infectious laugh, and he was the sweetest dude I've ever known. They found him, they say, in the fetal position. They say he must have crawled across the floor from his sleeping bag and got all the way to right *there* where I'm pointing. By that fire escape. But the door was chained. *That* door. The fire was started by the owner of the building, a douche by the name of Archibald Guzman. Known popularly as the Gooze. I'd call him a demon but that'd make him sound special when he's not, he's just a douche. How'd he get his money? He found some trick or something that lets him spread these buildings all over town that are ugly as shit yet people actually pay to live in them. He just keeps building them and nobody can stop him. But this place here was falling apart so he burned it down for the insurance. And Luke was sleeping up there. Luke did odd jobs for the Gooze, he'd clean up construction sites and shit. When you work for the Gooze, you get shit wages but also perks,

like you get to camp out in his empty buildings. But when the Gooze decided to burn
this down, he was so excited to slosh gaso-
line everywhere and light that match, he
forgot there might be somebody sleeping up
there. Luke, he drank a lot and couldn't
hold a real job. Everybody knew he was
bipolar, and he had a lot of bad days. But
on his good days, God, he was so happy.
He was like when a little kid makes a drawing of the sun with crayons."

As she's telling this to the camera, three
children show up behind her, in the alley,
standing at the fence. Neighborhood kids,
maybe ten years old. They gawk at her. They
press their foreheads against the chain-link.
She tries to ignore them.

She says, "He couldn't always pay for his
beers, but sometimes he'd get work doing
life-modeling, or he'd turn a trick with some
businessman from Macon or something,
and then he'd come in and give me a big
tip. I'd go, Luke, you find work? And he'd
go, Oh yes, I'm everybody's dream. I'm in
such demand. He was always in love with
straight boys, and they'd hit him up for
loans and he'd give them whatever he had.
He loved to talk about boys. Any boy I
wanted, he'd rate for me. He'd try to warn
me off the treacherous ones. One time he

43

said, Yeah, *now* he's got you creamin — but soon you'll be *screamin.* And he'd laugh, and oh my God, his laugh. When he laughed, everybody would laugh. And those that he loved, he *really* loved. His murder was a Savannah kind of murder, I mean just a total fuckup. Just because some rich asshole didn't really give a shit about anything but his bank account. I think of Luke crawling across the floor and seeing that iron chain on the door and then I hate the Gooze so much it makes me crazy. And mostly this town doesn't care. I've been saying this town is some kind of fable or fairy tale, but what it really is, it's a pit of vipers."

The kids, their stare.

Doubtless other folks are watching too, from their porches.

She's making a spectacle of herself, and somebody must be calling the cops by now. She's still got her fury up, feels the flush on her collarbone, and it's intoxicating; she doesn't want to quit. But it's time. She collects her camera and tripod, and climbs back over the fence, and hands her backpack down to one of the kids. Might as well put him to use.

The kid's got a grin on his face.

He must know that somebody died in that house. Yet he's chuckling like there's some kind of joke here.

She jumps down and retrieves the pack. The kid says, "That was great."

"What was?"

"That stuff you were saying. You high or somethin?"

All the kids laugh. She unlocks the bike and pedals off, and she can still hear them laughing.

Christ, she thinks, they're right. I really am entertaining myself, aren't I?

Ransom drives his mother down Waters Avenue in her classic 1989 burgundy Caprice. It's a slow, majestic ride. He's wearing the sports jacket that she dug out of his closet in the turret ("We need to make a certain impression, darling"), and it still fits though it dates from his college days, and the car is warm and he can smell the old leather of the seats, also her Iris Poudre fragrance. The outing has a formal feel, like the church trips of his boyhood.

As ever, the Caprice has the responsiveness of an aircraft carrier.

They don't take Abercorn Street because Abercorn turns into an endless strip mall south of Victory Drive: Morgana calls it "the largest repository of soul-destroying folderol in the universe." Instead they take Waters

45

Avenue. She loves Waters. It's all old-school Savannah, weird and ebullient the whole way. Rosette's Lounge (NO LOITERERS! NO DRUGS!); the Relentless Church of the Lord; Da Boyz in Da Hood Carwash (BEST HAND JOB IN TOWN); Cheryl-Ann's "Chinese" Take-Out; the Open Door Holy Deliverance Church (BEHOLD THE HAND — IT'S NOT SHORTENED THAT IT CANNOT SAVE!).

Also several businesses that were founded by Ransom's father and are still in Morgana's possession. At each of these she has remarks. For example, at Ottling's Fresh Crab and Seafood she notes that the cute little crabs on the sign have been replaced by a streamlined logo reading OTTLING'S FRESH, and she mutters, "Oh what has occurred *here*? Fresh *what*? Is this an accusation? Do they mean Ottling himself is fresh? This is clearly the work of some SCAD design student. They're all inculcated in that aesthetic of empty style; it sucks the meaning out of everything. I must speak to Hiram Ottling about this."

Then, when they pass the clutch of redneck loiterers about Pillow's Car Wash & Detailing: We give you the BIZNESS!, she wonders aloud, "Do you think our employees still wash cars once in a while, or is

46

the 'bizness' now strictly the sale of meth-amphetamine?"

The red light at Derenne Avenue. A hobo stands there. He's got tattoos and a dozen earrings and a blue mohawk. He's dressed in wounded-vet getup. And he's flying a sign, which reads:

FALLUJAH NOV '04
3RD BATTALION, 1ST MARINES
VICTORY?
YOU DECIDE

Morgana says, "One of your worthy companions?"

"Hatchet Head. Got a dollar?"

She digs in her purse and finds one, and lowers the window and passes it. Hatchet Head does a double take when he sees her, and another when he spots Ransom behind the wheel. He grins. He's missing some teeth. He offers Morgana a fist bump, and she returns a frozen smile.

At White Bluff they pass a billboard for one of Archie Guzman's crappy condo sprawls. Photo of the man himself, with a cutout crown on his head: LIVE LIKE A KING IN ROYAL CREST APARTMENTS!

"Your worthy client, Mother?" says Ransom.

Presently they arrive at the Chatham County Sheriff's Complex.

It's neo-brutalist, concrete and brick and crushed rock and approximately the size of Versailles. When stuffed to maximum capacity, which it is every day, it holds fourteen hundred prisoners. Ransom and Morgana lose an hour at reception with paperwork and fingerprints and waiting. She sits there, pecking at her phone, texting arrangements for tonight's big event. Ransom contemplates a heating duct. Wishing he'd told her to go to hell.

Though he finds, to his surprise, that he bears no special animus toward this place. He was an inmate here for seven months, and it was by no means pleasant but he made no real enemies, nor was the block of bland gray time particularly unhealthy for him. Though he didn't use the time wisely. He might have contemplated his future, formed some plans. Instead he spent the time brooding on the misjudgments and betrayals that had led him here. His release came suddenly, a total surprise. Just before last St. Patrick's Day, the bulls sprang a couple hundred inmates, to make room for what they called "the paying customers" — the drunken frat boys they'd soon be collecting from the festivities on River Street:

boys who all had daddies and mommies who would post fat bonds for them. Ransom still had months to go on his sentence, but suddenly he was out in the warm day, trudging down the long concrete driveway. He had no idea where to go. But he fell in soon with Billy Sugar, who had also been released that morning. "This is the third year in a row I've gotten the St. Pat's Amnesty," said Billy. "What a great city, that sets its alcoholics loose on St. Pat's."

The two of them walked together to someone's bungalow on Toomer Street to pick up Billy's dog, Gracie. She leaped up like a porpoise when she saw him. They went next to a convenience store to pick up a tenner of Icehouse. The world felt reborn. Like coming out of a dull, dark movie into the living day. They caught a ride with a roofer into town; Billy riding up in the front of the van, talking with the roofer, Ransom and Gracie sprawled in the back on a mess of shingles. A hot wind whipped around. Ransom sipped a beer and wondered what he was supposed to do now.

They drove to Billy's old encampment under the exit ramp of the Harry S Truman Parkway. Billy invited the roofer to join them, and they all walked under the ramp to the camp, a good-hearted place, easygoing. The denizens called it the Truman Marriott. A dozen folks were lounging on sprung sofas and milk crates and duct-taped office chairs. They greeted Billy and Gracie warmly, and were also welcoming to Ransom and the roofer. A woman called Boiled Liza brought them bowls of her "conflagration chili." Ransom met Hatchet Head for the first time: he was a former cat burglar and had great stories about his profession. The roofer turned out to be a true South Georgia redneck who spun conspiracy theories that even dyed-in-the-wool Q-Anonists wouldn't have swallowed, involving stolen body parts and the electrified corpses of rodeo stars. But he was kind and generous, and when they ran out of beer he volunteered to get more. He and Liza went off to the Jiffy Mart, and Ransom stretched out on someone's spare hammock. The traffic overhead lulled him into sleep: his best sleep since the night of the stone stairs. Or probably since he first met Madelaine.

Next morning when he woke, he decided that he would borrow money from his sister Bebe and move to Asheville, North Carolina, and start a new life — carpentry, or writing, or legal aid. But first he wandered with the vagabonds into town. They went to the Apostolic Social for the free breakfast and showers. It was full of folks from various camps.

Billy and Hatchet Head gave him a little tutorial: Savannah has some forty-odd homeless camps, arranged in an arc all around the city, with thousands of people living in them. There's a camp for families, a camp for drunks, a camp for psychos. There's a camp for white supremacist bikers, which everyone steers clear of, even the cops. "And above all of them," said Hatchet Head, "there's *our* camp, the infamous and irrepressible Truman Marriott, for deviants and malcontents only."

After breakfast Ransom joined the crew's migration over to Wright Square. He was aware that someone he knew might see him loitering with these folks. He knew that he might be sneered at — or worse, pitied. But he held to a kind of proud defiance. Fuck my family, he thought. I like these people. He found himself hoping that Morgana *would* drive past and see him. Or his brother, David. Or that Madelaine, the love of his life, would drive past and behold him with this band of lowlifes.

That night he slept in that hammock again. And the next. He never made it to Asheville. He got a part-time job working at a friend's furniture repair shop. He found a

51

tent at the Salvation Army and pitched it in the woods a ways off from the ramp, not far from Billy's tarp. Now it's a year later, and he still hasn't left. Though his sister Bebe begs him to, though his sister Willou scolds him viciously, though both of them keep warning: if you stay here, Morgana will find a way to get her claws into you and you'll be finished.

"Musgrove?"

A guard is standing there. Ransom and Morgana rise and walk with him to the security gate and then through a series of gray doors and gray corridors to a gray windowless cubicle.

Where the Gooze awaits them.

Fat mule. Pasty-skinned with a jailhouse beard and a cascade of faux chins. Slight stink when he rises to greet them. "Well as I live and breathe! The Queen of Savannah, come to visit poor li'l me in my humble abode."

He means to sound good ol' boy folksy, but it comes out stiff. Frightened. There are little shifts in his gaze. He gives Ransom's hand a few sweaty pumps, then Morgana's. "Glad you're here, Morgana. Sight for sore eyes. Some folks won't even *talk* to me."

They sit across from him at the wooden table. The bull withdraws.

"Been watchin the TV?" Guzman asks. "Readin the *Savannah Morning News*? Jesus. Am I the Antichrist or what? Now they callin me the Vulture of Victory Drive — you heard that one, buddy?"

Addressing this last to Ransom alone, as though they were old friends.

Ransom says, "I have heard that."

Guzman says, "I bet you have, but it's bullshit. Tell you right off, I'm a good guy. Some of my workers really like me. Some of my tenants I've had for years. That old woman on Tattnall Street, Hazel or something? Christ, *no* complaints. I treat her real good. I'm not the bad guy here; I'm the *victim.* That's a nice jacket, by the way. One of your daddy's? Elegant. Your family, you're always the stylish ones. But I don't need you in a suit. I need your ass on the street. You know? You got all those homeless buddies, right? Like the old guy with the dog, you know him, right?"

"What about him?"

"Nothin, just some folks know the score, know what I mean? Morgana, you gotta get your whole family on this. Your older boy? The big lawyer? Oh yeah, get *him.* Your daughter Willou, she's a judge, right? C'mon, Morgana. You know what my lawyer calls you? I better not say. But it involves

53

lady spiders."

Morgana keeps a tight smile. "You asking me to pull strings for you, Mr. Guzman?"

" 'At's 'bout right."

"Are you innocent?"

He tries to smile. "Of some things."

"That's a yes?"

"Could be. You workin for me or what?"

"Again, are you innocent?"

He sniffs. "I did not light that place up."

"So who did?"

He does a little noncommittal rocking thing with his head.

She lets it go and asks, "Did you know Luke Kitchens?"

"Not much. He worked for me sometimes. Day labor."

"Any trouble between you?"

"Nah. Who ever had trouble with Luke? You hear what they callin him? The Gentle Giant. Ha. That's how they playin it: Gentle Giant versus Gooze the Vulture."

"Did you know he was staying in that house?"

"Nuh-uh. Ain't even *seen* the kid for like a year. I mean yeah, sometimes I let my guys sleep up there — if they paintin for me, or polishin floors or shit. But Luke, he never did ask."

Ransom scrutinizes him. "Then how did

he get in?"

"Dunno. Maybe he copied a key?"

"And who put the chain on the fire escape?"

"Wa'n't me."

"Who else then?"

He shrugs.

Ransom shakes his head. "Mr. Guzman."

"Call me Archie."

"Mr. Guzman, this isn't plausible. It's a squirrely neighborhood; of course you'd chain up the doors."

The man takes a moment to size him up. "How would *you* know what I'd do or wouldn't do? Open your fuckin ears. No, I didn't chain the fire escape. That'd be *impeded egress.* Georgia Code, section one-zero-zero-three point one. Somebody pulled that shit once in a building of mine — made his place into, like, a nightclub, and chained the back door so nobody could sneak in. I went in with a bolt cutter. I nearly cut his . . . *member* off too, but I took pity. I only tossed him out on his butt. Shit. Wanna see crispy critters? One spark. I mean no fuckin way."

Ransom glances at Morgana and catches her doing something he knows well: her eye-drop. Sometimes when she's reading you, she'll drop her gaze to check out your

55

hands. Ransom follows her lead now, and sees Guzman chopping at the air nervously with his gestures. Which tells Ransom nothing. But when he looks back at his mother, he sees that she's pursing her lips thoughtfully. She seems to have arrived at some conclusion. Giving no hint, though, as to what that might be.

"Tell us," she says, "how your fingerprints happened to get on that gas can."

"Well, let's see. Maybe from my fingers? The can was in my garage. I probably used it, I don't know, two, three years ago, I don't recall. But my garage is easy to get into. Them bastuds coulda slipped in there anytime, swiped it."

"I see," Morgana says skeptically. "And planted it near the crime scene?"

"Wouldn't put it past 'em."

She lifts a brow. "And who are these people who would do this to you? These 'bastuds,' who are they?"

He shrugs. " 'At's what *you* gotta find out."

"You mean, should I choose to take your case?"

"*Should?* You shittin me? Your bank accounts are leakin like a sieve. I happen to know, don't ask how, that every business you own is losing money. Plus you got all

56

your *causes.* And granddaughters to help with their tuition. And that house is a big brick money-suck. And your trips around the world'n shit, and here's me come along with half a million dollars and you givin me *should*?"

"Yes," she says. "Before I take the case, I need to know what you'll be pleading. You'll maintain your innocence?"

Guzman shrugs. Hangs his head. "Yeah, why not?"

"Meaning what?" says Ransom. "Meaning you've been set up?"

Guzman seems distracted. Nervous. Glances up at the room's camera and shifts his chair, so the camera cannot see his face. Then he says, "What, now?"

Ransom presses. "Who's setting you up, Mr. Guzman? Who are your enemies?"

Guzman lowers his head. "My enemies?" He's stroking his chin and seems deep in thought.

Morgana finally loses patience. "Sir?"

Guzman raises his eyes. And does an odd thing.

He opens his mouth.

Dentist-wide. To show them both what's inside of it. There's a card, propped up by his tongue. The card says:

57

Framed by his rotting teeth.

Morgana and Ransom gape.

Guzman shuts his mouth again. He takes a moment to chew and swallow. "Really, y'all, I got nothin *but* enemies. Ask Billy Sugar."

Jaq cruises down Bull Street, one hand on the handlebars, the other holding a butter pecan ice-cream cone. Taking it slow, the wheels wobbling a bit. She's weighing a decision. She's so fed up with the conduct of the investigation into Luke Kitchens's murder that she's considering going to the Savannah Police Headquarters and lodging a formal complaint. It's a daunting idea. It is in fact insane. To challenge the Savannah Police Department? When she brings no expertise: not in forensics, not in psychiatry, not in criminal justice, not in anything? They'll smile and roll their eyes. They'll gaslight her, that's guaranteed.

Still. She did know Luke. And she knows that Guzman's lawyers are lying when they claim that Luke was a drug addict who nodded off with a lit cigarette. Luke never did drugs at all. The police need to know that, don't they? If they haven't bothered to interview Luke's friends about his drug use, isn't it her duty to tell them? She rolls into Forsyth Park, to the big fountain, where she dismounts and takes a seat on a bench, and considers her plan. Weighing out the pros and cons. Meanwhile polishing and trimming her ice-cream cone till there's nothing left.

She's enjoying this cone. It's strange to her how much pleasure, despite the gravity of this situation, she's managing to draw from this ice-cream cone. When she's done, she licks her fingers slowly, then takes out her phone and googles the Savannah Police Department.

Six minutes later she's got an appointment with a detective. Four P.M. this very afternoon.

Her stomach is aflutter but she's OK.

She aims her camera at herself.

"OK, I just made an appointment with a Detective Tuck at the Savannah Police Department Headquarters, known affectionately around town as the A-hole. I'm going to tell him the truth about Luke, and I might also raise the subject of why the police are evading the obvious guilt of Archie Guzman. I might even mention the overall corruption of the Savannah Police

Department. I know these are controversial subjects, so I suppose some . . . *trepidation* on my part would be fitting. But I don't feel any. Honestly, I'm looking forward to this visit."

As she puts the camera away she's thinking, hadn't those kids at the fence seen this in her? How she draws a kind of — not pleasure exactly, but anyway a kind of fuel or something from her outrage? Isn't this why they were laughing at her?

For the first two days after Luke's death she was annihilated. Unable to eat or emerge from her room, her pillow drenched in tears. Taking nights off from Peep's, and the other bartenders were pleased to cover for her because they knew how much she loved him.

But then on day three she took a look at the news. They still hadn't arrested Guzman. But bits and pieces of evidence were emerging, and his guilt seemed evident. She started checking for updates on her laptop. She checked the *Savannah Morning News,* WSAV, *Connect,* Lamar Raskins's *City Blog.* Seemed like the cops were casting for some way to let Guzman slide. His lawyers were concocting lies. So quickly they came up with that lie about Luke being an addict, which made her blood boil. On Instagram

60

she posted about it. She got likes and shares. For the first time in her life she tweeted — a small rush of excitement. Everywhere she went, she checked for Gooze News. On the TV at Peep's, on her phone at stoplights, on her laptop in the middle of the night. Hadn't those corrupt assholes snagged him *yet*? Jaq has two mothers, and at dinner that night she poured out the details to them. They gave her concerned looks. Then, the day of Luke's memorial service, although the service wasn't till 4:00 P.M. she got up at nine (painfully early, considering she'd been at Peep's till three), just to peek at the latest.

They'd done it.

IN CHAINS! said Lamar Raskins's *City Blog*. GUZMAN BEHIND BARS! said the *Savannah Morning News.* Immense relief. That morning Jaq's mothers were at work, and she had the bungalow to herself. She fixed herself a latte and a piece of toast with plum jam and went out to the back patio, and sat there, sipping and munching and looking at the stories on her laptop. Even the *Atlanta Journal-Constitution* had it: MURDER CHARGE IN SAVANNAH: ARSON GONE WRONG FOR WEALTHY DEVELOPER. The cops had taken him from his house, from his ugly mansion off Victory Drive near Thunderbolt, and there was video and she sat there, savoring it. Taking in all the details of his arrest, and munching her toast and drinking her latte, and the sun came through a gap in the bamboo and fell on her face so warmly, and the toast was disappearing and she realized she was not miserable at all.

Which gave her a small stab of remorse.

A sense that she was losing Luke. I'm not thinking about Luke anymore; I'm thinking about his murder; I'm thinking about the Gooze. And what satisfaction there is in his comeuppance.

She couldn't bear to think she was forgetting Luke.

The memorial was held in a room at the American Legion. Standing room only. Folks who wouldn't have given Luke the time of day were crowded into the back, standing there somberly and dabbing at their eyes. The only no-show was Stony — but everyone knew how private Stony was; she was probably off in the woods somewhere, tending to her grief. After a string of Luke stories, Jaq showed her favorite videos of him. Finally they all sang Lana Del Rey's "Young and Beautiful." Then everyone went to Peep's and right away they turned on the TV and watched the Gooze News.

She sent a silent message to Luke: we're not forgetting you; we still love you and you're not slipping away but we're all just so enraged; you can understand that, can't you?

Then last night she went to a club with the young man she's been seeing. Pivot, a hip-hop artist. He and his friends were coked up and making crude jokes, or not even all that crude but just pointless. She'd had no problem with that before, but now all the insults and wordplay made her feel lonesome. She sat there thinking about how this city was arranging for Archie Guzman to go free. She felt a great remove from Pivot and her friends. Yet she was sort of OK with that remove. When they left the club, there were throngs of drunken redneck boys on River Street, and she recalled how much Luke loved drunken redneck boys. But he won't love them anymore — because of you, Gooze. "Because you're a fucking murderer," she said aloud — and just that little flicker of outrage seemed to assuage her emptiness, for a moment anyway, and she went with Pivot to his place and they had wild sex: rough, daring, splendid.

It's all bewildering.

Now she's back on her bike and gliding

through Forsyth Park, passing many friends and giving them hellos, coasting past the Confederate Sentry (sorry, son, but I think your days are numbered), and on down the avenue of oaks that divides the great lawn. On the left, they've put up a huge circus tent for the upcoming Telfair Ball. She loves the Ball. Celebration of the arts, centerpiece of the cultural year, and attended by what feels like half the city. What other city has something like this? No other city. And this year, as always, her Aunt Willou will be the M.C. But Luke won't be there.

She does adore Savannah. All the conviviality and the outrageous beauty and the characters and the sunlight and the aromas. But she can't forget what happened to Luke.

At the bottom of the park she locks her bike so she can go into the café where, if she's lucky, that golden boy who works at the kayak shop will be hanging out. But when she lifts her eyes from the locking-up, she spots her grandmother Morgana's car.

The old burgundy Caprice, tooling up Bull Street from the south.

Morgana is perched in the passenger seat per usual: she's never learned to drive. But today her driver isn't Betty, Jaq sees to her astonishment, but rather her uncle Ransom. How in the world? He and Gram aren't even on speaking terms — not since he went to jail, since he's been living in the camps. Yet here they are together, coming up to the stop sign at Park Avenue, right in front of her. She gets a jolt of pleasure seeing her uncle. She loves him dearly, deeply, but he seems not to even notice her, nor does Morgana: so intent are they on their conversation. It's a little surreal, since they're close enough as they pass that Jaq can smell the iris of Gram's perfume (which gives her another jolt of pleasure and then a twinge of sorrow because Luke *loved* Morgana's perfume).

Ransom and Morgana are cruising down Park Avenue between the Sentient Bean café and Forsyth Park. He just wants to accomplish this errand without quarreling, but Morgana's got something else in mind — she wants his company at lunch. "I insist," she says. "I'm starving. And it's nothing to you, is it, half an hour one way or another? I need to debrief is all. This has been quite overwhelming. To the Gryphon then."

And what the hell, he thinks: he's hungry too. And just by chance he seems to have an opening on his calendar. So he takes a left on Drayton and drives her to the Gryphon Tea Room. As they're led to their booth (which apparently she reserved hours ago) she's animated and works the crowd: "Emmaline! *Who* did your hair? Did Charlene do that? You look like the Queen of Spain, I mean the young one, that fabulous one, oh you look *amazing.*" "There you are, Richard! I've a *devastating* tidbit for you regarding our Charleston garden rivals. Must tell you in private. Can we talk tomorrow?" "Oh Beatrice, I have not finished that book, I confess. I'm drenched in guilt but I simply haven't had a *minute.*"

But everyone is looking at Ransom.

Because it's big news: Ransom Musgrove out in public with his mother. Morgana rather basks in it, showing him off, helping him with the names: "You do remember Beatrice, don't you, dear?" "Ransom, I'm sure you recall the Tartanians?" She stands back to give him room to shine, to let him charm them with his small talk, but he can't come up with any. He seems to have lost that faculty. Yet she's quite undismayed and keeps moving him on to the next table, and the next, until finally they alight at their own.

She takes the pork tenderloin, he'll have the salmon.

The waitress is a pretty girl with pink

bangs and a nose ring, probably a student at SCAD. She seems quite pleased to take Ransom's order, and when she's gone Morgana murmurs, "She thinks you're handsome."

"How would you know that, Mother?"

"Don't they all? Haven't they always? They're all in love with you."

He rearranges the salt and pepper.

She tells him, "Beatrice is in our Flannery Book Club. I mean we've named it for Flannery but we never read her. Right now we're reading something called *The Shoes I Love, the Shoes I Walk In.* Yes, it's about two goddamn pairs of shoes. Really. Mostly we plod, says the author, but on occasion we may dance. And we must love ourselves even if our exes don't. Every *word* was an insult to my intelligence. What a strange meeting that was today. That man was perfectly odious, wasn't he?"

"Yeah."

"My ladies will *not* be induced to read Flannery. Last year I made them read 'A Temple of the Holy Ghost,' because it's all set in Savannah, but of course they didn't care for it. They say, But *Morgana,* her characters are all so *grotesque.* They're so *miserable.* I tell them, welcome to *life,* ladies. But they won't hear of it."

"And how do you know that story is set in Savannah? It doesn't *mention* Savannah."

"Still, I'm certain of it." She takes a bite of her pasta salad. "The little girl in that story is Mary Flannery herself. No question. Darling, have some of this. It's divine."

Holding a forkful before his face.

"Mother, I have some right here on my plate."

"But take some of *mine*. It's got this bright olive-y taste —"

"But it's the exact same pasta salad."

"But it's *heavenly*."

Wishing to not have her fork float there any longer, he opens his mouth like a baby bird and accepts the morsel.

"All right," she says. "*Stone Kings. Treasure*. What in the world?"

"No clue."

"He was looking right at you, Ransom."

"Was he? I still can't help."

"Some project of his? A new warren of repulsive condos? The Stone King's Treasure Palace?" She studies the sprig of mint in her tea. "Stone King, Stone King. Maybe he's peddling graveyard plots?"

The other diners are stealing glances. The downtown attorneys, rich wives from the Landings, the treasurer of the Yacht Club. Anyone who knows the story of the Musgrove family troubles (which is everyone) is fascinated to see the two of them together. Ransom imagines he can see the gears turning in their busy little brains. Morgana ignores them all. "And hiding those words in his mouth? What was that for?"

Ransom shrugs. "I guess that was his comment on the value of attorney privilege in Chatham County."

"But he overplayed it, didn't he? It felt like a game of some sort. I don't trust him."

"Good. So you'll turn him down?"

She reaches over and takes a bite of his salmon. "That marinade is quite good."

Which is her way of saying she's not turning him down.

The waitress comes by to refill their tea. Then asks if they'd care for something else. They wouldn't, but still she lingers. Scoops some crumbs off the table. Finally comes out with it. "Hey," she asks Ransom, "don't you hang at the Bean sometimes?"

"Yeah, sometimes."

"I saw you reading *Timon of Athens.* You're the only one ever reading a book. Everyone else has a phone or a laptop, you're always reading a book."

He smiles and shrugs.

"Actually he doesn't own a phone," says Morgana. "A situation that shall soon be

69

rectified." She offers her hand. "I'm his mother. Morgana Musgrove. I'd be happy to introduce you if you'll tell me your name."

"Alexis."

"Alexis, may I present my son Ransom?"

"Hi," says Alexis.

"Hi," he says back.

She turns beet red and hurries off.

"Oh these girls today," says Morgana. "They simply don't know how to flirt. Apparently it's a lost art. These days you go online, find someone you like, tap tap you're good to go. Gives me the shudders. Still, she *is* attractive. I'm sure I could get her number —"

"Mother, listen to me. Your man's a murderer."

"Oh? Is that quite proven though?"

"He set that fire."

"Did he? Well, I know one thing, he didn't chain that door. That little sermon he gave us about the building code — that was real. He truly believes that. He takes pride in adhering to all the little bylaws. Deep down no doubt he *is* a weasel or a vulture or whatever y'all call him. But he *imagines* he's full of virtue. Albeit a tough, no-free-lunch kind of virtue."

What ticks Ransom off about this speech

70

is what always ticks him off: her cocksureness, her iron faith in her ability to see through everyone's masks and divine their true motives. He might ask her how, since she reads people so well, she managed to screw up so many lives. But it's not worth it. He settles for: "He's going down, Mother. He'll be a fuzzybear for the inmates at Reidsville."

Still she keeps the mild face. "Beloved," she says, "won't you consider working on this a little? Just for a few days, till we know whether he's guilty or innocent?"

"No."

"But I *need* you. I need you to find out about these Stone Kings and their treasure and what's Guzman's interest in all this. You know you have laser vision when you want to. So tell me, what do you see?"

Hitting those switches as hard as she can.

"No thanks," he says. "Guzman doesn't want me, he wants you. Your spiderweb, all your pals. That's what he thinks is worth half a million. And maybe he's right. And anyway, what else is he gonna spend his money on? In his new life. Other than a jar of Vaseline, what will he need? Can we go now?"

He pushes his chair back.

"Now?" she says. "But we just arrived."

71

"But we're done. Let me drive you home."

She waggles her finger. "After dessert. First we'll have some dessert and discuss terms. *Alexis?*"

The waitress comes over. Morgana says, "What are your desserts today, dear?"

Alexis gives her options; Morgana picks the crème brûlée. She mutters, after the girl leaves, "She's still blushing. Let me invite her to the Soiree tonight; you two can —"

Ransom fishes the car keys from his pocket and places them on the table.

"Oh good Christ," says Morgana. "You'll abandon me? How the hell will I get home? Shall I suddenly learn to *drive*? Shall I stick out my thumb? Shall I take the *local bus*?"

"I'll drive you right now if you're ready. You ready?"

"Do you really imagine," she demands, "that you're Timon of Athens? Some kind of noble outcast? Are you too pure to engage with *hoi polloi,* is that what you think? Do you think you deserve *laurels* for cowering in the woods like a little spotted faunlet?"

"OK," he says, and rises. "Thanks, Mother. That was delicious."

Upon which he turns and walks away. With what seems like half of Savannah watching him go.

72

Jaq's meeting that cop. Telling herself, Don't lose it now, don't let him rile you. But Detective Tuck's desk sits beneath a crippled ceiling fan in the sepulchral Savannah Police Headquarters, and the fan as it goes round makes the light flicker, which makes Jaq crazy. Out the window is a view of the Colonial Cemetery, the mossy gray tombs, all gothic and unreal. Tuck is also unreal. He has a cowlick and he's pale and pink and she finds herself speaking to him as she might to a dull schoolboy: slowly, with big stresses and lots of repetition. "It was late," she says. "Ve-ry late. It was two A.M., but we were still busy, *so* busy, and Luke came in with a friend and I got them a beer and a mar-ga-ri-ta."

"Wait," he says. "Where was this again?"

Patience. "Peep's. Where I work."

"*Bo* Peep's?"

Don't ask him if he knows another Peep's in Savannah. "Yes, uh-huh, Bo Peep's."

"And you say you're a bartender?"

Only nod and smile.

He picks out the letters on his laptop with one finger, biting his tongue as he works.

Finally he looks up. "And when . . . was this?"

"Night he was killed."

"Right. You said that."

"Listen, Detective Tuck, can I just tell you one thing?"

"Sure."

"Luke didn't take drugs."

"No?"

"Guzman's lawyer says he was injecting fentanyl, that he shot up that night and lit a cigarette and nodded off, and that's what started the fire. Like, what a horrible thing that drug-crazed hobo did to the property of a fine upstanding citizen, right? But that's not what happened. It couldn't have happened, because Luke didn't *do* butter."

"OK."

"He drank. He drank boatloads. But he didn't do fentanyl. He didn't do carfentanyl, or smack, or anything. Never, none of that shit. And I saw him nearly every night, so I'd have known."

"OK."

"But Guzman and his boys, and by that I mean y'all, you got that lie going, and now we're told somebody found a hypodermic needle miraculously right near the body, right? So the Gooze is gonna get off?"

Ah shit, she can feel it. Her composure

draining away.

Tuck's eyes were small to begin with; now they're angry little beans. Getting this rise from him is rich, but she has to ignore that. She has to breathe deep and think only of reining herself in.

She takes a moment. Then she offers, "So, I recorded him that night, wanna see?"

He's not quick to reply.

Well, she thinks, you *will* see. She pulls her laptop from her bag. It has a sticker, a quote from Malcolm X, and Tuck's lips move as he reads: *If someone puts their hands on you make sure they never put their hands on anybody else again.* She pulls up the video she made at Peep's, and goes directly to the 41-second mark. Skipping the bit where crazy Stony says she lives in some kind of "Kingdom" with soldiers who aren't ghosts and aren't anybody's slaves and all that. Instead she goes right to where Luke is saying, "But you know who we just heard? Out there? The Musician."

Jaq: "Really? The Musician is out to-night?"

Luke: "And whistling so gorgeous, and I swear to God he did a duet with a *mocking-bird.*" His laugh. She's watched this video thirty times in the last few days, but still the sweetness of Luke's laugh makes her catch

75

her breath.

"And them tourists on the ghost tour," he says, "you know what they shouted at us? *Yo, Frankenstein! Yo, Witch!* That's *us.* I mean we're the stars of Savannah, Jaq! Ha ha ha!"

Now another cop has left his own desk and ambled over to watch the scene. This one wears a suit. In his late thirties. Long face, slightly horsey, with weary eyes and a big strong nose. He watches Luke on the video and then says, "Hey, do me a favor? Play that again?"

Jaq shrugs. "OK."

She slides it back to :40, where Stony is winding up her rant about the King's soldiers: "They're not ghosts, they're not anybody's slaves. You can't fuck with 'em."

The cop with the long face asks, "Who's that?"

"Friend of Luke's," Jaq says. "Stony. Kinda nuts. But wait."

The camera slides to Luke and he says: "Hey, you know who we just heard? Out there? The Musician."

The cop leans forward and gives his full attention. "I've seen photos of Mr. Kitchens. But never a video."

Luke says, "We're the stars of Savannah, Jaq!"

76

The cop smiles, and at first Jaq thinks he's laughing at Luke. But he says: "Think he was really OK with it though? The bullying from the tourists? Or was that just how he defended himself?"

She raises her eyes to him. "Oh. Probably that."

He offers his hand. "I'm Detective Galatas. Nick Galatas."

Not bad looking, she thinks, in a white-cop, worn-down-while-still-young sort of way.

"I'm Jaq."

"I've lost friends to violence," he says. "It's the hardest thing in the world. What you must be going through. I'm sorry."

She turns away from him, back to the screen. Tingle of tears. She doesn't need that now.

"I do know," he adds, "what you mean about rich people with pricey lawyers. But Guzman? I mean, Archie Guzman? I mean —"

He cuts himself off.

They keep gazing, both of them, at the laptop screen, at the last frame of that video. Luke's sweet face, as broad as a buffalo's.

Then Galatas lets it out: "Just FYI, the guilty party is not getting away with this."

She mumbles, "Really?"

"I come from a family of fishermen," he says. "My father owned a shrimp boat till the bank took it. I'm on your side. On this one, there's a lot of folks on your side."

She can sense that he has turned to her, but she's afraid that if she returns that look these tears might get loose. So she keeps her eyes locked on the screen. He hands her his card. "If you ever hear anything that could help us, will you call me?"

"Yes," she says. "I will."

"And thanks so much for speaking up."

In Wright Square stands a great loathsome milky-white wedding cake of a monument, erected in celebration of the lordly old slaveholder who founded the railroad that brought King Cotton into Savannah from the hinterlands. All day the tourists troop by and pull out their phones and snap selfies and marvel at the marble bas-relief of a choo choo train. Meanwhile, in one obscure corner of the square, there's a rock, a big shapeless rock to honor the memory of Tomochichi, the Yamacraw chief who was a friend to the first colonists. He was, by all accounts, fair, generous, and sagacious. Originally — back in the 1740s — the entire square had been dedicated to Tomochichi. Originally his tomb occupied the center.

But cotton and the character of Savannah intervened, and he was pushed off to this corner. Lucky to have gotten even this, this big black rock, to which the tourists pay little mind.

This is where the drunks and vagabonds like to gather, in the late afternoons.

Today Ransom joins them.

Boiled Liza is braiding the hair of Cyclone. Henry rolls a joint. Hatchet Head, bristling with tattoos, is reading *The Conquest of Bread* by Pyotr Kropotkin, his favorite anarchist. He looks up when Ransom takes the bench beside him. "Oh Ran. Your mama scrubbed you up so goo-ood, didn't she?"

Henry grins a toothless grin. "You so purty, Ran. Come ovah heah, sit with Papa."

Meanwhile Cyclone, snail-slow in everything he does, slowly pops open a can of Icehouse, pours it into a paper cup, fits the lid onto the cup, and puts Scotch tape all around the lid's edge. Because such the law demands. Then he passes it to Ransom.

The beer has a rotten-corn taste that says *swallow this and move on.*

Ransom says, "Hey, Hatch. Saw you flyin that sign. That veteran of Iraq con, that worked for you?"

Hatchet Head says, "Uh-huh. It was gold."

Liza guffaws. "Soliciting on the corner of

79

Victory and Waters — *day*-umn. How did you not get busted?"

"Because they can*not* bust me," says Hatchet Head. "They can*not* arrest a veteran of the Battle of Fallujah. Not with all them folks drivin by. Go viral in like two seconds. *What don't the VA want you to see? Heads woulda rolllllled.*"

Cyclone laughs his slow laugh. "Haw . . . haw . . . haw."

Hatchet Head adds, "Anyway, it paid for our beer now, didn't it?"

"Well yes it did," Liza allows. "I'll drink to that."

They all raise their cups and sip.

Then they fall silent. They listen to snippets of the carriage tours going around the square behind them. Ghosties and more ghosties. The guides don't dwell on the darker history of this square. The slaughter of the Native Americans, the century of slavery, the corpses hanging from these oaks (the old courthouse is next door), the Klan rallies, the desecration of Tomochichi's grave to make room for the Slavery and Railroad Tycoon: all that is set aside so they can focus on the ghosts. "Folks around heah all *sway*-uh that on moonless nights they can still hear old Tomochichi laughin and hollerin with his good pal General Oglethorpe, smokin the peace pipe together, red-man/white-man as one, livin in peaceful harmony. . . ."

The vagabonds sit there and drink it in. The sun sinks behind the oaks.

Finally Ransom ventures, "Hey, I got a question for y'all."

"Uh-huh?" says Liza.

"My mother asked for my help today. You know, she's got that little detective agency? Well, she's investigating the death of Luke Kitchens."

Liza raises an eyebrow. "You mean his murder?"

"Yeah. Exactly. And we got presented with this weird clue. Just some words on a card. The words are: 'Stone Kings. Treasure. Keep safe and give my love.' That mean anything to y'all?"

"Treasure?" says Henry. "I'm in."

Instantly the others all say, in unison, "I'm in."

Then they listen a while as another tour goes round. Cyclone refills their cups.

Liza asks, "Um, Ran, do we get a context?"

"Well, no, because *we* didn't. We just got those words."

Liza repeats them. "Stone Kings. Treasure. What else?"

81

Ransom adds, "Keep safe and give my love."

Cyclone asks, "Keep *what* safe?"

"The Stone Kings," says Hatchet Head. "You gotta love and protect the Stone Kings."

"They may be kings, and they may be made of stone," says Liza, "but they need love just like you and me."

"Haw haw haw," says Cyclone.

They're silent again. They drink.

Then Liza says, "Well, there's that woman. You know that woman Stony? The archaeologist?"

This triggers a faint memory in Ransom. "Black? Locs, kind of intense?"

"Uh-huh. I think her real name is Stone. And here's the thing. When she's drinkin she says she lives in a Kingdom."

Hatchet Head says, "Bear in mind, though, she is way off her nut."

When the beer's done Ransom offers to buy more, and everyone endorses that, and Liza and Hatchet Head go with him. They stroll out of the square and head over to Parker's Urban Gourmet on Drayton. It sucks they have to go to an expensive deli for bum-brew, but the 7–Eleven shut down years ago, and the Kroger is too far. They leave Hatchet Head outside so as not to spook the staff (he has that blue mohawk, and on his throat is a tattoo of Satan and the demons of hell). But the staff gets spooked anyway. *Uh-oh, here come the hobos.* Someone slips in behind them and mouses about, pretends to straighten the shelves while keeping an eye on them, follows them till they put down their money and go.

They rejoin Hatchet Head and amble back toward the square.

As they approach it, a girl on a bike comes around it, very quick, intent on her biking, pumping away, and is about about to turn onto Bull Street when she spots them. "Mine nuncle!" she cries.

She sails up to them.

"Jaq," says Ransom. He gives her a hug. They're both laughing. Ransom loves her laugh: she has the most radiant laugh. She seems so happy to see him, and to see them all.

"Hello, Liza," she says. "Hello, Hatchet Head."

Liza asks her, "Girl, where you goin like a bat outta hell?"

"Work."

"Peep's?"

"Morgana's. Tonight's the Spring Soiree. I'm tending bar."

Ransom says, "Wait'll you see her big floral thing. You'll laugh your head off."

Jaq says, "And guess what, guess where I'm coming from. You won't believe me. The A-hole."

"You *what?*" says Liza.

"I went to the A-hole *voluntarily.*"

"Oh girl," says Hatchet Head, "you need treatment."

"I went to complain," says Jaq. "The cops keep talking about Luke Kitchens like he was a drug addict. He wasn't a drug addict."

"No, he wasn't," Liza agrees. "He was just a drunk like me."

"That's exactly what I told 'em."

"But you didn't mention *me?*" Liza asks.

Jaq grins. "I didn't, but I could tell they were thinking of you."

"Speaking of drunks," says Hatchet Head, "your uncle just bought us some Icehouse. Would you care for a taste?"

He holds out his cup. Jaq accepts it, takes a swallow. "Thank you. That's really horrible stuff."

She starts to tell them about Detective Tuck and his cowlick and his stupid questions. But as she's talking, an open horse-drawn carriage goes clopping past them. The guide is giving his spiel, and it's a real performance, and Jaq falls silent. She and the others watch the guy.

Another ghost tour of course. He's dressed like a ghoul. He's bombastic, with a phony Oxford accent and expansive gestures, and Ransom knows him from amateur theatricals around town. He reins in the horse beneath a spreading oak tree, and rises and tells his passengers about Alice Riley, an indentured servant who was hanged in this very square back in 1734. "Right *there,*" he says, "beneath the limbs of that majestic oak. And her crime, my friends? She proved to be a faithless servant. Some say she was a prostitute, some say a Jezebel, some say a *witch.* Some say she cast a spell over her husband, Richard, and induced him to murder their master, to murder him by strangulation as he lay helpless in his bath. . . ."

Liza murmurs to Jaq, "You with us?"

Jaq grins. "Sure." She sets her bike against a tree. Joins the others as they approach the carriage.

The ghoul holds up on his tale when he sees them coming. Shakes his head and says, "Liza, don't do this."

But she ignores him, and addresses the carriage. "*I'm* Alice Riley, OK? Y'all wanna know what really happened?"

85

The tourists smile. Supposing she's an actor, that this is a part of the tour. But the ghoul keeps pleading, "Liza, don't. Please don't."

Already Hatchet Head has his hands around Ransom's neck. Ransom makes choking sounds, and Liza says, "The man being killed here is my employer, William Wise." Ransom's tongue lolls from his mouth. "He was a first-class douchebag in every way. He brought over young indentured servants from Ireland so he could rape them. He raped *me* nearly every night. I'm carrying his baby. Yes, I'm glad to see him die. But I did not kill him myself. The man killing him is my husband, Richard. As you can see, he doesn't need my help."

Hatchet Head throttles away, throttles with gusto, laughing and shaking his victim as a coyote shakes a prairie chicken.

Says Liza, "Does it look like I'm *inveigling* him?"

The tourists shake their heads.

The tour guide says, "Stop it, Liza."

Liza suddenly starts shrieking. "THEN *YOU* STOP IT! STOP TELLING THEM LIES! I'M NOT A MURDERER! AND I'M NOT A WITCH, AND I'M NOT A GHOST, I'M NOT ANYTHING CUTE! I'M NOT A DISNEY CHARACTER! I'M

JUST ANOTHER VICTIM OF SAVAN-
NAH SHITTERY!"

"Step away!" says the guide. "Step away
or I'm callin the police, I'm *serious*. . . ."

Meanwhile Ransom, zombie-style, has
arisen from his death and is trying to climb
into the carriage with the passengers. Asking them, "Won't you take me to the graveyard and bury me?"

They recoil. But they can't recoil far
because Jaq is climbing into the other side
of the carriage. "Won't you bathe me?" she
says. "Won't you take me to your hotel and
bathe me in rose water and then bury me?"

The tour guide has had enough: he snaps
the reins and the horse picks up its trot and
the carriage rolls round the square toward
Bull Street heading north. But still the
vagabonds shuffle after it, crying, "Please?
Won't you bury us? *Please* bury us! Please,
please, *BURRRYYYYYY USSSSSSS*!"

They stop. They laugh their asses off. The
carriage recedes.

"God," says Jaq. "That was sweet."

She reaches over and hooks Ransom's
head in her elbow and draws him in for a
hug and says, "Bye, mine nuncle. Bye, Liza.
Bye, Hatchet Head."

Gets on her bike and takes off. The three
vagabonds head back to Tomochichi's rock.

On the way, Liza says quietly to Ransom, "You should ask Billy."

"Ask him what?"

"He says he seen Stony that night. That night Luke got killed. He saw something bad with Stony."

"Really? Where is Billy? River Street?"

"Prolly. Since he ain't here. Prolly on River Street taking tourist dollah."

Stony in her living tomb waits to be killed.

Above her, bolted into the ceiling, is an LED bulb. When it's on, it throws off a metallic blue light that fills this little chamber. It coats the cot and the plastic mattress, the scoop chair and the wooden table, the litter box and the plastic jars of Kroger Corn Flakes. She hates this LED light with every atom of her being. It stays on about fourteen hours a day. Constantly it pumps forth the evil blue. It wears her down, turns her thoughts into gruel, sucks away her will.

But sometimes, suddenly, the light will snap off. No warning or preparation, just out it goes with a clap of darkness, and terror will boil up in her throat and she'll scream. Knowing by now, after so many cycles of dark and light, dark and light, dark and light, that her cries are utterly pointless, but still the roar will churn up out of her, and keep coming till her larynx gets ragged and she tastes blood and her shrieks die into sobs.

Then the blackness will start to soften.

Her nerves will loosen a bit. The focus will drain out of her terror, and memories will start to come. At first they'll be mere scraps, blurs, but after a few hours in the pitch black she'll slip into a state between sleeping and waking, a kind of floatingness, and the memories will become entire scenes, as rich as dreams — and, like dreams, entirely beyond her control. Drenched in emotion, full-blooded, more vivid than life. She'll drift from one vision to another and for hours she'll be perfectly content.

Then the light will switch back on.

She'll scream from the shock of it — just as she screamed at the shock of the dark. And regularly, soon after the light comes on, Mr. Kindness will make a visit. He'll ask her probing questions and terrorize her softly, and she'll say nothing. Not a word. And finally he'll leave her alone again with the blue pulverizing light. And another "day," courtesy of Mr. Kindness. She'll spend it staring at her palms. Hating that blue light. Trembling. Grieving for Luke. Fearing for the King's soldiers and for their loved ones. Replaying all her choices, regretting them, despising herself, praying for death.

Now and then she'll open one of the plastic jars of cereal. She'll eat and drink a bottle of water. Then she'll come back to this cot and sit.

This is how the "days" go.

However, she senses that this one is about to end.

She can feel it. She's been sitting forever staring ahead and tapping out time on her knee, pure time, and now she knows the hour has come. Soon Mr. Kindness will make his evening visit. She'll endure that and then if she's lucky he'll go away again and turn the fucking light off and give her "night."

But he must be getting impatient. All this restraint and gentleness: it's getting him nowhere. Soon, she knows, he'll start torturing her. He'll have to.

Unless — she imagines brightly — he elects to skip the torture and get right to killing her.

She gets up now, goes to the litter box, and does her business. Creates a little bouquet of stink, in honor of his coming visit. Then returns to the cot. Watches as the palmetto bugs burrow into her half-eaten cereal. She knows Mr. Kindness won't like that.

Come soon, Mr. Kindness. Pay your visit. Get angry with me. Finish this.

She hears his key in the lock. The door to her cell swings open.

"How you doing, Stony?"

He wears the mask he always wears. All she ever sees are his eyes, the pale skin around them.

"Are you staying warm?"

He swings the heavy door shut behind him. Starts checking on things. He likes to check on things. "Keeping clean? Using your litter box?"

He notes the palmetto bugs in her cereal bowl. "I gave you a plastic bag to keep the roaches out of your food. Why don't you use it?"

She won't lift her eyes.

He drags the one chair, a piece-of-crap plastic scoop chair, close to her cot and sits. She can feel his gaze.

"How's your sleep, Stony? Does the dark scare you? Hours and hours of pitch black, that'd drive anyone nuts."

She tries not to move a muscle.

He says, "I brought you something."

He holds a newspaper out before her. The *Savannah Morning News*. The headline reads: LUKE KITCHENS MURDER: INVESTI-

Bringing that night back to her. Luke, the knife, his suffering. But she shuts her eyes. She demands of herself: no tears.

"This was big news," he says, "a few days ago. Not so much now. But . . . you know, to most people, Luke was just a homeless junkie. It's too bad, but everybody's moving on. Everyone's forgetting."

She tries counting her breaths to see if that will drown him out.

He says, "Blame those two jailbirds. They were supposed to just bring you to see us, so we could talk to you. Instead they *roofie* you. And pull you out of a busy bar when half of Savannah was watching. And wind up killing your friend. Just so you know, I didn't hire those morons. Wasn't my decision at all. But now everything's fucked, you know? And we have to make the best of it."

She tries thinking of Jaq's smile. That radiant source of light. That should fade him some.

"I'll be frank," he says, "I don't like coming down here. You want to know where we are, Stony?"

Nothing fades him.

"I'll tell you. We're under the city, down in the storm drains. Amazing down here, isn't it? Miles of these tunnels. They dug it all out in the 1870s. Brickwork, arches, huge vaults. And these little surprising cubbyholes, just dug out of the clay. Bootleggers used to keep their booze down here. Ran all their booze under the streets. But now they got most of the portals sealed up pretty well, and it's hard to get down here. Nobody ever comes. Except me. So just pray that nothing ever happens to me, you know?"

She can feel his eyes upon her.

"Stony, you've got the treasure of the Kingdom and my partners need it. It's that simple. Tell us where it is and we'll let you go."

She knows if she were to tell him he'd kill her the next moment.

"You think I'd renege on that offer? I wouldn't. First, because my word is my bond. But also because I'm sure you've told someone else. Right? I'm sure you've got a backup. So I'll always have to be good to you. And I will. We're going to give you money, Stony: a hundred thousand dollars. And more help along the way, I promise. And the King's soldiers will always be taken care of. That I'll swear to you. You have my word. You hear me?"

She shuts her eyes. Why is he saying all

93

this? He said this yesterday. He said this the day before. He says it over and over. Why doesn't he just start torturing?

And then, as though he can hear her thoughts, he shakes his head gently. "What do you think, that I'll whip you? Or put bamboo shoots under your fingernails? Not my style. But yeah, the partners are antsy. Soon they'll force our hand. It won't be physical torture, I promise. It'll be much worse. Think. Who do you love, Stony? Think about it. Use your imagination. Or you can tell me. Just tell me, it's so simple."

Jaq opens the iron gate and walks her bike into Morgana's back garden. Fig tree, china-berry, dogwood: a latticework of branches that leads her to the rosette patio at the side of the house. Wafts of cookery from the kitchen: roasting ham and roasting apples. She unlocks the cellar door, pushes aside a droop of Lady Banks roses, and rolls the bike in. Her waitress uniform, apricot-colored with a white apron, sort of dowdy and flirty at the same time, waiting where Betty has hung it. She puts it on. She studies herself in the mirror. The light through the yellow roses: it's like she's in an old daguerreotype. Over her reflected shoulder is the big oak door that never opens. Morgana says it leads nowhere, it leads to a brick wall — then she'll change the subject. And Ransom won't talk about it either, and neither will Bebe. But other folks have told her that this door opens to a tunnel that descends to the storm drains and this was how Jaq's great-great-grandfather the bootlegger, back in Prohibition days, ran his booze secretly all over the city. She gets a shiver of fear from it now, which is sort of pleasing and sort of tinged with Luke's death: that confusion again. She locks the cellar and climbs the side stairs to the rear hallway, and enters the "keeping room," the room by the kitchen. Her cousins are here: Ginny and Lucia; they yelp with delight to see her, and exchange hugs and twirl to show off their outfits. They're in apricot waitress uniforms too. From the kitchen comes Betty, who wouldn't be caught dead in apricot (much too loud): she gives Jaq a hug too; meanwhile Marcel is pulling the hams out of the oven and bringing them here to the keeping room where Louis is carving them up. Right away Jaq pitches in and helps fill platters with the carved meat and the cloves and pineapple slices, while her cousins arrange heaps of biscuits in sweetgrass baskets.

As Jaq works she has only to lift her eyes

to see her favorite work of art.

It hangs between the two tall windows of the keeping room. Simple sketch of a horse race, from before the Civil War. The legend reads: *10B, Savannah 1856.* Only one corner of the sketch is reserved for the race itself, the barreling horses. The focus is on the grandstand: the mobcapped women, the waistcoated men, cursing, cheering, waving scarves. One crestfallen soul holds a busted ticket while the coquette accompanying him peeks out from under her big hat at some happier, luckier man.

"Hey," says Ginny, in her cautious way, "night before last, didn't I see you with some guy on River Street? In front of Bootleggers?"

Jaq smiles. "Pivot."

"That's his name?"

"Yeah, it sort of means he's a lookout. Like a gangster thing. He's a rapper."

Ginny grins. "He's sexy."

"Well. Yeah. But he does kinda deal drugs a little."

"Oh," says Lucia.

"Mostly just weed though."

"And he is *very* pretty," says Ginny, and they all laugh, and carry their platters and baskets to distribute them around the house. Jaq finds Morgana in the parlor, standing before the piano. Making a few last-minute tweaks to a grand arrangement of flowers, the sight of which makes Jaq bust out laughing.

At the base of the spray is a row of cancerous black blooms with long white whiskers. Above that, a tier of freesia, then clematis. And at the very peak, dominating all, an arc of what look like impossibly garish rocket ships. The whole edifice is unbalanced and nightmarish, and Morgana mutters, "Oh, ha ha is right."

"No, I mean, Gram, you've outdone yourself," says Jaq, and she gives Morgana's delicate bones a hug. "It's kind of a masterpiece."

It wouldn't be fair to say she's the only one *allowed* to hug Morgana. Others might get away with it if they dared. Her cousins Ginny and Lucia used to embrace her themselves, when they were little. But in adolescence they caught the terror of her like a contagion, and switched to the formal buss that Morgana's adult children all use, that everyone uses but Jaq. Only Jaq is still drawn to wrap her arms around her. And Morgana always hugs her back, after her fashion: a sort of arms-akimbo clutching, while emitting her high bird's laugh.

Now Jaq swings out of the embrace and

the two of them stand side by side, beholding the ziggurat of blossoms.

Jaq asks, "So who grew the black things?"

"Oh, guess."

"Miz Rundle?"

"Her new passion. They're called bat flowers."

"You've placed them perfectly, Gram. They're like a row of helmets. They're like bodyguards to the royal court."

Morgana smiles. "Yes. On a barge to the underworld."

"And the loud things on top?"

"Popsicle flowers. Papaya Popsicles from Rebecca Cressling. I know, they're inexcusable. Listen, Jaq, I'll need your help with her. And with Miz Rundle. Try to smooth out their first meeting with this creation? You're such a diva whisperer. You're so good at smoothing ruffled feathers."

Jaq shrugs. "I'll try."

Then she takes out her phone and coaxes her grandmother to stand in front of the flowers as she shoots a quick video. Morgana doesn't know it's a video; she thinks it's a still shot and she assumes her standard pose: power chin, frozen elegance — holding it for one instant then bustling off, mumbling, "So much left to *do* —" and Jaq congratulates herself to have caught such an essential Morgana moment.

Oh, she doesn't quite trust her, never feels quite safe here, but she does harbor a foolishly deep love for this woman.

She knows well that her mother Bebe resents Gram and claims she was monstrous to her and to Ransom and to Grampa Fred and to all sorts of people. Certainly Jaq has caught glimpses of that monstrousness along the way. But what she mostly sees in Morgana is her gift for social discernment, and her wit, and the burning energy she hurls at all sorts of noble causes. Within her sphere she's an inspiration. So many folks are glad to bust their asses for her charities. Louis and Marcel have worked these events for thirty years. Betty's also been here forever. And of course the TLG, the Three Loving Granddaughters: Lucia, Ginny, and Jaq do the Spring Soiree every year in their waitress outfits. Whenever they pose for photos (which they're obliged to do a dozen times per event), Jaq takes the middle, between her two white cousins, which piquantly asks the question: Which of these Loving Granddaughters is not like the others? Bebe hates these photos, hates the uniforms. She thinks them demeaning. "Don't you see, she's using you for virtue points. She's manipulating you. You treat it all like play, like dress-up — but you're still a young Black woman in a service uniform, working for an old, rich white woman."

Jaq thinks that's unfair.

Morgana has never insisted on the outfits. But Jaq is working at these events, she's staff, one of the TLG: she's happy to dress the part. And furthermore Morgana has never pressed her into this service. She always invites Jaq to come as a guest instead. Once or twice Jaq *did* come as a guest but had no fun. Kept wanting to jump up and do things. Had to stand around holding a sickly sweet cocktail (made by Louis) in one hand and a biscuit 'n' ham in the other, and engage in stupefyingly dull chatter, while her lucky cousins got to skitter around, rocking to their own beat and serving cheese straws and giggling at private jokes she was not privy to. Ever since then, she's volunteered every time. There's no pay, but contributions are made quietly to the fund for her MFA, and she gets to see Morgana flaunting her full powers, and she always has a blast.

Now she bears an Igloo cooler full of ice out to the porch. Marcel comes behind her with cases of soda, Louis has the liquor, and they set up the bar on the most beautiful screened-in porch in the world. All the tables and chairs are made of wicker, white and summery. Late sunlight comes through the dark green leaves of the fig trees. Wasps tap-tap on the screen. Male mockingbirds insult each other in the garden.

Aunt Willou, who's been busy doing the lesser floral arrangements, stops by the bar to say hello. She's Morgana's oldest daughter, and Ginny and Lucia's mother. Named for an Aunt Willow and an Aunt Louisa: Will-LOU. She's rail thin and wears her hair in a prodigious perm. She's a county judge with a reputation for toughness. She lives out at the Landings, the gated community on the water, and she's been called the greatest gardener since Capability Brown. Her husband is an analyst for Deloitte. She takes a spectacular array of mood pills. She drinks like a fish, is obsessed with the flaws of her own appearance, and has a mean streak. Tonight she asks Jaq about her time at Emory University: Was that good for her? Was it productive? When Jaq says she loved her time there, Willou casually tosses in: "Because Ginny's getting nothing from Duke. Nothing." She sips her drink and adds, "I mean, at least *you've* got a job; you got *some* thing out of it" — referring to Jaq's work at Peep's. It's Aunt Willou's efficient way of insulting Jaq and Ginny and the two colleges they went to all in one quick cut — plus throwing in a self-stab for good measure.

In return Jaq presents her with her first negroni of the night.

Knowing she'll be back for many more before the night is done.

Now it's six thirty. The first guest arrives.

Rayford Porter.

Morgana brings him to the bar. He's Morgana's age. Suave, large-boned, sharply dressed, with long, curly white locks of hair. In his youth, goes the story, he was blond and beautiful, with the physique of a prize-fighter. But he was also a drunken wastrel, and one night in Pensacola, Florida, he put on boxing gloves and got into a ring with a carnival bear. The animal soon grew tired of boxing, waded in and switched to wrestling, and Rayford was nearly killed. But returned home the wiser. He settled into investments and made a pile and now has a beautiful house out on Turners Rock.

Morgana says to Jaq, "You know what we want, don't you?"

They want her negronis. Everyone does. Jaq mixes them Savannah-style: a generous shot of gin topped by smaller doses of vermouth and Campari — just enough to impart "the color of the sunset outside" (plus a slice of Vietnamese orange, which Marcel's cousin sends up from Miami). As she pours, Morgana brags on her, talking up her movie.

"What's it called?" Rayford asks.

"May I tell him?" says Morgana eagerly, and when Jaq shrugs, goes on, "Well, you know she's applying for an MFA program. Documentary filmmaking, and so she's creating this movie that she calls *Some Town Out of a Fable.* It's sort of a documentary and sort of fiction. It's kind of a love letter to Savannah, isn't it, Jaq? All about the strange souls who inhabit this city. I've seen some of it and it's delicious."

Rayford gives one of his gentle chuckles.

Jaq hands him his drink. He takes a sip and shakes his head, as if to say, how unutterably *right.* She feels a jolt of pride. And she happens to know that Rayford is the anonymous donor who bankrolled much of her school tuition when she went to Emory, and she thinks, this is not a good time to mention that she has kind of stopped making *Some Town Out of a Fable.*

"I saw you riding out on Waldburg today," he says. "You shooting out there?"

"Oh yeah, I was looking for secret gardens," she lies. She doesn't bring up the burnt-up house.

103

Morgana says, "I'm sure Rayford would let you shoot his garden on Turners Rock. Best in the city."

"I'd be honored if you would," says Rayford.

"Oh, thank you," says Jaq.

"Though I gotta confess," Rayford adds, "everything I know about gardening I learned from your grandmama here."

He and Morgana share a happy look.

Imagine, Jaq thinks: having a friend who would still be your friend *in fifty years.*

Ransom, looking for old Billy Sugar, descends the steep stone staircase to River Street, which runs beside the wharves and has always been the city's center of commerce. It's now strictly for tourists, a fronting of adorable shops where you can buy Mamie's Real Cocoa-Pillows and Aunt Tessa's Real Hominy Grits and Lubba's Real Shrimp'n'Bacon Chips. In the air is the smell of burnt pig and burnt caramel, and last night's drunken piss, and the stench of the river mud. Ransom pushes through the crowd. He hates River Street. He never comes here. River Street is where he had the fight with his brother, the night that sent him to prison.

There, up there to his left, at the top of

those stone steps, his brother, David, accompanied by two hired goons, said repulsive things to Madelaine. Ransom should have held in his rage but didn't. Horror ensued. That ten seconds of memory: What do you do with it? You can't do anything. You're obliged to let it play. Your brain is a carnival and the star act is always performed by torchlight, performed over and over again by the same incompetent idiots, and the crowd is thoroughly sick of it; they jeer and catcall but then the curtain is drawn back and the cast trots out again, and the show must eternally go on.

He has to bump and dodge through the crowd nearly the whole length of River Street before he finally spots Billy.

Billy, with his dog, Gracie, on a park bench facing the water. Tourists have gathered round them. Ransom stands away and watches. When a child drops a dollar in Billy's hat, Billy says, "Say thank you, Gracie," and Gracie makes a deep stretch like a salaam. The kids gasp with pleasure. They line up to pat her. She accepts their worship with regal aplomb.

One child asks, "Mister, is your dog really saying thank you?"

Billy says, "Gracie, are you really saying thank you?"

105

Gracie makes a quick assured nod. The kids squeal some more. Fifty cents into the pot. Not much; these aren't first-rate dog tricks by any stretch, but they earn an old hobo some pin money.

The blast of a ship's horn. A mammoth freighter, its containers stacked to the sky, comes sliding down the river channel. The tourists drift off to the water's edge to watch it, and Ransom moves in and takes a seat on the bench.

Gracie's happy to see him. She wags her tail and lays her head on his knee. Billy doesn't look so pleased.

Ransom says, "I guess you two are ready for the big time."

"What you want, Ran?"

"Gracie, you need an agent. Not *his* agent. You're the star."

Gracie rubs her head against his thigh as he scratches her. Billy stares off at the ship.

Ransom says, "Well, I do have a question."

"I can feel that," says Billy.

"This woman Stony. You were at Peep's? You saw something go down?"

"What's this about?" says Billy. "Who you workin for?"

"I'm just asking."

Billy says, "Word is you and your mama paid a visit to the Chatham jail today."

"That got around quick."

"Workin for the Gooze?"

"Morgana *wants* to work for the Gooze. She thinks he's innocent. I want her to know he's guilty as sin."

Billy squints. "Why? What would that gain you?"

"I'm not sure. What did you see?"

Billy shakes his head. He's watching the approach of two train kids. They come sauntering up, and he mutters, "Have you met my new friends?"

"Train kid" refers to any dedicated hobo no matter their age. These are in their late thirties at least. They're both white. One is scrawny as a wizard, with dot tats under his eyes, a pointed beard, and a skirt worn over his trousers: half Buddhist, half psychopath. The other's short, stout, with a ring in his brow.

"Billy!" cries the Buddhist, and he grins. His incisors are filed. "T'sup my brutha Sugah?"

As friendly as can be. However, he carries an odor that Gracie doesn't like: she growls. In two seconds she'd explode, but the Psycho Buddhist tosses her a twist of Slim Jim, and she snaps the thing out of the air and is momentarily placated.

"Don't feed my dog," says Billy.

107

The Buddhist shows his sharp grin. "Take it easy, my brutha. Your puppy protects his papa, I like that, that's a noble thing. Hey, pooch, I got more."

Tossing her another tidbit.

Billy looks off at the freighter.

Then the Buddhist reaches into Billy's bag and takes out a can of beer. He doesn't fuss with the plastic-cup Scotch-tape ritual, just pops it open and drinks. But then makes a face. "Warm," he says. He spits it out. "Pissy." He tosses the can aside. Sits down on the ground before the bench, crossbones-style, and his buddy Stout sits next to him, and both of them stare up at Billy.

Utterly ignoring Ransom.

"So my brutha," says the Buddhist. "Don't mean to be pushy but I mean, you forgettin your promises?"

"Didn't make any," says Billy.

"Oh man," says the Buddhist. "Oh man, lying is bad for your soul." He shakes his head. Keeps that stare trained on Billy.

Finally Billy says, "What do you want? You want money?"

The Buddhist doesn't answer.

Billy digs into his pocket. "I got like, six dollars and change."

Graciously the Buddhist accepts the bills. "OK, you lovable old fart. Thank you. Keep the change though. Don't need your pennies."

"I got shit to do," says Billy, and heads off. When Gracie tries to hang back, hoping for more treats, he drags her with him.

The Buddhist calls, "Don't be cruel to your dog, Billy. We're watching you."

Then it's just Ransom facing the train kids.

He asks, "So what did Billy promise?"

For the first time, the Buddhist sets his full gaze on him. A long burning glare. "What he promise? He promise next time he sucks your dick he's gonna bite it off. Just stay out of other people's business, OK, Richie Rich?"

Ransom wonders, who's been telling this asshole about me?

At six forty-five, Lucia gives Jaq a heads-up (*"Rundle alert!"*), and Jaq whips up two negronis and carries them to the foyer just as Jane Rundle comes through the front door, leaning on the arm of Robert, her young "companion" (no one knows the exact terms of their relationship). She's eightyish and moves like a somber tortoise: sometimes extending her neck to peer at threats, sometimes retracting it. Betty's there to greet her, and Miz Rundle speaks to her in

109

the old, pure, nonrhotic Savannah accent: rich and haughty, with a floor of doom. "Well, Betty, we have suh-*viiived.* That's all we can say. We have suh-*viiived* anothuh *win*-tuhhh."

"Yes we *haaay*-uve," says Betty, in her country accent.

Jaq awaits her moment.

Morgana, she notes, is hanging back as well. She's up on the grand staircase, pretending to be in deep consultation with the auctioneer, but of course she's keeping a sharp eye on Miz Rundle. She wouldn't miss a drop of this.

Now Robert leads Miz Rundle into the parlor, which is wide-open to the foyer. All the guests watch as the two approach the arrangement.

Miz Rundle's neck lengthens. Robert scowls, ready to heap scorn upon Morgana's work. But at that very moment Jaq moves in with the negronis.

"Oh *yeesss,*" says Miz Rundle. Taking the drink in her long eager claws.

"Miz Rundle," Jaq asks, "did *you* grow those black flowers?"

"Those? Oh yes, those are my babies."

"Such *confident* babies." Jaq makes her voice low, conspiratorial. "The way they stand up before these . . . *other* flowers. Not surrendering to the cheap and tawdry. They won't tolerate bullying, will they? They won't put up with it."

Miz Rundle stands there, swaying, frowning. Jaq feels certain she took her flattery too far.

But then the old lady nods. "Why, *yesss*. They *whoan't* be bullied." And her head settles back into her shoulders, and she leans against her escort and makes an impatient gesture with her fingers, *get me to comfort.* Marcel and Louis bring over the wide shepherdess chair. They set it between foyer and parlor, to afford her a supreme view of her bat flowers, and everyone awaits the advent of Rebecca Cressling.

Jaq is reminded: you cannot flatter these ladies too much.

The trickle of guests becomes a flood. The house quickly fills. Everyone in their spring finery: flowery smocks for the ladies; seersuckers and gardenia boutonnieres for the men. The city manager, Harriet Mack, shows up with her husband, Ward. Then comes Mr. Warren Bledsoe, the owner of the Chatham Sugar Company. Also Bill Dunning, who has cerebral palsy and is seventh-generation Savannahian and vice chairman of the Board of the Society for the Disabled. The chief of police, Aaron

111

Swann: a Black man, big laugher, reputedly a true son of a bitch. He tries to flirt with Jaq. He makes a joke, and she grins and tells him, "Chief, you've got a line behind you." She serves a VP of Gulfstream, and the dean of the School of Fashion at SCAD. Lucas and Laurie Tartanian, old money. The founder of the ballet company, Carswell Bogdanovich, and his husband, Art Chandler, Morgana's CPA.

A man with a strong nose and kind of sad eyes steps up and asks for a seltzer water — and it takes her a second before she realizes: "You're the detective."

He smiles. "Wasn't gonna bring that up. What happens at the A-hole stays at the A-hole."

She hands him his seltzer. He murmurs thanks, and he's about to move off, but she says, "You know, I've actually seen you before today, now that I think of it. Here. At the Soirees."

"Uh-huh. I try to come. Everyone loves the Old Fort."

"And your name again . . . ?"

"Nick Galatas. Accent on the *la*."

"Right. And I'm Jaq."

"Hi again, Jaq. I'll let you work. Remember, anything you need from me . . . you got my number . . ."

Off he goes. And then Serena Underwood, a young blond debutante, steps up with two giggly friends, and they tell Jaq how much they *adore* her Instagram posts about the Gooze — and she's back to mixing negronis.

Next comes Gerson Hale, the famous photographer. Known for his portraits of south Georgia folks in grotesquely unhappy settings. He's Black and Native American, in his thirties, and stylish: three-quarter-length jacket, long hair. She says, "Hi, Gerson. Would you like a negroni?"

"Scotch if you've got that."

She pours one.

He asks very softly, "So how you doing with it, darlin?"

Takes her a moment to realize he's not talking about his drink.

He means Luke. Of course. Luke used to model for Gerson. Gerson liked him for his odd shape, and posed him in old trailer parks, in white-trash check shirts and skivvies. Luke hated these sessions but was desperate for the money. Afterward he'd stop by Peep's and drink a few shots in a row.

Now she says to Gerson, "I'm not too good. You?"

Gerson says, "Can't sleep. Sleep won't come."

She hands him his drink. "Gerson, tell me something. Will that fucker get off?"

"I guess. Time served or whatever."

"Jesus."

"They're all weasels," he says. "This is a sick little town full of weasels and they don't ever let you forget that."

Lucia passes by. She gives Jaq the word: *"Bec alert."*

Jaq gets to the parlor just as Rebecca Cressling is making her entrance in a yellow-and-black-striped smock and a knot-front hat, looking like a stoned bumblebee. As she approaches the great spray, Jaq angles in and presents her negroni and murmurs in her ear, "I have to tell you, Rebecca. Your Popsicle flowers. They triumph. I think they're a triumph of love over darkness. You know?"

Rebecca gazes awhile at the contrast between her happy blossoms and Jane Rundle's dour ones. She takes a sip of her negroni, which seems to please her; then she nods solemnly and says, "Lordy, you're right. They *do* triumph."

There's a little iron bridge that leads from Factors Walk to Bay Street, and on the far

114

side of it Billy and Gracie are waiting for him. The three of them walk together, in silence. Billy with his herky-jerky gait, looking like a badly strung marionette. Gracie sniffing everything, Ransom thoughtful. They take Oglethorpe Avenue nearly to the Savannah Police Headquarters. But Billy doesn't like walking past the A-hole, so they turn into the old Colonial Cemetery and follow the diagonal brick path through the mausoleums. The fragrance of tea olives. Ransom looks up at the imposing windows of the A-hole, and says, "So Jaq today, she went in there."

"In there? The A-hole?"

"Uh-huh. She went to complain about police conduct in the Luke Kitchens case."

"What, is she nuts?"

"She does have excess passion. That seems to run in our family. Hey, who were they, Billy? Those train kids, what did they want?"

"Dunno. They came around couple days ago. Askin me about that night — just like you. I say, Didn't see nothing of interest, gentlemen. They don't wanna believe me. They keep showin up. They tell me I promised 'em something. But I never did. They're sayin that just to needle me."

"They represent someone?"

Billy shrugs.

They come out of the graveyard near Perry Street, walking through a little playground. Billy says, "When I was a kid, I used to play on them swings. Over there?" He points to a ruined brick wall. "Used to be the jailhouse. The *old* A-hole. The inmates, they'd shout to us, Look here, kids. We got candy'n such. But I heard they had these long fingernails and if you got too close they'd snag you and pull you right up against the bars and cut your vocal cords so you couldn't make a sound. And then all night long they'd scoop your brains out with them claws, and you'd be found in the morning, except no head. So I never did go over there."

"Good Lord," says Ransom.

"Oh yeah. I grew up on shit like that."

They walk in silence down to Liberty Street, then to Wheaton Street, then to the CSX railroad cut. Down the tracks, through the woods. There's still light in the sky but a few stars are surfacing. They come to an oak tree. Four hundred years old, so it's said, dying, a great storm cloud of a tree. Somewhere off in the woods a bird starts singing. A song like a chuck-will's-widow, clear and haunting — but it keeps going and then takes a strange turn, kind of a flip and then sudden ascent into a melody so gorgeous it rearranges Ransom's insides. It's not a chuckwill's-widow, it's the Musician. Ransom stops and looks at Billy, who has also held up. Even Gracie has stopped: she has her ears up but she's not barking, just peering toward the music.

The Musician has his home back there. They can see it: a bit of blue tarp through the leaves. At night the Musician is generally abroad but sometimes just before dark he'll still be under that tarp. They stop walking; they just stand there on the tracks, listening. The music fades. The Musician must be headed the other way, toward town.

"Holy Mother of God," says Billy.

They walk on.

After a while Billy says, "OK, listen. I will say this one time. I won't go to no cops with it, ain't never gonna testify. But you wanna know what happened that night? At Peep's? So, I was hangin outside, like always. Stony comes out. She was in there with Luke but comes out in the company of some other guy. He had a jacket and a tie, but he smelled to me of Reidsville. And she's kinda leaning against him."

"OK."

"Not OK. Stony, she don't lean against nobody. But she was leanin against that one. Like she was real drunk, but she'd been in there less'n half an hour. She was fine when she goes in, but she comes out trashed. And walks off with that guy. Into the dark. Toward Madison Square. Then Luke comes out, and he goes right after them."

"And?"

"And nothing. All I seen. I shoulda kept my mouth shut. But maybe the next night I got toasted and let that story spill."

"Who'd you tell?"

"Do not recall. But now them train kids are ridin my ass."

Ransom asks, "If you saw that guy again, the guy with Stony? Could you —"

"Pick him out? I guess. If I cared to."

"You don't care to?"

"You playin? Don't play with this, Ran, you'll get us killed."

"Killed?"

"Do I stutter?"

Jaq and her cousins take turns showing off the auction things. They come down to the landing of the great staircase and look out at the crowd in the foyer and pitch away. Everyone adores the Three Loving Granddaughters. Ginny is crisp and snarky, and Lucia meanders like a spoiled child ("OK, here's a week's vacation at the Tartanians' cabin in New Mexico, and omigod if I

118

weren't so scared of snakes this'd be like *fabulous,* and see that hunky cowboy, yeah I'd bid a *crapload* — oops. I'm sorry"). The folks are quite entertained.

But Jaq is the real star.

She has a deep persuasiveness. Louis and Marcel wheel a plantation desk up to the foot of the stairs, and Jaq tells the crowd that this item was in Melissa Painter's family for six generations before tonight's generous donation. She points out a cigar burn, and tells how the authorities came for Charles Painter in 1848 for murdering his mistress, and how he set his cigar down *right here* while they were putting him in shackles. She's making this up on the spur of the moment, but it gets the crowd laughing, and everybody's in a merry, freewheeling spirit when the auctioneer, Bunny Willows, starts the bidding. The desk sells for sixty-five hundred — twice what they'd projected.

Next round, she peddles an original photograph from Gerson Hale's studio. "See this double-wide trailer? It's ninety-eight in the shade, and the boy on the couch is staring at the wall because he's bored to death and there's an emptiness in his life but also a sexiness, isn't there? Of course there is. Because this photo was created by the extraordinary Mr. . . . Gerson . . . *Hale!*"

Coaxing a big round of applause for him, and a winning bid of four thousand.

Then Morgana winds up the night.

She has lovely sly things to say about bat flowers and Popsicle Papayas and the women who grow them. Miz Cressling and Miz Rundle bathe in her praise. Each deigns to applaud the other. Then Morgana speaks of "the salt of the earth" in Savannah who support the disabled, those who give money but also those who give their love and time, those who advocate tirelessly, those who find their life's light in service. At the end of this address she brandishes an envelope that says top secret, and opens it and announces an anonymous gift of twenty-five thousand dollars. The audience cheers and howls, and everyone looks to Rayford. He stands mildly, bashfully, in the back of the room, swirling his third negroni, ignoring their gaze. And Jaq thinks: yes this town is a pit of vipers but there are also fairy godfathers here.

However:

An hour later, as the party has wound down and she's returning the Igloo to the kitchen, passing through the keeping room, she sees Gerson Hale gazing at the drawing of the racetrack, and she says, "I love that sketch."

"Really?" he says. "Do you know how long Morgana has had it?"

She sets the Igloo down. "Oh, it's always been here. It's an old family thing."

With a sober tone he offers, "It must be worth a lot."

"A lot?"

"Drawing of this quality, 1850s? Many thousands. Tens of thousands."

"Oh."

"Do you *know* about this racetrack?" he asks.

"Not really."

"Because this is the Ten Broeck racetrack."

"Oh. What's that?"

"It was just outside of town," he says. "Before the Civil War. Look here, by the artist's name: it says *10 B.* You see?"

She nods.

"That means Ten Broeck," he goes on. "It was owned by the Lamars. Your mother, Bebe, she descends from them, doesn't she?"

Jaq vaguely recalls that the full name of Bebe's father was Frederick Lamar Musgrove. She says, "I think so."

Now he presses: "But you really don't know what happened there? At that racetrack?"

"What do you mean, happened?"

He tells her.

She stares at him and wonders why he would say such a thing. Is he a sadist, to be fucking with her head this way? Is he pulling a prank? Is he warped, she wonders; was this some twisted attempt at a *joke*?

It's been a long brutal day at the ER for Bebe. At eleven, when her shift began, they got a nine-year-old kid who'd been shot in the foot by a drug dealer because he was working for a rival. They managed to save the foot. Won't walk perfect but will walk. Then at three a code blue came in, a fentanyl OD, a woman Bebe knew: Marie Jones of Port Wentworth. She'd OD'd on butter before; this was her third or fourth rodeo. The last time, Bebe had visited her in recovery, tried to talk her through her shit, keep her pride up. A month ago she'd run into Marie at the Kroger. Doing OK. Clean for a year. Working as a chambermaid at the Blue Sunshine Motel out on Route 17. Had even regained custody of two of her three kids. But in the long run nothing stands up to butter. Bebe was at Intake when the gurney came in, and could tell simply by the speed of the doors as they swung open (how they didn't burst but just calmly parted) that Marie was already gone.

Of course nobody quit. The team worked like dervishes: Dr. Krasnyk doing CPR, Wendy on the venipuncture, Bebe on the OPA. Slipping it so gently past the hard palate — doesn't want to tear that palate even though she knows what she knows. And every so often Ashley, working the paddles, would shout "All clear" and they'd all step back for the zap, and let Marie make another jump, then they were right back to work. Keep your head down and stay after it because you never know. Although you do.

Dr. Krasnyk called it at 3:47.

Yank out the tubes, the catheter, the conductives: not another minute with this nonsense. Move on. Patient's dead. Her kids will be lost to the winds, in six months nobody will ever mention her name except once a year when those kids will Instagram a picture of a pond lily and the words "Marie Jones, Never Forget" — though soon enough they'll forget to do even that. Then not another entry for all fucking time. Bebe went into the scrub room and washed herself like Lady Macbeth and then went to do rounds, and all day she's had no time to breathe let alone mourn. Until now. Now she's finally going home. Out in the parking lot, getting into her battered Santa Fe —

and still she has no time. She has to pick up her wife, Roxanne, at the Treutlan School, and as she's about to send a text saying she's on her way, she sees one from her daughter, Jaq:

Gram gave us a ham but I can't carry it on the bike can you come

Bebe would never have accepted that ham herself, because she won't take anything from Morgana. But if Jaq has already said yes, and if Marcel has already bagged it nicely, which he surely has, and if it's a ham from Mooney's, which of course it is . . . well, it *will* solve tonight's dinner question.

So all right, Bebe thinks, first I'll get Roxanne, then swing by the Old Fort.

She feathers the key, cranks the engine, texts them both, and goes trawling up Habersham. Kids on skateboards under the yellow streetlights. A trio of feral dogs, trotting along, mangy, heads low like they're on a mission. The big Kroger market and the sweet socializing all around it.

On Perry Street she pulls up before the Treutlan School.

Roxanne is the school principal. She gets into the Santa Fe and fastens her seat belt and releases a small *huff:* she's not a whiner

124

but you'll know by that little pushed-out huff how tired she is. She went to work at seven this morning and so has spent fourteen hours being beat down and pulverized by teachers, parents, children, and accountants, and Bebe senses it would be cruel to now unload on her about the kid with the damaged foot and the death of Marie Jones. So she keeps that to herself.

"How is she?" says Roxanne. Meaning Jaq. Roxanne is Jaq's birth mother, and she and Bebe have been together for fifteen years, married for five — and whenever they see each other the first question is nearly always: How is she? Particularly since the murder of Luke Kitchens.

Bebe says, "Gotta fetch her at the Old Fort. She worked the Soiree and Morgana's giving her a ham and she can't take it on her bike."

"A ham from Mooney's?" says Roxanne, a little lift in her voice. Then she asks, "Did you see her this morning?"

"For a minute. She ran out to shoot her movie. The secret gardens."

"She wasn't scrolling the Gooze News?"

"Not as I saw. Maybe she's getting better. How was your day?"

Roxanne grunts. "All parents are evil, but some parents are *cunningly* evil. You?"

"Survived."

The rest of the trip in silence. Till they pull up before the Old Fort and Bebe texts:

here

They have the windows down because it's such a nice evening. Memories for Bebe under every tree. That time with Lu Ann Farris under the brown turkey fig tree. They were playing sardines and hiding together and had a sweet kiss — though a few weeks later she caught Lu Ann making out with Ransom. Ransom was two years younger than Bebe and Lu Ann, but all the girls loved Ransom. God, it hurt at the time, but it doesn't hurt anymore, it just floats before her.

Text from Jaq:

Gram says could you guys come in for a minute

Good Christ.

Bebe reads the text aloud. "What new shit is she up to?"

"If it's OK I'll wait out here," says Roxanne. "I have emails to write."

"I'll be quick."

Bebe checks herself in the rearview. Two

drops of Visine. Slap some foundation on, that's it and fuck the rest, who gives a shit? Wish I hadn't worn this shirt though. Adds twenty pounds. Pray Willou isn't there: she'll give me that *how can you let yourself go this way* look. Which I can't deal with tonight.

Betty answers the door. "Oh Bebe! We *miss* you." They hug. Bebe knows of course about Betty's troubles, the sugar in the gas tank, and when she pulls back from the hug, she looks into Betty's eyes, wondering, how much is she medicating? Not too bad. Just slightly glassy.

"Betty, you OK? You need any help?"

"You know I'd call you. You shoulda been here tonight! Jackie was a smash!"

"Where is she?"

"With your mama. They're in the Turkish room. Waitin on y'all."

The words *Turkish room* give Bebe a chill.

It used to be that many Southern Victorian mansions had a Turkish room, a small and cozy chamber reserved for smoking, or for "intimate conversations." Morgana's Turkish room is the little round chamber in the ground floor of the turret, just off the foyer. There's a nod to Islam in the stenciled frieze: repeating Aladdin lamps, each with its own wisp of steam. Bebe has always hated this room. The sanctification of it. The way Morgana would show it off to guests: "Oh that's our Turkish room — for *intimate conversations,* you know?" You were never allowed in there unless something big was going down. Once, when Bebe was eight, all four siblings were collected here. She was placed on the settee between Ransom and Willou, with David in the Queen Anne chair. Father sat in the grandfather chair. Mother sat as always in the ancient leather armchair. When the children settled down, she announced their impending divorce. Then dismissed them. All her kids were sobbing. Bebe was sure Morgana had enjoyed the moment, had been delighted to use the room for such an *intimate conversation.*

A few years later the same team was mustered again (minus David, who was at Yale Law) for pretty much the same news. This time Bebe gathered her courage: "You really pulling the trigger this time?"

But it was another false alarm.

Seven years ago the summons went out again, and again they gathered — all adults now. Mother and Dad wore their long faces. Bebe drained her Madeira. "Please," she begged, "would you just fucking *do* it?"

Dad raised a hand. "My beloved children,"

he said, and told them he had cancer. Four months later he was gone.

Tonight, Betty slides open the wooden door to reveal Willou on the settee, Jaq next to her, Morgana on her leather throne. The grandfather chair has been left empty in honor of the fallen lord. A deathly silence. Why, Bebe wonders, does Jaq have her eyes lowered? Usually, after one of Morgana's soirees, she's stoked, bombing around in triumph.

Betty slides the door shut and pads away.

"Darling," says Morgana quietly, beckoning Bebe for a kiss.

Bebe figures why not play along if it'll help to get this over with. She bends; they do the side-by-side smacking thing. She gets a whiff of iris, the feel of soft down around her mother's temple, a vague memory of when her mother really felt like a mom.

She takes the Queen Anne. Her sister, Willou, smiles at her. Willou is at a particular moment on her arc of drunkenness, a time of complaisance before the evil settles in. If we can just move this along quickly, Bebe thinks, I'll get out of here with no real damage. She says, "So how was your Soiree?"

"Oh, wonderful," says Morgana. "The TLG did a fabulous job. Particularly *this* one" — meaning Jaq. "She put a spell on

129

Warren Bledsoe. Got him to buy one of Gerson's gloomiest 'Kodaks' for three times its value. Ha ha ha!"

She beams. Jaq wanly smiles.

"How much did you clear?" Bebe asks, trying to pretend she cares.

"For the evening? Oh, perhaps seventy thousand. When we add in the silent auction."

"That's great."

Silence.

"So what's up?" Bebe says abruptly. "Why are we here? You can't divorce him when he's dead, Mother."

Morgana shuts her eyes. Her "long-suffering" look, and Bebe knows she took it too far. Jaq will give her hell on the ride home. But it's time to poke this thing. "And so?"

"And soooo," Morgana drawls, "well, I'm sure y'all know about the young man who was burned in the fire?"

Jaq catches her breath. Soundlessly, but Bebe can feel it.

Willou says, "What about him?"

"You've heard they're holding Archibald Guzman for the crime?"

"Uh-huh."

"Well. He's asking our agency to investigate."

130

"Oh God," Bebe says. "By agency, you mean your little detective deal?"

Morgana makes an expansive gesture. *"Ours."*

"And you're taking him on?" says Willou.

"Nothing's signed. But I think we should say yes. He may well be innocent. Ransom and I went to visit him today at the Chatham jail, and some of what he said sounded persuasive."

Bebe narrows her eyes. "How persuasive?"

"Well, we can't know for sure until we really dive in but —"

"No, I mean how *persuasive*?" Rubbing her fingers against her thumb. "Cut the shit, Mother. How much is the Gooze coughing up?"

Morgana shrugs. "Well, of course we'd never take him on *at all* if we thought he was guilty."

Bebe glances at Jaq. The fury is evident in Jaq's eyes. Bebe says, "Mother, you do know Jaq was a friend of the victim? Right?"

"Well yes, so I'm sure she'll want to help. This will require all of us. The whole family. If we're going to find out the truth, I think we all have to pitch in. Mr. Guzman showed Ransom and me a note. Words that he was loath to speak aloud. The note said, 'Stone Kings. Treasure. Keep safe and give my

131

love.' Do any of you know what those words could mean?"

They stare at her.

Finally Bebe says, "Nope. Can we go now?"

"Hold on," says Morgana. "I have one more thing. There's a syringe: it was found at the burned house. Mr. Guzman's lawyers claim it's evidence that Luke Kitchens was an addict."

She's looking dead-on at Bebe now, and Bebe can sense where she's headed, but she tries to keep her gaze steady. "And what?"

"And," says Morgana, "*was* he an addict? Had he ever sought treatment? Do you know?"

"Mother. This is surreal. You really think I'd comment on that?"

Morgana's face fills with color. Her nostrils are slightly flared. "To save an innocent man? Oh, I do. Whatever you think of me as a mother, there's a principle here. It may be terribly old-fashioned and out of date, but there's still the presumption of innocence, which I don't think has been quite abolished yet. There's a fundamental principle —"

"Yeah right," says Bebe. "I can say it in four words. Rich. White. Men. Walk."

To which Willou replies, "Bebe, knock it off."

132

"Do what now?"

"It's a business. Mother owns a business. It requires her to find things out. She needs to know if the kid was addicted, because that will impact her client's freedom. Honestly, it's a reasonable fucking question. So she asks it, discreetly. That's how things get done in Savannah. What, does that get you all *triggered*? I'm sorry, little sister. Look, we saved some ham for you, so get off your high horse and take it home and have at it, take some biscuits too, get a big heap of mayonnaise —"

"Oh Jesus. Am I really being fat-shamed by a skeleton? This is rich. The ambulatory skeleton here calls me a pig, and claims to be related to me, while my fucking mother —"

"Children," says Morgana. "There's no call for this."

"No?" says Bebe. "I coulda sworn I heard somebody say, Tell your sister and your mother what raging assholes they are; it's important that they learn this. Jaq, it's time for us to go."

But Jaq raises her hand and says, "Wait."

She's staring at Morgana. Bebe has never seen her so still and taut. Morgana notices as well. "What is it, darling?"

133

"The drawing," says Jaq. "Of the race-track."

"Yes?"

"How'd you get it?"

"Get it?"

"How did it come into your possession, Grandmother?"

Morgana seems truly confused. "The sketch? It comes from Fred's family."

"You mean the Lamars?"

"I suppose."

"Charley Lamar?"

"Well, *that* I don't really —"

"It was his racetrack, Gram. You didn't know that?"

"What do you mean, his?"

"He owned it."

"Oh. Well I didn't know he *owned* that racetrack, no, all I knew —"

"I just googled it. It wasn't hard to find. Did you know about the slave sale?"

Morgana looks stunned. She slowly shakes her head.

"You didn't know he sold four hundred thirty-two enslaved people in one swoop — at that racetrack?"

"At . . . at . . ."

"Uh-huh. The slaveholder was Pierce Butler, who was Charley Lamar's friend. He needed a lot of money in a hurry, so

134

Charley kindly offered his racetrack as a venue for the largest slave sale in American history. They kept the enslaved folks in the stables. Split up all these families who had lived together all their lives, and sold them off to Louisiana and Texas. Yes, *that* racetrack. The one you keep in your 'keeping room' —"

Morgana sets her jaw. "Well, I surely did *not* know."

"You did though. Somewhere in your head, you must have put this together —"

"Did *you* put it together, Jaqueline?"

"It's not my sketch. Not my ancestors."

"Nor mine," Morgana snaps back. "That's my husband's family, not mine. The sketch doesn't really belong to me, I'm just holding it. It belongs to my children, my grandchildren. Everything here belongs to y'all. I'm just a *steward.*"

Jaq winces as though she's been slapped.

Among the sweetest things in Bebe's life has always been sliding open the door that permits escape from the Turkish room. Through the years the track of that door has been kept well oiled so it slides smoothly; it fairly jumps when you push it. Tonight when she pushes it, she finds Betty standing right outside, eavesdropping. Bebe and Jaq make a beeline past her, to the front

135

door. "Take care, Betty."

"Oh you too, Bebe. And oh Jackie, you were wonderful tonight, we're so *prouuud* a you."

Jaq goes down to the cellar and shucks her waitress outfit, which disgusts her now. She's frightened of the bare room and that big door to the underworld, and she quickly fetches her bike and rolls it out of there. Into the night air. In front of the house, the crappy old Santa Fe awaits. Roxanne behind the wheel, Bebe beside her. Jaq puts her bike in back, and climbs into the seat behind Bebe, and they drive off.

"Hey, Mama," she says. She calls Roxanne, her birth mother, Mama. Bebe she calls Mom. Outsiders get confused, but it feels perfectly natural to the three of them.

"Hi, angel," says Roxanne. Leaving it there. Not even asking about her day — so Bebe must have already filled her in on what just went down.

They drive past the big Kroger supermarket. It's lively tonight, folks gathered in the parking lot and somebody's playing Megan Thee Stallion's "Cry Baby" and a dozen folks are dancing or at least swaying. Jaq stares at them. She can't see them really. She can only see the sketch. She keeps hearing Morgana saying that word *steward.* For a while she shuts her eyes.

Then she opens them and says, "I mean the thing is, Mom, what you've been telling me about Gram all these years? You were right. You can't trust her. The way she keeps saying, Oh Jaq you're so *brilliant,* you're so *original,* you're so *born to command:* yeah, I admit that got to me. She's always like, Oh, let's be *of service.* Let's see if we can't wheedle fifty grand from Mrs. Cressling on behalf of the disabled, the disadvantaged, the fucked-over. Makes you feel you're in a noble band of outlaws, you know? Like you're riding with Robin Hood. But then . . . *this.*"

Roxanne says softly, "So what happened?"

Jaq takes a moment to gather it up. Then she says, "In Gram's house there's a sketch of a racetrack."

"Uh-huh," says Roxanne. "Near the kitchen."

"Yeah. You know what that racetrack *was?*"

"Why, is there some secret?"

Jaq takes a breath, which Roxanne picks up on: she asks, "I mean, is this the kind of thing that's going to make me drive into a tree?"

"Yes it is," says Jaq.

137

So Roxanne pulls over, across from the Salty Dog Tavern. Then turns in her seat, and Bebe also turns; the two of them face their daughter and Roxanne says softly, "OK. What?"

Jaq says, "So that racetrack was owned by Charley Lamar, that's Mom's great-great-grandfather. Right, Mom?"

"Something like that."

"It was his racetrack, and one time he used it for the biggest slave sale in American history. Four hundred thirty-two people."

"The Weeping Time," says Roxanne.

"Yes," says Jaq, and she asks Bebe, "Mom, you never knew that sale happened at Lamar's racetrack?"

Bebe has tears in her eyes. "Of course not."

"How could you not know?"

"I just didn't, I didn't know."

Roxanne asks, "How did you find out about this?"

"Gerson Hale told me. Tonight. So I went up to the guest room and googled it. It was called the Ten Broeck Racetrack, and it was owned by Charles Augustus Lafayette Lamar, and what a monster he was in every way. Rich fucking entitled bully. If he didn't like people, he'd beat them senseless on the street, and nobody said a word. He didn't like the law against the Atlantic slave trade, so he bought the fastest yacht in the world and went to Africa and brought back six hundred enslaved people, except two hundred died on the way, and all the white folks thought this was a great exploit, that he was a great hero. And then he had that slave sale at his racetrack. I thought, oh maybe Gram doesn't know about that, or doesn't know that was *his* racetrack. Right? Give her the benefit of the doubt. So I come back down, go into the Turkish room, and that fucking woman is in her judgment chair asking us to work for the Gooze. For the guy who burned Luke Kitchens alive."

Bebe says, "I'm so sorry, honey."

"And then, and then she *demands* that you betray your medical ethics. On behalf of that asshole. Which of course you won't do. I mean for *years* I've been giving you a hard time about Gram. I've always been like, why is Mom so mean to Gram? OK, so Gram *is* kind of manipulative, kind of a power freak, kind of a narcissist, kind of a meddling fucking duchess all the time, but so what? She's still so much *fun.* Right? That's what I always said. But now I can see her. The charities are all for show, aren't they? Really, deep inside, she lives for her privilege, doesn't she? Just *lives* for her position in this town, and she'd sacrifice anyone to that. And think of Uncle Ransom, your poor brother, who she *destroyed* with all her weird shit. I mean broke his heart and drove him nuts till he wound up in prison and now he's living on the streets. And she wants us all to work for the Gooze? She's a witch. I hate her. I hate her ancestors. I'm *so* glad I don't have that toxic fucking blood in my veins. I'm sorry you do have that blood in your veins, Mom. It makes me sick. I hate her."

She can't say any more though because she's starting to cry. Bebe gets out of the car and opens the rear door, and Jaq gets out, and Bebe takes her into her arms. Then Roxanne comes around and holds them both.

The three of them, in an embrace across from the Salty Dog Tavern.

Somebody driving by calls out, "Get a room!"

Detective Galatas after the Spring Soiree is out in his Sierra, cruising down Montgomery, just "peeping the town," he calls it. Stops at Channi's market to get some NOS Nitro Mango, which he's kind of addicted to. Three droopy white kids and one droopy Asian kid feeding gas to their Nissan. Rich kids, SCAD kids. Inside the store he runs into Floyd McDew. Black, lived here all his life, one burglary fourteen years ago but he's clean now and works at the pulp mill. Floyd is glad to see him because he helped him out of a jam once. Galatas asks about his wife and her choir — she sings at Smyrna Baptist — and Floyd says please do come see them sing, and Galatas says he will.

Then back out on Montgomery again, cruising.

That big green house near 38th has new paint — which doesn't quite compute because only an old lady lives there, Mrs. Vonda Ragsdale, who has no money — so does this mean her prodigal son is back? He's handy but stupid and hooked on heroin. He'll let shitheels stay in the carriage house. Need to be watching that.

Checking his city. Poking, measuring, weighing. Trying to get a fix on it, which is impossible, because it's always changing, always squirming out of his grasp.

On Burroughs Street he happens to notice fifteen-year-old Vernest Cleveland. He's hanging out in front of the Sweet Shed candy store. Now what's this story? Vernest is a "corner boy," a lookout for dealers. He ought to be keeping an eye out for cops like himself. But he's got his nose in a video game — and Galatas blows right past him down to Floyd Adams Park, where he gets right up on the action. Two on a picnic bench: Dante Ferrell and Angel Garcia. One Black, one Dominican. Negotiating with some white guy whom Galatas doesn't recognize but that's OK; he's not trying to bring down a drug ring, not tonight. He's just a bit worried about Vernest.

So he calls the kid's mother. While he's driving, he calls and lets her know Vernest's whereabouts. He says, no, the boy is not in legal trouble yet, but if you don't nip this in the bud he'll soon be dead. She's a good woman who cleans houses. She says she's on her way right now. Galatas keeps rolling in a wide arc around the town.

He's on 36th going east when he comes upon Officer Dayquon Orr in a police cruiser. Dayquon is Black, tough as rebar, used to ride in a Bradley Unit in Afghanistan, and there's even a picture of him up in a hatchway wearing night-vision goggles. When he came back home, he decided to keep fighting the assholes. Outdated notion, but that's how Dayquon lives. A great street cop. With a real nose for the putrefaction of souls. Galatas reveres the man. He eases up next to the cruiser.

Dayquon asks, "Is it true some girl came

to the station to complain about the Guzman case?"

"Uh-huh. Bartender at Peep's. She thinks we're gonna let him go."

"Ha," says Dayquon. "*You* won't."

"I tried to tell her that."

They talk about this and that. Cars collect behind them. These cars have room to go round but they're scared of going round a police car. So they just wait. No honking, no cursing. Good, thinks Galatas, learn some respect, learn some patience.

Dayquon says, "So there's this guy Lootie, homeless guy, up at the Yamacraw camp?"

"I know him."

"He says he saw Guzman toss that gas can in the dumpster."

"Yeah?"

"Yeah that's what he *says*. But he's looking for mercy on that intent to distribute, so I don't know."

"I'll look into it. But we need something that'll stick."

He drives on. Heading vaguely homeward.

He's on Habersham coming up to Troup Square when he spots the very wealthy Warren Bledsoe, owner of many mills and refineries, walking his King Charles spaniel. There's a cute little marble fountain in the

143

square, with a low bowl especially for doggies: that's probably where they're headed. Galatas pulls over. Lowers his window and says, "Hey, Warren." Bledsoe does deign to smile — though without warmth, because Galatas is only a cop while Bledsoe owns pulp mills and a sugar refinery. And serves on the Coastal Area Planning Commission, and has a brother on Wetlands and sisters on three zoning boards: so Galatas must defer. He says cheerfully, "You outbid me at the Soiree tonight. Those andirons. Those were impressive."

"Oh," says Bledsoe in a bored drawl. "I'm sure they're fake. I'm sure I paid too much."

But Galatas keeps cheerful, keeps deferring. "You know, I ran into Joe Holland the other day. He got himself a new Fabarm twenty-gauge shotgun. He showed me. Turkish walnut stock and a swamped rib barrel, and the trigger breaks like fuckin glass at four pounds. But I tell you *what,* Warren. You could still outshoot him with your old Benell."

But he feels Bledsoe tense up. A suggestion of: *this cop is not in my tribe and he's being too pal-sy here.* "Wait," says Bledsoe, "you and I been huntin together?"

"The Jaycees?" Galatas reminds him. "Quail hunt? Down by Midway?"

"Oh. Oh yes, uh-huh. I shot quite a few birds that day."

The spaniel is tugging at his leash and Bledsoe turns away then with a goodbye wave that's not really a wave, more a flick of the forefinger. Galatas does not merit a wave.

Nevertheless, he is not upset. He smiles as he drives off. He thinks, does Bledsoe forget that I shot nine quail to his three? Also, the gentleman has a nasty surprise in store for him, doesn't he? A little trap he's already fallen into but doesn't know it yet, but soon he'll learn that although the mills of the gods grind slowly, they grind exceedingly fine.

It's midnight, and Ransom is sleepless. He lies on his bedroll beside his tent, in the woods near the Truman Marriott, and looks up at a patch of sky, at the stars. It's quiet. Now and then a car will come off the Harry S Truman Parkway and take the long curve of the off-ramp. The woods will fill up with headlights. Then the car will turn left or right onto President Street and the lights will fade and the night sounds will come back: cicadas, bullfrogs, far-off train horns.

He's looping Madelaine. Memories of Madelaine.

The time she came to his dorm room at Duke, wearing that sunflower dress. She was twenty; he was twenty-four. He was in law school. She was an undergraduate who loved poetry and had just transferred from Hollins. She was of the Hilliards, an old Savannah family, and was engaged to be married to Ransom's brother, David, who was already a successful corporate attorney in Savannah. Of course when she arrived at Durham she looked up her fiancé's brother, to pay her respects or whatever, and invited him to a poetry reading. Sounded dismal but he agreed out of politeness. When he went to fetch her, she had a new plan. Another friend was performing at a comedy club, and they went there instead, and that was *truly* dismal; that was more hushed and funereal than any poetry reading.

But afterward, when they went to a dive bar to drank tequila rickeys, she said yeah, the show was excruciating, but still she liked that anyone was willing to brave such humiliation for a thread of hope. Though she agreed, it truly did stink. Ransom thought his brother had lucked out. Madelaine had a sense of justice, but dark wit as well. Also bright green eyes. She talked about David a lot. How enthralling she'd found his stories of Morgana, how charming he was with friends. They had another round of rickeys and talked about their favorite poets (John Clare and Annie Dillard). Quoted whole poems to each other. Then went to another bar where they told Savannah stories. They had generations worth of Savannah gossip to share. Not just what they had done or seen, but what their great-grandmother's cousins once removed had done or seen. Back and forth they went. She told of her great-aunt Edna, who was such a Southern belle that when her little daughter had sat too close to the fireplace and her skirt had caught fire, Edna had simply fled the room, leaving another child to put out the flames. Ransom told of a great-grandfather who was a chemist for the Union Bag Company and who had died of a heroin overdose in the arms of his mistress. Madelaine listened with rapt attention. She admired his drinking prowess; he admired hers. Later that week they skipped classes and drove with friends in a caravan up to the little town of Hillsborough and went hiking. Talked throughout the hike. Kept talking when they stopped for lunch at the Wooden Nickel café. Their friends went home without them. It was just the two of them heading back together in Ransom's car. She let something slip: she said David seemed maybe too *settled* for age twenty-seven, too deeply planted in the culture of Savannah law and power, too undisturbed by the easy corruption of the town.

Then, for a mile, there was silence.

Then Ransom told her the story of how when he was eleven, he had been goaded by David, fourteen, to steal a secret key from Morgana's jewelry drawer. They used it to unlock the big door in the basement that led down to the storm drains. They had one flashlight between them. They wandered for hours through the eerie brick tunnels and the vaulted brick chambers. But then David said, "Bet you wouldn't last a minute without the light." Ransom agreed with that. David said, "Don't you want to toughen up? Mom says you're too weak. She says you're a trembling leaf. She thinks you're such a loser." Keeping up with that line of abuse till Ransom agreed to one minute of absolute darkness. David switched off the flashlight and stole away. As soon as Ransom realized he was alone he panicked. He heard David run down a tunnel, and he went after him, feeling his way, screaming for him to turn the light on. Soon he got lost in the blackness. Lost for hours till he finally saw a glimmer of light up above, and climbed up a ladder to a drain hole, and shouted for help. The Savannah Department of Stormwater came and opened a manhole for him, and the police brought him home. His family was waiting on the porch, all beside themselves. But he ignored them. He went looking for David. He found David in the parlor, launched into him like a missile and brought him down and started pummeling him. David was much bigger than he was, but Ransom was inflamed with rage. Kept hurling those fists. David kept screaming, "Get him off! Get the psycho off me!" Until finally Rayford, who was visiting at the time, lifted Ransom up into the air and held him there — and he was still punching, still flailing away.

Ransom tried to paint himself as the fool in this story, as the bratty and panicky little brother who deserved a good scare. But Madelaine saw the tale in a different light. She saw David as a bully. Ransom took no special pains to disabuse her of that view.

The road they were driving on was through farmland. It dipped into a cool hollow and she said, "The air feels so clean here, doesn't it? Not like Savannah. To me Savannah always feels like my great-aunt's kitchen when she's boiling water for tea."

The next week they drove to the shore.

The pain was welling up in both of them now, though neither of them spoke of it. It was a labor to even converse, to choose a radio station on their drive, to choose a barbecue joint. Everything seemed tender; everything hurt. When they went into the ocean and splashed each other, that was like murder.

And it went on like that, unspoken, this untreated inflammation; it went on for weeks and got worse and worse until one morning she came to his dorm room and sat in the camp chair and managed to summon forth: "We've got a problem."

The next day they flew home to Savannah.

She went to her parents. He went to see Morgana, only Morgana because Dad was off hunting.

She was on the porch. The pineapple glasses, the pitcher of iced tea.

He told her, "Madelaine Hilliard and I are in love."

Her face went white, but her voice stayed calm. She evinced quiet curiosity. She inquired about his plans. He reminded her that he was nearly done with law school, and this summer he and Madelaine might journey to Asia together and follow the Silk Road.

Quite coolly she said, "And your brother?"

"Madelaine's going to talk to him. This weekend."

She nodded. She said softly, "Well, one thing to bear in mind is that if you should happen to go through with this bizarre scheme, it would kill him. We both know him. He'll drink himself to death inside of six months. Also it would annihilate your father. And your sisters. And everyone we love, and the Hilliards, all of them including Madelaine; not to mention your poor mother. For the rest of our lives our families would share nothing but disgrace and unimaginable grief. Do what you feel you must, but bear that in mind."

Madelaine got the same treatment from the Hilliards.

In fact, Morgana and the Hilliards soon joined forces. Ransom and Madelaine fought back for a while but then surrendered. Madelaine flew off to Europe, alone. David, who was told nothing of their love, somehow did find out where Madelaine had gone: the Greek island of Patmos. He flew there. He was careful to not be an asshole. He spent a week with her on Patmos, then they traveled to Turkey and then to Croatia and so on. They came back married.

Ransom did not leave town. His father got

him a job at the law firm of Schilling & Bates, making good money to pay down his law school debt. He thought, I'll take care of it in a year and I'll be out of here.

Three years later he was still at Schilling & Bates. And one day he got a letter, a real letter, in his mailbox, from Madelaine. Saying how sorry she was. And revealing the depth of her troubles with David, who had become abusive. Not physically, but when he got drunk — which was often — he turned into a vicious bully. She quoted him; the quotes reminded Ransom of Morgana. She said she'd understand perfectly if Ransom didn't want to write her back, but if he did, he could leave a note in the trunk of a certain live oak at the dairy farm, where she would find it.

Yeah, he thought. Not in this lifetime.

He went to the sink and burned her letter. I'm sorry, he thought, but there's nothing I can ever do for you.

Ever, ever, ever.

Now as he lies there looking up at the night sky, a single car departs the Truman Parkway and swings round the exit ramp. He watches its headlights in the trees and listens to the frogs and the cicadas. Then hears the shutting of a car door, way off, and then another.

He wonders, who'd be coming to the Marriott at midnight? Henry deals pills, but his clients never come around *this* late. Or it could be the police. But no, it won't be, the police don't come in pairs. When they come, they come in flocks. Then he recalls that Liza has a car and will often make late visits to the Salty Dog to see what she can turn up: someone must be getting lucky.

He drifts for a bit.

Then abruptly he's hearing voices. Coming from Billy's tarp, which is just thirty yards away through the trees. Billy and some other guy. Speaking quietly, but rapidly and without warmth, and Ransom silently rises and pulls on his trousers and shirt, and slips on his shoes and then his headlamp, though he leaves that switched off. He starts on the trail to Billy's tarp. Stepping carefully. Lots of roots. Barely enough moonlight to pick his way. Rustling through palmettos as he walks but the murmur of the frogs covers that. He's thinking: it could be one of Billy's grandsons. Billy has three grandsons and they're all troubled and they show up at odd times needing things. And there are many other troubled souls who latch on to Billy now and then: Maybe it's one of them? But why, he keeps wondering, didn't

Gracie bark? She should be barking her head off at any visitor.

Then when he's right up on Billy's camp, he hears Billy say clearly, with acid clarity, "Fuck you then."

A voice comes back, "Always such an attitude. Always treat us so *unfair.*"

Ransom knows it instantly: the insolent whine of the Psycho Buddhist. And as he comes closer, although the moon is faint and the campfire only embers, he can make out Billy sitting on an upturned milk crate and the Buddhist looming over him. The Buddhist holds a machete. Gracie is stretched at Billy's feet. She seems to be sleeping. But she can't be sleeping with that man standing there.

Ransom glides toward them.

Billy Sugar spots him. The Buddhist must have picked up something from Billy's gaze, because he turns, and says quietly, "Ooh, shit, it's the fucked-up rich kid. Ooh, here we go."

Ransom reaches up and switches on his lamp.

The Buddhist is wearing a mask, some kind of ghost mask, but there are holes through which his eyes are visible. They're sparking: he seems happy, jacked. He says, "We were waiting for you, weren't we, Billy?

154

Did you bring a gun?"

Ransom steels himself. When he rushes, the Buddhist will get one good swing at him with the machete — but in that instant Billy can jump him, and maybe the two of them together can bring the Buddhist down. If Ransom survives the machete.

But the Buddhist is laughing at him.

"You mean," he says, "you got no gun at all? You just came to watch? Well, OK, watch. Without a witness this'd feel pointless, wouldn't it?"

He raises the blade. It gleams in the beam of Ransom's headlamp. He's taunting Ransom. Making it clear there are no options now, no excuses — and Ransom accepts this and charges. With each step the light from his lamp leaps and falls. A glimpse of the slashing machete; then dark; then a frame of Billy's face opening into a howl; then dark again. Ransom slams into the Buddhist and the two of them go flying, smacking into the trunk of a palm tree. The headlamp flies off and goes cartwheeling into the night. He gets his hands on the Buddhist's neck. The Buddhist twists, jackknifes, but Ransom keeps all his focus fixed on his thumbs, on the grip that promises this fucker's death. He can feel the ligaments giving way, the soft tissue.

Then an explosion in his skull.

Some awareness that he's been kicked. Also that the same boot is swinging back to kick him again, and he's got nothing to stop it with. Again, the lightning. This time he's cajoled into leaving this world, letting go of it as a leaf lets go of a twig. He starts to sink, to flutter down through shades of gray mist. Stretching out his limbs as he goes, grateful for the change of scenery.

But Billy, he vaguely recalls, is still up there.

Billy and Gracie are up there somewhere, and he ought to see about them. Aren't they in some danger? He reaches back. Tries to get some grasp on the former world. But it's electric with pain: he wants to let go again, leave it.

But Billy's up there.

He concentrates. Opens his eyes.

His skull's on fire.

Billy's lying right beside him. Looking sleepily back at him. But not seeing. Ransom raises himself a little. Billy's head is beside him, but the rest of Billy is over by the gutted fire, by Gracie, still clutching her fur.

Ransom hears his own small voice say, "They killed Billy."

Then a little louder. "They killed Billy."

He fills his lungs with air. He hurls his

voice into the dark: "THEY KILLED BILLY."

Then he sees Gracie stir a little, or thinks he sees that. He crawls over and puts his hand on her chest, right beside Billy's hand. Does he feel something? Is she trembling?

Around him, the vagabonds are gathering. Cries of horror, keening. More and more folks, an arc of them, already in mourning. Ransom calls, "Who's got a phone?"

Nobody, of course.

He says, "Henry. Go to Monica's tent, tell her to call 911. Then the vet. Tell her to call Mary the vet, tell her we've got Gracie, tell her we're comin."

Henry moves off, and Ransom hoists Gracie up into his arms. "Liza, your car."

He carries Gracie; Liza and Hatchet Head follow. They take the path out to President Street, to Liza's old wrecked Impala. As they set off toward town, they pass the police coming in their cruisers: one, two, three of them, lights ablaze, sirens spinning.

CHAPTER TWO:
FLANNERY KNEW.
FLANNERY GOT OUT,
WHAT A LUCKY GIRL!

The Musician is not whistling tonight: there are people in Whitefield Square, and he won't work to an audience. He doesn't mind folks eavesdropping so long as he can't see them. If they're a block or three blocks away they can listen all they want, but when they're right there ear-gawking at him he gets nervous and clams up. And tonight there's a host of people, a steady migration of them going east to west through the square, their movement accompanied by an orchestra of distant sirens. They're homeless folk. They're all humping their stuff: backpacks, garbage bags, crates; and they all look outcast and exhausted, and here comes a woman carrying a child on her shoulders and the child's whimpers can be heard above the sirens.

Word's out there was a murder tonight at the Truman Marriott. The cops know they'll be getting shit from the citizenry tomorrow, so tonight they're going in force to all the Eastside camps, not just the Marriott but to all of them, one camp to the next and trashing everything in their path: they think that will mollify the public outrage. So everyone on the Eastside has gotta clear out and find whatever shelter they can. Some will tuck in under the benches in the squares. Some will find spots in the Westside camps: the cops are leaving them alone.

There's no rhyme or reason to any of this. Maybe tomorrow the police will trash the Westside camps. But those are the rules for tonight.

As he sits there and watches, a tune begins to worry him. The sirens and the crying child have disclosed part of a chord, and he's trying to find the rest of it. This chord, as it makes its way toward being born, feels like early Scriabin, pre-*Prometheus* but with some of the later harshness. He needs to express the thing. Powerfully in his mind he can hear the modulation from F♭ minor to E♯ minor, and he wants to wrap his lips around these notes. He's just about to get up and go find some privacy when Henry, one of the vagabonds from the Truman Marriott, plunks down on the bench beside him and says, "Oh Jesus. Shit I seen tonight."

The Musician says, "Oh."

Henry tells him that he saw the murder scene. He says it was Billy Sugar who was killed, and he was killed by drugged-up train kids. He provides details, although the Musician has not asked for them. He tells the Musician about Billy's severed head. He says that he saw Billy's dog, who had been dosed and is now, for sure, dying. The Musician knew Billy Sugar, and knew Gracie, and in his thoughts this event reshapes itself into an as-yet-unwhistled C# minor seventh.

The homeless refugees keep shuffling through the square.

Henry says, "Course *we* get the hammer. They're clearing out every camp on the Eastside except the white supremacist camp, 'cause the cops are scared of *them,* but everybody else has gotta go, that's twelve fuckin camps, brother. They got Hatchet Head and Boiled Liza at the station. And Ransom Musgrove, they're tryin to pin the murder on him."

The sirens keep rising toward the G#. They're unstable but their instability shimmers. And now some Savannah dogs are starting to howl the B. And there's misery in every face that passes. Henry says, "First we lose Luke and now Billy. They're gonna

160

kill us all, ain't they?"

After a moment the Musician thinks to ask, "Where's Stony? Do you know Stony? Do you know if she's safe?"

"Nah," says Henry. "Ain't seen Stony for a while."

They sit there quietly.

Then Henry says, "How 'bout you? Where's your stuff?"

"Oh," says the Musician. "I left it."

"It'll all get *took.*"

"I know."

All the Musician's stuff is under a blue tarp in the woods by the CSX tracks. He keeps many things under that tarp. Some of them — certain well-worn items of clothing, a beloved fry pan, a few keepsakes — are of great value to him, but it's too dangerous to go back there now, with all those rampaging peace officers.

Also, it was time to leave that tarp anyway.

It was beautiful there. Peaceful, in the trees, with an ancient live oak not far away. Easy walking to the center of the town. But it had a drawback. Not a stone's throw from the tarp is a portal down to the Savannah storm drains: a squat concrete cylinder with a slanted steel door. And every day lately there's a guy who's been using that portal. Going down into the drains early in the morning, really early, like 5:30 A.M., unlocking that door and going down into the darkness and then an hour later coming up again. Just as it's getting light. The Musician is an owl: he prefers to be abroad at night, wandering, whistling. He likes to get home around 5:00 A.M. Then he'll be on his hammock, just drifting off: and there goes that guy.

And late in the day, maybe 6:00 P.M., just when the Musician has had his breakfast and is about to start wandering, that man will come again. Same routine. Every day, twice a day. Who knows what he's up to down there? Probably involves contraband. Folks have been smuggling shit through those drains for 150 years. The Musician does not want to see any of this. He does not want to watch the comings and goings of criminals. He always pretends he's asleep, though his tarp is far enough back from the portal that probably the guy doesn't even notice him.

The biggest problem is that he's pretty sure he knows the guy.

He's made up his mind he won't be staying there anymore.

The loss of his home causes an intense sadness, but tonight everyone has lost their homes, and Billy Sugar is dead, and so long as these police sirens keep screaming into the night the Musician has work to do. He has a duty to compose against them. He says good night to Henry and goes looking for a place to perform in peace.

Jaq's in bed TikToking. Flicking from clip to clip, but not really seeing anything. She can't possibly sleep. First, because the night is full of sirens — something nasty is going down out there — but mostly because in her head Morgana keeps saying that word. *Steward.* Oh, steward is right, steward of all the shit. Those people at the Soiree tonight, that's what they do, they steward all the shit down through the generations. They keep it in their keeping rooms: their portraits, and their secretary desks, and their hierarchies and dynasties: they keep it all just as long as they can — and without thinking Jaq finds herself instinctively going to her Messages because she's desperate to text Luke about this.

But of course she can't text Luke about it.

Oh, she misses him abysmally.

And then, although she's promised herself she won't go back to that video, she decides she needs a taste. Just a little taste, a moment of his laughter. So she summons it on her phone. She tries to skip ahead, right to Luke, but she's impatient and starts too soon, at the moment where Stony is saying, "They're free people, OK? That's all. The King's soldiers are the only free people to ever live in the State of Georgia. They *live,* that's all. They're not on the Savannah Death Trip, they're not ghosts —"

She pauses it.

Drags it back and replays.

That clue. That weird clue from Guzman. Stone Kings, treasure.

How stupid she was to have not seen it. So wrapped up in her rage she hadn't even noticed. Stony's real name is Matilda Stone. And she was hanging with Luke on the night he died. So she could know something, couldn't she? She *must* know something. And the Gooze knows she knows.

And there's something else, something else that nags at her, something she remembers from a long time ago. About some treasure in Savannah. She lies there, trying to remember. Shuts her eyes and tries to conjure it. But still those sirens. Whining, whining. And a moth tapping against her window, tap tap. When all she wants is to remember. What is it? What is this memory that's teasing her? Tap tap. So hard to focus. Tap tap, that fucking moth. She slides her eyes to the window.

There's a face there.

Just outside, covered in blood, leering at her.

With fierce eyewhites, and demon tattoos crawling on the neck and the hair swept up into a blue crest. She sucks in all the air of the room.

But it's only Hatchet Head, she realizes. Just Hatch, standing outside her window.

She slides it open. "What?"

"They killed Billy."

She stares at him. "They what?"

"Billy Sugar," he says. "They cut his head off."

"Oh." Instantly her eyes fill with tears.

He says, "Train kids did it."

"Why?"

He shrugs. "They so fuckin cranked up all the time."

"Where's Ransom?"

"Cops took him. Acting like *he* did it. They're gonna try to frame him."

She struggles to take all this in. Holds up a palm: wait. Lets the curtain go and puts on her jeans and a T-shirt and a jacket in twenty seconds. Carries her sneakers because Bebe is a light sleeper. Tiptoes out to the kitchen and hears Roxanne snoring like the ocean, and under that is the windy sighing of Bebe, and the sound from both of them is deeper than usual — because tonight they're certain their little girl is safe, tucked away in her bed, which is something of a rarity; she's usually at Peep's or some boy's house. She knows she should not be doing this to them. But what choice does she have? She floats to the front door and out to the carport, the driveway. Nobody out here, perfect stillness. For a moment she entertains the thought that Hatchet Head's visit was a dream. But when she walks out onto 49th Street and stands there, headlights appear.

It's Boiled Liza's old Impala.

Jaq gets in the passenger seat. Liza driving, Hatchet Head in the back. Jaq asks them: "Where is he?"

"The A-hole," says Liza.

"What happened?"

They tell her. Most of what they say is incoherent, but the essential horror — two train kids at the camp, Billy beheaded — that comes through. "And Ransom," says Liza, "he heard these voices and goes over there. And they killed Billy right in front of him. And kicked Ransom in the head and knocked him cold, and when he comes awake he calls out and we all come runnin. Seemed like Gracie was dead but we took her to the vet. She ain't dead yet. Maybe by morning, though. You know that woman vet on East Broad? That's where we were when the cops showed up."

"Like forty of 'em at once," says Hatchet Head. "Had their *guns* out. Like we were murderers. Fetched us to the A-hole, and took us in one at a time."

"Tryin to cross us up," says Liza. "Kept askin about Ran. Was he pissed at Billy for somethin? Was he belligerent? That kind a shit."

Hatchet Head says, "They let us go but they kept Ran."

"They want to nail him so bad," says Liza.

"And now," says Hatchet Head, "they cleanin out all the Eastside camps."

The Impala rolls up Drayton Street. Ahead of them knots of homeless folks are crossing the road: hauling trash bags, pulling shopping carts. A whole family is already squatting there in Forsyth Park, right by the circus tent.

Says Liza, "Folks are everywhere."

They roll to a stop at Gaston Street, at the red light. It's warm out so they have the windows down, and Jaq hears, far off but clear, the song of a mockingbird — but the bursts of this song are disturbing and discordant, and she soon gathers it's really

167

the Musician, whistling. She wants to ask Liza to stop, but she's so moved she can't find her voice. But it's OK because when the light turns green Liza doesn't go: she's hearing it too. Hatchet Head also keeps quiet. They sit at the intersection and listen. The tune builds toward violence, and it feels to Jaq that her spine is being split open, from the nape of her neck down to her coccyx. Then someone comes up behind them and honks, and the spell goes off.

They're rolling again.

Her thoughts drift back to Ransom.

She turns to Hatchet Head in the back seat. "They won't beat Ransom, will they? They won't hurt him?"

"Nah," says Hatchet Head. "Not these days. You really gotta piss 'em off to get that. If you really piss 'em off, they'll say something like, Hey, let's get you to a doctor, and then they'll turn off the camera and do whatever shit they like. But Ransom'll be way too smart for that."

The detectives interviewing him are named Marsh and Tuck. Marsh is stupid but diffident, whereas Tuck is stupid and aggressive. Marsh is middle-aged, Tuck is a kid. Marsh has a beer gut. Tuck has a cowlick and the demeanor of a teenage bully. He's

168

having fun now, making Ransom grind back through the details of his story. Looking for inconsistencies, trying to trip him up. It's all a performance. He's playing up to the chief. Chief Swann made an appearance in this little room an hour ago. Said not a word, just folded his arms and let his august gravity pervade the room. Then he went away, but his presence remains. They all know the chief is watching them through the two-way mirror, and Tuck is playing to that. When he says, "Now, Musgrove, tell me again what motivated you to visit your pal at such a late hour?" he folds his arms just the way the chief would, leaning way back in his chair and looking out through one squinty eye and acting as chieflike as a cowlicky punk can. "I mean, what was so *un*-usual that made you go calling on him at midnight?"

"I told you. Those voices."

"Whose voices?"

"Again, Billy and that train kid. And also, Gracie wasn't barking. Billy had a visitor but Gracie wasn't barking, and that struck me as odd."

Marsh is taking notes on his laptop. "Gracie wasn't barking," he repeats as he types. "Gracie, that's the doggie?"

Ransom nods. Trying to stay amiable.

Then Tuck takes back the interrogation. "So you went over there?"

"Yeah."

"And found Billy with two guys?"

"I only saw one."

"Right, the ghost. The guy with the ghost mask."

"Yeah."

"And the other one? Was he a ghostie too?"

"Never saw him."

"Then how do you know he was there?"

"Something kicked me in the head."

Tuck doesn't laugh. He doesn't like being fucked with. He says, "You should have somebody look at that bruise, Musgrove. 'At's a bad one."

Enough menace in his voice that Ransom figures it's time for a lawyer.

Though he knows if he asks for a lawyer they'll get dark quickly. They'll lock him up and spread tales. They'll leak to the *News* and WSAV that the younger Musgrove son has been living at a homeless camp, has been there since he got out of jail for assaulting his brother, and is now mixed up in a grisly new murder case. Morgana will be mortified. Bebe will be worried sick, and Madelaine will have to read about him again.

But if he can hang loose and easy for a while, then, when they tire of toying with him, they'll likely just let him go.

Tuck asks, "Was there tension between you two?"

"Between me and Billy? No."

"You guys have a spat or something? A falling-out?"

"No."

"One of your hobos," Tuck says, "told us there's been kind of a tension."

"I wasn't aware of that."

"Tell us, where'd you get the machete?"

"Like I said, it belonged to the guy in the mask."

"Can you prove that?"

"How would I do that?"

"I mean you *are* covered in Billy Sugar's blood. You got bruises where he kicked you —"

"Not Billy. Billy didn't kick me."

"Oh right, the *ghostie* kicked you. The invisible one. I like it when these Two Ghosties show up in your story and *they* do all the bad stuff and it's *their* machete, and you and Billy were having no problems at all, you're just super close buds, right?"

One small solace now, a thing for Ransom to focus on, is that Gracie was sound asleep and didn't have to see what happened. And she's likely dead by now. So for the rest of eternity, she won't know. He tries to dwell on that. To keep his mind off the present nastiness.

"Says here you got a drunk and disorderly in . . . '06? Plus a resisting?"

Ransom nods.

"You were seventeen? And then another resisting, '07. Kinda young, weren't you? What's a matter, were the officers mean to you? Did they annoy you?"

Marsh laughs. Tuck tucks his tongue into his cheek and keeps reading. Finally gets to where he's going. Tossing out, as lightly as he can, "Here's one that says you assaulted a David Musgrove."

"That was the charge," says Ransom.

Tuck takes it slow and easy. "It's curious how similar that name is to yours."

"He's my brother."

"Oh. Got it. What was that about?"

"Family dispute."

"Says you assisted him in falling down some stairs?"

Let him play, Ransom thinks.

"On River Street?" Tuck presses. "Those stone stairs? They call them the Stone Stairs of Death, don't they?"

Ransom nods.

Tuck bunches his lips disapprovingly. "Mr.

172

Musgrove. Were you sleeping with your brother's wife?"

"No."

"You two weren't writing letters back and forth?"

Ransom holds the edge of the table.

"Because that's what this says. Says you and your brother's wife, Madelaine, were sending these love letters and your brother found out. And one night you thought he was outta town so you arranged to meet. You met her at the Amber Lantern, and you were comin out the back, up on Factors Walk by the stone stairs, and your brother shows up. Now it seems to me, if anybody's gonna blow their fuse in this situation, wouldn't it be him? But no, according to witnesses, it was you. According to witnesses he called his wife some names that may have been well deserved but still you went all nuts on him. Is that all fair and accurate?"

Ransom stares at the fleshy place where Tuck's chin meets his neck.

Tuck smiles. Inviting him to make a move.

Ransom drops his gaze and takes a deep breath. "I need a lawyer."

"Oh, *really*?" says Tuck, in a mocking bray. "No kidding. But first you need a doctor. That cut on your head is bleeding again.

Let's get you checked out." He turns and asks the dark mirror, "We off?"

The intercom replies, "Uh-huh. Off."

"OK then," says Tuck. Standing and leaning close. "Look at me, Musgrove."

Ransom raises his eyes.

"Let me ask you," says Tuck. "what kind of a shitbag fucks his own brother's wife? Was she just fuckin *hot,* was that it? Was she so smokin hot you just had to get your dick wet?"

That ugly smug face, hovering.

Ransom's fist lashes out. Tuck is ready though: he leans back and the punch does not connect. And instantly Marsh is behind him and has him in a bear hug, pinning his arms. Ransom arches to get free — spinning, kicking, his chair clattering to the corner. But still Marsh is holding him, and Tuck plants a blow in his gut and the wind flies out of him.

Marsh tosses him to the floor.

He lies there heaving.

"Yeah sorry," says Tuck. "Too bad you don't have your machete."

Ransom claws at the floor. Finally manages to gather half a breath.

The door opens and someone new steps in. A pair of shoes — and a voice: "Hey now, boys, let's take a little break."

174

Ransom squints up at the new cop.

Brown corduroy jacket. Long face, kind of horsey, friendly, assured. Seems to be higher on the food chain than Tuck or Marsh. "Musgrove, I'm Detective Galatas. You ready for a little walk? You up for that?"

Glint in the man's eye.

Plainly Tuck takes umbrage at having this suspect yanked from him. "Wait a minute, Nick. He swung at me. You saw that. He's gonna snap any second. We're right *there.*" Tuck sends the mirror a pleading look. But the mirror is unhelpful. Galatas reaches a hand to lift Ransom up, and Tuck and Marsh must stand by helplessly as their toy is stolen from them.

Galatas steers Ransom out of the room. Down the scum-green corridor. Is he planning to kill me? Ransom wonders. If he's planning to kill me he's being pretty casual about it. He's got no backup. Does he mean to do it by himself?

They get buzzed through another door.

Galatas says, "Your niece called me, Musgrove. Good thing she did, the way Tuck was getting to you in there. You wouldn't a lasted ten minutes. She saved your ass. Plus here's another lucky break. We looked at some surveillance video from the Jiffy Mart on Wheaton. Not far from the murder scene. Three hours ago. Couple a train kids, just like you said. Filed teeth and all, trippin balls. And we got folks on the street who know them. Apparently they've been leaning on Billy Sugar, stealing his lunch money. They were down at Thomas Square tonight copping a shitload of speed and fentanyl, and musta got it in their head to go pay him a visit."

At the front desk, the clerk hands Ransom the bag of clothes that Hatchet Head brought for him. He steps into a stinking little closet to change, and when he emerges, Galatas escorts him out to the night air.

Jaq is standing there by the Impala with Liza and Hatchet Head.

Galatas tells her, "Special delivery, ma'am, somewhat damaged but still functional I hope. You'll watch this idiot, right?"

"I'm in your debt, Detective."

Galatas laughs. "Does that mean a free beer when I'm off duty?"

Jaq grins, with all her lovely teeth. "Absolutely."

"Yeah but I never am," he adds.

And then he changes his tone. He gets crisp.

"So listen, Jaq, you and your uncle here, and your grandmother and your aunts and your fucking second cousins twice removed?

176

Y'all need to stay clear of the Kitchens case. Far away. You think the name Musgrove gives you immunity? As you see, it doesn't. Ransom, you keep away from the camps. My gut tells me somebody's ready to blow you out like a match. You hear? Hundred people disappear from those camps every year. Nobody knows where they've gone. Maybe they caught a train back home to Macon, maybe they're in the river. We don't know, we don't care. You hear me? Jaq, you need to trust us on this. We'll get Guzman; we'll get the goods. Now take this one over to your mom's, keep him close."

"All right," she says.

"OK then." He looks to Ransom. "Musgrove, get a fuckin job. There's dignity in work."

Then he turns and walks back into the station.

They drive through the still city, heading for East Broad Veterinary. Jaq's dying to get everything out: about how lucky she was to still have the card of the one good cop in Savannah, about Gram and the racetrack sketch, Stony and *Stone Kings Treasure*. But not here. Not with Liza and Hatchet in the front seat. She needs to get Ransom alone.

They keep passing vagrants on the move.

Ransom asks, "How's the camp?"

"Gone," says Hatchet Head. "Po-pos didn't waste no time. Already brought in a bulldozer. Middle a the fucking night. They gonna erase that place."

Liza says, "But we got most a your stuff out, Ransom. It's in the trunk."

"Thank you," he says.

Soon they pull up at the vet's. Ransom and Jaq go to the door and buzz, and Mary answers. She opens the door wide and there's poor Gracie. Standing up, though wobbly on her feet. She approaches. Flips her tail a little. Tucks her ears back when Ransom reaches out his hand.

But she's looking past them, looking for Billy.

Ransom says, "Doctor, this is my niece Jaq."

Mary says, "Uh-huh. I've seen you at Peep's."

"How's she doin?" Ransom asks.

"I induced vomiting. Used an IV, a diuretic, and I think we got her cleared out. I'd say she's fair."

"How much do I owe you, Mary?"

"Nothing." She eyes the new bruise on his cheek. "Shit. Cops did that?"

"Cops were sweethearts."

She turns to Jaq. "Your uncle probably

178

got a concussion from the guy who kicked him. And now this. You gotta get him to the ER."

"OK," says Jaq.

"And make him stay at a real home. Take him to your mom's?"

"I will."

"Ransom, you want to leave Gracie here for a while?"

"No, I'd rather take her with me, if that's OK."

Mary considers. "Yeah. Well. Wait."

She goes behind the counter and flips on a light switch, and counts out some pills. Comes back to the door.

"Two more doses of the charcoal, tomorrow morning and at six in the afternoon. With her food."

"OK. Any special thing to feed her?"

Mary shrugs. "What did Billy give her?"

"Right."

Back at Liza's car, they lift Gracie in. Get her settled in the back seat. Ransom and Jaq get in on either side of her.

Then Liza starts driving. "Where to?"

Ransom says, "You know the old lumberyard near the Bartow school?"

"Wait a minute," says Jaq. "We're going to the ER."

"No, I'll go there tomorrow."

"Mary said now."

"Well, now I need to go to the lumber-yard."

"Why?"

" 'Cause I'm gonna camp there and I'm worn out."

"You can't *camp.* You gotta come with me. I promised Galatas. I promised Mary."

"I'm sorry."

"Also I gotta talk to you," she says.

"Go ahead."

"It's private."

They take Oglethorpe Avenue to MLK Jr. Boulevard. Turn at the old railroad station, and drive past the ruins of old warehouses covered with kudzu.

She's gazing at him. A truculence in his profile. The way he clings to resistance, to his stubbornness: she's always admired that. How he lives in exile but never bitches about it. Doesn't bitch and doesn't preach, but keeps to his home in the woods and is loyal to his fellow vagabonds. She finds a chivalry in that and feels a kinship to him, as though they really do share a blood tie. In truth they haven't even spent much time together. She was eight when her mother got together with Bebe, and he was already in college. Jaq only knows him from a few trips to Sapelo Island, and around town, and scattered Christmases and Thanksgivings. But on one of those Christmases, when she was a sophomore at Emory, they were all hanging at the Old Fort and it was getting late and she quietly murmured to Ransom that she'd love a cigarette. They snuck out and walked to Kroger, where he bought a full pack of smokes just so they could each have one and toss the rest. They walked to Forsyth Park. They sat on a bench and talked — or mostly she talked and he listened. He was always a great listener but particularly that night.

She told him about her thorny love life. How it never quite worked out because she was always so restless and somehow never felt quite *matched*. He didn't tell her that was a conceited or arrogant attitude. Or that she was young and the condition would soon pass. Rather he told her it might be with her quite a while (he was right about that), but she should not surrender or compromise or settle in any way but keep her door open to love and just see if it came or not.

He didn't talk much about himself — not directly — but she could tell he was deeply troubled. Clearly his lawyering was getting him down: he was working for a rat-ass firm supposedly to discharge his college loan, but also, she knew, to fulfill the wishes of Morgana and Fred. She tried to draw him out on this: he wouldn't be drawn. But he did talk about her mother, Bebe, and Morgana and Willou, and his brother, David. Allowed her glimpses of his struggle, and talked about Savannah with love and rage, and she began to feel a deep, live connection to him, electric, the deepest she'd ever felt for anyone.

Of course since then she's learned there was something else going on. This was the time when he and Madelaine were leaving notes for each other in the trunk of an oak tree; he was pursuing that madness. But she didn't know that then. She just knew he was in trouble. And she knows it now. They drive through the dark city and she's desperately worried about him, and wants to take care of him and to share what she knows.

They turn right, cross the Central of Georgia railroad tracks, and pull over by a dense copse of trees. Liza pops the trunk; she and Hatchet Head help Ransom unload his stuff. He humps his pack up onto his back. He tightens the cinch, takes his tent-sack in one hand and Gracie's leash in the other, and when he's said his goodbyes to Liza and Hatchet Head, he turns to Jaq.

"So," he says. "You saved my life there."

She shrugs.

"Give my love," he says, "to your mom and your mama."

"Yep."

He starts off walking into the trees.

She follows him.

He takes a few steps and turns. "Where are you going?"

"With you."

"No you're not."

"You think I'm gonna tell my mom that after I saved you from the cops, I let you wander off into the fuckin woods again? Uh-uh."

He glowers at her. She glowers back.

Finally he pushes some air out. Looks back down the path and calls, "Hey, Liza, do me a favor? Could you and Hatch wait for a minute while I have a talk with my niece?"

Liza shrugs. "Yeah, OK. We'll smoke one."

Ransom and Jaq and Gracie walk to the fallen trunk of an oak tree. He takes off his pack and they sit. There's a faint illumination from a single distant streetlamp: just enough for her to see his eyes.

He says, "OK, why am I not going with you? Because I think somebody paid those train kids to kill Billy Sugar. And it has something to do with Luke's murder. And whoever set it up, I'm gonna hunt that fucker down. And I'm sure he'll come hunting me right back. So I can't stay at your mother's house, or my mother's house, or anybody's house. I'm not gonna bring this danger down on anybody."

She doesn't answer. She just pulls out her cell phone, queues up the video, and passes it. "I took this that night," she says. "It's Luke and his friend Stony. Just before they left the bar."

He watches the video while she watches him. When he finally raises his eyes, she says, "So that's Stony. I just figured she was crazy. But then tonight, Morgana gave us that clue: *Stone Kings Treasure* and all. Stone, that's gotta mean Stony. She was Luke's friend, and she knows he wasn't shooting up and knows the Gooze was letting him stay in that house. And she was with him that night. She'd be a perfect witness. So the Gooze has to silence her. That's why he's paying Gram half a million dollars. To find her. So we gotta find her first. Can we work together?"

He gives a weary smile. "No."

She says, "I mean, you hunt for Billy's killer and I'll hunt for Stony. But we'll hunt together."

"No."

"Why not?"

"Well for starters my sister wouldn't approve."

"I'm twenty-three. I do what I like."

"So do I. You want someone to work with, why not Morgana?"

"Gram? That's insane. She fucks with our heads."

"Yeah, but she's quick-witted and she owns a detective agency. Could be a big help when you're tracking a missing person."

"So why don't *you* work with her, Ransom?"

"Me? Nah. My pride and dignity and all."

"I got those, too," says Jaq. "If you don't want to work with me, fine, I'll do it myself. I'll find Stony and I'll put that monster behind bars and Gram can kiss my ass."

Betty wakes in her bed on the third floor of the Old Fort and hears faint music from somewhere. Fancy music. She thinks it might be coming from the parking lot of the Kroger down the street. Folks sometimes gather round a tailgate in the parking lot, and play their playlists and gossip and drink and dance till the managers chase them off. She's been to those impromptu parties herself. But when she checks her phone she sees it's 4:00 A.M. Kroger's been shut for hours. Damn and now she's wide awake. She was dreaming of her childhood home in Odom. The chicken farm, her dog Bonkers. God did she love Bonkers. In her dream, Bonkers survived the tractor; he was lame but alive. But now she's wide-awake and of course the tractor did what it did, and did it thirty years ago. But her grief is fresh, like it just happened. She lies there dazed and weakened, and soon the cheatingness of her ex-boyfriend Randy finds its way into her head — and now sleep is doomed. She'll need another hit of Ambien. Which is no good; she's running low. She has benzies, which would be better and might even bring her back to that farm for a few hours, but she has to ration those, too, since her doctor has been cruel and withholding lately.

Another gust of that weird music.

She puts her robe on and her Chinese slippers and goes to the top of the back stairs, where she can hear it better. It's singing, it's opera. Over a bed of static, so it must be Morgana playing her old Victor Victrola, which signifies that she's for real drunk, which she hasn't been for a long time, not since the night David went tumbling down the stone stairs and Ransom was arrested.

This isn't good at all.

Betty steals slowly down the grand staircase, and the music gets louder and there's also a strange slashing sound. She descends to the rear entrance hall. And then into the keeping room. From here she can see into the dining room.

Morgana is standing at the dining table, with her back to Betty. She holds a pair of scissors. The diva wails away on the Victrola, and the violins whimper. On the grand table before her, Morgana has four different kinds of wrapping paper and twelve different ribbons. She's talking to herself, loudly, and sobbing, and using her scissors like a sword, making long thrusts, and doesn't notice Betty standing in the darkness of the keeping room.

She says, "They're *poisoning* us, Fred. Your ancestors, oh Christ, they're rotting beneath us and they're poisoning us, aren't they? Look at these portraits. Look at your *people.* Your walls of monsters and toadies, I hate them every one. Oh, how was I so *seduced*? I thought I could triumph? Christ, I really did. Y'all seemed like such children to me. Like a whole city full of spoiled *impossible* children and I thought, I can make changes, I can educate them, *ha*! But your people, they lie down there and they

187

rot and they *breathe,* don't they? They breathe out their poison gas, and it just seeps up. And you can't *hide* from it. There's nowhere to hide. Can you hide in a homeless camp? Ha ha ha! That's the strategy of a coward and an imbecile. Can you immure yourself in an *emergency room?* No, the poison will come right in after you. Because it's in the *air.*" She lunges with the scissors again and again, and confetti is everywhere and she says, "Flannery knew. Flannery *knew.* Flannery got out, what a lucky girl! Oh, Fred, I am so sick of this rank *poison. . . .*"

Now Betty retreats, and thank God Morgana didn't catch her looking, because in this demon mode she'd surely have sliced her into long strips of confetti. I'm not saving the benzie, she thinks, I'm going upstairs and taking it right now and also a double-fucking Ambien and I'll sleep till someone throws a bucket of cold water over my head and that crazy monster down there can make her own fucking breakfast.

CHAPTER THREE:
MR. KINDNESS
OPENS THE DOOR

At the county courthouse on Montgomery Street, Superior Court Judge Willou Musgrove Lutinger works through the morning docket call. She and her bailiff have a rhythm going: *"Docket number so-and-so!"* the bailiff intones, *"Defendant Such-and-such!"* — and the name hovers in the air a moment, no response, and then Willou brings down her gavel and cries, "Bench warrant! Call that bond!"

And then just like that again, choppity chop: *"Docket number so-and-so! Defendant Such-and-such!"*

Then a moment of silence. Then BANG. "BENCH WARRANT! CALL THAT BOND!"

And then once again. Case called, no show. "BENCH WARRANT!"

She's been doing this for years and by now she's gotten to know many of the miscreants on this list quite well, and as she hammers away she has the sense she's looking down on this ceremony from afar, from some distant planet, and it seems other-worldly and tragic (though still monoto-nous), and she wonders, why the hell aren't they *here,* these defendants, how can they do this to their lives? — as she nods her head in time with the gavel and the sing-song. An appearance is just an appearance, can't you just take your medicine and move on?

But then the next name the bailiff reads is actually here — oh well, the string is broken. The defendant, a check kiter, shuffles forward with his public defender and pleads guilty, and Willou feels rather proud of him, just for showing up, and tries to cast him whatever scrap of mercy the law permits. She gives him a minimum sentence. She goes through the Boykin questions and wishes him luck and sends him on his way. The bailiff calls the next case, and as he does Willou drifts off. She recalls her mother's bizarre little charade last night: trying to rope her kids into helping her with that so-called detective agency, and she also recalls her sister calling her "an ambulatory skeleton," the memory of which causes her to suddenly double-bang the gavel, which throws off the bailiff for a moment — and while she waits for him to find his place, surreptitiously she flips open her makeup compact on the bench. The mirror tells her that what Bebe said is true. She recently had neck liposuction that was a bit too aggressive and it's caused what they call "skeletonization," which is particularly noticeable whenever she raises her chin. But raise her chin she *must* in this courtroom if she is to look appropriately regal, and oh, Bebe really knows how to wound her. To slip the dagger deep. Always has. She knows it's wrong to be checking her reflection while hearing cases, but it's the fault of her sister and the smug wokeness she's exhibited all her life, but it's gotten so much worse lately, although to be fair Bebe did say one other true thing last night. That their mother is *insane* if she thinks any of her progeny will help her with that fucking "case." The bailiff has finished calling the case and there's a long silence, and Willou looks up and is just about to cry out, "BENCH WARRANT!" when she realizes that the defendant is right there below her — has come forward with her sorry-ass public defender and is waiting to plead.

Gloria Ludd.

Willou stays her hand. "Oh. Hello, Miz Ludd."

She has a history with this one. She has sentenced her, or foregone sentencing, at least a dozen times. Still Gloria Ludd keeps coming back. Today she's charged for possession of a drug-related object, a crack pipe. Originally the charge was possession of the crack itself, but the state has dialed that down to a misdemeanor. The DA says there have been technical difficulties. The crack pipe has not been returned from the state lab.

A typical fuckup, thinks Willou, and again her attention drifts.

Then Gloria Ludd interrupts the man to say, "Your Honor, it's all bullshit anyway. That's not my crack pipe, that's my sister-in-law's crack pipe."

Miz Ludd is heavier than the last time she was in this courtroom. She wears what looks like a bustier and her muffin top is showing.

Willou inquires, "How's your job at the poultry plant, Miz Ludd?"

"Not good, Your Honor. If I may speak frankly. I left that job. Because it required me to get up at like four thirty in the morning to drive to Claxton, which frankly I'm not capable of, and one a these days I'm gonna drive off a bridge, Your Honor, if I may be so frank, and besides which it ain't my pipe, I've never used such a shitty-ass crack pipe in my life, and may I get so justice for once?"

Willou can't help but smile.

How, she wonders, did Gloria attain adulthood without realizing that society does not ever serve "justice" to the slobbish, the whiny, the weak, the indolent? She scowls and happens to catch a glimpse of this frown in the little round mirror. It is indeed the countenance of an ambulatory skeleton. She needs to be out of here. She cuts Gloria off and gives her thirty days suspended, which, considering her record, is quite generous, and when Gloria tries to complain her attorney shushes her.

Willou reads out the Boykin questions, makes sure Miz Ludd has enough bus fare to get home, and wishes her luck.

Tosses a final BANG onto the gavel.

Then rushes down the long hallway to her chambers, where she shucks off her robe in a hurry. Leaves the courthouse. Goes around the corner to where her Escalade is parked, gets in, locks the door. In the deep blue of her SUV, she vapes. Pops a Klonopin. Does a mini crossword on her phone. Tries not to think of her sister or her mother. Composes herself. And, after one more Klonopin, is headed back to the courthouse and passing the window of an empty storefront on Montgomery, when she catches in the glass the reflection of her new hairdo, which looks like a helmet. I look like Kaiser Wilhelm for God's sake, if Kaiser Wilhelm were an ambulatory skeleton. She pauses, and tries to fluff, to muss, to give her hair any sort of life, and then a voice nearby says, "Hey, Judge?"

She turns.

She knows this one.

A no-count hoodlum from one of the ultra-white trailer suburbs of Effingham ("Methingham") County. He often operates in Savannah because there's nothing worth stealing or fencing in Methingham, unless you're stealing your neighbor's pseudo-ephedrine, which would be a high-risk undertaking and not for a run-of-the-mill slimeball like this one. No, of course he brings his business to Savannah. He's been hauled before her for auto theft, for receiving stolen goods (or rather violating parole on that conviction), for selling fake IDs on River Street, for all manner of picayune little crimes, and she has no time for him and gives him a curt nod and brushes past him and is about to cross the street when he says, "It's about your niece."

Her nerves come to attention.

She turns back. Erases everything in the

world that's not this weasel.

Because she knows instantly that he's not come on his own accord. He's from a world that loathes and abominates judges and would never voluntarily call on one. Even now he's sliding his eyes around to see if anybody's looking. Tension in his lids, rigidity: he's scared. He's here because he was *sent* here — and anyone with the power and the gall to send him on such a mission is properly to be feared. Even by Willou.

But she mustn't let on to being aware of that.

She says, with an offhand air, "Which niece? I have a few."

"Jaq."

"Oh, uh-huh. What's the problem?"

He closes the space between them. "She's been sniffin around. Askin about Kitchens, how he died and all the necessary circumstances and shit, and I personally got no problem with it, Your Honor, but some people, you know . . ."

These words have been rehearsed. He doesn't deliver them with any clarity or dispatch, but it's plain he's worked over them. She asks — knowing she'll get no answer but hoping maybe the nonanswer may tell her something: "What people?"

"Ah. Jes' shit on the street. You know.

Quack quack."

It does illuminate. That he won't give her *anything,* not even the flavor of his source, underscores the depth of his anxiety. She considers. She might try to trump his fear with some of her own brewing. She could whip up a charge right now, find some narrow chamber and a flexible cop and threaten him with two years in the most exclusive wing of Reidsville, with infinitely more years tacked on for bad behavior: *forfeit your fucking* life *if you don't tell us this second who is threatening my niece.*

But she can see already that such an approach won't work. She can tell by the look in his eyes that he's really, really scared of somebody.

She can't crush him if he's precrushed.

She's thinking this as he mumbles his obligatory: "Jes' wanted to give you a heads-up, Your Honor, 'cause you been so good to me, you coulda come down harder than you did but you didn't and I'm grateful —"

"What's your name again? Buddy something? Buddy Jenks?"

"*Bubba* Jenks."

She turns and walks away. No point in any niceties. She goes back to the courthouse and into her chambers and shuts the door behind her, and stands there breathing.

Beside her is the framed portrait of her ancestor Charles Augustus Lafayette Lamar, the esteemed ghost. Also her own ghost, her reflection in the glass, the Kaiser helmet, the walking-skeleton neck, and just a tiny glint of fear in the skeleton's eyes.

The loveliest of nights, Stony thinks. It started in terror of course, with Mr. Kindness making his visit and then the light snapping out and her shrieking into the dark. That was followed, after he was gone, by the usual tide of regret. Why had she been such a fool as to trust Lloyd from Statesboro? *Why? Why? Why? Why?* Then floods of grief. The loss of Luke. Loss of the Kingdom. Loss of the King's soldiers. All those torments lingering for a long time, whirling like moths, but finally her mind settled and in the blackness she had a memory.

From age four or so. Of an old woman in the little Holiness church down in Tatemville. The woman had silver braids and sang hymns a cappella so beautifully that Stony would start crying as soon as she opened her mouth.

Then came another.

She was ten or eleven. There was this old guy Martin and he taught her things. How to change the oil in her mother's car; how to find lion's mane mushrooms. One day at an old dried-up creek bed they went hunting for arrowheads. At first it was fun. He told her to keep a lookout for stones of a different color, or stones that had "ears," or a certain kind of bulge. But all the stones were gray and dull and misshapen. The day dragged by. They found nothing. Martin kept cheerfully searching, kept picking up one stone after another and peering close, then tossing them aside. But Stony was bored to tears.

But something happened to catch her eye.

"That one there," she said. "That one has ears."

He said, "Which one?" but he wasn't really paying attention.

She knew, though. The thing was almost completely hidden in the creek bank, but she was certain. She kept pointing.

When he saw it, he grinned. He said, "Pluck it out then."

She did and he spritzed it with his water bottle. With the dirt washed off, the thing was brilliant. The glowing spine of it, the serrated flakes, the pointy ears. It thrilled her to hold it in her hand. It almost had a face. Martin said, "That's a beauty. Feel the knapping? That's a Putnam, middle archaic.

Somebody lost that thing five thousand years ago. Think of that. Some guy shot an arrow and missed. And he walked all around here lookin for it, and he must have been so mad. Such a bad day. First he misses the buck, now he's lost his precious arrow. His life seems just *ugly* to him. You feel his presence?"

"Yes sir."

"And five thousand years later *you* come along and say, 'Why, there it is, right there.' Make him look like *such* a fool."

Now in the blackness her mind rises from that memory, and floats to another one.

She recalls a visit she made just a few months ago to her friend the Musician, at his tarp in the woods. She went to talk to him about the soldiers of the King. The Musician never drinks a drop of alcohol, but he served Stony a gingery tea, and she sat on a tree stump and shared with him all the secrets of the Kingdom. Because she needed to tell somebody, and he was the only person other than Luke she could trust. She told him where the treasure was. She told him what to do if anything ever happened to her. When she was sure he had that information down cold, she left. Or pretended to leave. Really she only went a little ways and stopped. Hoping he'd start whistling — that she'd catch an impromptu concert. But after standing there about two minutes he called: "Stony, I know you're still there. I'm not gonna whistle now. But it was great to see you and I won't forget what you told me. Come again soon."

She floats away from that vision. She doesn't know where she's going, but she's not afraid. She feels weightless. She feels herself spiraling into space, and she thinks, if I can go anywhere, why not go to the Kingdom?

So she does.

She's a child. She's a little girl running with other kids through a great garden of corn and yams and peas, running up to the wall made of logs, then down to the gate where they say hello to the sentries. They pass through and go sprinting together to the edge of the marsh, to the pluff mud that sucks in their toes. Hermit crab. Heron. Snake. *"Snake!"* she cries. *"Snake! Snake!"* and the other kids take up the shout till the men come. One of these men is her father. He hovers over the snake with his bayonet like he's ready to kill it but then he doesn't. Suddenly his hand flashes out and he scoops it up and makes her hold it. "It's a good snake," he says. It tries to writhe out of her grip, but she clutches. Her father lifts her onto his shoulders. His name is Sharper and he's the captain of the King's soldiers. She's his princess. He carries her, and she carries the snake, and they go back through the wooden gate into the Kingdom, and she floats past the little log houses, past the folks who have come out to look. Contentment spreads through her neck and cheeks. Partly she's thinking she really is a child, partly she knows she's just Stony, dreaming in her living tomb. Whichever, she's having a great time.

Then the LED light switches back on and burns her eyes, and she screams till her voice gives out.

Then a minute passes. Then a key turns in the lock.

Mr. Kindness opens the door.

He comes in and does his "inspection." The cereal, the powdered milk. He clucks at her messiness. Peers at her feces in the box of cat litter. Brings the chair close and sits. It's hard to read his intentions behind that mask, but she can see his eyes and they don't look so gentle today. He seems disturbed.

He says, "I found out about you and Jaq Walker."

He pauses to let that settle in.

"Folks at Peep's, they told me how much

you love her. That's good. We won't have to use your mother. Jaq's easier to get to. You know? She's always riding around on her bike, she's kind of careless. You know what she's been doing? She's been looking for you. No one else gives a shit but she does. She loves you. She hates that you might be in danger. Speak to me, Stony."

Trying to keep back her tears.

"Look at me," he says. "I want you to see me. Raise your eyes."

When she does, he pulls off his mask.

He's that detective. Galatas. The friendly cop in town, the one who always wants to help you out. Not that she'd ever believe any of that. But lots of folks do.

He says, "You know I can do anything I want. She trusts me. She'll go anywhere I ask. She's so young. Any trauma now will last her whole life. Have some mercy on her."

The veins come out on his pasty forehead. This gives her a little hope. He's vexed and it seems like he wants to punish her. She tries to tell him with her eyes: do it. Do what you're aching to do. Let's get this going.

But then abruptly he pulls back from her.

He says, "Enough, Stony. We try to treat you fairly, but you're too good for us, you're so pure and righteous, OK. You're the dealer, let's see the hand that you dealt Jaq. I'll bring you a picture of it."

And he goes.

Jaq is swimming against the change-of-class flood at the Treutlan School. Down the wainscoted corridor with all its memories and echoes, the kids giving her long stares, making her feel like an alien. She looks into their wide eyes and remembers when she was first a student here, a freshman, and how the upperclassmen were so adult, and how they cowed and frightened her. Now they seem like little figurines. How in the world, she wonders, could she ever have been intimidated by these porcelain-smooth miniatures?

She steps into the principal's office. JoAnne, the secretary, is on the phone but looks up and says, "Oh, Jaq!" Rises for a buss. "Your mother's in with somebody, but hold on a minute."

Jaq takes a seat in an old shiny-seated wooden chair next to four students solemnly awaiting their fates. Above them is a wall of photos — of kids mainly, but Roxanne's broad beneficent face keeps showing up. She's been principal of the Treutlan School for six years and assistant principal before that, and she has a huge presence here.

At last some kid and his mother emerge from the office with troubled countenances, and Jaq gets nodded in. Roxanne's very happy to see her — Jaq seldom visits — and they hug and Roxanne says, "Hello, angel."

"How are you, Mama?"

"Oh, they're trying to kill me," says Roxanne, as she settles behind her desk again. "I just met with a mother regarding her son. The boy is fine, but she has severe developmental issues. If I could only expel *her,* I would in a heartbeat. How are *you,* Jaq?"

"I'm OK."

"Last night was brutal. I didn't want to say too much because I don't want to get between you and your Gram."

"I know."

"But she did put your mother through years of pain. Years. And now she's causing *you* a ton of pain, and I'm . . . I'm still standing by, but I'm starting to resent having to."

Jaq nods.

Roxanne says, "But you're holding up?"

"Kind of."

"You working on your movie today?"

"Well, yeah, but the deadline's like a month away. I got a lot of stuff but it's not coming together."

"Well, you'll get there. Just gotta get back

in the groove."

Jaq nods. "Hey, listen, Mama, I had a memory last night of something I heard when I was a little girl. Do you remember the soldier of the King?"

Roxanne thinks. "You mean our ancestor?"

"Yeah, maybe. Who was he?"

"It's just something that's been passed down. My grandmother Ellen, she talked about him. She got it from her grandmother. Herriat. You remember that recording of Herriat?"

Jaq dimly recalls that once her mother played for her an audiotape that someone named Herriat had made in the 1940s. "I don't remember what she said though."

"Well, she spoke the Geechee dialect," says Roxanne, "and she was hard to follow, and you were like eleven, and you wanted to get back on your bike. She was your great-great-great-grandmother. She was born into slavery. Lived into her nineties, into the 1950s. She always said her grandfather was a soldier of the King and a free man."

"But what does that mean?"

Roxanne shrugs. "I don't know."

Jaq asks, "You think it was religious,

somehow? Like maybe he was a disciple of Jesus?"

"Could be. Why are you so interested now?"

"I'm thinking maybe I could use him for my doc. Was he really a *free* man?"

"I don't know, angel."

"Does that tape still exist?"

"Probably. At the Historical Society."

"OK, I'll go there. But I gotta ask you something else."

"Mm?"

"Why didn't you warn me about Gram?"

"What? Warn you how?"

"I mean stop me from going over there. I mean Mom always tried to stop me, but you were like, Oh, don't be so harsh on Morgana. Oh, let Jaq go over there. Let her wear the demeaning waitress outfit."

"That's simply not so."

"Which part is not so?"

"Every word. First of all, Mom never tried to stop you from seeing Morgana. She personally despises her. But she doesn't think you're *endangered* by her. When Mom and I first got together, we made the decision that if Morgana wanted to be a real grandmother and be loving, we wouldn't interfere. And she *has* been a real grandmother. And as for that uniform, we told

206

you not to wear it. Your Mom was quite adamant. You screamed at her. You said, 'Why not? Why can't I wear what my white cousins wear?' "

"Well, what about *you,* Mama? Why didn't you step in?"

Her mother gazes a moment. Weighing whether to speak or not.

"Jaq," she says, "you know where those outfits come from?"

"No."

"Morgana wore 'em when she was a waitress. She and her sister. For years. So that's what they are."

"Mom never told me that."

"Your mom doesn't know. Morgana doesn't talk to her children about her waitress days."

"So how do *you* know?"

"I went to complain. About you wearing that damn uniform. She told me where they came from, and she said it wasn't up to her whether you wore them or not. She said it was entirely up to me. And I was glad she said that. But really — no, Jaq, it's entirely up to you."

Her phone buzzes.

Jaq says, "What, you gotta go?"

Roxanne kills the sound. "Nope."

"Aren't there students on death row out there?"

"There are always students on death row. They can wait. I want to ask *you* something."

"OK."

"How much have you been thinking about Luke's murder?"

This is surprisingly intrusive for Roxanne. And hits a nerve, because of course Jaq has been thinking about Luke all the time. "I don't know. I mean it's always in my thoughts. But, sometimes it's up front and sometimes it's in the background."

"How much up front? An hour a day? Two?"

"I don't know. Not all in one chunk, but I guess if you add up the minutes, then, yeah. Hours."

"And which do you think about more? The loss or the outrage?"

Jaq mulls it over. "Well, I think about the loss a lot. But mostly I'm thinking about how we're letting that monster get away with murder. Why do you ask?"

"Because sometimes you get a thing like that in your head and it won't let go. If you're anything like me. I don't want it to eat you alive. OK? Just try not to obsess about it."

"OK," says Jaq. "I'll try."

"I hope Herriat gives you what you're looking for."

Ransom, with Gracie on a leash, rings at the Old Fort door, and waits for Betty. But when the door swings open, it's Morgana herself. Looking brittle. Her makeup has been recently freshened, but the mask is transparent to him. The filminess in her gaze. The faint aroma of Scope mouthwash. She was drinking last night.

Nevertheless, he gets right to his business. "Mother, I want to work with you."

"Gracious me," she says. "Well, come in then. But you'll have to leave that creature outside."

"I can't. This was Billy Sugar's dog."

"Who's Billy Sugar?"

"The man they killed last night."

"Oh! I heard that on the radio. The poor man in the encampment? Was that *your* encampment? Lord, aren't you just a *magnet* for misfortune?"

"Yeah, that's true. But I still can't leave her alone."

She draws a breath. "Oh well." And she calls: *"Betty?"*

Betty comes shuffling from the kitchen.

"Uh-huh?"

"We have to clean the feet of this animal. Bring a dish towel?"

Betty's astonished, and a bit over the moon. "A *daaaw*-wug?" She comes to the door and gets down low and makes a goofy face.

"And apparently," says Morgana, standing behind her, "we must invite it into our home."

After a while Gracie takes a tentative step forward, reaches out her tongue, and gives Betty one shy, sad lick. In return for which Betty gives her a big hug — but then looks up and sees Ransom clearly. The big purplish bruise above his cheek. "Ransom! What happened to — ?"

"I walked into a door."

"Oh no! A *door*? That's terrible. C'mon, let's get you cleaned up."

"First," says Morgana, "you must scrub that dog's paws. Before it tracks mud into this house. Ransom, you go upstairs and change, and be quick. Have you put Neosporin on that?"

"The vet did."

"Really? Are you a beast of the jungle? Good Lord. Wash up and come to the Turkish room and I'll deal with it."

He makes no objection. He hands the leash to Betty, and wends his way up to his old bedroom in the turret. It's just as it was when he was a boy. The posters, the bust of Lucretius, his catcher's mitt on the sill. The cedary smell of the furniture polish. Maybe, he thinks, this frozenness is a sign of Morgana's love for him. Though more likely it springs from her virulent distaste for any sort of change.

He takes a quick shower, and clips his beard close, and puts on a fresh shirt and jacket. When he comes downstairs, Betty's in the foyer, wiping Gracie's paws with a dish towel dipped in warm water. Gracie's being patient with her, allowing her to lift her paws one by one. "Oh what a dirty *daaaw*-wug," Betty says. "What a dirty dirty *daaw*-wug."

Morgana awaits him in the Turkish room.

She has an open card table before her. It bears a gift. A box of some kind, gorgeously wrapped in two shades of green. The ribbon is a soft new-leaf green; the paper is darker, like a hemlock forest. Every fold and tuck is pin-neat. "That for me?" Ransom asks.

"For Jacqueline. She and I had a little set-to last night. Now sit and be still."

He does. She examines his wound. Loads her fingers with Neosporin, and the first touch buzzes with pain and takes him deep into his childhood. She works the salve in

211

gently. She seems sober enough, confident, and he sits there with his eyes closed and listens to Betty's incantations from the other room: "Your filthy little paws, *look* at 'em, so *filthy,* ain't you a-*shaamed* of yourself?" — and they're so lilting he almost drifts off to sleep.

But then Morgana wipes her fingers with a towel, and sits in her leather chair and says, "Very well then. Report."

He tells her everything. Taking his time. As he speaks, she listens with full Morgana intensity, pressing her lips together such that they're slightly mismatched: a sign of her perfect attention. Now and then she leans forward and lifts her hand, cueing him to pause so she might beg a detail or a gloss. "What did the 'Buddhist' fellow say again? 'Without a witness this would feel pointless?' What in the world could *that* have meant?" And: "What did Billy say about the man walking out with Stony? 'Smelled of Reidsville?' Translate that." Her manner is imperious, but he doesn't care; he's so battered from the long night he's glad to surrender. Let her have whatever she thinks she needs.

As he's finishing his tale, Gracie slinks into the room and lies at his feet. Morgana doesn't seem to notice her. She asks Ransom, "And you wish to work with me, I suppose, so I might help you track down whoever hired those . . . 'train kids'?"

He nods.

She casts a quizzical look. And finally says, "Tell me, why do you imagine they didn't kill you?"

"What?"

"Seriously. What stopped them?"

"I guess they were in a hurry to get away."

"You were unconscious. It would have been no trouble for them."

"That's such a lovely thought."

"It just strikes me as odd."

"OK. May we change the subject?"

"Of course."

"What have *you* learned, Mother?"

She shrugs. "Nothing of value. Johnny thinks the 'Stone Kings' could refer to a contractor up on Route 21 who calls himself the 'King of Concrete.' He's been up there investigating."

"Oh good. So he'll have a report by year's end?"

"Oh, don't rush him."

"And Guzman?"

She raises a brow. "What about him?"

"He killed a man. Aren't you curious as to why? And why he's looking for this woman Stony? Why he's so desperate for us to find her?"

But her attention seems to have wandered. Abruptly she calls, *"Betty?"*

Betty calls back, "In the kitchen."

"Bring us a little a morsel of meat?"

A pause. "A what?" Another pause. "You want a ham sandwich?"

"I mean a gobbet of something for this poor creature."

"Oh! Yes, all right."

Morgana turns back to Ransom. "You really believe Guzman would have us find Stony only so he could murder her?"

"Or compel her silence. I wouldn't put that past him."

"Well, you should. Can you not get your head out of the narrative it's stuck on? I'm reminded of when you were little. You begged me to tell you stories of monsters. You loved those tales. I couldn't vary them by so much as a syllable."

"Yeah, I recall. You'd come home smashed at three A.M. and climb up to the turret and wake me to tell me a story. I was cool with it so long as the stories weren't too sloppy. But they usually were. You couldn't remember the characters from the night before. You'd get them confused with people you'd met at cocktail parties. I had to give you prompts."

"Perhaps that's what I need now, my beloved. Some sort of prompt."

"OK. Archie Guzman, with a match."

"No, as I told you, if he were lying I'd see through it. I'm afraid that, just as he claims, he's being framed. Though by whom? And why? Also the real mystery remains, doesn't it: why has he retained *us*?"

Betty comes bearing a small silver platter, with a Spode china plate. On the platter are three strips of leftover Mooney's ham.

"Thank you, dear." Morgana takes the plate and tips it toward Gracie to let her see. The dog is wary but tempted. Her gaze focuses. Morgana takes up a piece in her long fingers and holds it out and causes it to dance a little. Whereupon Gracie, ever so slowly, approaches, sniffs, and takes it gently in her teeth. Retreats a step. Looks away sheepishly, and wolfs it down.

Morgana says, "I believe Mr. Guzman offers that outrageous fee because he thinks we enjoy some kind of . . . shall we call it . . . privilege? In this town? And he wants to purchase some of that."

Then she shuts her eyes. Thinking. He doesn't interrupt her. A murmur comes from the kitchen, Marcel talking to Betty. Gracie comes up and quietly devours the rest of the ham. Then curls up at her feet.

There's a brown thrasher singing outside, and the low chatter of a bus tour, from the street.

Finally Morgana stirs and shakes her head. "No. I can't quite grasp his reasoning. He's not a simple man. He's a fool but not simple. Most frustrating."

The doorbell sounds: its bright jarring trill.

As a boy he loved whenever it went off: it always meant something exciting was up, one of Morgana's weird friends or passive-aggressive rivals or addled tenants, some new *story*. But just now he only wants to follow Morgana's train of thought. He doesn't want to deal with Beverly the cat lady, or Whit who lives in the carriage house and imagines he's a bear cub and hangs honeycombs around his apartment to entice his boyfriends. Ransom hears Betty pad across the foyer in her slippers. The creak of the door and then a voice they know.

Willou comes sweeping in. "Ransom! I heard the news about the murder. Was that *your* camp?"

"Yeah."

"Are you all right?"

"Fair."

Then she sees Gracie. "Oh good Christ."

"Her name is Gracie," says Morgana.

"Give your mother a kiss?"

"No, no kisses for you." She takes the settee. "There has never been a dog in this house before."

"Not quite true," says Morgana. "Recall the time I allowed Aunt Clara to hold that hideous Mexican thing on her lap?"

"Not really. But anyway, wouldn't that have been . . . forty years ago?"

"Yet the odor lingers. Harry Stump informed me that the animal was eating feces off the street."

Willou has had enough. She turns to her brother. "So, Ran, what brings you here? Same as me? Our mother's adventures in criminology?"

"Oh goody," says Morgana. "does this mean you've also come to help? We'll work as a family?"

"No and you're batshit to think it. I'm here because I got a threat today. Someone gave me a 'tip' about Jaq."

"Jaqueline?"

"Apparently she's asking questions about the Kitchens case."

"Who told you this?"

"A thug from Effingham. He was just a messenger. Someone sent him to warn me. Jaq is pissing people off."

Morgana rears up a little: her cool indignance. "What has this to do with me? She doesn't work for me, as well you know —"

"Yeah but he meant you too, Mother. You're also pissing people off."

"Really? Did he *say* that, or is that merely your conjecture?"

"Your snooping stirs shit up."

"My 'snooping,' as you call it, is my profession."

"No it's not, it's your play. You inherited that annoying little toy of an agency from Daddy, and it amuses you but you're putting us all in danger —"

"Nonsense. A threat from Effingham County, you say? I don't listen to Effingham County. And anyway I know nothing about these 'questions' Jaq is supposedly asking. Ransom, do you?"

Ransom is looking down, chucking Gracie under her chin. Does not want to be dragged into this. "Well. I believe she thinks —"

"Stay out of it," Willou warns.

"Do not bully your brother," says Morgana. "You're always too quick to play the bully, Willou. It's not attractive —"

"*I'm* a bully? Good Lord. Mother, you eat everyone's *air*."

"Ungainly metaphors do not advance your cause. Have you spoken to Jaq about this?"

"Not yet. Haven't been able to find her."

"Well, good luck to you. And when you do, would you do me a favor; would you give her this?"

She hands Willou the pretty wrapped box. "And you should tell her mother about these threats. Get her to talk to Jaq. Of course Jaq would do anything her mother asked of her — she's a good obedient daughter. As, I expect, you shall learn to be. Probably not before I'm dead, however."

Galatas in his Sierra cruises down Jefferson, trying to float like he always does, eyes on the town, taking note of everything he sees, but it's tough because he's got Stony's silence under his skin. When he's been trying so hard to help her. Give her all this care, keep her fed, clean her waste, keep her safe, visit twice a day. Tired as shit in the morning but he drags himself out of bed while it's still dark and drives out there and takes all that risk, and slogs through those wet stinking tunnels so he can beg for her help, wheedling and cajoling her to just be *sane.* Struggling so hard to make everything work out for everyone. And she won't give him one fuckin *word*?

Stays mute like her tongue's been cut out? And she's doing this, he knows, to show contempt for him and all his dreams. It's her way of saying, I don't care if you *are* bringing prosperity to this town. I don't care, because I'm pissed off and I think you're cruel.

He has the urge to go back down there right now and show her what real cruelty feels like. I'm capable of it, he thinks. I've done worse when provoked. I'm a good man and will always take care of my people, but if you threaten or endanger my people, then I'll be the monster you want me to be, you smug royal bitch.

But then he'd have to kill her.

And he still wouldn't have the treasure of the Kingdom. Whatever the fuck this treasure is. And all his work would be wasted.

No. Everything's OK, he thinks. She'll snap soon. Those were real tears today.

He's coming up Habersham past 37th and out of the corner of his eye he spots a vaguely familiar vehicle, a black Expedition parked in a tidy little parking lot — and he slows, and wonders, who is that? But he thinks he knows. He loops around the block again. Gets a good angle on the license plate and snaps it with his ALPR. Runs it, and it comes up registered to one Lonnie Hall of Springfield, Georgia. *Yes,* he thinks, right, good news. Lonnie Hall is an Effingham county commissioner, and the tidy parking lot belongs to Davina Morris, a rather high-tone hooker who owns 1125 Habersham. He can lean on her tomorrow. He expects that Lonnie Hall will be delivered up to him. That will come in handy down the road sometime.

This, he thinks, is how leverage is gathered.

Patiently.

Sometimes it takes years to gather enough. Sometimes you never get enough. Then you might have to add a secret something. But in the meantime you just keep collecting and collecting and you can't collect too much leverage if you're ever going to rise up in this town, with all the assholes above you trying to push you back down.

Message comes in on his burner phone. The Big Partner. One word.

No

It's enraging. But he has to swallow his anger. The time will come, he thinks, but not yet. For now he smiles wanly and taps out a response with one thumb:

Thanks for the suggestion

A moment later he gets:

You can't touch her. She's immune. Anything happens to her and the US Cavalry
will descend on this town

Galatas writes back:

Ha ha. Maybe the only way tho

Eyeblink later:

No. Never

We'll see about never, thinks Galatas. But
he can't pursue that train of thought just
now, because as he's coming around Troup
Square and passing the elegant Bledsoe
residence, he spies the gentleman himself,
Warren Bledsoe, right there up on his handsome raised terrace, holding forth to some
flunkies in suits. Men who were no doubt
flown in this morning from New York and
Atlanta for some business meeting. And
there's that annoying King Charles spaniel,
running up and down the balustrade and
barking, and Bledsoe shouting, "Rascal! Be
a good boy!"
Poor fucking Warren, thinks Galatas.
The man imagines he's like a god in this
town with his pulp mills and his refinery
and his forests to the west and all his

councils and boards. He sneered when the Big Partner invited him to assist their enterprise. He called it a pipe dream, said they'd never get the permits. And it seemed he was right to sneer. The Big Partner gave up right away. Saying, Warren Bledsoe has too much money and too much power and what leverage do we have?

Well, sometimes you have to add a secret something.

A few weeks ago Galatas arranged to have Warren Bledsoe's laptop lifted from his office, seeded with photographs of naked children, and quietly returned. Now Bledsoe carries that bomb with him wherever he goes. His own personal doomsday, ready to be triggered at a word from Galatas.

Soon, he thinks, I'll make it clear to you what I have. Then I dare you to destroy that laptop, which would only make it worse for you. As we've already copied your hard drive. I dare you to say you've been framed. No one will believe you. Everyone will abandon you. You'll be thrown to the wolves. Rascal will join the feast.

Dare you to do anything but play along with us. For the rest of your life, do what we say, be a good boy.

He swings around the square, drives back to Gaston, heads toward Forsyth Park.

There, he chances upon a lovely and serendipitous sight.

Look who's right there at the corner of the park. Outside the Georgia Historical Society, chaining up her bike.

Pulling her camera out of its adorable bag. His gut clenches.

How self-assured she seems. And how entitled — like all Musgroves, Black or white. She's wearing her cute well-worn jeans, and she struts as she walks up to the base of the marble steps and sets up her camera; and her skin is glowing and she radiates the sense that she *knows* things. She thinks she knows what justice is, and how people work, and how to make them share their stories with her. She thinks she knows all about the subtle mechanisms that govern the running of the city of Savannah.

But really, Little Miss Immunity, you have no inkling.

Jaq stands at the foot of the impossibly steep staircase to the Georgia Historical Society. Narrow Doric columns, hulking pediment, sparkling marble: it's like the entrance to an Egyptian mausoleum. She says into her camera, "Kind of forbidding, isn't it? I don't know why it feels that way. Really it's just a big room full of books. I like books. But

I've always been weirded out by this place. Well anyway, here I go."

She mounts the steps, swings open the great door, and enters. A death quiet: the click of her boot heels echoes in the vast empty chamber. Three small rodenty old white women look up from their work. She goes up to the desk, and thank God her friend Arthur is working today. Black, nerdy glasses, small. He lifts his eyes and grins. "Jaq! What are you doing here?"

"Research. Would you like a piece of Orbit gum?"

"Sure. But you have to shhh."

He indicates, with a slight nod, the three ladies. And on a slip of paper he writes: GENEALOGY. ALL DAY. THEIR FUCKING DYNASTIES.

He has such big eyes and big glasses. Jaq thinks he looks like some cartoon animal, and feels comfortable in his presence. She points to her camera and whispers, "Do you mind if I shoot you?"

"Not supposed to."

His glasses slip down his nose. He pushes them back up.

"I won't tell anyone," she murmurs, and she starts recording. "I've been given to understand, Arthur, that y'all have an audiotape of a woman, she was my great-

225

great-grandmother, maybe more greats. Her name was Herriat, she lived off Bonaventure Road in the 1950s when she was very old, but she was born into slavery, and after the Civil War she worked —"

"Herriat Crawford?"

"Yes."

"We've got her. Her narrative's been digitized. Wanna hear it?"

He leads her to a desk with a creaky old computer. Locates the audio file as she puts on the headphones. "You ready?" he says.

She nods. He taps the arrow and leaves her to it.

A stretch of thick scratchy dead air. Then the plummy Atlantic accent of the interviewer, one of Alan Lomax's acolytes. He introduces Herriat and asks about her childhood. Her answer is no-nonsense. She was born in about 1857 but doesn't pretend to remember slavery days. She has only a few scattered memories of the Civil War, of the Yankee soldiers on the wharves, of everyone fleeing the big fire. But she recalls vividly the time after the war. Life on Montmillan Plantation after the freedmen and freedwomen took it over, which she calls "a good life, the best life." The website has her photo: her broad face. She was nearly ninety when this recording was made. She speaks in the Geechee dialect, which is nearly unintelligible to Jaq, but there's an English translation on the screen. She tells of the man she fell for, Prince, who was brought over as a child on the slave ship *Wanderer* by Charley Lamar in 1858. When Herriat says "Mistah Charley Lamar," she cuts the syllables strictly.

The interviewer asks about her family. She had one grandmother born in Africa, and recalls a handful of words the woman used, also some tales of her grandfather Sharper. She says she never met Sharper because he died in Florida before she was born. But, she says, he was "a soldier of the King."

The interviewer asks, "What does that mean?"

"The soldiers of the King, they were free men. They weren't slaves. Sharper, he lived in the Kingdom, and he was a free man."

"What was this Kingdom?" says the interviewer.

Herriat says, "Where the free people lived. Everybody knew that."

Jaq is aware, as she speaks, of vibrations from her cell phone.

She looks down. Aunt Willou. Been texting her for hours.

Need to see you.

Jaq goes back to Herriat.

Until the recording is finished. Then Jaq takes off her headphones and signals Arthur, who comes over.

"I want to ask you something," she murmurs.

He leans in. She picks up his smell, which is fresh, happy, breezy, a mix of bubble gum and pop tarts. She says, "Herriat says her grandfather was named Sharper and he was a soldier of the King. Do you know what that means?"

He thinks.

"Maybe," he says. "Wait."

He goes off to the shelves, and comes back a few minutes later with two old maps and three old books. He sits beside her. Then the two of them spend an hour studying. Squinting at faded script on the maps, wading through military reports, letters, trial notes. Slowly, things come into focus. The world seems to transfigure itself around these old papers. The three old ladies pack up and depart, scowling at Jaq and Arthur as they go. They leave the place empty. The great room now belongs to Jaq and Arthur alone. The looming shelves, the dour portraits of dead slaveholders. Jaq tries to keep focused. She bows her head and digs deeper into the lives of the King's soldiers and their families. But it starts to feel like too much. She's overwhelmed. She feels an emptiness inside of her, an aching void.

Finally she looks up at Arthur. "Fuck," she says. "Was Savannah always this bad?"

"Oh. Yeah." He shrugs. "Well no, actually, General Oglethorpe, he was a pretty good guy. But he was chased out just a few years after he founded Georgia. And after him, yeah, they were all criminals."

They sit for a while.

He adds, quietly, "I mean that's what these books are all about. The crimes of Savannah. Every book in here. They're all just the sickest crime stories you can imagine."

"*Every* book?"

"Uh-huh." He rises and beckons her to follow. He stops at a shelf and pulls out an old book. Opens it to a random page, and holds it out so Jaq's camera can get a look. It's a long list of names, in graceful script. "Yeah, see this? This is the register from a slave auction. Scrupulously documented. Half this shelf is slave auctions."

He snaps the book shut. Replaces it. Turns to the camera lens and gazes into it, not seeing it, lost in thought. Then abruptly he strides off to another bookcase. Takes down a big brown volume with a portrait of a Native American chief. "This guy, this is William McIntosh. He was part Savannahian and part Creek Indian. He betrayed his people in exchange for some prime bottomland. Gave away the whole Creek Nation to the white settlers. Consigned all his people to starvation and to the Trail of Tears. For some *real estate*. I'm telling you. These dudes, they take your breath away."

He crosses to another shelf, tips a volume with one finger.

"This here? This is all plantation birth records. You see the calligraphy? Yeah. Look. Beautiful handwriting. Half of these children were born of rape. There were millions of rapes. I'm not exaggerating. Millions. Every slaveholder thought it was his Christian duty to rape all of the Black women all of the time, except most of them weren't women, they were little girls, they were like twelve or thirteen years old, and some of them were little boys. Those avenues out there? These streets, these squares?" He gestures toward a fancy illustrated map of the city. "Most of them are named for prominent child rapists. I mean those fuckers. They completely got away with it."

Silence.

Finally Arthur says, "But you still don't believe me. You don't believe it's *every*

230

book. You think there are books here that are innocent."

"I don't know," she says. She's still overwhelmed by the thought of all those rapes.

"Well OK," he says. "Find one."

"What?"

"Pick any one."

She walks to the nearest shelf. She pulls out a big random volume.

Heritage Kitchens of Old Savannah. She hands it to him.

"Oh yeah," he says. "This one is actually quite popular."

He opens it to a chapter of table settings, silver services. He shows it to the camera. "Every day we get these little old ladies: they're so sweet, they're so polite and sweet, and this is the kind of shit they always want to see. They say, 'Well *ah'm* investigatin' the pedigree of my antebellum sil-vah-way-uh. That ah inherited from mah great-great-granddaddy's plan-tay-tion? Y'all have any books about antebellum sil-vuh-way-uh?'

"And I give 'em this book and they're happy.

"I always want to say, 'Ma'am, the *source* of your silverware, the true *pedigree* of your silverware, is the profits from your great-great-granddaddy's cotton plantation. And you know what led to those profits? The

231

advantage your great-granddaddy's cotton had over the rest of the world? It wasn't the climate. It wasn't the soil. It wasn't your great-great-granddaddy's noble bearing, though I'm sure he had that. It was simply the amount of labor he could extract from his enslaved workers — relative to the cost of the corn required to feed 'em. Before that, East India *owned* the cotton market. But they just couldn't get their coolies to work like that. Not like the enslaved folks of the American South. So the South prevailed. And your great-great-granddaddy got very rich, and now you've got all this fine silver, and bless your heart.' But of course I don't say that. I just hand over the book."

Which he shuts now and returns to the shelf.

A boop from Jaq's phone. Willou again. She ignores it. Arthur doesn't even hear it.

He says, "And the particularly sick, brazen, and twisted element of these crimes is that those committing them maintained that they were doing *kindnesses*. Working for God's kingdom. Look here, look at this. This is a collection of the sermons delivered at Christ Church. The most pious and appalling shit you'll ever read. Basically what the preachers were saying was: Our patron, Charley Lamar, wants slaves. All his friends

232

want slaves, and they want cheap slaves. They want the resumption of the Atlantic slave trade. They want to secede from the Union, and take over Mexico and South America, and build a great Empire of Slavery. And God wants this too. And so *you,* you artisans of Savannah, you bricklayers, you chandlers and wheelwrights, you Irish and Germans and Jews, all you little nobodies: if you want God's love and you want there to be somebody lower than you on the social order, you better let Charley Lamar and his pals have all the slaves they want. I mean when they wink, you better wink back."

Arthur winks at Jaq with one of his great big eyes. She keeps the camera close on his face.

"And all this winking," he says, "it's never stopped. Crime after crime. I mean, *this* book, this tells how Jim Crow was a *good* thing. You know? And *this* one tells how the massacre at the streetcar protests was *sadly necessary.* And every white soul in Savannah believed that shit. There were no exceptions. There were no holdouts. *Everyone* winked. Right? And the mills. Lemme show you the mills!"

He marches to a shelf, finds a book, flips through pages till he comes to a photo of

233

workers in a textile mill. White and Black, men and women.

He says, "The mills came here in the 1920s because there were no unions here, and here they could pollute as much as they liked. The Union Bag Company stuffed the city council with company bosses. They took *every single seat.* So all the mills, Continental Can and American Cyanamid, they could just shit away at will into the Savannah River. The river was *glowing.* DDT levels off the charts. And then ten years ago the Chatham Sugar refinery blew sky high. The workers knew *that* was coming. See this?"

He shows her a photo of the Chatham Sugar refinery. More smiling workers. On the floor, snowy drifts of sugar.

"Place was like the inside of a candy floss machine. OSHA told them, again and again, Hey, guys, you know sugar dust is *combustible,* right? And the bosses said, Hey, oh, sorry, yeah, we'll take care of that right away. But you know how you get busy and you just postpone things? So they put off that proper cleaning for about ninety years. I'm not kidding. *Ninety years.* When it exploded, sixteen people were killed and fifty were horribly burned. Workers came staggering out with the skin dripping off

234

their bones. The owner, ol' Warren Bledsoe, he had to declare bankruptcy. A very creative bankruptcy designed by your uncle David. So that when Bledsoe brought the company out of bankruptcy, lo and behold, somehow he still owned it! With no liabilities! Wink wink, right? The winking never stops. I mean, Jesus, Jaq, you don't have forty hours, I know, so let me shut up. But yes, I meant it. Every single book in here is a crime story."

Willou is infuriated by the sight of her niece standing there on the corner of Forsyth Park holding her bike and flirting with God-knows-what-boy, utterly oblivious to her aunt's discomfiture. Or anyway pretending to be oblivious. Willou taps the horn.

Jaq gives her a glance and holds up a finger: one minute.

Keeps talking.

Willou's ire grows. She *does* know the boy, after all: it's that young Arthur Haverty, who wants to be a historian. Too nerdy for Jaq, Willou assesses. Jaq prefers dangerous guys, guys who live on the boundaries. And Jaq knows that, so why is she teasing him? And why is she making me wait? Willou loves the girl, has loved her from the start. She saw right away that little Jaq was intensely curious, and frank, and drawn toward justice. And of course she's family. But just now, thinks Willou, she's really pissing me off.

Finally Jaq gives the boy a kiss on the cheek, and wheels her bike up to the passenger window of the Escalade and says, "Hi, Willou."

"Put your bike in," Willou demands. "I'll drive you home."

"Sure." Still that attitude. "If you like."

She puts her bike in the back, and gets in, and off they go down Gaston Street, toward Bull.

"So," says Willou. Tamping down her fury. "What brought you here?"

"Research."

"Are you . . . seeing that boy?"

"*Seeing?* I don't know what that is. No, I went there to find out something about Stone Kings. And I did. Stone is a woman named Stony, and she lives in a Kingdom and I just found out where it is."

"You're not serious."

"I am. You know, the Historical Society is quite wonderful. It's truly a temple of knowledge and progress."

Still with a snarky edge to her tone. It's hard for Willou to keep her equanimity. Particularly because she's stuck now behind a horse-drawn carriage tour, which has paused to allow a gaggle of bridesmaids to use the crosswalk at Bull and Gaston. They're drunk, they're screaming. They carry a giant inflatable penis, holding it up for everyone to adore. And once they've finally staggered along on their way, the horse decides to take a dump. Takes its sweet contemplative time about it too. Meanwhile Jaq keeps going on about her research. About "Stony" and her "kingdom," and how Guzman doesn't want us to know about it so he's trying to murder Stony, so "we have to get there before he does" — on and on in this vein as though Jaq has any idea of how criminal cases are really pursued and prosecuted, until finally Willou can't hear another word and breaks in to say, "You cannot be this fucking stupid."

Jaq turns to her.

"It's a *police matter,*" says Willou. "Involving arson and murder and *maybe* a missing person, and there are right now many people working on it. If you're honestly worried about Stony, just go to the cops. They'll probably find her in twenty minutes, though likely she's skipped town, which homeless people tend to do, you know, so it might take a little longer."

"Go to the cops?" says Jaq. "Going to the cops again would be like going straight to the Gooze."

"Oh for Christ's sake, will you shut up and *listen*? What do you think, I'm just whiling away a lazy afternoon carting you around the city? That I have nothing to do? I canceled a *court session* today. The afternoon docket. Do you understand how fucking serious that is? I did so because this morning I was approached by a man who claimed to be worried about you —"

"Wait. Worried about me? Why would —"

"Do *not* interrupt me. This man didn't come to me out of the goodness of his heart. He was hired by someone. To send a message. The message is: you and your grandmother need to stay out of all these investigations —"

"I've got nothing to do with Gram's detective games."

"Really? That's what *she* said. *I've nothing whatsuh-evah to do with what Jaq is doing* —"

"You saw Gram?"

"Just now. I told her to stop."

"And will she?"

"Of course not."

"And will *I*?" says Jaq. Casting a burning glare. "Will I stop?"

238

Willou returns that glare — and then looks back to the street, where that horse is still trying to finish its apparently difficult shit. It's a disgrace, Willou thinks. That animal is clearly *unwell.* She wants so much to honk. But restrains herself.

At last she shrugs and says, "I don't know, I suppose you won't. I'm wasting my breath, aren't I? Here." She reaches into the back seat and fetches Morgana's gift and places it on Jaq's lap.

"What's this?"

"From Gram. Don't squint like that, you'll get age lines. I guess it's some kind of peace offering. Apparently she was up late last night wrapping it. I think she was drinking as well. Wrapping and drinking, that's her favorite thing. Also venting, no doubt, her imperial victimhood to the four walls. Open it."

Jaq won't look at the package. She looks out the window instead. The horse moves along at last, and Willou is free: she zips down Gaston Street. Turns right at Abercorn and goes sailing southward and tells her niece, "Please do open it."

"No, I have no interest," says Jaq.

She presses the button on her armrest, to lower her window.

"What are you doing?" says Willou.

239

"You're not thinking of tossing it? Do *not* fucking toss it. If you toss it I swear to God I'll strangle you."

"What do you care?"

"I want to know what's in there. All that effort in the middle of the night? I want to know what my mother is up to. Don't you? Don't try to tell me you're not even curious."

"I'm not."

But after a few blocks, Jaq does give an experimental pull to one end of the ribbon. The bow unravels. She looks down. Lets the ribbon go and it slides off her lap like a snake. With a steeling-herself sigh, she slips her finger into a tuck of the wrapping and tugs.

Softly rips, unpeels. And reveals an old, square-topped velour box.

By now Willou has quietly pulled over.

Both of them gaze at the box.

There's a little brass catch, which Jaq releases. She flips open the lid.

The box is full of confetti.

Scraps of paper. Willou instantly knows — knew all along, really. But Jaq is puzzled, and picks up one of the scraps, and examines it. "It's a face," she says. "It's a girl in one of those, what do you call those? — mobcaps? Oh, wait. Is this . . . ?"

"Uh-huh," says Willou. Speaking in a murmur, but she detests her mother and wants to scream.

"Holy shit," says Jaq. "She cut it into pieces?"

Willou reaches up and adjusts the rearview, locates her face. Her bug-like glasses, the helmet, that too-noble chin. But it's not a good light for seeing the tendons and hollows she's looking for, and she gets peeved and pushes it back to more or less where it was. "That sketch," she says, "was appraised for thirty thousand dollars."

Jaq turns to her. "What?"

"You heard me." She puts the car in gear again, and eases back onto Abercorn, and they drive in silence.

They're nearly to Victory Drive when Jaq suggests, "Well, it *was* hers to give."

"Not to mutilate," Willou snaps right back. "It was hers to be passed down. She was supposed to be a *steward*. As Daddy always said: *we're stewards, that's all we are.* But Morgana suits her own whims, doesn't she? And she's not even in the Lamar bloodline."

"Um. Neither am I."

"Sure, OK, but you wouldn't have destroyed the thing."

"Oh, yes I would. If it were mine. They

241

had a slave auction there."

"Then sell it! If you don't want it, sell it! And give the proceeds to feed starving kids or whatever. Good Lord, we could've fed the whole friggin town. But no, Mother has to make her gesture. Everything she does is a meaningless gesture. Everything is dramatic, everything is high-minded, everything is a fucking manipulation."

As she rails, though, she notices in the corner of her vision that Jaq is studying the scraps. Picking them from the box one by one, peering at them. The flanks of a racehorse. The mustache of some dandy. Some jockey's brandished crop. Willou quits talking; she's not being heard. They cross Victory and drive for a few blocks, then Jaq says, "Hey, Aunt Willou? I have something I really have to do. Could you drop me here please? Right here?"

Ransom has always found refuge at Rayford's. In his boyhood, whenever his mother had ceased to draw pleasure from reviling Fred's uxoriousness, or David's ploddingness, or Willou's "dullness of discernment," or Bebe's plumpness and clumsy devotions and virtues: whenever she had tired of tormenting everyone else, then she would draw her youngest into her sights, and set

242

to work on him. She'd work with relish, for it seemed that everything about Ransom was wrong. He was lackadaisical, he lacked flint, lacked drive, was a "carnivalesque perversion" of all her hopes, was "the baggage handler of his own doom," was "the idiot camel carrying on his back his own future misery." Deep in her cups, late at night, she'd spiral up to the turret, click click click in her heels, to tell him things. Sometimes they were loving things. Sometimes she'd just chat or tell stories. But quite often she came for cruelty. Once she ascended the stairs and said, "You know, all the way down in the parlor I could feel your lassitude. Don't you know it simply shrouds the entire house? I can't bear it. I'm afraid the floors will collapse." She let her words sink in while she stood there, breathing arabesques of gin into the room. Then, work done, she spiraled down again, click click click.

Whenever her assaults overwhelmed him, whenever he sank too profoundly into despair and silence, Bebe, his loving protector, would make a call and then walk him down to the Kroger parking lot, and Rayford would come pick him up in the Range Rover and take him off to his house on Turners Rock.

Ransom's sanctuary.

The precise symmetry of the stone terrace. The shrimp boats spreading their wings over the Wilmington River. The shell-shaped platter of biscuits and ham and Cokes (till Ransom was sixteen, then lime rickeys till he was eighteen, then bourbon). The houseful of fossils, the blooms that Rayford had collected from all over the world, the hours-long bouts of gossip and stories.

This afternoon Ransom gets a ride from Liza and Hatchet Head in Liza's mottled Impala. They take Victory Drive past Thunderbolt, over the bridges, under towering stoop-shouldered clouds. The day has turned quite warm. The spring mildness seems threatened. Buzz on the radio about a coming heat wave. There's no AC in the car so they keep the windows open and don't talk because the wind is too loud. They let Ransom out at the Turners Rock turnoff, and drive on toward the day-drunk bars of Tybee Island.

At the gate he rings up the house. Tells the camera, "Hi, Boris"; the barrier arm lifts, and he strolls up the long drive.

His spirits lift a notch with each step. Soft crush of oystershells. A nod to the turkeys poking around by the birdbath fountain.

The four different kinds of bougainvillea, the six different kinds of wisteria: somehow harmonious. Up to the beautiful modern house, which is all glass and shimmer, and Boris comes out to greet him with a roar and an embrace. Boris: the unlikeliest of butlers. Latvian, lanky, loud, with a Trotsky-sharp beard. And right behind Boris comes Rayford himself, bestowing a full Rayford bear hug. Then the three of them head into the great room with its glass vitrines full of fossil sloths and Triassic turtle shells and ibex horns, and, under the glass of the coffee table, the bones of both species of triceratops.

When Ransom was a boy, whenever he thought of being rich and weighed the pros and the cons: the con was Morgana, the pro this house on Turners Rock.

On the terrace they take their hammock chairs, and Boris brings them bourbon lowballs and a platter of oysters. Salt breeze from the river. Rayford points out a couple of birds flying low over the water, smears of bright pink. "Roseate spoonbills. Wasn't none ten years ago. But now look, they comin north. They say it's a sign the world's goin to hell. But how purty they are!"

They chat for a while: this and that. Rayford's grown children, Ransom's sisters.

245

Rayford mentions that he saw young Jaq at Morgana's Soiree. "She tol' me she's making a movie about the city. Said Savannah's like a fairy tale or somethin. Somethin out of a storybook. My good Christ. She'll learn, I expect."

They drink.

It's time to get down to it.

Ransom says, "So you've heard about my mother and the Gooze?"

"Oh. Somethin, uh-huh. She workin for him?"

"Yes, and I'm sort of helping her."

"All right. Well, that's news."

"What's your take on him?"

"On the Gooze?" Rayford shakes his head. "I guess my take is that man fucked up royally. Burned down that house of his for the money and burned that boy up in it, and everybody knows it, and what's he got for a defense? A hypodermic needle? Jaysus. That's a flophouse in East Savannah — and they only found *one* needle? Nah. They ain't got shit. So the Gooze, he tries the usual. Jiggers up some vast conspiracy, dark forces etcetera, big frame-up. But ain't nobody go' fall for that."

Rayford's father owned the kaolin plant on the river, and when Rayford was a boy he spent summers in Sandersville loading the kaolin slurry into tank cars. Picked up half his accent there: the *ain't*s and the chopped-off *t*'s. And he's never bothered to refine it much — though he can swing into a higher tone if he needs to.

Ransom asks, "Rayford, do you know a woman named Matilda Stone?"

"Uh-uh. Rings no bell."

"Archaeologist?"

"Oh. OK, maybe. Colored lady? They call her Stony? She look for old graveyards and all?"

"Uh-huh. That's right."

"Well, I seen her around but I don't know her. Why you ask?"

"She's gone missing."

"Oh shit."

"And Guzman's looking for her."

"Yeah? How come?"

"That's our question. He won't tell us. Maybe she's a witness of some kind."

"Jaysus. Man's so slimy. He won't tell you what he wants with her? How do you work for a client who won't be straight with you?"

Ransom shrugs. "I don't know. It's my mother's deal. Which raises another question."

"Uh-huh?"

"Could you tell me what my mother's up to?"

Rayford laughs. He sits in his shambling bear posture, a little slumped, bourbon in hand, with his rich curly white locks, which used to be golden, and his big, expressive, wide-open face, and he plays it, as always, Southern-slow and cagey. "I mean . . . *yaw* don't know?"

"I don't."

"We-ul, *I* sure don't. Gooze gonna deal her a few bucks?"

"Two hundred grand. Up front. Three hundred more if she proves his innocence."

"Hoo shit!" Rayford grins, and takes a drink. "I mean ain't that your answer then? Ain't she been worried about her bank account, all them causes, all them contributions, all that flying with Hattie Bainbridge to Barcelona? Plus bailin Betty out of jail, payin Betty's lawyers? And you know she's always been panicky about money. Even when your daddy was in his prime; when yaw had money comin outt'n your ears, still, when she'd drink, she'd get them panics. She'd say, Why, we all gonna wind up living with the *hobos.*"

But he must sense the sting that carries for Ransom, for he reins in his laugh.

They turn to the oysters. Use a screwdriver to jimmy them open. A dollop of horseradish, down the hatch. While they're at it, a solemn procession of pelicans passes up the river. The sun has gone down but the birds' wings are high enough to catch the light.

"But you know," Rayford finally allows, "with Morgana it's always hard to say. I mean maybe it ain't the money at all. Maybe it's just her general pissedness. You know? She is what we used to call a scrapper. Always has been. Even when she first come to town. She and her sister Elsie come here from . . . what was that little town they was from? *Surrey?*"

"Surrency."

"Surrency, right. And Surrency was known for one thing in them days. They didn't have a stoplight in Surrency, but they had two flashing lights, about two blocks apart, and you're comin along at night, I think that's Highway 341 and maybe you're on your way to Hazlehurst, and why you're goin to Hazlehurst in the middle of the night is another story, not nothin you're proud of, but you're comin along flat and straight and there ain't nothin on the radio but fahr-and-brimstone preachin, and you see this flashing light from out about ten, eleven miles out, and it's goin *blink . . . blink . . . blink . . .* and you don't know it's two lights, 'cause from ten miles out it looks like *one* light.

249

But you go a mile and the light starts to . . . *stretch,* seems like, and now it's goin buh-*blink,* buh-*blink,* buh-*blink,* and you go another mile and the light keeps stretching and you just don't know what the hell you're lookin at. Is it aliens? Is it an alien spacecraft? Am I gonna get myself anally probed here? And lots a folks, after about seven, eight miles a this they jes' get hypno-tized by them lights and they run off the road into a pine tree and boom they dead. And that's what Surrency was famous for, until your mother and your aunt Elsie came outta there.

"So they come here to Savannah and they get waitress jobs at Johnny Ganem's, which in those days was where all the town bosses went for steak and shrimp and oysters, and they drew attention, them girls, 'cause they was both quick and funny, and Elsie was good-looking and Morgana was, well I guess the word is *stunning.* But also, she could be mean. You didn't want to pick a fight with her. And so smart. What I noticed straight off was there was no country in her speech; no *r*'s and no twang at all. Elsie still had her twang but Morgana, she sounded Savan-nah from the jump. Because Savannah is what she had decided to be. You know? And oh, the boys was fallin. I'd bring her over to

Herb Buchanan's little soirees on Jones Street and the boys would jes' gather round. Sometimes if Johnny Mercer was in town he'd come play and play Herb's piano, and those nights were magic. He'd play 'The Days of Wine and Roses.' That was one of his tunes, you know that one? And he jes' loved Morgana, and I sometimes thought he was singin it right to her. And the boys was all lookin at her. And I was lookin too. And I recall telling myself, Rayford, you better watch out now, you better keep checkin under your ribs, see that nothin's *missin.*"

He swirls his bourbon in its potbellied glass.

"But Jay-sus, what a *student* she was. Of people. She was still a little coarse, untutored, but she was learnin all the time. She'd be watching folks all night, and Christ, the things she *noticed.* Drive her home and she'd tell me her theories. Her notions. As to who'd be setting up with whom, who'd be getting his heart broken, whose love affair was going to take place despite all protestations to the contrary, who'd be risin in the world and who'd be losin all his money. She had a way of seein folks' futures. I always figured she was guessing but she wa'n't. Turned out she was nearly always right. Though some of them fates she called out, they didn't show up for *years.* But she knew. She nailed 'em.

"But I asked her once and she says, I'm not readin out what they'll *be,* Rayford. I'm just tellin you who I think they *are.*"

He takes a swig, stays with that memory a moment. Then goes on:

"Then she started takin *me* to parties. I thought it was my town, but it was already hers. Took me to the strangest places. Places I never knew existed. Juke-joint trailers in Port Wentworth and secret gay bars on Tybee, and fish camps and strip clubs and VFWs, and you name it, every night somethin new, she knew 'em all. One time she says to me, somethin like, Savannah's not just *one realm,* Rayford. It's a great many realms. But they work together to keep us in thrall."

Ransom laughs. "Jesus, she really said *realms?* She said *in thrall?*"

"Uh-huh. 'At's how she talked. Jes' flipped them words right on out there. This is a girl with no college education, but her mother was a teacher and she'd been readin since she was three years old. She'd read everything under the sun, my God. Smartest girl I ever met. And yet the old guard, the money set, they still wouldn't give her the time of day. She seemed just a little too

252

hungry for them, a little too quick. Like who the hell does she think she is, shows up here from Shitsqueeze, Georgia, and grabs Harmon Rutherford and Lucas Tartanian to squire her around? And even then she drank too much. She drank *religiously.* And she had a vicious wit, which I don't need to tell you. Round 'bout three in the morning she'd bring out the knives, and she'd fillet one of them dimwitted society girls in three minutes and have us all laughin our heads off. Result a which, she'd have a new enemy. Before long near every woman in town hated her."

He shakes his head. Reflects.

"I tell you what. One in particular who hated her was our friend Rebecca Cressling. Rebecca may pretend to be a bohemian but she's always enjoyed her money. She always gets a kick out of her properties and her heritage and her place in this town and all. And from the get-go she had her eyes set on Fred Musgrove. I 'member when Fred started to get flirty with your mother — and Rebecca, she about lost her shit. I recall at Chrissie Dunning's funeral, when Rebecca saw your mother in the receiving line and said, Oh, there's that little country slut with the city tone. Ha! And all the young ladies giggled. But the boys kept right on lovin

Morgana. They jes' *swooned* for her. And Fred Musgrove was a boy like the rest of us."

And in this peaceful hour with so much brought out to dry, Ransom finds it reasonable to ask something he never has before: "And you, Rayford? Did you swoon for her too?"

Rayford pauses and pours another oyster down his gullet.

Sips his bourbon.

Then allows, "Oh, completely. I mean I was . . ." His voice fades out. Comes back: "*Gone.* God. It's forty years and I still *dream* about her. I dreamed about her last night. I can't — oh Lord it's about *time* you got out here, you lazy bastard."

This last spoken to Boris, who has shown up to refresh their drinks. "Apology, apology," says Boris. "I am watching the television. The politics. What a show of shit! Ran, where your damn mama? Where your damn sisters?" It seems Boris has been drinking himself. Ransom tries to get him to stop filling the glass but he insists. "I cannot leave your glass empty, Ransom, do not ask me for that. Ha ha ha!"

When he has topped off both glasses, he turns toward the river, spreads his arms, stands there a moment with the bourbon

254

bottle in one hand and the tray in another, exulting in the sunset. Then lurches away.

"By the way," says Rayford, "Yes I *do* remember that Stony woman. I believe she was at one time in Rebecca's employ. Diggin up some kind of hidden loot on her land somewhere. Oughta go talk to *her,* Ransom."

"OK. Thank you. I will."

"And the point I'm tryin to make, in a nutshell, is that folk in this town all look down their noses at Guzman, and Morgana has always resented those fine folk. She has learned to be more polite — but she's always up for a scrap. So maybe she wants this case just to spite 'em all?"

Jaq turns the door crank, and the bell trills, and while she waits for Betty she hears a tour bus behind her, trawling down the cobblestones. She turns to look. The guide has a phony-ass Scarlett O'Hara accent: "Now this mansion heah, why, we-all heah in Savannah, we-all call this 'the Old Fohht,' uh-huh. It was built in 1883 by Richard Musgrove and his wife, Mirabelle Lamaaah, of the famous Lamaaah family. It's an *ex-*quisite example of the style known as red-brick Romanesque. Note the faces of those

ghoo-uls in that wall beneath the parapet
—"

They're not ghouls, Jaq thinks, they're
angels. But lately all tours have turned into
ghost tours, even tours in broad daylight,
even garden-and-magnolia tours, and you
just *have* to work *ghoo*-uls into your spiel,
and get *ghastly* in there too, and *blood-curdling* (pronounced as "bluhd-cuddling"),
and by now all the tourists on the big fat
streetcar-bus are gaping at her and she
gapes right back: You with your bloated
corn-fed faces, I think *you're* the *ghoo-uls.* I
have my own tour guide right here in my
skull who tells me all about you.

Then the door opens. Betty.

"Jaaaq!" she cries. Going for a hug. Jaq
tries to step back because she's covered with
sweat but Betty says, "No, I'm gonna get
ya," and she hugs hard and holds on.

"Gram here?"

"In the garden, sweetie. You want iced
tea?"

"Yes please."

First Jaq stops in the little bathroom
tucked beneath the stairs, fills the sink, and
immerses her whole head in the cool water.
Dries off with one of Morgana's luxurious
towels, and looks at her face in the mirror
to see if she can spot any of the change she's

feeling. She can't. She just looks tired. She goes out through the foyer and into the keeping room (which looks naked without the sketch) and into the kitchen, where she says hello to Marcel, the cook. Betty has brought the iced tea pitcher out of the fridge, and fills a glass for her, which Jaq inhales.

"Another one?" Betty asks.

"OK, thanks."

But then Betty notices the clock: five thirty. "You know what, Jaq? It's time to bring Morgana a little somethun. You wanna switch to white wine?"

"Of course I would." Betty pours one for Jaq and one for Morgana, one for Marcel and one for herself. "And are you hungry, darlin?"

"I ate at the Bean," says Jaq. "No appetite lately but I got a salad down."

"Here you go then." Betty hands her the two wineglasses. "I'm so glad you're *baaackk.*"

Jaq says, "I'm not back."

"OK. I'm glad anyway."

Betty holds the side door open for her, and Jaq goes down the steps and walks round the corner of the house and finds Morgana in the long garden bed on the south side. She's kneeling in the soil, in the late, soft sunlight. She's wearing her garden overalls and planting pansies. She sees Jaq and smiles — though not too broadly, because after their quarrel that would be inappropriate. "Jaqueline."

"Brought your wine."

"Oh! Thank you."

"I came to say thanks for the gift."

"Well. It was far too late. Should have done that years ago."

"I appreciate the gesture."

"I'm glad."

"I opened it in front of Aunt Willou. She didn't take it well."

Now Morgana can't suppress a fuller grin. "I wish I'd been there to witness that."

"She pointed out that you might have sold the sketch and given the money to charity."

Morgana considers. "Well. I might have. But then it would still exist."

Jaq sets her wine down carefully, pushing the base a half inch into the soil, and kneels beside it.

"Dear!" says Morgana. "You'll get your shorts all soiled."

"They're already soiled. May I ask you a question?"

"Of course."

"Do you really think Guzman's innocent?"

"I do," says Morgana without hesitation.

"But what do *you* think?"

"I think he set that fire and I think Stony knows about it. Ransom told you about Stony, right?"

"Yes."

"I think she was a witness to Luke's death. That's why the Gooze has to find her. That's why he hired you."

"All right," says Morgana. "That sounds reasonable. Tell me about Stony."

Jaq looks down at the pansies. Their faces stretch along this wall for half the length of the house. Morgana is selecting seedlings by color from an array of little cartons. Some already have a single bloom, but for those that don't, their smiling photo from the seed packet is neatly pinned to each carton. Jaq has always loved helping Gram to plant her pansies. "God," she says, "they look so happy."

"Don't they? I found this Polish website. I can't read a word, but I just tap a picture and they send. See these packets? I'm sure they're telling me useful things, if I could find anyone who speaks Polish. But I just plant away and they seem to do fine. They keep popping up with their odd little grins and then I just have to order more. Would you care to put one in, Jaqueline?"

She passes Jaq the trowel. Jaq hollows out

a space, selects a violet pansy with a yellow face, and presses it down into the earth, which is still warm from the long day.

"So, Gram," she says, "I've decided to trust you. Well, sort of, but not really. I just want to find Stony. She hasn't been seen since the night Luke died. Nobody's really worried because we're all used to Stony coming and going, but if Guzman's looking for her, well . . . I want to make sure she's safe. If you'll help me find her, I'd like to work with you. But will you swear to me, that when we do find her, you'll never tell Guzman where she is?"

"Sure," says Morgana. "I can promise that."

"So you want to know about her? She comes into Bo Peep's a lot. She likes margaritas. Her real name is Matilda Stone. She looks fifty but maybe she's not that old, maybe she's had a rough life. She's what they call a 'contract archaeologist.' When the city wants to build some new twelve-story garage or a new jail or whatever, first they have to prove there's no Native American burial ground. So they hire her. But she doesn't seem to get many jobs. Sometimes she digs up arrowheads and sells them. But mostly she's broke. She always stayed with Luke when she was in town. She and Luke found empty buildings to hole up in."

Morgana raises a brow. "When she's in town?"

"Yeah because mostly she's not here. You ask her where she lives, she says her home is some Kingdom somewhere. I always thought that was just craziness. But then you told us about Guzman's clue, Stone Kings and all, and I had a thought, and I went to the Historical Society today and found out some things. You want to know what I found out?"

"Yes."

Looking at Jaq with her intense gray eyes. Jaq says, "No one else can hear?"

"Oh. I don't know, maybe Betty. She's so often listening." She calls, "*Betty?* Are you eavesdropping?" No answer. "So perhaps not."

Jaq draws a breath. "Well OK. Did you know that in the Revolutionary War there were Black soldiers who fought for the English side?"

"I didn't."

"You know much about the Battle of Savannah?"

"Much?" Morgana chuckles.

"Yeah, well," says Jaq, "same for me. Zero. But today I found out the British won that battle, and Black soldiers were key to that victory. But then the British wound up losing the war, and the Americans took their plantations back and wanted their enslaved people back. But the Black soldiers were done with that. They still thought of themselves as soldiers of the King of England, and they still had their muskets. During the war they'd lived in the wild, and they'd learned all about the Savannah River. They knew the tricky parts, the swampy parts, and where there were hidden islands. So now they went back to one of those islands, about fifteen miles north of here, and built a kind of secret fortress. And many other enslaved folks ran off from their plantations and joined them. Till there were maybe two hundred people in that village, and rows of wooden cabins, and public buildings and gardens, and a breastwork that went all around it."

Morgana raises a brow. "What's a breastwork?"

"I don't know. A wall of some kind?"

"I see. And this village: they were *allowed* to build it?"

"Of course not. But no one could find it. And everybody knew the King's soldiers had muskets, that they were dangerous, so they left 'em alone. And the people planted fields and corn and beans and yams and all, and they fished and gathered oysters and trapped, and once in a while they stole a cow from one of the local plantations. They were led by these two men: Sharper and Lewis. And they were thriving. The Georgia militia came out; the King's soldiers fought them off. But then some bad stuff sprang up between Sharper and Lewis, they had some falling-out, and Lewis betrayed the village. A new militia came out to fight, from South Carolina. There was a big battle, and some of the King's soldiers were killed and some were caught, and the village was burned. Lewis was put on trial. He made a sort of a confession and then they cut his head off and stuck it on a pole overlooking the river. And it stayed up there for years.

"But now listen to this. Sharper and his wife, Nancy, and a bunch of the others got away. They went south. They walked down through the jungle for night after night, for weeks. They fought at least one fight we know about, with the militia who were hunting them, and some of them were killed, but the rest got away, and they made their way down the coast. They hid from people, and forded the rivers, and got past the little farms and the little villages, and got all the way to Florida. Which was ruled by Spain in those days. Sharper and Nancy petitioned the King of Spain for sanctuary. That petition was granted. That's all we know. How many were with them we don't know. We just have a few lines on a document. Sharper and Nancy: petition granted. Then they disappear from history. But it looks like they made it to freedom."

Morgana is rapt. "Lord."

"And Sharper's my ancestor. And his granddaughter Herriat, she made a tape, back in the 1950s, where she talked about him. She heard about the village when she was a child. Everyone called it the Kingdom. She said the people in the Kingdom were the only free people who ever lived in the State of Georgia. Those were her exact words. Now wait. Look at this."

She lifts her phone. She has the video cued up. When she presses the arrow, it goes right to Stony at Bo Peep's, saying: *"The King's soldiers are the only free people to ever live in the State of Georgia."*

Morgana looks up. "What's this?"

"I made that when Stony came in with Luke. That night, the night he was burned. I taped Luke too. Wanna watch?"

"Yes. Would you play it all for me?"

"OK." She takes it back to the beginning, and they watch together.

Then Morgana says, "And would you

kindly send me a copy?"

Jaq works her thumbs a moment. "Sent."

"So who else knows about this village?"

"Arthur. At the Historical Society. Also I tried to tell Aunt Willou, but she didn't want to hear. I think she thinks I'm nuts. She also thinks this is too dangerous for me."

"It is."

"So I'll stop. As soon as we find Stony."

Morgana brushes a few wisps of hair from her eyes. "This island — do you know where it is?"

"I think so." Jaq taps into Google Maps on her phone, satellite mode. Bird's-eye view of Savannah. She drags the picture over the squares, over River Street, over the wharves and the broad gray river, following the water north. Over the derricks, the big bridge, the oil tanks, the gasworks, which are lit up like a Christmas tree, the dark satanic sugar refinery. Then a wilderness of marshes and swamps. She feels Morgana beside her, her iris smell and always sweet breath (hint of mouthwash today). The evening is warm, and on the other side of the garden hedge someone is rolling a supermarket cart down the cobblestones, a kind of high-hat concerto.

Her scrolling takes them at last to a green blurry smear of trees. "See this island? The general of the state militia, he said the encampment of 'the runaway slaves' was on an island southwest of Dubbey's Ford. Dubbey's Ford would have been right *here*. This island — this could be it. It's called Montmillan Island. It's still completely wild. I think somewhere in there is the Kingdom."

"I know of Montmillan Island."

"You do?"

"A friend of your grandfather owns it. Or did. They used to hunt quail there. I'll get Johnny on it."

"OK. And I might check it out myself."

"Don't."

"I'll be all right, Grandmother. I'll be very careful."

But Jaq does have a thought then. It occurs to her that she might be safer with a gun. The guy she's been seeing, Pivot, he's a hip-hop artist in town, a performer at the Starnite Lounge, but to supplement his income he deals weed. So naturally he's a little paranoid, and he keeps a pistol in a desk drawer. She's seen it there. Maybe she could borrow it? She's been avoiding Pivot since the other night on River Street when he and his friends were so coked up and dull and annoying, but now as she thinks of him her thoughts are fond.

Yeah, she thinks, I'll pay him a visit.

Meanwhile Morgana is putting her things into a wheelbarrow: the bags of soil, the empty cartons, the trowel. Jaq rises and slaps the dirt off her shorts, and follows her into the basement. They take turns washing their hands at the old sink. Cooler in here, the smell of ancient grouting. That spooky door that's never been opened, which supposedly opens to a tunnel that goes down to the storm drains. She imagines that labyrinth now, right beneath her, these tunnels that undermine the whole city, and she feels off-balance; she puts her hand on the doorjamb to steady herself. And stands there watching silently as Morgana dries her frail hands on a little striped towel.

Willou crosses the bridge over Lazaretto Creek, then takes the hairpin turn down toward the marina. Her tires crunching on the oystershells. Pulling her Escalade close to the big boatshed, where cars passing over the bridge won't be able to see it. When she opens the car door, she can feel how the weather is changing. The air's getting warmer even after the sun's gone down. And sticky. Feels like a dog's breath. She walks out to the wooden dock, and the rhythm of her shoefalls marks her urgency.

She walks past fancy speedboats, luxury

yachts. This dock used to be all shrimp boats, but those are gone now. The old seafood shack is also gone. Morgana and Fred used to take the whole family here on Saturdays. One of the shrimp boats was owned by an old Greek guy named Galatas: he'd invite them all aboard, show them the big nets and the coolers, while the crew snapped off shrimp heads, snap snap. The man is still alive but lives in a home somewhere. The community of Greek fishermen is scattered. She knows the old fisherman's son: Nick, a Savannah cop who's always trying to do her favors. Gives generously to her charities. Apparently he'd like to enter polite society. But how would a cop enter polite society? Something in his face gives away his eagerness. Poor guy. Though she *is* glad for the favors.

One big yacht after another. They're all owned by Yankees or Atlanta bankers. Smoked glass, sleek, dull. They mostly just sit here. There's only one boat she really likes at this moorage: a sailing sloop at the end of the dock. It's old, from the 1940s, and graceful. Belongs to a high school boyfriend of hers, Murphy Drayton, a broker who now lives in New York and lets her use his boat whenever she needs it. Whenever she requires a truly private meeting. There's no privacy in Savannah, nowhere you can go where you won't be seen. Except Murphy's yacht.

Down she goes three steps into the salon.

Her brother David rises to greet her.

He doesn't look well. He used to be handsome. Now he's corpulent, overtanned, and oily; he looks like a bored walrus. Still she loves him deeply and is always glad to see him. Always she feels she can detect his true spirit under the armor. They give their buss, then stand back from each other and exchange sly little grins: we're still playing at life, aren't we? He's made them both old-fashioneds with fresh orange peel (someone comes in here every week and keeps the bar stocked). They sit facing each other, beside the big port window with its panoramic view of the river. They clink glasses.

He tells her, "Maddie sends her love."

She hates Madelaine, which he knows. But she says, "You give her my love right back?"

"I will."

Willou's the one who called this meeting. It's up to her to get it going. But she hems and haws until he snatches the reins. He says, "I heard about Mother."

"Heard what?"

"That she's working for the Gooze. At

269

some preposterous fee. For whatever reason."

"How'd you find that out?"

"My mysterious sources." He takes a swallow of his old-fashioned. "Actually, Burt told me. Guzman's lawyer. Is that why we're here?"

"We're here because today a thug from Methingham County came to my chambers. He's working for somebody, but I don't know who. He had a message. He told me Jaq has been snooping around the Guzman case, and needs to stop."

"You mean Jaq our niece? Bebe and Roxanne's Jaq?"

"Uh-huh."

"I don't get it. Why is Jaq —"

"She was a friend of the victim. Of Kitchens. She went to the cops and told them Guzman's lawyers are lying, that Kitchens was never a drug addict. And she's been following all the Gooze News. And now she's going to the library and researching madly and making big discoveries and running around like a chicken with her head cut off."

"And the Gooze is all worked up about *that*?"

"Weird, right? Makes no sense. Maybe it's a message for Mother. To stay out of this."

"But . . ." He squints. "Why would any-body care . . ."

"Because maybe the Gooze is telling the truth. Maybe he *is* being framed. And somebody doesn't want that truth to come out."

"Are you kidding?"

"I'm not," she says. "Does the Gooze have any enemies?"

"You mean other than everyone?"

"I mean someone who would hire that thug. Someone who's a little crude, some-one who will go to any lengths."

"You're telling me you actually believe the Gooze's I-wuz-framed shit?"

She shrugs. "I want to figure this out. I want to find out what fucker in this town would target my niece. And I want your help on this."

"No."

"Yes. For Jaq."

"Right. Hold on."

He gets up and carries their empty glasses to the little galley, where he prepares two more. Sets Willou's before her, sits again, and again they clink glasses and drink.

He drains half of his in one go.

Then he says, "Yeah, look, I'd do anything for you, for Jaq. Unless it's also for Mother. Mother knew Ransom was trying to fuck my wife. Apparently they had something going even when they were at Duke. All those years. But Mother never told me. Even now, she does not exactly take my side in that affair. Even after my brother tried to murder me. She's always treated me like a little bit of a monster who's bullying her sweet prince. Story I've never told you before. I was maybe fourteen, and Mother calls me into the Turkish room. And she's drunk of course, and she tells me she knows I'm gonna grow up to be very powerful. 'Very powerful in this town.' You know, it's about the nicest thing she ever said to me. But then she says, David, you must always use your power to protect your fragile little brother, to protect his creative genius. Will you promise me that, David? Like that was, that's the *purpose* of my power, that's the *meaning* of it. Then she goes up to the turret to tell her prince bedtime stories. She can go to hell, Willou. And Ransom too. I'm sorry about what happened to his friend Billy, but in my opinion they cut the head off the wrong hobo. And if Jaq wants my help on this case, well here's my help. Tell her to grow up real quick and realize what town she's living in. Tell her she's lucky she got a warning. Savannah doesn't give out many of those."

■ ■ ■ ■

Jaq's passing Forsyth Park, pedaling west. Pauses outside the Sentient Bean café to text Pivot.

up for a visit?

Somebody calls to her; she looks up. Boiled Liza and Hatchet Head are hanging at a table in front of the Bean. Jaq says hello and takes out her camera and asks Liza where she's staying, now the Marriott has been closed. Liza says she's at the shelter on Bee Avenue, "just a classic hellhole." Hatchet Head says he's at the 44th Street Shelter, which is "precisely like your armpit's asshole if your armpit had one." Then Jaq feels Pivot vibrating in her pocket. She checks her phone.

zzzz. tomorrow?

The *zzzz* conjures an image of him in bed. He sleeps in the nude, and the thought of that hangs ripely in her thoughts. It's too damn early for him to crap out. She bids her friends good night and rides on over there. He lives on Montgomery and 48th: it takes her nine minutes. It's a two-story house with a big porch. Lights on. She locks the bike, glides up the steps.

The door is open.

She steps in and hears, from above, banga banga bucka banga.

Oh no.

His grunts. Then the whimpers of some girl. Jaq stands quietly at the foot of the stairs and tries to guess who's with him. Oh God. Charlynn? It *is* Charlynn. Jaq can smell her perfume hanging in the air. Knows she should be feeling betrayed, crushed, as Charlynn's her good friend. Actually, Jaq *introduced* Charlynn to Pivot. Exposed all her secrets to that sneak, and this is where trust gets her: bucka banga bucka banga. But on the other hand there *is* a certain convenience to this. It gives Jaq the drop on Pivot, and a sense of guiltlessness as she steals into the little room by the parlor that he uses for an office and opens the desk, which he always, unforgivably, leaves un-locked, and takes out his Smith & Wesson and slides it into her waistband. Feels huge there. She also borrows three bullets, while right above her Charlynn is wailing like a cat left out in the rain, which Jaq finds somewhat comical. She floats outside and transfers the pistol to her backpack and puts the backpack on and feels the new weight against her spine as she takes off. It's comforting, and she rides a block before pausing to text:

you and Char riding the zzzzz stallion or I'd have said hello

Ransom's awake in the dark, in his sleeping bag, playing back that visit to Rayford in his head — when suddenly there's a wasp in the sleeping bag with him, a furious buzzing and he jumps, and Gracie at his feet leaps up also, and starts barking into the night, and he's struggling to get his legs out of the bag when he hears the buzz again and realizes it's a phone.

His new cell phone. Which is all lit up.

"Hello, Mother."

"How'd you know it was me?"

"Who else has the number? You just gave me this today."

"Are you awake?"

"Half."

"I got a visit from Jaq," she says. "She'll work with us."

"Oh. OK. Doesn't that worry you?"

"Yes. But it's her decision."

Then she tells him about Jaq's research at the Historical Society. About "the soldiers of the King" living on Montmillan Island.

She says, "That used to belong to Monty Reynolds. But maybe not still. Could you check it out, Ransom? I'd send Johnny but we just don't have forever."

"All right."

"How was Rayford?" she asks.

"He thinks Guzman's guilty."

"Well. So does everyone."

"He also said that Stony used to work for Rebecca Cressling."

"He said that? Rayford said that?"

"Yeah, and that she's been looking for some 'treasure' or something related to her family. And she hired Stony to help her. And we should really go talk to Rebecca."

There's a long silence.

"Well well well," says Morgana. "How intriguing."

CHAPTER FOUR:
THE TURKISH ROOM

Early the next morning Jaq gets on her bike and heads north. Takes Bay Street past the wharves and over the railroad bridge, past the wastewater treatment plant, past three bedbug motels. It's hot this morning. Even this early she's sweating. Truck horns go Doppling by, their shock waves nearly blowing her off the road. She keeps pumping those pedals. A strip mall with only one open storefront: an office of the Georgia Division of Family and Children Services (long line out front). She bulls through the miles. The city starts to thin out. Lots of slash pines, which her grandfather Fred always called toilet-paper pines. Grampa Fred knew about all the pine trees and had pine plantations of his own, and he said most pines were paper-bag pines, or sometimes rec-room pines, but these bristly starveling trees on Route 21, he called these "toilet-paper pines."

She laughs to think of it. She passes a Stuckey's Fruit and Fireworks stand, and then the hulk of a Sinclair gas station, and then the rotting carcass of a strip club. PARADISO EXOTIQUE / WHERE YOUR PASSIONS COME TO LIFE! Then more toilet-paper pines.

Then she comes to a washed-out sign that reads:

CAP'N STAN FISHIN
DOLPHIN TOURS
BOAR-HUNT!!!
"GATOR HUNTIN" 1.3 MILES

An arrow points to the left. She follows it. Old road, blacktop faltering to oystershell. Her bones take a beating from the bouncing. Then the road switches to sand, and now it feels like she's pushing through molasses, and it's ungodly hot and the sweat comes off her in torrents. Finally the sand firms up some, and the scrub pines give way to live oaks, primeval forest, and she arrives at a clearing overlooking a slow brown creek.

Wooden dock. Fishing boat with an outboard. Big open shed.

She dismounts and props the bike against a palm tree.

"Captain?"

Cicadas.

Under the metal roof of the shed are seine nets, tackle, traps, gutted outboards. Also, in the shadows, two dogs. They bestir themselves. One of them trots right up to her. Big red-coated coonhound, friendly. The other is skinny, silt-colored, and skittish. Wants to approach but is too nervous to do so. Makes a broad arc around her and whines.

Then Jaq hears a snore.

Her eyes cut to a cot in the shadows.

The man sleeping there is sunbaked, still young, early thirties maybe but wizened by the sun. Bearded. He wears no shirt and he's brawny with golden-red fur and he's got pirate-flavored tattoos — anchor, mermaid, parrot — and a big scar on his belly; he's kind of ugly-beautiful and she enjoys looking at him.

Finally the shy dog stokes up courage enough for two belated barks. The man opens one eye.

"And who are you?" he says.

"I'm Jaq."

"Uh-huh. What you need, Jaq?" Working the other eye open. This takes him a while. Then the business of focusing. "Want a dolphin tour? You look like you want a dolphin tour."

279

"Well, you look like a bad actor playing a wingnut Viking fanboy. No, I don't want a dolphin tour."

"What *do* you want?"

She thinks a moment. She's not ready yet to open up about her mission. "Something to drink."

"I got bourbon," he says, and reaches for the bottle, which sits on a milk-crate kind of night table.

"What kind a bourbon is that?"

He shows her the bottle. Southshot. The label has a bald eagle perched upon a cannon, and a cheap, fallen-nobility, Lost Cause look.

"I don't know this one, Cap'n. I know a hundred kinds of bourbon but not this one."

"It's pretty cheap. But it'll get your buzz on."

"What I need is water."

He points to a little fridge. There's a bottle of cold water inside, which she drains down her gullet. Refills it at the sink and puts it back. Then takes the towel that's hanging there and soaks it under the tap and rubs her face and her hair.

She looks round and sees there's one chair available: a captain's chair. Plastic, but it does have the word cap'n embossed in gilt letters. She drags it over and sits. She asks,

"Hunting boar, what's that like?"

He's sitting up now, still trying to gather his wits. "What you mean, *what's it like*?"

"I mean, is it hard?"

"Nah. Not really. Dogs do all your work for ya."

"*These* dogs?" She snaps her fingers softly, and the big red goof comes to her. She rubs its furry neck. "These are like secret boar-seeking missiles?"

" 'At one there is. 'At's a redbone. Real good pigpicker."

"And the other?"

Cap'n Stan sniffs. "In truth? Ain't much use."

"Why not?"

"Too jumpy."

"How come he's so jumpy?"

"She. I dunno, she has just always been jumpy."

"And how do they hunt boar?"

He shrugs. "Sniff out a pig, go in, flush it out. Then you come shoot it."

"Wow," she says flatly. "That sounds thrilling. Is there any risk?"

He shrugs. "I dunno. You could miss."

"Oh boy. Then what?"

"Shoot it again, I guess. Or I'll shoot it for you."

"So zero risk."

He laughs. "Why you want risk so bad? You got a midlife crisis? Tell you what, you could juke it."

"What does that mean?"

"Use a knife. In the jug'lar."

"Won't they bite?"

"Uh-huh, they will do." He grins. Surprisingly great set of teeth. "Hey, not to be annoying, but what. The fuck. Do. You. *Want?*"

She shrugs. "I'm looking for Stony."

He squints at her.

"Don't you remember?" she asks. "You two came to my bar a couple of months ago. To Peep's. I'm the bartender."

"Oh yeah?" He sits there hunched over, slightly rocking, trying to recall. His eyes open a little wider, as though something is coming back to him.

"But you were very drunk," she says. "You were drunk to begin with and it got worse. You showed everyone that scar."

"This?"

"Uh-huh. How'd you get it again?"

"Knife fight. Should see the other guy. That sumbitch livin with the angels."

"At Peep's, though, you said a gator tried to swallow you."

"I did?"

"That was cleverer than the knife fight

282

story. You came with Stony. You friends with her?"

"Drinkin buddies."

"Seen her around lately?"

"No ma'am."

"OK. Well, no one has. I'll give you a hundred dollars if you'll take me out to the island."

He sniffs. "I don't think so. It's just too fuckin hot today."

They sit there. The dogs droop their heads.

He says, "Two hundred, though."

"Deal," she says, "if you bring your bourbon."

Ransom is in the Recorder's Office of Effingham County. A deep hush in here. Wall-to-wall carpets, smoked glass, chilled dead air. The clerk, a blonde with nifty cat-eye glasses, looks up and says, "Well hello, Ransom."

He recalls her from high school. "Hello, Rhonda."

She's appraising him. Probably she's seen him recently, on the streets in his vagabondage, because she's giving him a look that says, *You've cleaned up very well.* She says, "How can I help you? You practicing law again?"

He hears in her voice a certain sweetness, a flirtation, and it brings him back to the old days, to summers home from college, long before Madelaine, when diversions could still divert.

"I'm looking up a deed," he says.

He gives her the coordinates for Montmillan Island, and they check the plat map and note the code, and she walks him into the shelves. Pulls out one of the great books, and leaves him to it.

He turns the pages till he finds all the transfers of Montmillan Island, starting with a charter from the Trustees of the Colony of Georgia to a Viscount Montmillan in 1758. Twenty years later it was bequeathed to another male Montmillan; then down it went through generations of male Montmillans, then to generations of folks with Montmillan as their middle name, then in 1968 to Reynolds Montmillan Hollis, whom Ransom remembers from his childhood. Old Monty, friend of Ransom's dad, steadfast member of the Oglethorpe Club. Politically you'd place him on the right wing except he was too ornery to share a wing with anybody; rather he had his own bizarro wing. He was a crusty old son of a bitch fifteen years ago. Must be much worse now.

He held on to the island until just two

years ago, then sold it to a company called Sand Gnat Holdings, of which the deed notes only that it's incorporated in the State of Georgia and represented by the local firm of Schilling & Bates.

Deep in the jungle of Montmillan Island, half an hour's thorny, buggy, sweltering hike from where they left the boat, Jaq and Cap'n Stan come to a cleared space under a roof of live oaks and moss and resurrection ferns.

Before them: a row of six shallow trenches. Each ten foot by eight foot. Each marked off primly with low planks and string.

They stand there, passing the bottle of Southshot, gazing at the excavations, and Cap'n Stan talks.

He's been talking nonstop for the last hour.

Took Jaq a while to get him started. He was tight-lipped and untrusting on the boat ride, but she kept asking him to pass that Southshot, and when he did she'd pretend to take a drink, wiping her lips on her arm before passing back the bottle, and then each time he'd take a swallow himself, a big captain-size swallow. She was patient. She kept posing easily answerable questions (*Is that an egret? What's that over there — are*

those the eyes of an alligator?), and laughing at his bad jokes, and passing the bottle
back and forth, until she sensed he was
ready to spill. Then she floated, "So, Stan.
How'd you meet Stony?"

He gave her a sullen look. She changed
the subject. Found some excuse to praise
his dogs and then his boatmanship, and
asked a few more dumb questions. Ten
minutes later the dam broke. He started
talking about Stony. And once he began
there was no stopping him.

Stony, he told her, had just showed up at
the shed one day asking for a ride to Montmillan Island. She said she was an archaeologist; she wanted to explore. He told her
the island was private property. She said she
wasn't gonna hurt nothin. And she offered
him a hundred dollars. Stan himself had
been going there for years, taking the occasional boar or gator, and the old dude
who owned the island, old Monty, had never
minded. So Stan did take Stony over that
morning and came back to fetch her at
dusk, and she was covered in mud and eaten
up by chiggers and horseflies but very
pleased with herself. She thought she'd
found traces of some ancient village. Just
what she'd been looking for.

Next day she had come back and hired

Stan to dig with her.

Now Jaq and Stan are standing there, looking over the fruits of that labor. Stan says, "We dug all this shit in five months. Just the two of us. Stony, she's a tough boss. Never worked so hard in m'life. And she talked like a preacher alla time, like this was all about freedom and salvation and all. She said this is where runaway slaves hid out. Black men and women and children who would not live in servitude. And she went on about how we're *still* living in slavery days and how we all gotta rise up, not just Blacks but whites too, all of us, we gotta rise up. Want some?"

She smiles. Takes it, faux-drinks, passes it back.

The dogs are off barking their heads off, tearing through the brush, constantly on the move, picking up one scent and then another.

Jaq says, "What did you find?"

"A few little things. Belt buckles. Pieces a pottery. Part of an old musket. Thimbles."

"Thimbles? Really? Are they worth anything?"

"Doubt it. Rusted bad. Salt eats 'em. Stony thought there'd be a lot more good stuff in 'at open field, but we can't dig out there, because anyone flying overhead could see we'd been diggin."

"Did you ever find gold?"

He laughs. "You mean like doubloons 'n' shit?"

"No gold? None at all? No treasure?"

"Thimbles. Buttons. Sorry."

"Would you pass the Southshot?"

He does, and she takes a pull, a genuine pull.

"But I tell you what," he says. "Couple months ago, Stony stopped comin. Just stopped. And I admit, I started to miss her a little bit. And then one day I'm out at the Hard-Earned, you know that bar? On Route 17? And Stony's there with some guy, this young guy, real big guy, and she been drinkin. And she goes, I found it, Stan.

"And I go, Found what?

"And she's like, I found the treasure of the Kingdom.

"And then her buddy, the big guy, he goes, Shut up, Stony. And she does, but she says to me, Don't ever take nobody to the Kingdom. I told her I wouldn't. But I just did, for you. But you got me drunk, didn't you?"

Jaq weighs this charge. "I think you got yourself drunk."

"Ha. Want some more?"

"No, I'm good."

"You want to, um —"

"What?"

"I mean, you got a boyfriend?"

"Wait. Stan. I've known you how long? Three hours? And you're coming *on* to me? No. No, I'm sorry, I gotta get to a meeting. What time is it, do you know? Can I possibly get back to Savannah in like, two hours?"

Bebe is working her shift at the hospital, doing paperwork at her desk, when she catches, out of the corner of her eye, a sight that makes her blood run cold.

She shifts her eyes away, hoping the apparition will disappear.

But when she looks back, it's still there.

It's her sister. Willou. In full power attire. Her blazer and pencil skirt, her pumps, her small pearl earrings.

She has never come to the hospital before.

In fact, she's never come to visit Bebe anywhere, on any occasion.

Bebe gets up and gives her sister one *follow-me* flap of her hand, saying to the other nurse on duty, "Brionna, I'm off the floor now." Doesn't look back but knows Willou is behind her by the click of her heels. Wishes she'd worn her new scrubs because these are washed-out and droopy and it kills her to know her sister is back there sizing her up — but who could have predicted this visit?

They go down the bright hallway to the little chapel. "This is the only place we'll get any privacy."

There are eight tiny precious pews and a little altar.

It's deathly still when Willou shuts the door behind them. Bebe arranges her countenance and faces her. "What's up?"

Please, she's thinking, whatever this is, don't let it be about Jaq.

Willou clears her throat.

"It's about Jaq," she begins.

The door crank rings, and Betty shuffles in her slippers to answer. At the door is a fat white man. "Morgana round?"

Trying to seem self-assured, but he's got blotchy skin and sweat stains on the armpits of his jacket and Betty doesn't think him confident at all.

She says, "Who are you?"

He chuckles. "Jes' tell her her favorite client is here."

She finds Morgana on the long screened-in porch, in the wicker rocker, reading Flannery. Only an electric fan to cool her, but she prefers that to air-conditioning: she despises air-conditioning. She has her feet up on the ottoman and iced tea in her hand, and she's smiling at the prose as her eyes flick through it.

Betty says, "A man who calls himself your favorite —"

"I heard," says Morgana, not looking up. "Bring him here."

Which Betty does. Leads him to the porch and then lingers, assuming there will be a drink order, and also because she loves to listen.

"Mr. Guzman," says Morgana, reluctantly tearing her eyes from the page, and gesturing for him to take the wicker settee. "I take it you've been sprung?"

"Oh yeah." He doesn't accept the settee but instead plunks himself into one of the delicate bistro chairs. It whimpers under his weight. He's looking all around him, taking in the beauties of this porch and garden: the stained glass sailing sloop, the Lady Banks roses climbing the trellis, the lush lawn, the wisteria high in the hedges. "Sure is nicer here than in that fuckin hole. So how's our li'l case? What have you nosed out?"

"Nothing."

"Nothin?"

"Mr. Guzman, nothing is what I've been

paid for."

Guzman laughs. "OK. Fair enough. So lemme take care a that right now." He pulls a checkbook from his breast pocket. "So what'd I say again?"

"You offered a retainer of two hundred thousand."

"That much? Really? *Day*-um. Well, still a lot less'n I just handed over to the State of Georgia."

Betty now takes the opportunity to ask, "Sir, would you care for some iced tea?"

"How 'bout a Scotch? How 'bout a Scotch with lots a soda and ice, uh-huh, I ain't had Scotch in a *while*."

Betty goes out to the liquor caddy in the dining room and prepares the man's drink and freshens Morgana's iced tea, and works quietly so she can attend the conversation on the porch.

She hears Morgana ask, "How much did Judge Collins squeeze out of you?"

"Million point two. Even then, D.A. fought like six cats in a gunny-sack. Burt Randolph had to smooth that situation. But here I am."

Betty brings their drinks. When she hands Guzman his Scotch, he thoughtfully asks, "Hey, Betty, how's 'at li'l legal thing of yours?"

"You know about that, sir?"

He winks. "I know ev'athing."

"It's not good."

He winks and says, "Morgana'll take care a you, just like she takes care a me."

Morgana has tired of this exchange. She says sharply, "Betty, would you fetch us the Guzman?"

Betty goes into the parlor, to the great secretary desk, takes the contract from its pigeonhole, and carries it back to the porch.

"Please wait," says Morgana, "we'll need you to witness." She passes it to Guzman. "Two hundred up front, three hundred more if I uncover evidence leading to your exoneration or release from charges, et cetera, et cetera. Though I'm sure I'll never see *that*."

"Why? You think I'll weasel on the bill?"

"No, I think the executor of your estate will."

"What's that supposed to mean?"

"That you're in grave danger, sir. I'm highly suspicious of your sudden liberty. You could have been kept in jail but, miraculously, you've been released. I hope you've arranged a good place to hide."

"I don't need to hide."

She looks upon him with scathing contempt. "Very well. Look that over then. Also

293

there are our expenses, which may be quite high."

Guzman tries to focus on the words of the contract. But his eyes glaze over quickly and his lips pucker into a frown — and he's still on page one. After a moment Morgana shows him mercy. "Oh, *enough,*" she says, and hands him a pen. He signs. Then writes out the check for two hundred thousand dollars. As he gives it over he murmurs, "Don't you worry now, you'll get the rest."

"How reassuring."

"They ain't gonna get me."

"Who is they?"

Guzman smiles. "You mean, who *are* they?"

"Good Lord, you'll teach me grammar? Your *they* was a vague entity of indeterminate number, so the singular was correct, though I'll excuse your impudence as you're a complete idiot. But if you cannot be frank with me, Mr. Guzman, our collaboration will be a waste — an utter waste of both your money and my time. Again: who is 'they'?"

"They is the fuckers that framed me. Who wanna kill me now."

"Why?"

"Member that clue I gave you?"

"Of course."

"Sniff out what it means yet?"

"I suppose I've some notion."

"Then where is she, Morgana?"

"Matilda Stone? I don't know."

"Well, best you find her in a hurry. 'Cause they're showin her some pain right now, you can count on that."

"Why are they doing that?"

" 'Cause she's got the treasure. The treasure of the Kingdom. And she won't give it over."

A sumptuous maidenhair fern hangs near to the porch screen, and Betty is inspecting it now, searching for aphids. There aren't any that she can see. She's not sure what an aphid might look like, but there's nothing at all on this fern, and she's only here because she couldn't bear to miss any of this exchange. Fortunately, both the Gooze and Morgana seem oblivious to her. Morgana has set her gaze on the Gooze, and the Gooze is fixing her right back.

Finally Morgana says, "Mr. Guzman."

"Ma'am."

"How do I serve you?"

"Well now, I b'lieve I serve *you*, Morgana. I give you the big bucks, I give —"

Morgana presses. "But how do I serve you?"

The Gooze is puzzled. "Just do your

detective thing is all."

Morgana leans forward. "I'm being played. Aren't I? I seem to be a token of some kind, a pawn in this game you're playing. But what *is* the game? And who are you playing against?"

Betty is disturbed to see that Guzman is not the least bit cowed by Morgana's fierceness. He glistens with perspiration but his grin shines through. He chugs down his Scotch and soda and softly belches, and glances up at Betty and says, "That hit the spot, I'm obliged." Then he looks at Morgana. "You think I'm an idiot? Lot a people have that opinion. And that *helps* me. Member when I wanted to build them town houses on 56th street, and the entire old guard of Savannah rose up in arms against me, and ev'abody thought, oh, the ol' Gooze is sunk this time. How much did I win the zoning board by? You recollect? One vote. Six to five. Why not seven to four? 'Cause 'at woulda been too *expensive.* Them zoning votes has been getting *pricey.* It's an outrage. And on the other hand, how come it wa'n't five to six? 'Cause then I'd a *lost.*"

She doesn't speak, and he keeps up his gaze.

"I like to win. And I'm gonna win here, same way I always do. I know the price. I'm payin it. And you and your family, now you do your job, you find Stony for me, you take care a that treasure. Betty, thank you for the Scotch, a real pleasure. And you ever need any help with that ex-boyfriend a yours, you jes' gimme a ring."

He takes himself to the door and walks out.

Ransom and Hatchet Head sit in Ransom's rental, which is parked on Abercorn Street catty-corner across from a grand Victorian house. There's a florid sign in front of it: SCHILLING & BATES, ATTORNEYS AT LAW.

"What do you see?" says Ransom.

Hatchet Head squints. "Ground floor's wired. Second floor got them iron grates. Be a bitch."

"Look higher," says Ransom. "See that pecan tree?"

"That big sucker? That's a pecan? Well, you taught me something I never knew."

"See that big limb?"

"Uh-huh," says Hatchet Head, but he's shaking his head. "You're not thinking we could climb onto the roof that way?"

"Don't know. You're the professional."

"I'm not professional. I haven't burgled a thing for years."

297

"Didn't you break into that house in Tybee?"

"It was nearly empty. I got a kid's booster seat, which I gave to my cousin. That's all I got. I'm a professional panhandler now. I fly signs for a living."

"OK."

They keep gazing at the big house.

A smartly dressed lawyer pulls up in a shiny Porsche Taycan, gets out, and strides up to the broad veranda steps.

Ransom says, "That's Jack Schilling. That's the boss."

Years ago, just after getting his degree, Ransom was a lawyer in the employ of Jack Schilling. Most of his hours were spent dealing with the aftermath of the explosion at Chatham Sugar. Jack Schilling represented a company that had a maintenance contract with the Chatham Sugar refinery and that was responsible for keeping it clean. It had not been cleaned properly. When it blew up, Chatham Sugar itself was protected by Georgia's caps on workmen's comp. But third parties were fair game. So the victims all brought suit against the cleaning company. Ransom's job was to go out and negotiate with the widows and the kids who had lost parents. He had to go into nursing facilities and take depositions from burn

victims and offer "generous settlements."
This negotiating was unquestionably the
worst job on earth. It nearly killed him. So
why didn't he just quit?

Hatchet Head pulls Ransom from his
reverie. "Ran, you ever done any second-
story work?"

"No."

"Because what you see from the ground is
not what you'll see when you're up there.
That looks like an easy step, right? From
the tree to the roof? Wait'll you get up there.
You'll think it's the Grand Canyon. It's a
step you'll never take."

"OK."

"But I look in your eyes and see you really ain't listening."

"I'm listening."

"No, you're hellfire to take on these sons
a bitches. Get you some vengeance, I see
that. But maybe I know an easier way."

He opens his door and gets out. Reaches
back in for his knapsack and asks, "Yeah,
that island, what's it called again?"

"Montmillan."

"And who's supposed to own it?

"Sand Gnat Holdings."

"Meet me at the Salty Dog at nine," says
Hatchet Head, and he goes up the stone

steps and into the law offices of Schilling & Bates.

At five o'clock Jaq arrives at the Old Fort door, and turns the crank and the familiar chirp is answered straightaway by a howl. She hears Betty saying, "Gracie, shut *uuuup!*" Then spots them through the wavy old glass and the gauze curtain as they approach, Betty with a strong hold on Gracie's collar.

The door opens. The moment Gracie sees Jaq she pins her ears back and tries to jump up.

Betty says, "Get down, Gracie! Hi, Jaq. 'Mon in. They're all here."

And they are: Morgana, Ransom, Willou, old Johnny from the detective agency, all sitting in a circle in the Turkish room. And with them is Bebe, on the settee, glowering at her.

"Mom, I'm sorry," says Jaq. "I should have called you back. But I was on an island . . . and there was, it was bad reception —"

Bebe cuts her off. "So my sister tells me your *life* has been threatened? Because of Gram's shenanigans? Your grandmother is endangering your *life*?"

300

"Well, that's a bit unfair —" Morgana begins.

"Not a word from you," says Bebe.

"But it *is* unfair," says Jaq. "Gram's right. She's not endangering me — I am. It's *my* choice. I'm sorry this is scaring you, but Stony's missing and nobody's looking for her, nobody's even *thinking* about her and I just think I should do something because if I don't, who will? And if nobody —"

"Oh shut up, child," says Willou. "Your mom's not here to stop you."

"She's not?"

They all look to Bebe.

"Well, if I thought it'd help," Bebe says, "I'd raise a fit. I'd threaten to throw you out of the house. But you've made up your mind and I see that. The nasty old widow here has you in her web. Got my little brother ensnared too. And my sister."

"And you too," says Willou. "So there you go. So what are we gonna do?"

Bebe folds her arms.

"Good, then," says Morgana. "That's all out of the way. Shall we begin? Jaq, sit."

The shepherdess chair is empty, and Jaq takes it.

"Report," says her grandmother.

"OK. Well. There's a place that Stony — Matilda Stone — there's a place she called the Kingdom, and I just got back from there." She likes the sound of that; she gives it some space. Then goes on, "It's on Montmillan Island, which is in the Savannah River swamps, about fifteen miles north of here. It's a hidden jewel, is what it is."

Then, in a rush of words, she tells everything. Cap'n Stan and the dogs, the excavations, Stony the taskmaster, the thimbles and muskets. And how Stony, at some bar on Route 17, told Cap'n Stan she had found the "treasure of the Kingdom." And as Jaq is relating all this, she notes the mismatching of Morgana's lips. And Ransom is also hanging on her words, which is a golden liquor to her, and her aunt and her mother are also listening closely. And even though Betty is out in the foyer, feeding snacks to Gracie, surely she's listening in as well.

Jaq tries to feel a cool indifference to all this attention. But that's not possible.

As soon as she's finished Morgana declares, with a clap of her hands, "Oh, extraordinary! How *brilliant* you are. I think your expedition was simply a coup. Don't you all agree? Ransom, do we know who owns that island?"

Ransom shakes his head. "Working on it."

"All right then. Is it five thirty yet? I believe it is. I believe it's time for a drop of

Madeira. Who would like a drop of Madeira?"

At first, no hands. But then, in a why-the-hell-not way, Willou raises hers. And another hand goes up, and then three more. *"Betty!"* Morgana calls. "Six for Madeira!"

"Uh-*huh,*" Betty calls back.

Morgana tells them, "And now, Johnny, shall we give them our report?"

Johnny straightens himself. Hands her a case file.

She takes out a photo and holds it up. It's a still shot from Jaq's video.

Morgana says, "In Jaq's video of Luke and Stony — the one she shot the night of the fire — I happened to notice a figure in the background. Can you all see *this* gentleman? The one with the tie? I thought there was something a bit unnerving about him. So I had Johnny ask around."

Johnny says, "Yeah, so I sent a lot a emails, made a lot a calls, but got nothing. Nobody knew him. Till just out of the blue, this buddy of mine in Brantley County — used to be the sheriff there? — he pegged him. The guy's an ex-con from Valdosta."

He raises his phone and shows them a mug shot. The same bland weaselly face.

"In and out of prison," he says. "And then a few years back they let him plea out of a murder charge. He got five years in Reidsville. Somebody just whittled that way down for him. He was released a month ago."

"Which means?" Willou asks.

"Which means," says Morgana, "Stony's surely in peril. This is the man who took her out of Peep's. Presumably he works for hire. Presumably someone is paying him."

Betty brings the bottle of Madeira and a tray of rose-crystal glasses, and starts to pour.

"One more thing," says Johnny. "There's a woman in the Southside, in Tatemville, name's Louise Stone, I think she's Stony's mother. I got an address."

"All right," says Morgana. "Willou? Would you take that?"

"What do you mean, *take* that?" says Willou. "You mean go to Tatemville? Such a vile neighborhood."

"Well, thank you for enduring it. Now one last thing: Ransom went to see Rayford yesterday. And he spoke of Rebecca Cressling?"

Ransom nods. "She said Stony once worked for her. Something about digging up a family treasure, and we should look into it."

"Rayford is quite sharp," says Morgana. "Always has been, and he knows Rebecca

304

Cressling very well. I think she'll be well worth a visit. Bebe, would you care to stop by Rebecca's, see what she knows?"

Bebe glares at her.

"I know," says Morgana, "but would you anyway? Very well then. As we all have our assignments, may I propose a toast?" She raises her glass toward the portrait of Grampa Fred on the wall. He's up there wearing his army uniform: second lieutenant, Vietnam War. Quite handsome. She says, "To my beloved husband. Are you looking down at us, darling?"

"I pray to God not," says Willou, and they also drink to that.

Galatas glides past the cars parked outside the Old Fort.

Caprice, Santa Fe, Escalade, rental, bomb.

Which means: Morgana, Bebe, Willou, Ransom, Johnny.

And, up on the porch, Jaq's bike. So they're all in there right now. The whole clan, trying desperately to sort things out. To draw a coherent picture of their foe. Which they'll never be able to do. They're such idiots, that family. He drives on. Comes to Forsyth Park, the big circus tent, and heads downtown. He's stressed. He's exhausted. There's too much work for him.

And it's been so hot today. He keeps the AC off when he's cruising because he likes to hear the city: snatches of music, shouts of kids, the trains. And somehow the heat, brutal though it is, feels right to him. It reminds him that things are coming to a boil. The right measures are being taken. Stony is starting to crack. She won't last another day. There's a tracker under Ransom Musgrove's rental car, so Galatas knows all the places he goes. Knows for example that for twenty minutes today he was parked across the street from the law offices of Schilling & Bates, in the company of his blue-mohawk friend. That information will be followed up on.

Also, his informants tell him that Stony was quite close to that guy they call the Musician. As soon as we find him we'll bring him in and see what he knows about the Kingdom.

Also, Archie Guzman has been released from jail, and is now at his home on Victory Drive near Thunderbolt. He's a brave man, and disdains security. He has a maid and a gardener, but they'll be going home soon.

And sweetest of all, Galatas knows that Jaq will soon be pedaling alone on the streets of Savannah.

■ ■ ■

In her foulness of mood, Bebe arrives at the famous Browne-Cressling house, which is on Jones Street just off Lafayette Square. Gray, ivied, and domineering, it boasts a Charleston-style side porch, which overlooks a lush and glorious garden.

"Oh, you!" cries Rebecca when she opens the door. "I'm so *tickled* to see you!"

Bebe goes for the cheek-buss and is assaulted by an array of fragrances. Orchids, face cream, hairspray, cologne, and something from below, an astringency, an asafetida or such. Also, wafting in from the great foyer, comes the smell of lilacs, parrot shit, a cinnamon-scented candle, and some cabbagey thing on the stove. It's all a profusion and a mess, as ever. Bebe recalls her mother saying when she was little, "I can tell you've been to Rebecca's. You reek of it."

Not that she had ever *wanted* to go to Mrs. Cressling's. She went because Willou made her. Willou had "a job" there. She was "employed" by Mrs. Cressling as her "gardening protégée," and she brought her little sister "only for some company." Except that Bebe wound up doing the serious work. All the weeding and rooting and wheelbarrowing was left to Bebe — while Willou found better company gossiping with the boys on Jones Street, or with Mrs. Cressling on the famous Charleston-style side porch. Bebe didn't much mind. She liked being left alone with a garden spade. But she dreaded whenever Mrs. Cressling would look down upon her from the high side porch and make one of her faux-concerned comments: "You're not going to be a Cinderella, are you? You're not going to let your sister laze about while you're toiling away?"

Why was it, Bebe always wondered, that whenever she stole a single moment to wipe the sweat off her brow and crouch discreetly over a Reese's Peanut Butter Cup, *that* would be the moment when Rebecca would choose to appear above and remind her: "Oh darlin, darlin, would you like to join me for dandelion salad?"

Now Bebe is back, and those feelings are back.

Rebecca leads her through her parlor filled with loud paintings of Savannah gardens (many of them gardens that Rebecca owns), and she rattles away about various crises she's having with this mansion of hers, which she calls "this terrible eyesore" — replacing the *r*'s in that phrase with mouthfuls of tortured air — and leads her out to the side porch, her puce scarf fluttering in her wake. "Oh darlin, we missed you so at Morgana's Soiree!"

"Did you? I never go to those things. But I saw your flowers, Rebecca."

"The Popsicles? They were *spiritless!*"

"I thought they were quite colorful."

"They looked utterly cheerless and downtrodden! Possibly because someone overwatered them." Meaning Morgana of course, though she leaves that unspoken.

On the porch there are filigreed wrought iron chairs and a tea service that the maid has left. They sit and look down upon the splendors of the garden, and Bebe compliments Rebecca on her hyacinths and roses and snapdragons, and Rebecca says, "I'm told you have no garden at all."

"The things people talk about," says Bebe.

"Wouldn't you like to grow a few blossoms? So much happiness! I'd be delighted to give you some."

"Yeah, I don't really have time."

"Oh, I know you're such a heroine at the hospital. Everyone says so. But you must take time for beauty. Life isn't all suffering."

"Pretty close. But I like your flowers, Rebecca."

"Remember when you were little and you

and your sister would come over and work in the beds? You were both such *lovely* girls."

A little extra breath when she says "lovely" — and on that wind rides her unspoken judgment: *before you got fat of course, because although Willou was the prettiest and always will be, how far you might have gone had you stayed slim!* Bebe lets this slide by. So Rebecca goes a step further: "Although I do recall what a worker you were; you were so conscientious, you were so . . ."

"Bullied," says Bebe. "Look. Rebecca. I'm here to ask you a question."

"Of course."

"You remember a woman named Stony?"

"What now?"

"Matilda Stone?"

A darkness flits over Rebecca's features.

But she quickly brightens. "The excavator?"

"Archaeologist."

"Well, I think not a *full-fledged* archaeologist, is she? But anyway, yes, she worked for me once. Why?"

"What sort of work did she do?"

"She dug."

"Dug what?"

"Mother was certain that my grandfather buried some money in our garden. You know about his secret money, don't you?"

"Maybe. Was it something scandalous?"

Rebecca laughs. "Well, not scandalous in this town. He was a bootlegger. Like *your* great-grandfather Will Musgrove. They were both considered heroes. They were also rivals, did you know that?"

"I'm sure I've been told and forgotten."

"They had secret tunnels that went down to the storm drains. You see that door, darlin'?"

She points to a slanted door on the side of the carriage house.

"Right," says Bebe. "I remember. Goes down to the drains."

"It did once. The tunnel's been filled in. But anyway that's how our grandfathers got their liquor around. Through the storm drains. The cops would never go down there, because they knew they'd be killed. Grandfather made lots of money, which he turned into gold because he was afraid the feds would track his bank account. And in Mother's opinion he buried that gold. When I was growing up, she said that over and over. So that's why I hired Stony, to see if she could find it."

"And?"

"Well, she dug lots of little holes and trenches but she wasn't very focused. Frankly, she's a drunk and I had to let her

311

go. Why do you ask about her?"

"She's gone missing."

"Really? Oh, she probably just passed out at some motel in Pooler. Ha ha!"

Finally Bebe gets out of there. Gets into the Santa Fe and starts home.

She calls her mother.

"So what did she say?" Morgana asks.

"That she hired Stony to look for some gold that her grandfather buried."

"What? He buried gold? Why?"

"She said he didn't want the feds tracking his bootlegging money. So he turned it into gold."

"But that's bullshit."

"Why do you say that, Mother?"

"Well, first because everything Rebecca says is bullshit. Also, if there was buried gold, Jack Cressling would have told me."

"You sure?"

"He was in love with me. He knew I loved spicy stories. He'd have told me."

"So she's lying?"

"Yes. What else did she say?"

"Nothing."

"Bebe, report. I need details. *Report.*"

"I have reported. Now I'm going home."

"Don't fail me now. Now is when we need clarity. Granularity."

"OK, well, to be completely *granular* with

312

you, Mother, I can't do this for you any-more."

"So then do it for Jaq."

"Even for Jaq I can't."

"Well, then for poor Matilda Stone."

"Good luck to her," says Bebe. She pokes at her phone and ends the call.

Jaq finally gets to shower. She runs the water forever, pounding it into her scalp: it seems to settle the whirl of images in there. She rotates slowly for fifteen minutes, try-ing to cobble together a measure of peace. She'd stay even longer but she's supposed to work a shift tonight. Would love to get out of it but she's been missing so many shifts lately.

So, with a great act of will, she shuts off the faucet.

Towels off. Checks her phone and finds that while she was showering a text came in:

Jaq, this is detective Nick Galatas. Call me at this number?

She goes into her bedroom, shuts the door, and calls.

"Hello, Jaq."

"Hi."

"Well, so, there's a woman named Matilda Stone? Stony? And I think she's a friend of yours. And I have some news about her. But, if I can be frank . . . I don't necessarily want the Savannah police to know we're having this talk. Does that make sense?"

"Yeah."

"I hope that doesn't scare you, Jaq."

"It scares me a little."

"Well. It's really OK. Can you meet me?"

He gives her an address on Waters. Used to be a storefront church. The Resurrection of the Righteous.

He says, "Just come around back. There's a yellow door, it'll be unlocked. I'm sorry, but this just has to be private. You got any time now, Jaq?"

It's easy to escape her house; there's no one here. Roxanne's still at work; Bebe's gone on the errand Morgana gave her. Jaq texts Holly to warn her she'll be getting to Peep's late. Gets on her bike, zigzags to Waters. Night's coming on. North of Victory there's a row of boarded-up storefront churches. Church of the Eternal Salvation, bankrupt. The People's Church of Perfect Redemption: just a peeling sign. Then the Resurrection of the Righteous.

She swings round to the back alley, coasts, spots the yellow door. Locks her bike to a dumpster. Kudzu draping over a broken-down van. Long, long shadows. She pulls at the door, and it opens.

She wishes somebody knew she was here.

Willou drives down to see Stony's mother. She takes Abercorn Street south, out past the Savannah Mall and a half dozen other repellent malls, through the zone of novelty shops and strip clubs and used-car dealerships, past the rotting fairgrounds (Morgana brought them here once, to a traveling carnival, in the company of some young artist with whom she was likely having an affair. Bebe and her siblings thought the place creepy but Mother said, "These are the fairgrounds Flannery wrote about!"). Then she's in Tatemville. On a cinder-block stoop a man in banana-colored underwear is holding an infant. She knows him. Tyrus Richard. A warrant out on him for domestic battery, and she could make the call right now but she has too much on her mind. So she drives right past. He gives her a look though, so knowing, so sneering, that she must check herself in the mirror just to make sure there's nothing out of place. You're judging *me*? Good Christ. You've got flies orbiting your head like electrons. Your yard has not a single flower. Go in now and pass the kid to your wife and sit in your bedroom and find young starlets to threaten online, whatever you need to vent your rage but do not beat on your wife again because next time you do that I'll make you disappear.

Christ, she hates Tatemville.

A few slow blocks on Stump Lane and she's come to her destination. Shotgun house, small but with a tidy lawn and hydrangeas and geraniums. Bluebird decals on her mailbox, and letters that spell out: L Stone. And a huge orange cat stretched on the stoop, not making room for Willou, so she has to reach to get to the doorbell.

A Black woman opens the door. Sixties, white hair. Wary.

"Ms. Stone?" says Willou. "I'm looking for somebody, um, that I'm worried about."

"What? Who's that?"

"Your daughter."

This earns her a long stare. "And who are you?"

"Willou Lutinger. I'm a Superior Court judge but that has nothing to do with why I'm here. Stony's not in trouble with the law. It's just that folks haven't seen her in a while —"

"Folks?"

"My niece Jaqueline. She works at Bo Peep's bar? She knows Stony from there —"

316

"Jaq?"

"Yes."

"She's your *niece*?"

"By marriage. And adoption. And she hasn't seen Stony around and she's a little worried."

Louise Stone keeps looking at her.

Doesn't say anything, just glares.

Willou wonders why she ever agreed to this nonsense, why?

Finally the woman says, "You were *my* judge."

"I was?"

"You don't remember? I got a whole parlor suite from Furniture Jamboree and shouldn't a borrowed on time because it was no money down but a whole lot of interest, and I mean they were gonna take it all. But you told 'em, you said, You're not taking a folding chair from this woman. You. Are. Predators. And you told 'em, You have wound up in the wrong courtroom, predators. And you said to me, You can go now, ma'am, you'll never hear from these people again. And I never have."

"Oh. I do sort of recall this case, now that you mention it."

Louise Stone wedges one foot under the belly of the orange cat and lifts it, swings it away from the door, and sets it down softly.

Then holds the door open for Willou.

It's cool and dark in here, the AC is throbbing, and there are flower arrangements and photos in gold frames. Willou sits on the sofa that Louise bought at Furniture Jamboree. Louise brings her a glass of ice water. They talk about the heat, and about the neighborhood. When Willou mentions she just saw Tyrus Richard in front of his house, Louise shakes her head and says, "And I had to raise my little girl around a man like that."

That brings them to Stony. Willou repeats her concern, and Louise tells her she's worried too. "Matilda, she likes to come and go. Whenever she feels like. And she never gives you no idea what she's up to. But I been worried. I wish she had a damn *phone*. She camps out a lot, and that means snakes. And spiders. And the *po*-lice. And I been hearin about wild dogs, there's packs a wild dogs runnin loose, you know that?"

"Yeah, I've seen them. They're scary."

"And then that friend a hers that got burned up. That Luke boy."

"Were they close?" Willou asks.

"Oh yes, she loved Luke to death. I don't know why. He was just a boy. Half her age and drinkin all the time, and who knows how he *paid* for that liquor. You know? Boy

318

never took a step that wa'n't into trouble. You know what I'm sayin? I say, Matilda, you stay away from that kid. But Matilda never has listened to me. Well that ain't quite so, she *listen,* but then she do *ee-zactly* the contrary."

"Sounds like my daughter," says Willou. "My older girl, if she's seeing a boy who's bad for her I have to say, Oh he's wonderful! He's so . . . *earthy!* He challenges our primitive ideas of success and worth. So *please* date him. If I talk like that enough, she'll dump him."

Louise laughs and shakes her head. "Earthy. I'll use that."

Willou smiles. Sips her water. "Louise, did your daughter ever say anything about a *treasure?* A *King's* treasure, maybe? Or else a King's soldier, or —"

"The Kingdom, uh-huh. She talks about that all the time. Says she found this secret Kingdom and it's keeping her very busy. I think she's nuts. Livin in the woods'll do that. She says she found a treasure there. I say, well thank God a'mighty, we're rich at last, bring it to Mama, darlin. But she never does, does she?"

"Does she ever talk about Archie Guzman?"

"Oh yeah. Uh-huh."

319

"Is she scared of him?"

"Uh-uh. No ma'am. She likes him. Does good business with him."

"Business?"

"She surveys his properties. When you build houses for the city or whatever, first you gotta do your archaeology. Make sure there are no graveyards or whatever. And he always calls Matilda. She likes workin for him, 'cause he never asks her for no short-cuts. He don't try to fudge no results. He built that project on Cuyler? She *did* find graves. He had to hire a crew to move 'em all. He held up the work for months and months, but he never complained."

"Wait. Louise. You're saying Guzman is honest?"

"Uh-uh, no ma'am, I ain't sayin that. I don't know the man. Matilda, she just say he's fair. Everyone else messin with her. Not Mr. Guzman. He takes her out for drinks sometimes."

"Really? She drinks with Archie Guzman?"

"Out in some bar on Seventeen that nobody knows, they go there. He's a perfect gentleman. That what she says."

"What about all the nasty evictions? They don't bother her?"

"Well she say, Guzman's a hard man.

About contracts and all, and the letter of the law. If you ain't gonna follow the contract, you better not sign nothin. But if you pay your rent on time, you got no problem."

"But not everyone can pay their rent on time, Louise."

" 'At's the truth. *I* know that. But she says he's fair."

"You have any idea where she might be now?"

"No ma'am. But if you hear from her, will you tell her to call her mama?"

"Yes of course."

That seems to be all. Willou rises. But Louise says, "Now hold on just a minute, Your Honor. One more thing."

"All right," says Willou, and she sits again.

Louise asks, "You know the Musician?"

"Which musician?"

"*The* Musician. That's what Matilda calls him. I don't know him. But she said, Mama, if anything ever happens to me, you gotta find the Musician. He knows where the treasure is."

"But what *is* the treasure?"

"Dunno. Doubt it even exists. But the Musician knows where to find it."

Jaq sits in a pew of the dark church, waiting for Galatas. Most of the windows have been boarded up so there's only a little streetlight coming in through the open door and a single unblocked window. Even *living* churches creep Jaq out. But this dead one, with its mural of worshippers kneeling and looking to Heaven with cartoon eyes and praying to be raptured there, plus the impossible heat and no AC in here maybe for *years,* and the stench of dead things rotting in the walls: this is terrifying. And he's late. And maybe he's not coming.

No, he's not, she decides. Something must have come up. He's a cop, and things always come up for cops, and he's not coming, and I need to get out of here before I lose my shit —

But then there he is, at the doorway.

Smiling. "Hey, sorry I'm late. Oh, my God, you're sitting in the dark. And in this heat! Jesus, I'm an idiot. Wait."

He finds a fuse box and flips a breaker, and the lights come on. And the blessed hum of an AC. He goes back to a little room and comes out with two bottles of water and gives her one. Maybe he senses that she's nervous being alone with him, because he doesn't take the same pew as hers. He takes the next one up, and turns to her.

He says, "Well, remember when you showed me that video of Luke? And there was also this woman in it? Stony. Well, I wanted to find her because I thought she might know something about what happened to Luke. I've been giving out my number to everyone who knows her. And I know a lot of people were getting worried. But anyway. Well today I got a call. From Myrtle Beach, South Carolina. From Stony herself."

Jaq is stunned. Overwhelmed. "You *talked* to Stony?"

"Yeah."

"Oh my God."

"She says, You lookin for me? I said, *Lot* a folks looking for you."

Jaq asks, "Why did she go to Myrtle Beach?"

"She's hiding. You know why? 'Cause she thinks Guzman wants to kill her. I told her, You're safe here, Stony. She says, No I'm not. Anyway, we talk back and forth and finally she tells me everything. She says she was pretty friendly with Guzman. He was sort of supporting her while she dug up this old village she called "the Kingdom." She was finding lots of great buried things, and everything was good. And so one day, she was coming into Savannah and she asked Guzman if she and Luke could stay at his empty house, and he said sure, because he

323

wasn't using it, and in fact, he said, he was never gonna use it, and it was such a money-suck, and he was gonna burn it down for the insurance money. She thought he was joking. But after the fire, she realized he'd been dead serious. And he must have forgot telling her she and Luke could stay there. And so that night she met some guy at your bar and went off drinking with him. She didn't have sex with him, they just got drunk, but that's why she wasn't in the house when it burned down. That's why she's alive. And Guzman called her and threatened to kill her if she ever testified. So she got outta town. I told her, Stony, we'll protect you. But please come back and help us nail this guy. And she says she's thinking it over."

"My God," says Jaq.

"She wouldn't give me her number, 'cause I'm a cop. But I asked her to call you, and she promised she would. Frankly I get the feeling she's getting sick of Myrtle Beach, South Carolina."

Says Jaq, "I just, I can't . . ."

"When she does call you, try to work your magic on her. OK? Tell her, we understand she doesn't trust the police here. But I'll organize security personally. Tell her I'll send a car for her. Tell her I'll send a stretch limo."

Jaq laughs a little. But still shakes her head. "I mean I can't —"

"Yeah I know. This is not your grandmother's theory of the case."

"No, it's not."

He says, "You know Occam's razor?"

"Look for the simplest answer."

"Exactly. Kind of my guiding rule as a detective. And the simplest answer is staring us in the face."

"The Gooze."

"Yeah. But my colleagues don't want to admit that. Because the man's got too much power in this town. He's got a lot of things he knows about people. And then your grandmother, she won't admit it because . . . I mean honestly, I gotta tell you, she and your uncle Ransom have one thing in common: they both love drama. But *you* saw it from the beginning, Jaq. That man's as guilty as sin. Have you ever talked to him?"

"Uh-uh."

"Well, I did. Yesterday. His lawyer was there, so he couldn't be broken, but you can feel how fragile he is. He *wants* to confess, you can just feel it. *You* could break him, Jaq. He'd trust you. I think if you talked to him he'd break. He's over there in that big ugly house of his. You could get the truth out of him. I mean, I'm not suggesting you do that, by any means. I want you to stay out of this shit. I'm just saying, he'll never tell the truth to Morgana. And she won't even let *you* talk to him, will she?"

"Wait. You really think I could get him to talk?"

"No, no," he says. "No, I don't want you going over there. Why can't she send that detective, what's his name, Johnny?"

"Johnny?" She shakes her head. "Johnny's lost in space."

"I just can't stand to see Guzman going free. And maybe he will go free. His lawyers are so smart. But, Jaq, don't you go there. It's just way too dangerous. Look I don't want to disparage anyone's faith, but this place is spooky, isn't it? And I've got a wife and kid to get home to. Let's get out of here. May I drive you somewhere?"

"I'm good."

"Really? On your bike? It's so hot."

"No, I'm fine. Thanks for sharing that."

Ransom is nursing a beer at the Salty Dog, and Hatchet Head comes in and takes the next stool.

"How'd it go?" Ransom asks.

"Aight. Talked to your former boss."

"Jack Schilling?"

"Uh-huh. I told him the VA is refusing to treat me on account a my Republican politics."

"Or maybe because you're not a veteran?"

"You've got the soul of a clerk, son. Mr. Schilling got quite turned on. He's taking the case. On the way out I stopped to use the jakes. And waited. And two hours later when everybody was gone, I came out and dodged them security beams and broke into the file cabinets and got what you asked for. And made copies. And put everything back all neat and proper. Ta-dum."

He places a file folder on the table.

Which Ransom now opens.

First up: the State of Georgia Articles of Incorporation for Sand Gnat Holdings. Showing that it's wholly owned by another enterprise in Atlanta: Bobcat Investment.

Ransom muses, "So Sand Gnat's just a shell."

"Uh-huh. But conveniently for you, Bobcat Investment is also represented by Schilling & Bates."

The next document tells Ransom that all outstanding stock in Bobcat Investment is owned by another firm: Tarantula Enterprises.

"Jesus."

"Yeah, three shells and still no bean," says Hatchet Head. "And Tarantula is represented by some firm in Charlotte, North Carolina. So dead end there. For all our trouble, all we've learned is that somebody is going to great efforts to keep the ownership of that island from prying eyes."

"Right."

"Which, why would they do that, unless there was some fuckedness afoot?"

There's nothing so hateful as Victory Drive for biking in the dark. Four lanes, no bike trail, and Jaq has to cling to the curb the whole way while the traffic bends slowly around her, and all the faces are pissed off and sullen as they slide by. She's worn out and nightfall hasn't cooled things any. The air is still baking and she's pumping away and glistening with sweat, and scared to be trying this. And what if the Gooze just refuses to see her? Still she has to try. Galatas is right: she has a certain gift for drawing folks out. Folks tell her things they wouldn't tell anyone else. But he's also right when he says Gram herself would never let her do something like this.

And so what if the Gooze refuses to talk to her? His loss, fuck him.

But she's got a feeling he won't refuse.

She takes Victory because there's no other route to the village of Thunderbolt. She sets her jaw, and puts everything into the rhythm of her legs, and the cars keep honking and the faces keep leering, and finally through the trees she sees it: the Gooze's nest.

Like a McMansion, only uglier, with spindly columns that go three floors up to a slab pediment. The whole facade looks like it was ripped off a condemned Holiday Inn.

She pulls off on the narrow shoulder.

Holds up her camera and records. She says, "This is as close as I want to get with a camera. The cops might be watching this house. I don't want them to see me snooping."

She holds the shot for a while.

It's a good shot, hellish, with headlights from the traffic playing on the trees, floodlights on the columns, and the burning sky behind. She tells the camera, "I'm a little scared, I won't lie. But I've got a weird thirst for this. I think I'm the one who can pry the truth out of him. I really think I'm the one."

She puts the camera away.

The front gate is open. She rides right through to the front of the house. Leaves the bike. Steps up to the broad concrete veranda.

The front door is slightly ajar.

There's a piece of paper taped to it. A torn-out page of notebook paper, and a handwritten note.

IM SORRY, says the note, in a childish script. *Didnt mean to kill the boy. Didnt know he was up there.*

The confession goes on, but Jaq doesn't finish it. She pushes the door open and calls, "Mr. Guzman?"

Silence.

"MR. GUZMAN!"

Echoes. She steps in. Calls again, nothing. Passes under a grandiose arch into the foyer.

Then the great dining room.

The dining table has been pushed to one side. Chairs pushed over.

From a massive gold Russian-mafia-style chandelier, Guzman sways.

His eyes are bugged and his jaw open. A look of startlement. Jaq commands herself to quit looking. But she can't obey. She knows she's burning a bad image into her brain, but she can't stop. That expression. He's been trapped for all time in one moment of surprise and horror. It's too much for her, yet she has to keep staring. Has to keep drinking it in and drinking it in. Voices behind her, running footsteps. The static of a police radio. And then a soft voice. "Jaq?"

She turns and it's Nick Galatas and his face is so gentle, and everything he's saying has turned out to be true. He *told* her not to come. He's always been trying to take care of her, and she melts into his arms and weeps like an infant and he says, "It's OK, Jaq. Everybody's safe. You're safe, Stony's safe, Guzman had to do that, you know that. It'll all be OK."

Stony can't look at it. She keeps her eyes shut. She can feel his breath beside her, and it's clean breath, it's happy breath, it's almost a chuckling, and he says: "Come on Stony, look. Jaq saw it. You can see it. Come on. Do this for Jaq."

He came here in the middle of the "night." While she was drifting so happily in the blackness, while she was working so happily in the garden of the Kingdom, the light came on, rousing her back to hell. And the door opened, and Mr. Kindness came to tell her Jaq had found the hanging body of Guzman. He has pictures on his phone, he wants to show them to her. He says she *must* look. But she won't.

"You really should, Stony. You should open your eyes. You should see how much pain you're spreading. The amount of hurt that you're giving Jaq is *unbelievable*. I got

331

to that house and she was standing there just looking at him and she's . . . she's damaged. For life I think. I'm sure for life. You've really given her something. She just flowed into my arms. She needed my strength, Stony. She's in so much pain and she wept like a baby in my arms because the sight of that man hurt her so much and will stay with her forever, but you know what? That's really *nothing*. There's so much more in store for her if you won't help us. Stony. All you have to do is *cooperate*. . . ."

He goes on of course. And on. But she can't hear him.

She can't hear him because her ears are full of Sharper. The father of her vision, Sharper, is speaking to her now, and his voice is so powerful that everything else sounds like crickets in the distance.

He says, The man's lying.

He says, They always lie.

If you trust them for an instant they'll steal everything. They'll rip the soul right from your body.

Now you're a soldier of the King, he says. Never surrender. Never trust them.

Never listen to them. No matter what they say.

They're always lying.

332

CHAPTER FIVE:
A DOOR MARKED NEVERMORE, THAT WASN'T THERE BEFORE

The ER has been slammed all week. The heat. This oven of heat is baking up waves of violence, and every day Bebe and her colleagues must work their asses off to stay even with it. Gunshot wound, fentanyl OD, eye gouge from a jealous husband. Then a fifteen-minute break during which she goes out to the car and breathes for a moment, huddles over her coffee and Cremora, texts her daughter and tries to sound upbeat.

crazee day, how you?

Shrapnel from a drive-by, road rage, van-flip in a police chase. Bebe grabbing ten minutes in the crummy nurses' lounge, texting Roxanne and Jaq:

Campari and the bandit in 3 hours, YAYYYYY!

Three gunshot wounds come in from

three different parts of the city, in one afternoon, all three of them thigh wounds. Someone apparently is hunting human thighs. And an OD was just called in, but it's six o'clock on the button and she's free; she leaves Wendy to handle it, just hustles on out to the Santa Fe. Too hot to even touch the door, but she bunches the hem of her scrubs into a kind of glove and manages to yank the handle up and get the door open. Reaches over without getting in and inserts the key and starts the engine and the AC, then moves off to stand in the shade of a hospital palm tree till the car cools a bit.

Then she drives up Habersham and collects Roxanne at the school. On the way home they talk about Jaq. Roxanne never comes right out and blames Bebe or Morgana or any other Musgrove — but it's clear she thinks Musgroves are at the root of her daughter's misery.

At home they shower and set up the board for a game of Settlers of Catan. Jaq comes out of her room. They play the game over and over like it's a drug. Rolling those dice, collecting those sheep. For a few days after seeing the Gooze's body, Jaq couldn't do anything, couldn't laugh or even talk, but now at least she can play this game. Though that's about it. They order pizza from Vinnie Van GoGo's and drink Sparkling Americanos. As soon as they finish one game they play another. Her two mothers can picture, every second, the image that Jaq is trying not to remember, and if pretending to like this game will help distract her from that, well then they'll pretend to *love* this game. They cackle whenever they make a good roll. They cackle as they steal one another's crops. They play on and on and stagger to bed around 2:00 A.M., and thank God when Bebe goes to check on her twenty minutes later, she's dropped off to sleep. Bebe goes back and gets in bed with Roxanne and says, "I think it's getting better."

Five P.M. the next day and Jaq's still in bed. Gloomy day out there, heavy, a few splashes of rain. Scrolling TikTok all day, an endless thread of it, looking for something to divert her. But it's all just rolling shit and doesn't begin to fill the pit inside her.

Now and then texts come in. Detective Galatas writes:

Not to bug you, Jaq, but please, the moment you hear from her

Which is very kind but she almost hopes

335

Stony doesn't call — because what would there be to say to her? All that matters is she's alive.

There are folks out there, good folks, encouraging Jaq to go back out into the world. A message comes from Arthur:

Might get my hands on an extra ticket to the Telfair Ball. Care to be my guest?

How sweet. But she's in far too much pain, and doubts she'll ever leave this house again.

Back to the infinite TikTok.

Nothing from Ransom. She knows Bebe has demanded that Morgana stay away from her, never wrap her in her dangerous nonsense again. And she understands Ransom might think that proscription binds him as well. But she misses him. Every moment. Loves him as deep as ever and always worries about him. Even as she lies there marinating in loneliness and shame and confusion.

The main confusion is this: Stony is alive and well and therefore Jaq should be over the moon. And part of her is. But mostly what she feels is humiliation. She's humiliated that she ever bought into her nutty grandmother's weird theories about Guzman for a second. Humiliated because in the tweets and FB posts regarding Guzman's suicide, everyone seems to know that Jaq's the one who found the body, and that Jaq's "step-grandmother" Morgana was working for Guzman — and some are even speculating about what Jaq might have been "up to" with the Gooze. It's all only innuendo, but as there seems to be nothing real for her to cling to, it's unbearable.

Now her phone lights up again and by habit she glances at it.

Ransom.

A message from Ransom:

Need to leave you alone and we will, but just want you to know we're thinking of you

Which doesn't help. In any way. In fact these words make her feel more desperately lonely than ever.

Then right away comes another one.

also we're not giving up, we're getting closer

Bebe puts the dishes into the machine and Roxanne cleans the counters, and now the rain has picked up and there's lightning. On

337

the TV news they're talking up this storm, which has blown in from the Atlantic and will be pushing its nastiness all night. Bebe and Roxanne don't talk, they just clean. Neither is willing to burden the other with her worries. They work silently and listen to the thunder and the TV. Then Bebe starts setting up the board, and Roxanne calls Vinnie Van GoGo's and orders a large pie with pepperoni, artichokes, and black olives. She brings out the Campari and sweet vermouth for their Americanos. And as she's taking down the lowball glasses, suddenly Jaq appears.

Which should be a good thing because she hasn't been out of her room all day.

But over both mothers comes a sense of dread.

Jaq has put on her gown, her long silver gown, and she's rebraided her hair and applied her makeup, and she's breathtakingly beautiful. She has her backpack on and her bike helmet.

Roxanne says, "What's this?"

Jaq says, "I'm going to the Ball, Mama."

The great circus tent has been deployed on the big lawn of Forsyth Park, under what the tour guides would call the "watchful gaze" of the Confederate Sentry, up on his tall bronze pedestal. In spite of the inclement weather, *tout Savannah* has come to the Telfair Ball. They're dressed to the nines. They've come in their dinner jackets and tulle gowns, their diamond stickpins and diamond tiaras; they've come to glorify the beaux arts. The theme tonight is *The Circus*! There are contortionists and acrobats, wire walkers and clowns, an escape artist, a juggler, and Lady Godiva in a nude bodysuit who comes riding in sidesaddle on a white mare, and the audience is bedazzled and well fed and already a touch drunk, as Willou rises from her power table and mounts the stairs to the podium.

The band plays a fanfare.

As it does, Willou places her compact on the podium and flips it open for a last quick glance. Repulsed by what she sees. The circus gaslight seems to disclose a new depth of horror to her face, a depth hitherto unseen. She seems to be a perfect death's-head — albeit with a new poofy hairdo. This revelation is bracing but also strangely *satisfying:* the confirmation of something she's known all along but kept from herself. Now that the truth is fully upon her, although she's tempted to burst into tears, she elects instead to carry on — and a small smile crosses her features.

The fanfare dies away.

But for the constant drumming of rain, the great tent is still.

She leans into the mike and says, "Ladies and gentlemen, the immortal W. C. Fields . . ."

Then, massively projected onto the canvas behind her, comes a scene from an old movie, *The Fatal Glass of Beer*. W. C. Fields opens the door of a lonely cabin, looks into the teeth of a blizzard, and declares, "And it ain't a fit night out . . . for man nor beast. . . ." Whereupon a handful of snow is tossed into his face.

The audience laughs and there's a round of applause, and Willou says: "But . . . under this lovely tent, *we're* safe, aren't we? We're all still a bit damp, but we're safe. Safe from the wind and rain, safe from the darkness, and we've truly created a realm for ourselves, haven't we? A realm of beauty, a realm where the arts are revered, where creative aspiration is cherished, where we can forge deep bonds of community around the celebration of genius and imagination. . . ."

On she waxes, reading from teleprompters, memory, and the inspiration of the moment. It's the same opening, more or less, that she gives every year, so part of her attention is free to scan the crowd and see if her big pre-Ball worry is being borne out, if this circus tent is proving too vast a venue for the Ball, too unwieldy. But it's not, really. It seems to work quite well. Despite the rain, the acoustics aren't bad at all. The crowd isn't chattering, the waitstaff isn't clattering. Even at the back of the tent, folks are listening quite politely. Though maybe, she thinks, it's because the speaker is a death's-head?

She gives a shout-out to Paula Wallace, the founder of SCAD, and to the chairman of the Telfair Board, "my very wonderful brother David — stand up, David." He does stand, and gets a fair round of polite applause. She's still furious at him. His wife, Madelaine, is wearing some long *belle dame sans merci* thing. Willou's furious at her too — but soon her attention, and her patter, moves on. Alights upon Rebecca Cressling. "And here we have our very own real estate diva," she tells the crowd. "Please do give Mrs. Cressling a big hand, because she *is* your landlord."

Her target, a good sport, wags a finger at them all warningly, which earns a huge laugh.

And then Willou spots a late arrival, coming right down the main aisle.

Jaq.

Good Christ.

Isn't she supposed to be locked in her room?

But no, here she is. Simply shocking in her beauty and poise. She's wearing her only gown, the silvery silk one with the belt, but oh, it always looks good on her, it looks amazing, and though she's trying to be inconspicuous, nodding demurely to the people on either side of her, still she can't help but draw attention, from the men of course but also the women, because she's such a blazing comet.

Wherever her gaze pauses, Jaq knows someone. There's Harriet Mack, the city manager, giving her a wave and a small bow, and the nameless city politicians at her table also wave to her. There are the fabulously wealthy Tartanians: they nod, and she nods back. There's Aunt Willou up at the podium making rude jokes and getting away with them because she's so easy in her skin, so assured and content up there. Willou's husband is traveling for business, but Ginny and Lucia are here, and Jaq pauses for hugs and to share a quick burst of gossip. Then she presses on. She says hello to the contortionist, to Lady Godiva, to the stilt walker (she knows a great many people in this town: everyone goes to Bo Peep's sooner or later). As she's passing Rayford's table, he rises for an embrace: his look says he fathoms her troubled heart. "I'll say just one thing: soon you'll be gettin back to makin your movie. Not tomorrow but whenever. And when you do, you're gonna take some of this pain and put it in there, and it'll be better for it. Maybe it won't be *Savannah's a fairy tale* no more —"

"Fable," she corrects.

"Right. But there'll be more truth in it. And that's all I'm gonna say about that. Look, you gotta bring *both* your mammas to the house. I'll cook venison. I know both of 'em love venison, you *promise* to bring 'em?"

She moves on. She comes at last to the table of the Georgia Historical Society, and slips into a seat beside Arthur.

"Jaq," he says. "Thanks for coming."

"Thanks for asking me. I really needed to get out of that cell."

He introduces her to his tablemates, but they mostly know her already. They give her solemn looks, supposing Guzman's death has left her irreparably damaged. But Arthur, thank God, leaves all that alone. He banters with her. He reminds her of school trips they took together, idiot things their teachers said. Dumb pranks they pulled. The repercussions of those pranks. He gets her to laugh.

The waiter comes by and fills her wineglass. It's quickly empty again.

She asks Arthur if he's seen any more little old lady genealogists lately.

"Flocks," he says with a laugh. "Every day."

Her gaze keeps drifting. Hovers a moment at the table of her uncle David. David himself is off pressing the flesh, but his wife, Madelaine, sits there looking splendid. She wears an antique tea gown, pale and flowing and collarless, and her hair is long and her neck swanlike. She's so beautiful, Jaq thinks. No wonder Ransom is so drawn to her.

But then Jaq glances at Arthur and finds he has some question in his eyes.

"What?" she says.

He leans close and murmurs, "Did you find anything?"

"What do you mean?"

"On that island," he prompts. "The Kingdom."

"Oh. Right."

She catches the eye of a waiter, and he comes and refills her glass.

She takes a deep swallow of wine.

Then tells him. Fills him in quietly about her day on Montmillan Island. As she talks, he fixes her with those great big eyes. His avid gaze, plus the act of recounting: this gives her a measure of succor. A dish is put before her, lamb lollipops with mint pesto. She scarcely notes it. Her wineglass is refilled. Then coq au vin. She manages a few bites: it's good, but soon forgotten. She's immersed in her tale of the island and Cap'n Stan, of the dogs and the dig.

"Jesus," he says when she's done. "If that's true . . . if that really is the village of the King's soldiers . . ."

"I'm sure it is."

"God. I keep thinking about them, Jaq."

"So do I."

"It drives me crazy that nobody's even heard of them."

"I know," she says. "Why won't they talk about the Kingdom?"

"This whole city's supposed to be about history, nostalgia. Right?"

"Right," she says, "and here you've got these people who built a fortress, and fought off the Georgia militia, fought for their freedom and died for their freedom while the good white folks were enslaving and raping and doing all their standard shit."

"But no one even *mentions* the King's soldiers."

"I mean I understand," she says, "why they'd hush that up in slavery days. A free community of Blacks, thriving? A fortress? Right in the heart of the South?"

"That went against everything they knew."

"It went against their *Bible*. I get why they had to keep it quiet *then*."

"But why," he asks, "can't they talk about it *now*?"

"I mean what the fuck?" she says. She feels that sense of loss inside her, that place of emptiness: it's sharply painful. But it's endurable now that she's sharing it with Arthur.

Bunny Willows, the auctioneer, steps up to the podium. He starts pushing a two-week trip to Cancun. Emmaline Taube is intoxicated and screams her bids; Art Chandler is also intoxicated and screams his bids back. Money versus money: the crowd is amused. Jaq watches the show for a moment, then turns back to Arthur.

"Well, maybe it'll change," she says. "If Stony really has those relics, maybe that will bring some attention."

He gives her a puzzled look. "Where *is* Stony? Have you seen her?"

She shakes her head.

He says, "She used to come in the library pretty often. It's been quite a while. Where do you think she is?"

She's pondering how she might evade this when she feels a tap on her shoulder. She turns. Galatas.

"Hi," he says. "Glad to see you out and about."

"Oh," she says. "Yeah. I thought it might do me good."

He's wearing his long, sorrowful face. He says, "Arthur, how are you?"

"I'm well, sir."

"A word?" Galatas murmurs to Jaq, and she rises and steps aside with him. He says, "So. I guess if you'd heard from her you'd tell me."

"Yeah, of course."

"And when she does call, the second you hang up, you'll call me?"

"I will."

"I feel guilty, Jaq. I was the one who persuaded you to go over there."

"No, you told me *not* to go."

"Right. OK, I guess I did. But I — I know what you saw."

He's still holding her in his concerned gaze. She considers letting the truth out. But her eyes are roaming and she spots Morgana, standing by her table: she's in

347

conversation with Hattie Bainbridge, but she's looking over here. Looking at *me,* Jaq realizes. Morgana gives her a small, regal flip of her fingers, a come-to-me gesture.

Jaq turns back to Galatas.

"Yeah, it's a struggle, Detective, dealing with that memory. But thank you so much for giving a shit. I'm sorry, my grandmother is summoning me. But I promise to call the moment Stony calls me."

She makes her way toward the podium.

When she arrives, Hattie Bainbridge has already been dismissed, and Morgana stands alone. "How are you, my beloved?"

Jaq shrugs. "OK. You?"

Morgana smiles. "Shall we pretend we're discussing trivialities? For example, did you know that Murphy's Oil, which we all use on our furniture, is not really an oil?"

"What?"

"It's a *soap.* In fact it's called Murphy's Oil *Soap.* Fred's mother used it, and Betty wants to use it too, because it smells so good. But I don't care to slather soap on my antiques."

"Oh," says Jaq. She's having trouble staying focused.

Morgana urges her, "Do show more interest. At least a dozen pairs of eyes are upon you this very instant."

"Oh." Jaq brings forth a half smile. "OK, well. I don't know . . . your house, that . . . that fragrance, what is that? Is that cloves?"

"Right. Exactly. Now what did that cop want?"

"The detective? He was just showing concern. You know, because I found the body."

"Ah yes. Was that awful to behold?"

Jaq shrugs. "Yeah. I'm OK though."

"I'm sure you are. You're far from fragile."

"You think so? My mothers don't. They think I'll get all ravaged by PTSD. I mean, it *was* gross."

"Were the eyes all . . ." Morgana's fingertips are bunched: she opens them to suggest *popped.*

"Yeah. But the Gooze wasn't exactly high in my esteem, so . . . I mean I'm sorry he killed himself, but —"

"He didn't kill himself."

"Oh Gram. You can't *still* believe —"

"He was murdered. But don't look so troubled. Do you find beeswax leaves an unpleasant residue?"

Jaq stares at her. "How do you know?"

"Well, it yellows your furniture."

"No, Gram, how do you know he was murdered?"

"He wasn't remotely suicidal. He enjoyed

the fight. He thought he had his enemies on the ropes."

"You're saying Detective Galatas is lying?"

"Oh yes. As you were coming up here his eyes followed you. With a rather worried look. I suppose he's in on the affair. But he's not the boss. That's something we do need to figure out: Who *is* the boss? Also, what in the world is this treasure? And what have they done with your friend Stony?"

Morgana's gray eyes are full of fire and restless, and they keep moving, conning the crowd. "Look over there," she says. "You see Rebecca Cressling's table?"

"Uh-huh."

"Who's there? Do you know all their names? Start with the man she's speaking to."

"Chief Swann?"

"Uh-huh. Deputy chief in Jacksonville, Florida, but there was some hint of corruption so he resigned and came here. Of course, where else? Savannah is a magnet city for corrupt cops. Who's next?"

"Gerson Hale."

"Seems so brilliant. But all those troubled models. I think he's the source of their trouble. Who's next?"

"Um, a judge, but I forget his name —"

"Collins. The one who let Guzman go.

With dubious cause."

"And . . . is that his wife?"

"Sally, born a Drayton. Old Savannah money, very old, and we know where that came from."

"And then Warren Bledsoe."

"Who, with your uncle David's help, took Chatham Sugar through bankruptcy, dumped the liabilities — meaning the workers he burned up — and is now doing splendidly. Anyone left?"

"An old guy talking to Rebecca. Who I don't know."

"*Whom* I don't know," Morgana corrects. "But I do. He's on the Chatham Zoning Board."

"Why do you want me to look at these people?"

"To learn how the city works. How the power clusters. Where it clings."

Just then a woman named Margaret Rose, a local chanteuse, steps up to the microphone and taps it a few times, and greets the crowd, and starts to sing "The Days of Wine and Roses." Some of the folks get up from their tables and start to dance.

Jaq asks, "So one of those people at the table is the boss?"

Morgana laughs and shrugs. "Oh no, be *careful* with mineral spirits. A little goes a long way, and *always* remove it immediately. And let's see a smile."

Jaq tries. As much of a smile as she can muster.

"We still don't know," says Morgana. "But we're close."

"We?"

"Mostly Ransom. Johnny looks things up. Willou consults. I stay home and plant my pansies."

"Where's Ransom now?"

"Well he wouldn't come *here,* dear. He'll never go where David is. Where Madelaine is. No, he's gone up north. That man Montmillan has finally returned our calls."

"Wait," says Jaq.

"Yes. Used to own the island. Ransom's gone to see him."

"May I go with him?"

She grins. "He's already on his way. Also, your mothers devoutly, *devoutly* wish me to leave you alone. God, listen to that."

Margaret Rose is singing, *"Through a meadowland, toward a closing door . . . a door marked nevermore, that wasn't there before. . . ."*

Morgana says, "Johnny Mercer used to come to Herb Buchanan's apartment over Jones Street and play for us. What an original man. I think he's the best thing to ever happen to Savannah."

They listen and watch the dancers, and Morgana sways a little.

Morgana says, "That door marked nevermore — that hails from Poe, doesn't it? Quite Southern. With all that wistful sorrow. You know for me the days of wine and roses are those days: when Johnny Mercer was singing to us. There was a young man in love with me back then. I didn't know if I quite loved him back, but I loved to be . . . in his regard, you understand?"

She's looking now, Jaq notices, at Rayford Porter's table. Rayford is eating his bananas Foster and chatting with some other nabob, and oblivious to her gaze.

Jaq says, "Was Rayford the young man?"

Morgana smiles. "Well. I hadn't even *met* Fred then."

The grand dowager Jane Rundle is coming to visit her. But Morgana raises a finger sharply — *one minute.* Jane's head extends on its stalk. But she does wait. As Morgana leans close to Jaq and says, "Listen, my darling. There is *one* thing you might do for us."

"What's that?"

"Do you know someone called the Musician?"

"The guy who whistles?"

"Maybe. Stony's mother told Willou that someone called the Musician is a good friend of her daughter's. Would you inquire of your contacts?"

"Of course."

"But just phone calls. Don't go looking for him, please. And do not under any circumstances tell either of your mothers or your Aunt Willou. They'd murder me."

Ransom drives north in the rented car to Effingham County. Through the maelstrom. Maybe he's on something called Old Clyo Road or maybe it's just a cow path: hard to tell through the impressionist wash of his windshield. But if that scary garage-like structure over there, if that's a church, then he's supposed to turn here, according to Monty's instructions. So he does. Finds himself on a sand-and-shell lane that's turned to mud, and the car slides and fishtails for nearly a mile till he arrives at an old plantation house. Truly *old.* From the 1820s. Simple and spare. Illuminated by a single porchlight. As Ransom gets out of the car, a crack of lightning reveals a spectacular view of marshes and river bluff and oak trees and ancient barn, and then comes the crash of thunder and an inhuman howling from old Monty Hollis, standing there on the porch.

Ransom sprints to its shelter. Monty stands there laughing. Firm handshake for such a gnarly old man. He says, "You look better'n I thought you would, son. Word is, you gone and turned yourse'f into a hobo and a wastrel and a bum. But it don't appear so."

Ransom grins. "I trimmed up for you, Monty. You're looking good too."

"Nah, I know what *I'm* gone to. Dried-up snakeskin soaked in dog turd. 'Mon now, take a load off, we'll watch the apocalypse. Want some a this? It's moonshine, but from a fuckin *boo*-tique distillery in Clyo. You believe that? Flower children cookin shine out here and peddling it on the internet? Ain't half bad though. World gets nuttier. Care to top it off with a few drops of CBD oil?"

"You serious?"

"Smooths out the rough edges."

"Well then, please," says Ransom, and Monty doses two jarfuls of shine with an eyedropper.

They sit in rockers on the porch and watch the weather.

Monty says, "I'm sorry this place is in such disarray. My wife just up and died a while back. How's your mama, son?"

"She's OK. I'm sorry about your wife."

"Uh-huh. Fourth wife. Bit of a loose cannon. I dreamed of your mother the other night."

"Rayford just told me the same thing."

"Ha. Lots of us. They used to call us Morgana's Bananas. Ha ha ha ha! I hear ol' Guzman hired her to get him off that murder charge. Didn't work though, did it?"

"Mr. Guzman lacked patience," says Ransom, as he takes a sip of the shine. It tastes like turpentine, but a refined turpentine.

"He has patience now, son," says Monty. He notices that Ransom is looking up at a great rack of antlers hanging from the porch rafters. "My wife bagged that one. In the Yukon. Used to fly up on a Friday, back by Monday. She was a firecracker. You knew Rosalie?"

"Sort of. I was a little kid."

"Second wife. Your daddy went on one a them trips. Lousy shot."

"I think I've heard that."

"And your mama always treated him like shit. That I do recall. You want to know why I finally called you back?"

Ransom nods.

Monty says, "I got a call the other day. Some gentleman I'd never met. Warning me

356

to keep my mouth shut about the sale of my island. It had been my intention to do just that. But not after that call. Is that what you've come to ask about?"

"Yes."

"Well, what do you want to know?"

"May I ask who bought it?

"Yeah, ask away. But I will never tell you."

"Why not?"

" 'Cause I got no fuckin idea."

"What about Sand Gnat Holdings?"

Monty shrugs. "Dunno. Some lawyer from Atlanta drives back here one day, offers me nine hunnert thousand for the island. Outta the blue. Taxes on that place were a nutcracker. Every fuckin year. And the State a Georgia kept threatenin to take it for wetlands. I kept tellin 'em, Well, take it then, you Communist rat bastards. But they were all talk and no *consummation*. And in the meantime, who else gonna buy it? And I was sick of it. So I told that lawyer, make it a million, it's yours."

"You know what he wanted it for?"

"I had a guess. Which was confirmed by Archie Guzman."

"Guzman."

"Uh-huh. Week before the closing, the Gooze hisself shows up at my door. Tells me Sand Gnat Holdings is a front for some folks who want to build a big-ass resort on the island. Clubhouse, condos, hotel, marina, spa, the whole enchilada. Get Tiger Woods to design the eighteen-hole golf course. I told him, yeah, I figured that when they offered me a million dollars. Then he tells me *he* wants the island. And offers me a million and a quarter. And promises much more tasteful development. I thought, oh shit. Yaw seen his house. Imagine how he'd fuck up an *island*."

"What'd you do?"

"Bumped him up a little. Got him to one point four. Called the Atlanta lawyer back. Bitch comes down all pissy and huffy. I told him to bump up or get off my property. He goes one and a half. I say, what a true gentleman you are! Next day, Guzman comes howling back through. Ups to one six. It's a pissing contest for my delight and entertainment."

"But who was the Gooze pissing against?"

"I told you, I don't know. Whoever it was, he hated 'em — you could hear that in his voice. But he would not say."

"Why not?" Ransom asks. "The Gooze wasn't known for being discreet."

"Well, no. But somethin had him spooked."

Just then a fierce bolt of lightning crosses

the sky. The marshes, the oak limbs, the far riverbank. "Gawd *DAY-UM!*" Monty shouts, just as the thunderblast rattles the old beams around them. "HA HA HA! That is fuckin what we're still here for!"

He drains his drink.

Gets up on his spindly bowlegs, goes to the caddy, and fetches the bottle. Tops Ransom, fills his own.

"So, yeah. Smartass lawyer tells me he'll jack up to two even if I'll close the next fuckin day. I figger the Gooze will cough up s'more, you know? But I don't really wanna sell to the Gooze. 'Cause he's a greasy asshole. Much rather sell to this other greasy asshole. So I signed. Gooze comes round the next day, oh he's *hoppin.* That big pasty-ass face, them red blotches. He says, Monty! I'd a giv'n you another half million! I says, Archie. I'm polite, I don't call him the Gooze. I say, Archie. A half-million dollars is not to be sneezed at. But I live for my delight. And the *delight* I'm takin right now, in seeing the misery on your ugly face, is worth far more'n a half-million lousy dollars."

Monty's laugh starts out low and ratchets up to a barking shriek, and Ransom laughs with him.

"HA HA HA HA HA HA HA HA HA!"

When finally the two of them have collected themselves, Ransom says, "And how did he take that?"

"He did not take it at all *well.*"

Long sad pause.

"HA HA HA HA HA HA!"

Jaq fetches her anorak raincoat and her backpack from the coat check. Then stops in the fancy portable toilet to change from the gown into jeans and T-shirt. Puts on her sneakers. Pulls the hood up on the anorak, and braves the downpour. With head lowered she charges across the park toward the side of the Mansion Inn, where she has chained her bike. But when she gets there she notices, parked on the other side of Hall Street, a midnight-blue Escalade, with the door ajar and the interior light on.

Aunt Willou.

In there vaping and drinking and checking her makeup in the mirror.

Jaq comes to the passenger door. "Auntie?"

Willou jumps.

"Jesus! Jaq? Scared me to death. Get in here. Get out of the goddamn rain, are you a moron?"

Jaq hops in the passenger seat.

Willou hands her a towel to dry her face.

"What are you *doing*?"

"My bike's right here. But I guess I can't ride in this."

"You can't. But you can sit with me."

"OK, thanks."

"Sorry, I'm vaping. Want me to roll down the window?"

"No, I don't mind."

"I guess I should still be in there. But the show's over, I'm done with begging, what would I do? Want a drag?"

"Yes please. Thank you."

Jaq doesn't really vape, so the single pull carries quite a kick. Makes her feel that void within herself vividly. She returns the vape pen and tips her seat back a notch and says, "You were great, Willou. That speech."

"Just my standard. We love you, you love art, Savannah's your nest, gimme gimme gimme. But you, my dear niece, you were truly terrific. That entrance."

"What entrance?"

"You came in like a star. Everyone's terrified of you."

"Of *me*?"

"You seem to know your own mind. That's quite intimidating."

Jaq's unused to being praised by her aunt. She chuckles nervously.

Willou sips her cocktail, something clear

361

and ginny. And asks, "You OK? After what you saw?"

"Yeah. I mean not really. I still see him hanging there."

"Such a sleaze in everything he did, wasn't he? Even his suicide was garish and ill-planned. You'd think Mother would have paid some price in this town for defending him so stubbornly, but she hasn't really, has she?"

"No."

"Actually," Willou adds, "I think everyone's impressed she got such a handsome check. I mean, assuming it doesn't bounce."

"Yeah."

They sit quietly a moment.

Jaq knows she can't tell Willou what Morgana just said to her. Can't mention the investigation, because she'd have a fit. And she'd tell her mother Bebe, who would also have a fit. So she keeps quiet.

Then Willou says, "Did you notice Madelaine tonight?"

"Yes," says Jaq. "So beautiful."

"Uh-huh. That flowing gown. How tragic."

Jaq says, "You don't like her, do you?"

Right away Willou comes back with, "She's my sister-in-law, of course I love her." But speaks with a calculated evenness of tone. She takes another sip of her drink, focuses a moment on her vape pen — on making the tip glow, and then says, "You're not recording this, are you?"

"No."

"I don't want to be in some documentary about the Musgroves of Savannah."

Jaq smiles. "No."

"OK. Well, then, frankly, Madelaine's a manipulative bitch. She destroyed Ransom. I don't blame her for falling for him. I mean he's charming and God he's good-looking, and David wasn't right for her in any way. He *is* a bully, and he *is* a drunk, and that was a terrible mistake, her engagement to him. So she made a grand lurch to try and get out from under that mistake. I can understand that. I forgive her for that. I also forgive her for then knuckling under to her parents, and to Morgana, and going back to David. I mean the mysterious dynastic powers of Savannah were being invoked. Right? When Savannah really goes to work, when it's got its cauldron going, well you better submit; you're not going to beat it. Certainly Ransom wasn't gonna beat it. You know he's willful and romantic, and dashing and all, but has no real spine."

Jaq says quietly, "That's an unkind thing to say."

Willou raises a brow and sets her eye on

Jaq. "Yeah but it's true, don't argue. Anyway the point is, Madelaine knuckled under and married David, and had those two lovely kids and that should have been that. But . . . you know about the letter she sent, right?"

"I don't know much."

"Well, your mom does. She never told you?"

"She doesn't share that sort of thing."

"OK, well. One day Ransom got a letter. While he was working for Jack Schilling — that horrible job, and he was so unhappy. And he gets this letter from Maddie. Saying how sorry she was for what she'd done. And oh, she says, by the way, what an asshole your brother is, and how psychologically abusive, and how he'll get the kids if she ever tries to leave him 'cause he knows all the judges, etcetera. She goes to Ransom with this. I mean, that little bitch. I mean, why not find yourself a shark of a lawyer and leave my little brother out of it?

"I'm sorry if I sound bitter. I am bitter. I am so sick of my two brothers going at it. Always trying to kill each other, and spreading that poison, and I'm tired of it. I know it's not all Maddie's fault. It's not even *mostly* her fault. The fault is mostly with my mother, Morgana. But still, it chaps my ass, that letter.

"Anyway she told him that if he cared to respond, he should please leave a note in the trunk of the big oak tree out at the dairy.

"Which is so romantic! Right? And so twisted. Because she was never really gonna leave David: she's addicted to that lifestyle. And of course Ransom was still besotted, so he did leave that note, and they went back and forth with these little . . . I don't know what you call them, they weren't exactly love letters. I mean they weren't fucking. It was just this platonic tragic bullshitty thing. And anyway David somehow started suspecting her of cheating on him. He hired Screven Security and had her followed. And they intercepted the notes, which led to that disaster on the stone stairs. And now Ransom's broken into pieces, and my mother's holding those pieces, and there you go, there's another sordid chapter in the saga of the blackguard clan you've been shanghaied into, you poor girl. May I take you home now?"

"No, I'm OK. Thanks. The rain's stopped."

"Might start again. Lemme drive you."

"No, but thank you, Willou. Thank you for telling me that."

"Oh. Anytime. I got lots of these gruesome tales."

■ ■ ■ ■

The rain has turned to mist by the time Ransom pulls up at the Old Fort. A few of the windows glow with soft light. The oriel window, the gossamer-web fanlight and sidelights that surround the front door, all this welcoming light as though the place still wants to be his home.

Betty opens the door.

"Hi," he says. "Where's Gracie?"

"Up in my room. Listen. Hear her?"

The dog's mournful wail comes pouring down the staircase.

"She don't like the thunder. I better get back up there. Your mom's in the Turkish room. With Willou."

Off she pads in her Chinese slippers.

"Oh my beloved," says Morgana, as he steps into the Turkish room and bestows formal busses on her and on his sister. "We've been so worried about you in this storm. Did you see Monty?"

"Sends his love. Told me he still dreams of you."

"Goodness. Well, let him dream away. Report."

He does. And as he does, she sets her lips and draws him in with her gray eyes. At one point she bids him pause a moment while she fills three tiny rose-crystal glasses with cognac, and hands them out. Then she begs him to continue.

When he's finished, she says, "Good. For me that answers everything. Or nearly so. We still lack the identity of the boss, and we lack that treasure, and of course we lack Stony. But at least the *essential story* of this crime has become clear."

Willou straightens. Exchanges glances with Ransom. And asks, with a slight sardonic smile, "What is the essential story of this crime, Mother?"

Morgana says, "Oh, typical Savannah foolishness. Willou, do you recall Daryl, our gardener, when you were a girl? Well, Daryl lived in a trailer down in Richmond Hill. He had many brothers, and like many enterprising families in Richmond Hill, they were all engaged in distributing methamphetamine. So one day Daryl was at his trailer and he got into a dispute with one of his brothers. Some profits had gone missing. Contentious issues were raised, and he wound up taking a baseball bat and bashing in his brother's skull. He then called a second brother on the phone and asked him to come help him dispose of the body. Which the second brother was willing to do, as Daryl was in a bad spot, and it was a tight-knit family. But they quarreled over whose vehicle to use. The brother didn't think it was fair to use his, since his had just been washed and detailed. Daryl didn't have a car, he only had a van, which was filled with gardening supplies, so there wasn't much room for a body. Back and forth the argument went, and it grew more heated until finally Daryl killed the second brother as well. Same way. Same bat.

"Then, a third brother happened to stop by. Daryl explained what had happened. The two of them rearranged the crime scene to make it look like the two dead brothers had killed each other. But finally Daryl decided this was never going to work, no matter how the bodies were posed, because the third brother was weak and would quickly fold under interrogation. And it was a painful realization, because he was fond of this third brother. But he saw no way forward; he had to use the bat again. Then he called his girlfriend and took her bowling. Bowled two strong games, I'm told, before the police arrested him.

"Crimes like this happen regularly here. At the heart of these crimes is always the same thing: a man, a stupid man, who thinks he can manipulate the world to his satisfaction. A man who is drunk on himself, who believes he knows things he doesn't. Something triggers in him a bolt of entrepreneurial energy. He hatches some scheme in his head. He pursues it. Everything goes swimmingly until it doesn't. His plan hits a pothole and loses a wheel. This enrages him. He feels the world is against him. He becomes terribly angry and then violent. Blood is shed. A cover-up is required. This cover-up is invariably ill-planned. More accomplices are needed, and these turn out to be incompetent. This riles him still further. More blood is shed. Which calls for another cover-up, which demands more blood, and so on until you've created a sequence of really quite breathtaking slaughter. All utterly pointless, stupid, senseless. This happens in Savannah perhaps once a year. I do believe there's a poisonous vapor in this town, a sort of miasmal gas that rises from the storm drains and leaches into our homes and into our blood. Would either of you care for cheese straws?"

Willou passes. Ransom takes a few.

"Take more," Morgana says. "Aren't you starving, darling?"

"For Christ's sake," says Ransom, "will you tell us the story of *this* crime?"

"Oh. Well, of course. Though it's only my

surmise."

They wait. She ponders a bit.

"Well, we've learned from Monty's tale that a group of investors bought his island and aimed to develop it, and Guzman got wind of that and tried to cut in. There was a bidding war that grew personal, heated. Guzman was outbid; he became irate. I don't know how he and Stony found each other, but they did, and somehow his interest in Montmillan Island came up. She mentioned that Montmillan Island was probably where the King's soldiers had their secret village, and she believed she could find that village. He was intrigued and decided to bankroll her excavations. Didn't cost him much; Stony came cheap. But then she actually did find something out there. Dug something up, some kind of "proof" that indeed, a long time ago, runaway slaves had lived there. Had built not just a village but a secret fortress, right in the heart of the South, and had lived there, hundreds of them, in absolute freedom, for years. Sounds kind of like an American Masada, doesn't it?

"I mean, because honestly, they must have known what they were doing was suicide. Yet better that than going back to slavery.

"So Guzman somehow found out who the

investors were. He told them about Stony's evidence. This evidence must have been persuasive. They must have seen that if it ever got out, this proof of a free and thriving Black nation in the heart of the Deep South . . . well, that story would become . . . explosive. Media would be all over it. And they'd never get their easement. A billionaires' resort? On top of a sacred village? Permits would have been tricky to begin with. Now you could kiss them goodbye.

"I suppose Guzman tried to cut a deal with them. Suppressing Stony's evidence in return for some percent of the enterprise? Say . . . ten percent?

"But the group thought it would be easier and cheaper to just lean on Stony. So they arranged to do that. They hired that ex-con from Valdosta, that joker with the tie, who went, as they say, over the top, and wound up killing Luke. And God knows what they've done to Stony. And then they decided, OK, well, let us double down on the brutality: let's frame the Gooze. So they tossed Luke's body into one of Guzman's vacant buildings and burned it down. And Billy Sugar was a witness to their crimes, so they arranged to have him killed. And then they killed Guzman himself. It's the typical Savannah debacle. You look at the carnage, you look at the butcher's bill, and you inquire, Why in the world is this bill so high? And the butcher shrugs and says, Oh, I don't know. Things got out of hand."

Her children are silent, trying to digest all this.

Finally Willou says, "Well. It sounds no stranger than the cases that come to my courtroom. But don't you think you should go to the police?"

"I would," says Morgana as she refills her tiny glass, "except for my certainty that some cops are in on this. As well as some other folks."

Ransom says, "Who?"

"I can't speak to that yet. But at the Ball tonight I noticed an entire table full of possible suspects. Goodness. Hard to choose. They all looked just as guilty as sin."

Jaq gets a rush of familiarity when she pulls up her bike beneath the pantaloons of the neon shepherdess and her neon sheep. She locks up, and bestows high fives and hugs to the folks in front. Plenty of these, because the rain died just a few minutes ago and everyone was jonesing for a smoke, so they're all out here. They tell her they've been missing her. They say service has gotten slow and surly since she's been gone.

Nobody mentions the Gooze. But they all know, of course. She goes from one friend to another and when she finally gets done greeting everybody outside, she goes inside and greets everybody there, and Holly gives her a beer.

This takes half an hour. Then she goes out to her bike and unlocks it and rides away.

Of all the folks she spoke to, none had heard the Musician tonight.

She asked every single person at Peep's. But he's just not out, which is perfectly understandable considering the downpour. No one knows where he's staying. Some recall that he used to stay under a tarp in the Eastside woods, but no one knows if he's still living there, or its precise location.

OK, she thinks. Good time to go home, since her mothers will be really worried by now. She can find him tomorrow.

She pulls over and checks her phone. Messages from both Bebe and Roxanne. She texts them back:

I'm good waited for rain to stop. Home soon

And then, spur of the moment, she texts Ransom:

Saw Morgana at the ball. Told me things.
You coming back tonight? Wanna meet?

Waits a minute. No answer. So again she heads home. But she doesn't want to go home. Maybe she'll make a quick stop at the Salty Dog Tavern because one of the bartenders there, Wally, he might know the Musician.

But at the Salty Dog she finds Wally's not working. And nobody else has heard the Musician tonight.

Still nothing from Ransom.

So OK, home. Time to go home for real.

Ransom has rented a room at the Thunderbird Inn, and he heads there now, so worn out that he doesn't even stop at Peep's or the Legion for a drink, but just takes Oglethorpe past the Greyhound bus station right to the motel and pulls into his parking space.

On his phone, a message from Jaq. She wants to meet. He'd love to see her, tell her all about Monty, pick her brains. But Bebe wouldn't like it. Particularly at this hour.

But maybe just for a quick one? He writes:

OK, yes. Legion? 20 mins?

And he's about to drive there but there's

374

a rap on his window.

Hatchet Head.

He unlocks. Hatch slides in and says, "Developments."

"How'd you know I was here?"

"Who *doesn't* know you're here? You've decided to enjoy the luxuries of civilization, we all know that. The Thunderbird. Wow. This place is like *money,* man. Swank. Who's payin, your mamma?"

"It's cheap, Hatch."

"More'n *I* can afford." Hatchet Head seems to be a little drunk.

Ransom says, "I figured I'd get killed in those woods."

"I hear you," says Hatchet Head. "You got the bad juju all right. So what did old Monty say?"

"He said a lot."

"Yeah? Well, I got somethin too. You know the Musician?"

"I know what he sounds like."

"Yeah, well, I seen him tonight. Went to the Emmaus House to score some supper, and there he is. Normally he don't go to the shelters or nothin, but the man's *hungry.* He asks me, do I know where Stony is, 'cause he ain't seen her. I say, Ransom Musgrove's kinda lookin for her too. He says, Oh yeah? And I shoulda shut up then, but I

375

didn't. I told him about that 'treasure' thing. He says, Oh yeah, the treasure. I'm holdin it for her."

"He's what? Holding it?"

"Stony's treasure. Got it in a trunk. Stony asked him to keep it for her."

"What is it?"

"He didn't say."

"Where is he?"

"I dunno. His tarp, I guess."

"You mean out by the tracks?"

"Yeah, I guess."

"Then let's go."

The American Legion is closing up. So Jaq must stand at the entrance, in the doorway, waiting for Ransom. Sheaves of rain, and the lightning is back too. One of the bartenders comes out carrying a bag of trash, and she asks if he's heard the Musician tonight. He hasn't.

Then a police cruiser comes trawling up Bull Street. Very slow. She's got that gun in her bike box, so if they stop her she'll be in for deep shit. She turns so the hood will hide her face. Gets out her phone and stares hard at it, and feels a terror in her bones till the cops pass by. She draws a deep breath. Message from Ransom:

Hey sorry ran into hatch. Says stony gave musician the treasure. Going to his tarp to check out. let's meet tomorrow?

In a flash she types back:

Wait take me. Meet me at the Cathedral? Pick me up in 10?

Ransom and Hatchet Head are walking on the CSX railway tracks, and Hatch is talking too much and Ransom has to ask him to keep quiet. Hatchet Head says, "Cool. Cool." But then whispers, "Do you hear him?" Meaning the Musician. But all they hear are bullfrog peepers, legions of them, a constant roaring, and the rain and wind, which have kicked up again.

They come to the old stormcloud oak tree.

He flips his headlamp on.

There's a thin track going off through the pines. They take it. Past a NO TRESPASSING sign put up by SAVANNAH DEPT. OF STORM-WATER. Then the concrete portal to the storm drains, with a slanted steel door, padlocked. Ransom can hear the suck of water pouring through the grilles.

And from here, looking through the trees, he can see the Musician's blue tarp. Not twenty yards away. Ransom says, "Do you know his name?"

Hatchet Head shrugs.

Ransom calls, *"Hey, Musician! It's Ransom Musgrove! We talk?"*

No answer.

"About Stony! I'm looking for Stony!"

Bullfrogs.

Something's wrong.

What's wrong is that under that tarp, best he can tell, there's nothing. No hammock, no stove nearby, no dishes or pots or pans, no sleeping bag, no cinder-block fireplace, nothing. It's not a living camp.

It's dawning on him that he's been betrayed.

He turns and catches Hatchet Head in the light of his headlamp. Hatch has a hurt-animal look and his mouth is elastic like a fishmouth, and he says, "Hey, I'm sorry."

Ransom takes one step back. Then he wheels and tries to blast out of there, except it's all mud underfoot so he slips on the push-off, on the very first step — and the demons are already upon him. Some stinking animal wraps big arms around him and he bites at that arm, and gets a piercing shriek in his ear, which inspires him to sink his teeth deeper, which cranks the bellowing up higher, and Ransom twists and tears himself free of the creature. But right away, something else snatches at his face. Like a motherfucking bat, grabbing his face. He can't shake it off and he can't breathe. And then there are more bats, a confusion of bats and brightly colored reptiles, and he's stretching out in the cool grass and thinks, I can't fight all of them, can I? Maybe it's better to lie right down here and rest a while, look up at these stars, maybe get some sleep?

Jaq stands at the top of the steps to the Cathedral of St. John the Baptist at the great Gothic doors, just out of the rain. It's falling fiercely again and the wind is blowing and she's wet. Her anorak has kept the top of her dry but her jeans and sneakers are soaked through. Ransom's not coming. She knows that now. She's been waiting half an hour, she's sent him two messages, nothing. He must have turned his phone off. What an idiot. She's annoyed at him, and lonely again, and feels that emptiness inside her. And she's scared. If Morgana is right and Galatas is only a liar, then Stony may be dead or in captivity somewhere, and Jaq has done nothing to help her. And the Gooze still dangles before her, still looks astonished at how everything turned out for him. The lightning and thunder racks her nerves. And her mothers must be worried sick. But she's sent them enough notes. Pointless to send another; she just needs to get home.

If I go fast I can be home, she thinks, in seven minutes.

But maybe if she waits a little longer the rain will ease up.

A car shows up, coming around Lafayette Square, and she thinks, maybe this is Ransom now, OK.

But the car keeps going north.

She stays at the church door, sunk in gloom.

Then she hears a flurry of birdsong.

In the middle of the storm. Birdsong. Astonishingly near and the notes are coming with dizzying precision. For God's sake, it can't be.

But it is, it has to be. The next swirl of notes ascends effortlessly and banks and swoops and she would run toward it but where's it coming from? Seems like from above. From the bell tower? She's peering up into the heart of the rain, as though she'll find him flying around up there. And then three notes right beside her, and she lowers her eyes and here he is.

On the sidewalk, strolling past.

A little troll-like man with a huge beard and a rain slicker and rubbers, whistling his sonata till he happens to look up. He sees her and stops. He says, "Oh, excuse me."

"Please don't stop," says Jaq.

"That's OK, I'll finish later."

She says, "Will you come up out of the rain for a minute?"

He looks dubious. But does mount the steps. She moves a little so he can stand next to her. "I'm Jaq."

"OK. I'm Larry."

She laughs. But quickly says, "Sorry, I'm not laughing at your name, just that you *have* a name. I shouldn't laugh at that either though. Were you with my uncle just now?"

"Your uncle?"

"Ransom? Ransom Musgrove."

"Oh. I know who you're talking about. But I haven't seen him."

"Really?"

"Was I supposed to?"

"He wrote me to say that he was going to see you, because you have the treasure of the Kingdom."

"No. I have about three dollars."

"But you do know Stony?"

"I know her and love her, yes. But I don't have that treasure."

"Did you tell Hatchet Head you have that treasure?"

"I didn't."

"Wait," she says. "Look at this text from Ransom, look."

She shows him her phone. He puts on his reading glasses.

Hey sorry ran into hatch. Says stony gave musician the treasure. Going to his tarp to check out. let's meet tomorrow?

He spends a moment pondering. Then he says, "Is your uncle looking for that treasure?"

"Well, not really. He's just looking for Stony."

"Why is he looking for her?"

"She's missing. I mean nobody's seen her since the night Luke died. Except Detective Galatas told me she's *not* missing, she's in Myrtle Beach, South Carolina, but I don't believe that anymore. Have you seen her?"

"No." He turns to her. Squints, sizes her up. "But I have seen Galatas. Just this afternoon. At Dixon Park. Do you know Dixon Park?"

"Not really."

"Well, it's usually pretty empty, so that's where I like to whistle. But tonight I saw Galatas there. In his car. His . . . SUV, I guess you call it. He's always driving around having meetings with people, collecting information. Collecting tips."

"Galatas."

"Yes. He likes when people come up to his car. He gives them money and favors. He likes to distribute favors. If they're violating parole, he can fix things. He puts pressure on people. Unbelievable pressure."

"Oh."

"And today the man standing at his car was Hatchet Head."

"Hatchet Head."

"Yeah. And Hatchet Head got into his car and they drove off."

"Oh," she says. A terror begins to settle in.

"And listen," he says, "if Ransom did go to my tarp, then he's in trouble. I don't live there anymore. I moved. I moved because I was living next to a portal to the storm drains, and every morning, just before dawn, Galatas was passing my tarp on his way to that entrance. You shouldn't be watching a cop when he's doing things like that. So I moved away."

She thinks about this. "What's he doing in the storm drains?"

Larry shrugs. "Nothing good."

"You think he could be holding someone there?"

"That sounds like him."

"Could he be keeping Stony there?"

"If she's got something he wants. Yeah, then he would do that."

"Could he be keeping Ransom there?"

"If he's got something Galatas wants."

The curtain of rain pours down right before their eyes.

She asks, "Does he go there *every* morning?"

"Yes."

"What time?"

"Five thirty. Or so. Just before dawn. Just when I'm going to sleep."

"Where is this exactly?"

"Oh you don't want to go there."

"No, of course. But would you tell me where? Would you show me on the map?"

She moves close to him, so they can look at her phone. She pulls up Google Maps and goes to Satellite View. He gestures. "Take it up more," he says. "Over. No, over this way."

When she's hovering over the CSX tracks, he says, "Now can you go closer?" She zooms in. He says, "Look. You can even see it. That blue thing? That's my tarp. See that white disc? It's really a cylinder. It's the portal to the storm drains. He comes from this direction, you see? And then he goes down."

"OK. Thank you."

"But don't go by yourself."

She says, "Of course not."

"I better move along now," he says.

But he doesn't go. He looks up into the shimmering silver sheets of rain in the church floodlight. He says, "By the way, I don't have that treasure but I do know where to find it."

"You do?"

"Stony told me not to tell anyone unless something happened to her. I guess it's time."

"Where is it?"

"The. Treasure. Of. The. Kingdom. Dot com. One word, no spaces, no caps. Thetreasureofthekingdom dot com. I hope Stony will be OK. I hope your uncle will be OK."

And off he goes.

Stony is in the Kingdom. Her father Sharper is teaching her how to kill a boar. The dogs are holding a boar at bay in the middle of a creek bed. She and her father wade out there. Water swirls at their ankles, and her father hands her a bayonet and says, "You can do this." She says, "No, I don't think so." But he waits. And the dogs wait, and even the boar waits —

The LED light switches on.

She screams.

After a few minutes, when her screams finally fade, the door opens. It opens slowly: there's a foot of water in here. Three men come in, and they're carrying another man, who's unconscious. The three men wear masks. She doesn't know who they are, but she's sure that none of them are Mr. Kindness.

They wade into the chamber. They swipe the cereal containers and other trash off the wooden table. They lay the man on the tabletop.

Then they go away and lock the door. Never speaking a word.

She looks into the face of the sleeping man. Oh, she's seen this one before. This is Jaq's uncle. Jaq loves him. She always talked about how much she loves her uncle Ransom. She's always said he's beautiful.

He *is* beautiful.

But why is he here? she wonders.

A minute later, the light goes out again.

She gets some toilet paper and makes a wad of it. She wets it, and presses it gently to his face.

What does Mr. Kindness want with this man?

After a while he opens his eyes. He says, "Who are you?"

"My name is Stony."

"Oh. I've been looking for you."

"Well, you found me."

"There's no light?" he says.

"No. You're Ransom, aren't you?"

"Yes. I'm Jaq's uncle."

"I'm pleased to meet you."

A minute later, she goes wading back to the bed. It's still above water, but only by a few inches. She stretches out.

He says, "There's no light in here at all?"

"Sometimes there is. Don't wish for it though. You think you want it, but when it comes it's really awful."

"Why? Is it blinding?"

"Yes, at first, but after that it's just ugly. It stops you from dreaming."

"What is this place?"

"A room in the storm drains. It's wet now, there's like a foot of water. You're lying on a table. I'm on a cot. The water keeps rising. I guess it's raining out there?"

"Really pouring."

"Well, I guess that's why then. I guess if the water gets high enough, we'll drown. What else? There's a lot of palmetto bugs, but no rats. That's one good thing. Except I guess it's a sign of how shitty this place is. I mean even rats would never come here."

"Do you know who's keeping us here?"

387

"A cop. Galatas. You know him?"

"Yeah. What does he want?"

"From you, I don't know."

Actually, she thinks she does know. She thinks she's figured it out. She thinks Mr. Kindness has had Jaq's uncle delivered to this room so he can torture him, and make a record of his suffering, and threaten to show that to Jaq. Because he knows Stony won't be able to hold up against that. She thinks Mr. Kindness is cleverer than she thought.

She can't tell him this though. It's too painful to say.

Ransom asks, "And what does he want from you?"

"The treasure of the Kingdom."

"What's that?"

"I think it would be better to not discuss that at present."

He doesn't argue with her. They sit in silence. She listens to him breathing. It's so sweet to hear the breathing of another soul. She finds that if she holds her own breath, *his* breathing just keeps right on, and this makes her quite happy. What a phenomenon: a man's breathing.

After a while she says, "Anyway, I don't even know if you really *are* Ransom Musgrove. You're just a voice, you could be

388

anybody. You could be working for him."

"OK."

"Or, even suppose you *are* Ransom Musgrove, maybe the place is bugged. But listen, you have to be ready. He'll try all sorts a shit on your head. He'll threaten Jaq."

"Has he hurt you, Stony?"

"Not physically," she says. "Not yet. He's working up to it. He'll get there."

She's quiet for a while.

Then she speaks in a voice that's hardly more than a whisper, "But the thing is, he wants to be thought of as good. I mean that's something about him. He wants to be justified. Not completely evil."

This time the silence lasts several minutes. Then she gets up and feels her way to the table. She reaches out and touches his face, and gently feels round till she locates his ear. Slowly she lowers her face until her lips are very close. She can feel her own breath now because her lips are within an inch or two of his ear, and she can smell him, and he's shivering of course because he's wet and cold, and she says as quietly as she can, so that no bug could possibly pick up her words: *"That's his weakness."*

Jaq, still at the cathedral door, is visiting a website on her phone: thetreasureofthekingdom.com. Watching a video. In a scrubby, hot-looking field, full of palmettos and Spanish bayonets, beneath a washed-out sky, a large man kneels and tinkers with a drone aircraft. The camera closes on him. He glances up: it's Luke.

The voice of Stony (who's clearly operating the camera) says cheerily, "So, y'all, welcome to Wing-and-a-Prayer Archeological Surveys, Incorporated. Wherever you are, we hope you're not getting eaten alive the way we are on this godforsaken island. Let me introduce you to the team. I'm Matilda Stone, your grand instigator." She turns the camera to her face for a moment, grins, and nods. Then back to Luke. "That man there is your chief engineer. Wave, Luke."

He ignores her. He's busy affixing a black box to the drone's undercarriage.

"Hey Luke," she says, "your ass crack is showing."

He keeps working and asks, "Does that turn you on, Stony?"

"Normally it'd thrill me to the bone," she says, "but at the moment I'm distracted by that incredible aircraft. Isn't that our DJI Matrice 210 V2 RTK from Da-Jiang Innovations, which is the sine qua non of aerial archeology?"

Jaq has never seen Stony like this before. The easy wit, the needling, the confidence: she's in her element. Not a trace of her usual anxiety. Jaq huddles in the church doorway, and the rain pour down in torrents around her, but she holds the phone inches from her face at a slight tilt so she can hear every word, and she's completely immersed in this video.

"Now tell us," Stony asks Luke, "what is that mysterious black box you're attaching to that drone?"

"Puck," he says.

"That's right," says Stony. "That's the Velodyne Puck, which holds the LiDAR sensors. There are sixteen lasers, folks, and each one has its own detector, and each produces six-nanosecond pulses at nine hundred and three nanometers, generating how many pulses per second?"

"Three hundred thousand," says Luke.

"Is correct. You 'bout done there, beautiful?"

"I'm not."

"Well, I'm bored. Let's just cut to the chase, OK?"

Instantly, the video switches to THE TAKE-OFF.

The drone rises from the field with an escort of adoring dragonflies. Luke can faintly be heard saying, "Huzzah."

Then another cut: SO, TWELVE DAYS LATER.

Here's Stony in an office. Her laptop on the desk before her. She's looking into a camera, which is presumably being held by Luke.

Stony says, "So, y'all, we now have our results. As you can see I got bags under my eyes and I look like a Jamaican zombie, and we work and work and then drop and sleep five hours, and get up and work some more, and I won't go into the nightmare of 'ground classification' and 'color ramping' and retiling the LiDAR point cloud with our Headwall Hyperspec Nano; I won't even start. But, y'all, would you care to see what we got?"

The camera turns from her and takes in the laptop screen.

Stony says, "So to start, here's an aerial still shot of the area we call the Kingdom of Montmillan. Through the leaves, here you'll get a glimpse, just a glimpse, of our excavations. But as you can see, we have performed no excavations here, in this open field, as yet. Now then. We shall overlay that photograph with our LiDAR results."

That overlay happens on the screen.

As it comes up, Jaq's jaw falls open.

Stony says, "LiDAR reveals the outline of some twenty-two cottages in the field area, and another twelve in the forested area, which we believe was not forested when the Kingdom was flourishing in the 1780s. We also see this large building here, which for now we're calling the Gathering Hall. Further, we can see traces of three other large structures, *here, here,* and *here.* These were possibly for grain storage or food preparation or devotions. Also visible, of course, with such amazing clarity, is this outline of the great breastwork that surrounded the Kingdom in the late 1780s. It's nearly six hundred yards long by one hundred yards wide. Within this enclosure were three smaller enclosed areas, which we believe were used for garden crops and possibly even for keeping cattle, and . . ."

Betty's in bed with Gracie in her arms because the poor dog is frightened. Every time there's a crash of thunder Gracie squirms from her arms and tries to get under the bed, and her whines turn into wails, and Betty has to get up and drag her back up onto the bed. Holding her. "It's o-*kayyy,* it's o-*kayyy,* my love." But still Gracie howls, and Betty says, "You gotta shush up. Please shush up. If you don't shush up, I don't get to keep you." She's weeping because, except for her dog, Bonkers, she's never loved anything in her life as much as she loves this dog. And then BOOM — light fills the pier windows again and thunder shakes the house and again Gracie is slithering out of her arms and trying to squeeze under the bedframe, and howling.

Her phone starts to chirp.

Oh no.

Please don't let it be Morgana calling to complain.

But she looks, and it is. Morgana.

"*Maaay*-am?"

"Come down, please."

Betty puts on trousers and a shirt and gives Gracie a big embrace and says, "I'm gonna have to leave you here, my princess. But I'll be right back."

Though as soon as she's out of the room Gracie opens up like a pack of moonstruck Arctic wolves.

So Betty goes back and puts the leash on her. The two of them go down the broad staircase together.

Morgana's in the parlor, sitting on the piano bench, staring out at the storm.

Betty says, "I'm sorry. I'm sorry she keeps howling. I do eva'thing to stop her but she's scared."

But Morgana is far away. "Get the keys to the beast," she says. "And my black raincoat and umbrella."

"Oh yes ma'am."

A minute later they're headed out the door, but Betty doesn't know what to do with Gracie. "Should I lock her in the kitchen?"

Morgana opens the umbrella and says, "I don't care."

Betty says, "Can I bring her?"

Morgana walks down the steps into the rain.

Then, when the three of them have settled into the Caprice, Betty looks to Morgana for directions and she says only, "Victory."

They drive through the rain. The silence is hard on Betty. She's never liked silence much. And she's worried because Morgana's tone is so somber. They turn onto Victory Drive and Betty says, "I just don't want her to be a bother. I mean Gracie, she's too sad, isn't she? She's got such sad eyes. I never seen nobody so sad. 'Cept my sister. My sister Nonny was just that sad. She went to Alaska and she married a man, he was a *trapper.* I would not like to be married to a trapper. But I think he died. Now I don't know *where* my sister Nonny has —"

"Betty."

"Yes ma'am."

"I received a call. Someone is holding Ransom and he's in grave danger. We are going now to Turners Rock, because we require Rayford's help."

"Oh, Rayford," says Betty. "Rayford's always so helpful —"

"Now you must shut up, Betty."

Ransom and Stony sit atop the table together, in the pitch-black. The bed is gone. The water is now two feet high and rising quickly.

She says, "Are you thirsty at all?"

"Yes," he says. She opens a bottle of water and passes it to him, and he drinks.

She says, "Have you been able to revisit the past?"

"No. Not really. Is that what you're doing?"

"Uh-uh. I go to the Kingdom."

"Oh. Well, maybe I worry too much."

She says, "There's something I want to tell you."

"OK."

"I'm in love with Jaq."

He draws in a long breath.

But he can't really think about Jaq, because if he thinks of Jaq he'll start to crumble. He only says, "I believe she loves you as well."

"She doesn't," Stony says. "I'm well aware of the hopelessness of my situation. But thank you for saying so. I like hearing your voice. I like talking to you. I could tell you in general about the Kingdom, about the people who live there. Would you like to hear that?"

"Yeah. I'll try to listen. Tell me."

Boris comes out to the Caprice in his robe and opens the car door for Morgana. As she emerges, she murmurs, "Stay with me, Betty." Betty tells Gracie, "Stay here and be a good girl," and follows Morgana inside.

Through the soaring foyer, into the great room with all its spooky bones and fossils.

Rayford crosses to embrace Morgana. "My darlin," he says. "Why do you need me? What's the matter?"

Morgana takes one of the sleek Linley chairs. Betty takes the other. Rayford sits across from them. Boris asks if they'd care for something to drink. But Morgana waves him away and tells Rayford, "I received a message. They have Ransom."

"Who sent it?"

"I don't know, they didn't say. I suppose they want me to simply wait. But I'd like him back *now.*"

"Of course you would."

"So give him to me."

He frowns. "We have to think, darlin. Put our heads together."

"You did hear me, Rayford. What's the point of this charade?"

He gapes at her.

She repeats, "Give me my son."

He doesn't reply. She gives a quick shrug. "All right then — Betty, I don't have my phone. Would you look on yours? Look for the *Savannah Morning News,* then look for the *City Blog:* you'll find Lamar Raskins's home number. Call it. He'll be most pleased to get a scoop on three murders committed by certain Savannah grandees."

"Yes ma'am."

She takes her phone from her jeans pocket.

Rayford sighs. "Awright, Morgana. I believe you."

Morgana makes a sign, and Betty leaves the phone on her lap.

Rayford says, "But Boris gonna scan y'all first, you good with that?"

Boris crosses to a cabinet and produces some kind of device, something like a fat cell phone, and approaches Morgana with it. She won't deign to look at him. She tells

Rayford, "I'm not wearing a wire, you pompous asshole. Does that seem like something I would do?"

Rayford keeps one brow poised. He won't back down.

And after a moment she offers a small contemptuous wave of submission. And stands, and lets Boris pass the wand close to her bosom and around to her back. When he murmurs, "Would you lift your arms?" she has a look of fiery indignation but does what he asks. He scans every inch of her and when he's done, he does the same to Betty.

Then he pockets Betty's phone. Nods to Rayford.

"Awright, then," says Rayford.

She leans forward and says, "Ransom told me you'd tried to point the finger at Rebecca Cressling. I knew that wasn't like you. It was inelegant. Rude. But I kept arguing with myself. No, it couldn't be, I thought. It couldn't be that you'd panicked and tried to deflect suspicion onto poor useless Rebecca. But then tonight, I saw you keeping your distance from Rebecca's table, keeping away from Warren Bledsoe and Swann and all. I'd never seen that. You're always swaggering around and poking your finger at people but not tonight. And when

399

they played 'The Days of Wine and Roses'? Whenever they've played that in the last forty years, you've always raised your eyes to mine. But tonight you were afraid of me. You were afraid I'd see through you, which I do. You've always been utterly transparent to me. Which is why I would never marry you."

He rolls his eyes.

She says, "Does Rebecca have money in this affair?"

"Oh."

"Does she?"

"Lots of folks got money in this."

"Have I?"

He shrugs.

"How much?"

"Fifty grand."

"Oh. Yes. I recall that. An investment opportunity in some . . . offshore island. I wrote you a check."

"I said an island *somewhere.* I never said offshore. I also said it was dicey and I'd keep your investment quiet. Which I will. But yeah, you're very much involved."

"And Rebecca's in for how much?"

"Same."

"And Gerson?"

"Bit more."

"And my son David?"

400

"Not a cent. He wouldn't bite. Cagey boy, your Davy."

"And where's my son Ransom?"

"I got no idea. *I* ain't holdin him."

"One of your partners?"

He doesn't answer.

"Galatas?"

He still won't speak. She says, "Oh for God's sake, Rayford. Either you're candid with me or —"

"Awright, yeah. Galatas."

"Why in God's name did you make a deal with that worm?"

"Swann brought him in. We needed some muscle. All them committees, all them councils, all them damn permits."

"What a fool you are." She considers a moment. "And so what do y'all want now?"

"It ain't what *I* want. It's what —"

"*They* want. I got that. What is it?"

"Well. I could tell you . . . I mean I could tell you what a deal might *look* like."

"So do that."

"Well. Start off, you and your family, you gotta drop everything. Forget everything."

"Ransom goes free?"

"Uh-huh. Nobody wants to hurt him."

"And Stony?"

"Stony goes free too. Nobody wants to hurt nobody. You know, Morgana, y'all just backed folks into a corner. Make this deal, we'll get them safe, do it quick."

She ponders. She says, "Tell me one thing. How much did Guzman want?"

"To bury Stony's evidence? Fifty percent of the deal."

"Good Lord."

"I'd have given it to him. Figgered he had us by the short hairs. I thought, if he lets Stony's stuff out to the world? Would a *vaporized* our resort. And Chief Swann, he got that. He'd a folded. But Galatas? Galatas is a nobody, right? Minor partner. Who expected him to fuss? But he got his back up right away. He said, no no no. He said we're choking. He said we're makin too much of this. He said, That was a camp of runaway slaves. Lasted a few years because nobody cared. 'At's all it was. He said he was gonna turn Stony. It was gonna be easy. He'd dealt with dozens like her. He wa'n't gonna hurt her, he wouldn't have to. Jes' lean a little. And offer to move all them bones respectfully. And give her money, lot a money, get her a position at the college, pull strings. He said, Calm down, boys."

Rayford falls silent for a moment.

Morgana prompts him. "So you went with this plan . . ."

"Uh-huh. And Swann found that idiot

from Valdosta. He screwed up with Stony at Peep's, and wound up killin Luke. And then Galatas pulled that shit with leaving Luke at the Gooze's house, framin the Gooze. Thought he was smart. He thinks he's *playin* this town. He tells me he's got Stony, he's holdin her, and he's gonna . . . *persuade* her to turn over the treasure."

"But he hasn't done that," says Morgana, "has he?"

"But he keeps promising. He keeps sayin, any day now, she gonna crack. Meanwhile he's 'taking care a things.' I know he had Billy Sugar killed — he didn't tell me in so many words, but I know. And he had the Gooze strung up. And he was threatening Jaq and Ransom. I kept telling him, they're immune. But they kept askin questions, and I could see they were pissin him off. He was goin nuts, an I had no way to protect 'em. I got that guy from Pooler to go to the courthouse, talk to Willou, 'cause I thought she could shut Jaq down. But it didn't do no good at all. And then, last night at the Ball, Galatas tells me he's had enough of Stony, and enough of Jaq and Ransom. Said it's time to put the real squeeze on. So here we are."

"Here we are," she echoes.

"So what'll it be, Morgana? We make that deal?"

"I don't know, I need to think."

"You can't. No time."

"Don't you tell me what I can or can't do. If you hurt Ransom, it's true I'll lose, but so will you. You'll fry. Murder, kidnapping, extortion, and Galatas will fry too, and Swann, and Rebecca and whoever else you've entangled in this knot of snakes. And knowing that, with that leverage, did you think I'd just *surrender*?"

That infuriates him. "Morgana! You don't *see*? Galatas and his boys, they're holding a gun to your boy's head."

"Then tell them to use it. Kill him. Do whatever the fuck you need to. But *I* need to think and I need to use the bathroom. Stay with me now, Betty."

She walks out of the room, Betty scuttling after her, trying to keep up.

Jaq waits for Galatas in the rain, at the portal to the storm drains. She's taken the gun from her bike box, and her headlamp, and left the bike itself in the bushes near Wheaton Street. She's walked down the railroad tracks and then along this path, and arrived at this dismal gray concrete cylinder. Now she crouches behind a hedge of bamboo, lowers her head, looks out from her hood, and waits.

It's five in the morning.

The rain hammers away. Spring frogs shout and shout, and the racket exhausts her, and there's that gaping emptiness inside her and her fear.

A flash of lightning.

Another flash. Another. More.

She loses track of time.

Then comes the glimmer of a light. A headlamp, floating up the path.

She crouches as low as she can. Watching the light as it nears. The tread of heavy boots. A lightning flash catches his profile. Galatas. Then the darkness slams down with a crash of thunder.

There's one scoop of light, from his head-lamp: she sees him approach the portal. He fiddles with the padlock. Swings open the slanted door, steps in. His light descends; he must be going down a ladder. She touches her forehead to be sure of her own lamp. The gun is in her hand, loaded. She comes out into the open and steps up to the concrete cylinder, the open door, and looks down. His light is below at the bottom of the ladder. He sets off into a tunnel and instantly the light fades.

It's nearly pitch-black down there, and

she can't climb down the ladder with this pistol in her hand. And the anorak's pockets are too small. If she puts it into the belt of her jeans, it might slip out and he'll hear it clattering against the rungs of the ladder, and come back and kill her. But there's no other way. So into the belt it goes, and she swings onto the ladder and descends. As gently as she can. At the bottom she steps into water and sucks in her breath. Cold water, up over her ankle. She takes a long breath, and swallows the shock.

Takes the gun in hand again and follows the glow of that lamp.

She's in a tunnel that is eight feet high and seems to slope slightly downward. Pushing through that rainwater. Trying to be as quiet as she can, but to move quietly means moving slowly. She's losing ground. The glow of his headlamp is fading. If she wants to stay with him, she'll have to pick up her pace. But with every step deeper into the drains, the water rises, and she can hear herself sloshing. What saves her is that he makes a lot of noise himself, kicking with his heavy boots. That covers for her. But if he ever stops moving, he'll hear her.

If he does stop, she thinks, if he ever pauses and his light turns back this way, I can't wait. I have to shoot right away. Aim for just below that lamp and shoot.

Recalling what Grampa Fred taught her, when she was twelve years old and he took her quail hunting: Aim low. *Squeeze* the trigger.

But she has only three bullets in this gun. And who knows if she loaded them right?

The water is above her knees now, and it has a current; it's all going downslope and it pulls her along. The tunnel seems endless. There are high grilles on the left and on the right, pouring more water in all the time, and the cold is like pincers on her calves and stealing her strength, and still she has to keep striding forward, chasing that lamp. And every second struggling to keep quiet. Her anorak raincoat is hanging down, slapping the water behind her as she pushes forward, and anyway it's soaked and useless against the cold. So she loses it. Shrugs it off her shoulders and tugs it down at the sleeves until it falls behind her.

She's cold but no colder than she was.

On and on. Keep quiet. Keep up.

But then she has a thought. Maybe turn back?

Yes. Back.

That's smarter, isn't it? Go to Gram's? Gram can marshal a lot of folks in a hurry, and Betty can bring them port wine and they can wait together for good news. Why didn't I think of that in the first place?

Why am I following Galatas by myself?

But if she doesn't follow him, and if Ransom and Stony are locked in some room down here, how will they ever be found? Galatas won't tell. He'll just deny and smile. And this water will keep rising and they'll drown, and what is she supposed to do, what's the best course, she can't think, she's worn out, she's freezing, she doesn't know what to do —

Something changes in the sound of Galatas's strides.

It's gone up a note. And sounds fuller, why?

Has he come to some wider chamber?

Then suddenly his light veers to the right and is swallowed by blackness.

She rushes after him, fast as she can, she can't lose him. A moment later she herself comes to the big chamber. Vaulted brick ceilings. Glimmer of light from above, twenty feet up. There's just enough to see that there are many different tunnels leading off from this chamber.

Down one of them is the glow of his headlamp.

She follows. Deeper, up to her thighs, as quick as she can. But the current is strong behind her and keeps her unbalanced, shoving her forward. She holds out her hand to steady herself against the wall. She can feel the brickwork, the slimy brickwork, and something crawls onto her fingers and up her arm. And it's not just one creature, it's many creatures. She nearly cries out, and shakes her arm, and slips and stumbles. Pitches forward and splashes into the cold, cold water. Goes under, all of her. Even the pistol.

She brings her head up and gasps. The water running off her hair. She stands.

And suddenly, up ahead, the light goes out.

He must have heard her.

Silence, but for the swirl of the water flowing past.

If that light comes on again and it's aimed this way, she has to shoot. Will this gun even work when it's wet? But she has to pull the trigger the moment the beam is in her eye.

But the light doesn't come. The tunnel stays dark.

She thinks, he's coming for me. Through the dark. He's walking straight toward me. It's so dark I'll never see him. He'll reach out and snatch the gun from me and then I'll belong to him.

She tries to step back. But the flow is so

strong, she nearly falls again.

Maybe I could just shoot straight ahead into the black, maybe I'd hit him. Maybe he's standing right in front of me right now.

Then she sees another glow. A bluish light, coming from the left side of the wall up ahead.

She strains to see.

Galatas is standing up there, just where he was before. He seems to have opened some kind of little door in the tunnel wall, a door to a kind of cabinet, and now he's turned something on; he's looking into a blue glow. A screen? It's like the blue-gray of a TV screen, and his face is caught in the glow. He's intent on the screen.

He hasn't heard Jaq at all. Doesn't know she's here.

She draws a deep breath. And then her leg cramps from the cold and she reaches a hand to steady herself, but the wall is closer than she thinks; she makes a little slap.

He switches on his headlamp, and turns to her.

"Who's there? Oh. Jesus. Is that *Jaq*?"

She stands there shivering, holding the gun. All she can see is the light shining at her.

"Hello, Jaq. What are you doing here? Where's Ransom?"

And then, because she doesn't speak, he says, "Maybe don't aim that gun at me? Jaq? If you'd put that gun down please. We got a tip that Ransom is down here. He's being held down here. By somebody. This here is the security box, I'm checking all the cameras, but I'm not seeing him."

His headlamp seems to move a little. It floats to one side. Maybe he's taken it off his head? If he's holding it away from him, what can she aim for? She reaches up for the button on her own headlamp, but pushing it doesn't do anything. The water's killed it.

And now he seems to be coming toward her.

Coming very slowly, but coming.

He says, "Jaq, I really need you to lower that, OK? I understand. You're scared. That makes sense. But really, I'm here to protect you. I trust you and I know you're not going to use the gun, I know you won't hurt me. And I won't hurt you. You can trust me, OK, and I'll trust you."

So gently he comes. Gliding, gliding. Not ten feet away and she can see him a little now. He's holding the lamp to one side. She sees the outline of him first, then his face. Just faintly. His kind eyes. "You're so fearless to come down here. Jaq. I can't believe

411

you came here in the dark. And you look so cold, you're shaking, we gotta get you warm."

His voice bringing forth her tears as it always does.

She lowers the gun.

"I truly trust you," he says.

She hangs her head. He gently reaches for her.

She takes one deep breath, raises the gun, and pulls the trigger.

The sound in the tunnel is deafening. The headlamp drops from his fingers into the water. He shrieks: "YOU BITCH! YOU FUCKING LITTLE BLACK WHORE!"

Then he's quiet for a moment, breathing heavily. Searching with one hand for the headlamp. The light of it comes up through the water, casting a wobbly glow on his face. He's groaning. But saying in a faint voice, "It's OK. I'm all right, Jaq, I know you're scared but I really am on your side and we'll get through this —"

He leaps at her.

Springs out of the water like a living demon and grabs her arm, and his other hand goes to her throat and squeezes, and she falls backward into the water and he's above her: they're thrashing and he's squeezing her throat and the strength is going out of her. But she still has that gun. And she pulls the trigger and the shot is thunderous even under water. She feels him shuddering. He still has her by the throat but his grip loosens a little. She struggles, slides out from under him, heaves into the air. Fills her lungs. Grabs him by his hair and pulls him close and puts the gun against his face and fires again, and there's another clap of thunder and she feels the fragments of him flying against her.

She claws at his hand, gets it off her throat.

He falls backward. Sinks under the water and she draws another breath, coughs and breathes again. Stumbles toward the headlamp, which is still underwater and still glowing.

But the moment she touches it, it dies.

Darkness settles in.

Now there's only one source of light in this tunnel, the faint glow from that monitor, that TV screen he was checking.

She goes toward it.

There they are on the screen, Ransom and Stony. Huddled together on what looks like a raft, but maybe it's a table. Just inches clear of rising water. Boxes and bottles float around them. Ransom with his arms around poor shivering Stony. She says, "Ransom, can you hear me? Stony? *RANSOM!*

413

STONY!"

But they can't hear.

The keypad has three buttons with incomprehensible hieroglyphics. She tries one button: the screen goes dark. Touches it again, it flickers back to life. Another button, another view of the room. A third: another view.

Still they can't hear her and she can't hear them.

She scrolls through the views again. And in the third view, the one from behind their heads, she discerns the outline of a door.

She touches the wall beside her. An insect crawls onto her hand, but she steels herself and leaves her fingers on that wall, and starts to walk, slowly, through the blackness, running her fingers along that wall and keeping her touch as light as she can because she's feeling for a crack, for any pause in this wall, while she peers downward for any light. She walks until she comes to a hint, right *here,* of a seam. Maybe. Yes. A vertical seam, and when she peers down through the water, she can see a faintly glowing line of light, light coming from beneath a door.

She feels for a door handle. Finds none.

But there is, three inches in from the seam, a slightly raised coin of metal. When she nudges it, it slides to one side and reveals a keyhole.

Keys. She'll need that fucker's keys.

She kicks her way back down the tunnel, counting her steps as she goes, back to the monitor and farther, stepping carefully, probing the water in front of her with each step till her knee encounters Galatas. He hasn't floated far yet because he's floating facedown and his feet are dragging on the tunnel floor. She reaches around and finds his front pocket, and puts her hand in. Nothing. Tries the other pocket. No. Keep the despair under control. Has to pat the dead man's butt, but the back pockets have nothing but a wallet and she slides her hand around to his front and there it is! — hanging from his belt. A set of keys. She unhooks them. Careful, she thinks, you're shivering and frozen but you must not drop them, if you drop them you might never find them again.

In the darkness she counts her steps back, feeling the wall. The seam, the thread of light, the keyhole. But terror and the cold are making her shake. She needs both hands to pick out a key. Make sure she's holding it right and slide it into the hole. It won't go. Of course not, it's a house key. Feels the ridges of the next one. Another house key.

Next one is a car key. Palpating them one by one until she comes upon a key that's heavy and oddly shaped, and this she holds to the keyhole, and pushes, and it slides in. Turns it, the door clicks and she leans against it, and the water in the tunnel helps her and the door opens.

A little room. On a wooden table sit Ransom and Stony.

Staring at her. Ransom says, "Jaq?"

Stony says, "Holy shit."

"What the fuck are you doing here?" says Ransom.

Jaq smiles. "I followed him. Galatas. I killed him. We gotta go."

Ransom pushes himself off the table, then helps Stony.

Jaq says, "We do have a problem, I think."

"What's that?"

"No light out there." She points to the light on the ceiling above. "Can we take that with us?"

"It's bolted down," says Ransom.

"Well OK," says Jaq. "The drains are filling, so we better just go. I mean there's a few tricky turns so we might get lost and we better stay together. Stony, you're not scared of the dark, are you?"

"No. I don't mind the dark at all."

"We'll get you warm soon," says Jaq. She

recognizes her tone of false chipperness: it's the tone Morgana uses when she's making you do something you don't really want to. "Shall we start, then?"

The water keeps rising with every step they take. Now it's above Stony's waist and they're fighting the current, striding into the pitch-black unknown, so Stony has to take giant kick-steps, and though Jaq and Ransom are right there holding her hands and pulling her forward, she's starting to give out. Her legs feel like tin legs, stiff and cold and bloodless. They pass gushing pipes in the darkness, more water keeps blasting into this tunnel and the level goes up and up, and she's only moving because Jaq and Ransom are making her move.

And they're nearly as worn out as she is.

Jaq says, "Maybe we missed a turn back there."

"But we're going against the current," says Ransom, "so this should be right. We must be going uphill."

They're silent for a while. The rhythm of their march.

Then Jaq says, "Wait, look. That's light up there. Do you see? It's pitch-black behind us but up ahead is a little lighter, you see that?"

Stony's too weak to turn her head around to compare. She takes Jaq's word for it.

"So come on," Jaq says. "Hurry."

Ransom says, "Stony, can you go faster?"

She squeezes their hands as if to say, *sure*. But that's a lie and they must know it. It's true that as they go the faint light grows stronger. She can even discern their silhouettes now, Jaq on her left and Ransom on her right. But the current keeps getting crueler and crueler, every step feels like climbing a mountain, and if they weren't gripping her hands so tightly she'd gladly slip back into the dark.

She says, "Guys."

"What?" says Jaq. "We can't stop."

"Listen to me. About the Kingdom. I have to tell you where the treasure is."

"I know where it is," says Jaq. "It's a website. Your LiDAR, I saw it."

"You did? You saw it? Really?"

"Yeah. The Musician showed me."

"Then it's safe?"

Such a relief flowing into her heart.

But Ransom says, "No. It's not safe at all, *no*. You're *not* gonna give up. You have to get out of here or they'll erase the Kingdom. You hear me? Look. That light? That's *sunlight*."

And it is: faint sunlight. They slog forward

for another five minutes and then step out of the tunnel into a chamber of some kind. A big vaulted brick room. The water's just as high as it was in the tunnel, and the flow is nearly as fierce. But at the far end of this room, there's a ladder. Going up right out of the water. Stony can't see the top of the ladder, but it's illuminated by a soft glow of daylight.

"My God," says Jaq.

Stony shuts her eyes. She thinks she'll never reach that ladder; it's far beyond her strength. And even if she did make it, she could never climb it. She's thinking, I could go to the Kingdom instead. They'll be in the river today, all the kids, they'll be hauling the big net through the tidal river to catch crayfish and crabs, and I can be with them. It's time to be with them. I've done what I have to. The Kingdom's fate is with Jaq and Ransom now.

I'm going to let go, she thinks.

But then Ransom is at her ear and he's very loud. "No fucking way," he says. "The Kingdom needs you and we're going up that thing, we're all together so wake up, Stony."

Percy Mulker, fourteen years old, Black, is walking to church. He's going to the early morning service at Bolton Street Baptist

419

because his grandmother insists on his attendance. He's walking alone. He's dressed in his Sunday best. He's already bored. The day is bright blue and sunny but there still are big puddles from last night's storm, which he has to walk around. He's on the sidewalk, on Price Street between East Bolton Street and East Bolton Lane, looking up because he's passing a skinny tree with little birds like sparrows. They seem to be a family and they're quarreling, and flitting about, and they amuse him.

Then he passes that tree, and he's about to cross Bolton Lane when he hears a voice.

"Hey, kid!"

A weird echoey ghost-voice.

He looks to his left. Just Bolton Lane, nobody stirring. Looks the other way. Parked cars, quiet houses. He turns back to the little tree with the sparrows. They're still fussing.

So where did that voice come from?

"Here."

He spins around.

"We're right *here*."

The *here* echoes.

"Down," says the voice. "Look down."

Percy does. There's a drain hole at the corner, a drain hole maybe a foot high and three feet wide. Just a black drain hole.

"Yeah. You see us?"

Fingers come waggling out of the drain hole. Then he sees eyes. Glimmering in the dark, looking up at him.

Two pairs of eyes, side by side in that hole.

The eyes of mud-ghouls. He cries out in horror.

The voice says, "Hey, could you help us? We can't get out."

Percy considers running. Running seems the sensible thing. But he finds himself asking, "Um . . . how . . . how d'you get down there?"

Now the voice of a young woman. "Listen, we're trapped down here, OK? We're on a ledge, we're like twenty feet up and we're cold and we're tired. OK? Stony, stay with us, stay awake."

Another pair of eyes come open. Now it's three pairs of mud-ghoul eyes that Percy's facing. And the young woman says, "All we need is a phone. Do you have a phone?"

He does. But he's loath to surrender it to the spirit realm.

"I'm sorry," he says. "I can't give it to you."

"That's OK," says the voice. "Could you just call a number?"

Betty is walking Gracie around on Rayford's

big lawn, hoping the dog will pee, but Gracie keeps getting distracted. First by the big flock of turkeys, then by the smell of the river. Then by the sun when it burns through the river mist. Then by a kettle of big black birds circling overhead.

Finally, though, she squats and takes care of her business.

Then Betty leads her back to the Caprice, and sits in the driver's seat with the door open. Gracie sits on the grass. Morgana is in the passenger seat, staring forward, as though she's taking some long journey.

Finally she draws a breath and says, "You know every day in Savannah you make compromises. Mostly just little shitty compromises. Ugly flowers in your flower spray to mollify the mean old dowagers. Things like that. But sometimes big things. You keep thinking, I'll just make one more compromise here and I'll be done. But there will be more compromises tomorrow. And you *have* to make them. If you don't make them, you'll be erased. There were lots of people, maybe millions, who didn't make the compromises, but they were erased."

"Yes ma'am," says Betty.

"If you do compromise, you're a coward. If you don't, you're a fool."

"Yes."

"Ransom will disown me. Jaq will never speak to me."

Betty doesn't answer that.

"Still," says Morgana, "I don't see another path."

She gets out of the car and starts toward the house.

Then a phone rings.

It's not Betty's phone. It's Morgana's. It's in her purse, on the console, where she left it.

She comes back and hunts through her purse, and answers.

"Yes. . . . Who? . . . Say again? . . . Percy? . . . Wait a minute, Percy, say that again? . . . Yes . . . Yes . . . Yes, tell me *exactly* where you are." And she's walking off on the great lawn toward the birdbath fountain, still speaking into the phone, and the turkeys watch her, and Boris watches her from the front door.

A half minute later she goes striding toward the great house, calling, *"Betty!* I need you *now."*

Betty shuts Gracie in the car and goes running after Morgana.

When Betty enters the great room, she sees that Morgana already has her arms above her head, letting Boris scan her again, and she's telling Rayford, "Well, I'm informed that my position has improved a bit."

"I heard sort of the same," he says.

"Really? What did you hear?"

He says, "That right now the Department of Stormwater is removing a manhole cover at the corner of Price and Bolton Lane."

"Yes." She turns to Boris and says, "You done yet?"

He nods, and starts on Betty.

Morgana sits. "And Ransom is safe. And Jaq and Stony are safe. And Galatas is dead. And Rayford, I'm afraid you're fucked."

Rayford says, "I'm glad they're safe. Truly."

Betty's watching his eyes.

He keeps his gaze locked on Morgana and he says, "But you know, if Galatas is really dead, Ransom will go down for it. You know that. They'll come after him like the hounds of hell. Ransom Musgrove, the crazy man with anger issues? The rich hobo? Why was he even allowed outta jail after what he did to his brother? And after he killed Billy Sugar in a fit of rage? They'll find six homeless folks who'll testify to the bad blood between those two. And then he kills a policeman, a virtuous man — lures him down to the storm drains and murders him. And now Ransom's rich mother wants to set him free? And will concoct any bizarre story to bring that about? My, my, the corruption in this town."

Betty waits for Morgana to raise her eyes. She doesn't.

"And Jaq," Rayford goes on. "What'll they do to *her*? Jaysus. I mean, all over social media, think about it. Was she just workin for Guzman, or was she fuckin him? Was she runnin a con on him, she and her gram? Was she just datin a drug dealer, or was she dealing herself? Was she —"

Morgana makes a gesture then. Waves her hand in front of her eyes, like a windshield wiper, cutting him off.

He falls silent. Waits. Betty watching her. Morgana is reading the knuckles on her hand, the brown spots, the veins. Running her finger along one of those veins, as though following a blue river on a brown map. Lost in thought.

Finally she raises her eyes.

"I don't underestimate you, Rayford."

"Good," he says.

"I grant you could crush us. Yet not without pain to yourself. I'm not without resources. The FBI will be looking into the storm drains, into Galatas's business. Massive ugliness will turn up. Your name will be woven into everything. Galatas was a sloppy narcissist; so are you all. You'll come out looking like slobs and fools and criminals."

She stops. She glares at him. He glares back.

Finally he says, "So do you have a proposal?"

She lets it hang for a moment.

Then she says, "You want a deal? You want a deal from me? But not just from me. You'd need my whole family to sign on, wouldn't you? And that's a great reach. My daughters, yes, they're perhaps persuadable. Even Ransom. I hate to say this, but I do believe . . . though it will require an infinite amount of very precise . . . pressures . . . I do believe I could deliver him to the cause of silence."

Rayford nods.

She goes on: "As for Matilda Stone, I don't know. I've never met the woman. I have some thoughts. But I assure you of this. Jaqueline will never deal. Never. You'll just to have to live with that. She may not scuttle a bargain if she knows that speaking out will mortally wound the people she loves. She'll leave this town and won't speak to any of us again. But she'll never sign on. After a year or two, she may decide to blow the whistle. Or after ten years. You just won't know. Whatever pain it causes her, and that pain will be incalculable, she will not deal."

Rayford lowers his eyes.

"So," she says. "A proposal? You want my price? OK, I'll name my price, but it will strike you as fabulously expensive. I assure you it's cheap. If you so much as blink, I'll walk out that door. Bring me down as you threaten — you'll bring yourself down as well. That will have to be my consolation."

Now at last Rayford speaks.

"Just tell me what you want, Morgana."

EPILOGUE:
TO SEND THE FOX OR NOT

A year and a half later, on a brilliant day in October, two hundred guests — one for each of the King's subjects — come walking in a loose procession, under oak trees and soaring frigate birds, to the edge of a field on Montmillan Island. They've been brought in a flotilla of boats, led by Cap'n Stan's eighteen-foot fishing boat. And it's also Stan himself, with an old-fashioned admiral's hat worn Blackbeard-style, who leads the walking procession. A marching band plays Geechee-inflected ragtime, and the crowd winds out onto the cleared field. Near a cluster of excavation tarps, rows of folding chairs have been set out. There's a makeshift stage for certain distinguished guests. The folks spend an hour drinking champagne and eating wild-boar sand-wiches and hoppin' john, and listening to the band. Then they take their seats.

The news crews start their cameras.

Willou steps to the lectern and commences.

"This is a sacred site. This is a sacred island. This place is our American Masada. These hallowed grounds must always be protected and preserved; for here, right *here,* a great struggle for liberty was fought, some two hundred and forty years ago —"

From the woods nearby comes a great caterwauling of dogs. They seem to be chasing some doomed thing. Willou holds up a moment, and rolls her eyes, and says, "Um, Stan, I think your pooches are looking for lunch." Everyone laughs. Presently the barking fades into the distance.

Willou then brings to the lectern Diane Rawlings, the chair of the Emory University Department of Anthropology, who introduces all the other distinguished guests on the stage. Anthropologists and archaeologists from all around the country, as well as a congresswoman, a governor, a Supreme Court justice, and the pastor of the First African Baptist Church.

Next comes Arthur Haverty, the assistant director of the Kingdom of Montmillan Foundation.

He tells the story of the Kingdom. How it was created in the 1780s, its triumphs and tribulations, and how it came to be rediscovered. He speaks with great passion and the crowd is enthralled. Then he mentions some of the donations that have made possible these excavations and the proposed museum:

A gift from Mrs. Rebecca Cressling for $400,000, in memory of William Dennings, aka Billy Sugar.

A bequest from the late Reynolds Montmillan Hollis, "Monty," who generously willed his entire estate of $2,000,000 to the Kingdom of Montmillan Foundation.

A donation of $250,000, in memory of Sharper and Nancy, from Gerson Hale.

An anonymous gift, honoring the memory of Luke Kitchens, for $3,000,000 (there's a rumor that this has come from Rayford Porter — who is not present today).

Finally, a gift from Morgana Musgrove for $500,000 in the name of her granddaughter Jaqueline Walker (the mention of whose name brings up a huge cheer — but Jaq is not here either).

The governor of Georgia rises now and reads his prepared remarks. They are droning and dull and everyone drifts off.

Then a fox comes out of the woods.

The fox is pursued by three dogs. It scurries over the stage and into the audience, with the dogs on its tail, and there are shrieks and chairs upended and flying dogs and squeals and cursing and laughter. Till the fox darts back into the woods again — making a clean getaway.

When everything settles, the governor resumes his remarks.

While he speaks though, Ransom, sitting in the third row, is troubled. He has a decision to make, a difficult one. He managed to record that interlude with the fox on his phone; he got it all, and while everyone was recovering he snuck in a rewatch, and he knows that video's amazing and now he has to decide whether to send it or not.

Everything else today, he knows, will be posted publicly. The speeches and the toasts and all will soon be on the internet.

But only he has that thing with the fox.

Betty, who's sitting next to him, takes his hand and squeezes. He knows what she thinks: she thinks he's brooding over the deal. Because he's always brooding over the deal. He submitted to the deal, but was the deal worth it? No one was ever really punished; no one knows what happened. The chief of police suddenly resigned and left the state. A much-liked police detective went missing: months later his carcass washed ashore on the Savannah River near Fort Pulaski. Animals had chewed on it but there was evidence of gunshot wounds: maybe he'd been shot by drug dealers. Savannah carried on.

On the other side of the ledger, Ransom was not crushed and Jaq was not crushed, and there was no resort built and instead *this* happened: the restoration of the Kingdom of Montmillan.

Is this worth it?

The question is always looping around in his brain. But not so much now. Now he's mostly trying to decide whether to send the fox or not.

And as he ponders this, the governor of Georgia introduces the executive director of the Kingdom of Montmillan project, Matilda Stone.

Everyone stands. They applaud and cheer her for a long time. Also, all the folks onstage want to embrace her, so it takes her quite a while to get to the lectern. But at last she gets there and unfolds her speech, which shakes in her hands, and the audience finally falls silent, and she puts on her reading glasses and begins: "There was . . . There was one . . . very dark . . . time —"

Someone shouts, "We can't hear!"

Whereupon the pastor of the First African Baptist Church steps up and adjusts her microphone and murmurs, "Stony, speak up just a little?"

She murmurs, "Well, I'm a little scared of all the cameras —" and *that* does get picked up by the mike, and the folks give her another wave of applause to bolster her.

She draws a deep breath. She reads:

"There was one very dark time, not too long ago, that now seems to me like a dream. During that time, I was sustained by the love, and the kindness, and the laughter, of the loyal soldiers of the King of England and their families, who lived here, long ago, in what we now call the Kingdom of Montmillan. Sharper, and Nancy, and others whose names we know from militia records and trial records: Jemmy, and Juliett, and Lewis, and Cupid, and Fortune, and Chicheum, and Peter, and Little Coke, and Patience, and Joe, and Betty, and Dembo, and Pope, and Peggy, and Little Sharper, and Frank, and Dick, and Fatima, and another Nancy, and Hannah, and Phyllis. There were also hundreds of others whose names we don't know. They all lived right here. They lived free. In my opinion they were the only free people to ever live in the State of Georgia. The rest of us are required to submit, in one way or another, to the yoke of powerful interests. But these folks wouldn't do that. They made a choice — to

433

be free even if that meant almost certain death. And in my opinion they are *still* free and still alive in this Kingdom, and they still possess a great treasure, which is their story.

"And when I say they're still alive I don't mean they're ghosts.

"You can't put 'em on a ghost tour. They're not bits of floating ectoplasm. They're not glimmering performers in some spiritualist, ritualist, Lost Cause séance or mummers' show designed to amuse us, to distract us from Savannah's brutal crimes. No, when I say they're alive, I mean they live within us. Because now we know their story. And as we keep uncovering that tale, as we tease it from the earth and puzzle it bit by bit out of old documents, as we cherish that narrative of unbelievable courage, all the people of the Kingdom arise within us and flourish. That's what I mean when I say they live.

"Now let me say thank you to everyone who loves them as I do, who have started us on this road of renewal and celebration and freedom. Thank you to my mother, who warned me ceaselessly about the snakes and panthers and wild boar I'd encounter here, and since she'd never actually been here before today, she can't be blamed for not knowing that the real menace is the bugs. The mortal threat, Mom, as you'll find out when the sun gets just a little lower, is the no-see-ums.

"I mean, they're coming. So let us get out of here. And let me wrap this up if I may by thanking just one other person: someone who can't be here today, but whose sheer love for life, whose bliss, whose hatred for injustice presides over us now, and always will. Jaqueline Walker — oh Jaq, you're here too."

At the New York Film Academy in Manhattan, down in Battery Park, Jaq loads up the back of an Uber with her equipment — lights, filters, batteries, tripods — and gets in, and the driver heads toward an address on Bushwick Avenue in Brooklyn.

He says, "OK to take the Brooklyn Bridge?"

"Yeah," she says, "I don't know. Sure."

His name, she sees on her phone, is Ludovic. After a while she says, "I like your name. How do you say it?"

"With a *k,*" he says. "Ludo-VEEK. What's your name?"

"Jaq. Also with a *k.* Short for Jaqueline."

"Hi, Jaq," he says.

"Hi, Ludovic. Where are you from?"

"Romania. Little town in the mountains. Poplaca."

"You ever go back there?"

"One time. Show my kids. Old farms, beautiful."

She likes how he lingers on each syllable of *beautiful.* "But you wouldn't live there again?"

He shakes his head. "Ha! Too small."

They drive over the Brooklyn Bridge. It's a cold gray day. There's a message tone on her phone and she tenses up. Just don't look, she thinks. But the chime hovers in the air and won't fade. She gazes out at the barges on the East River, and tries to think about her homework, and about a boy she's seeing (though not, she's afraid, for much longer), and about what wine she'll have with dinner. But finally she makes a little defeated gesture with her shoulders and draws out her phone.

Ransom.

That familiar blasted feeling in her gut.

He's sent her a video. And she knows she shouldn't watch it but also knows she'll give in eventually, so what's the point of tormenting herself? Still. She does torment herself. She looks out at the city streets and tells herself: Mistake to look. Terrible mistake. Don't be a fool. Mistake, mistake, you're an idiot. She thinks that over and over again for about two minutes and then surrenders.

The video runs maybe fourteen seconds.

A crowd of people are in folding chairs before a wooden stage in a field. Of course she knows what they're there for. She's thought of little else for a year and a half but this coming day, and now here it is. Somebody is up onstage giving a speech. But the camera isn't focusing on the speaker. The camera is following a quick little animal, a cat or something, that has come out of the field, and is trying to escape some dogs who are hot on its heels. It jumps over the stage and runs right into the audience. It disappears under chairs on the far side of the center aisle, but you can tell vaguely where it is because the people there are screaming and jumping onto chairs to get out of its way, and the dogs barrel down the rows and make hairpin turns and bark and snap and nothing will stop them.

Suddenly the animal appears again.

Right in the center aisle, right *there*. Coming straight toward the camera and it's a fox! Is what it is. It's a red fox with a bushy red tail, and it runs right under the camera and everyone on this row lifts their feet, which gives it a clear path, and the dogs come right behind it. Jaq knows these dogs of course. The first is Cap'n Stan's "jumpy" dog, leaping over people's laps. The next is Stan's redbone, bounding within inches of the camera lens. Then here comes Gracie, howling as she crashes along, and Betty who is sitting next to the camera-holder tries to tackle her, which is insane: Gracie twists in her arms like a marlin on a line, and frees herself and goes careening down the row, and chairs and people are falling every which way, and amid the screeching is a lot of laughter; particularly she hears Ransom's laugh, which is loud and close: "HA HA HA HA!" because of course he's the one's recording this, and each HA *pierces* her, each is a dagger thrust into her heart. How can she endure this loneliness? There's a glimpse of Boiled Liza. There's Stony's mother. There's Marcel the cook, on his ass, laughing. And then the camera steadies and we're watching over the shoulders of the crowd as the fox shoots back into the woods. Jaq is furious. How could he have done this? How could he have sent this to her? What the fuck was he thinking?

The taxi comes to the end of the bridge and gets onto the BQE. Takes the exit onto Myrtle Avenue and follows that a long way.

Though maybe she half-forgives him

because how could he *not* have sent it?

Then Ludovic asks her, "And you? Where you from?"

She says, "I'm from Savannah, Georgia."

"Oh. I been there."

"Yeah?"

"Spent a day there. My wife and kids. Going to Florida."

"Did you like it?"

"Oh yeah." He pauses, remembering. "Lots a ghosts."

"Did you take a ghost tour?"

"Yeah yeah. But after it's over my kid says to me, Dad, I don't think them ghosts were all *real*."

She smiles.

He asks, "You ever go back home? Back to Savannah?"

"No."

"Too small?"

And then, because this man is a stranger so why not say it, and because this day has been so brutal and her thirst for justice is still like a pit in her stomach and she can't imagine how she'll survive another hour of this, let alone another year or the rest of her life, because she needs to speak *something,* she says: "No, I mean, it's just, there was kind of a corrupt deal going down and I was supposed to, I don't know. Wink? I

439

don't know. Everybody else did, so why not me? But I wouldn't, so. So I had to get out of there. And I think I can never go back."

"Man," he says. "That's rough."

"Yeah."

She wants to watch that video again. She looks down at her lap. There it is, waiting.

With her thumb she deletes it.

Then abruptly draws her camera from its bag and says, "Sorry, I'm just upset today. Could I record *you*?"

"Me. For what?"

"Tell me about your little town?"

He glances at her in the rearview mirror. She's trying to keep her face behind the camera, but it must be evident to him that she's crying.

Though he's polite enough to not mention it. He says, "You mean Poplaca?"

"Yes," she says. "What memory of Poplaca is the most vivid to you? What is it that gives you the most bliss?"

But she can't hold the camera steady any longer.

"Jaq?" he says. "Are you OK?"

A FEW HISTORICAL NOTES

Chapter One:
Some Hideous Compromise

- The founder of Georgia, General James Oglethorpe — truly a jewel of a man, a rare nonmonster in Savannah history — intended for Wright Square to be consecrated to the memory of Tomochichi, the Yamacraw chief who had befriended the new colony (thus assuring the quick destruction of his tribe, though neither he nor Oglethorpe imagined that). But in the 1870s the local Lost Causers decided to move Tomochichi's grave from the center of the square to the corner and replace it with a monument to the man who ran the company that built the railroad that carried the enslaved people from the coast to Middle Georgia and the cotton back to Savannah. Tomochichi got the rock. I don't mean

441

to disparage that rock. It's a nice one, black and weighty, and if you run around it forty times, chanting softly as you go, "Tomochichi, mico of the Yamacraw, will you give me what I seek?" then he will grant your wish. My friend Edgar Oliver and his sister Helen used to run around the stone all the time when they were children. The kids mostly stay away now because the homeless people creep them out.

- Alice Riley was hung in the square in 1733, for the crime of murdering her "master," who had brutalized her and many others for years. The ghost tours that I've overheard often skip over the brutality and go straight for what a witch she was. I don't know why they do that. She wasn't a witch. Also she probably didn't kill him. The real murderer was her husband: a man named Richard White. Former tour guide Elena Gormley tells of the witchification of Alice Riley in this sharp-edged article from Vice: https://www.vice.com/en/article/3dxmy5/ghost-tours-turn-womens-abuse-into-family-friendly-entertainment.

- There is resistance to the relentless fictions of ghost tours and antebellum

442

mansion tours in Savannah, and this resistance seems to be growing. See Tiya Miles's *Tales from the Haunted South: Dark Tourism and Memories of Slavery from the Civil War Era.* Ariel Felton, in *The Washington Post,* tells of the Black tour guides and historians who are sharing Savannah's true stories; these guides include Vaughnette Goode-Walker, Patt Gunn, Amir Jamal Touré, and Karen Wortham. Felton's excellent piece can be found here: https://www.washingtonpost.com/life style/travel/savannah-african-american-history-guides/2020/11/25/61ac0eb4-1933-11eb-aeec-b93bcc29a01b_story .html.

- I've barely scratched the surface here of the monstrosities committed by Charles Augustus Lafayette Lamar. In the 1850s Lamar was a narcissistic bully and one of the richest men in Savannah. He had a dream: he'd provoke the South into seceding, then conquer Mexico and Cuba and South America, and give birth to a new Empire of Slavery, which he'd populate with millions upon millions of freshly enslaved Africans, all of them working and sweating and dying under the iron rule of Emperor Charley Lamar.

It was a bloody, evil, unhinged fantasy. But he nearly pulled it off.

He was a pioneer in the art of "inflaming the base." He committed a series of outrages, each designed to garner scathing headlines in the Yankee press, which Lamar would then declare "perjurious" and "false," to engorge his followers with a sense of their victimhood. In 1858, just before he hosted that slave auction at his racetrack, he relaunched the horrors of the Atlantic slave trade, kidnapping some six hundred Africans and carrying them to Georgia aboard his yacht *Wanderer* (only four hundred or so survived the journey). In 1859 he beat an opponent within an inch of his life before a crowd of stunned onlookers. Then challenged the editor of *The New York Times* to a duel. In 1860 he joined with other "Fire-Eaters" — the pro-slavery leaders of the South — to split the Democratic Party and bring about the election of a Republican president, knowing this would trigger secession. Lamar and the Fire-Eaters *engineered* the Civil War. They were proud to have done so. They did not, however, expect that England would abstain from supporting their Southern brethren and were astonished when Yankee farmers took up arms on behalf of "Lincoln's tyranny." Lamar was killed in perhaps the last engagement of the war, and the Fire-Eaters' cause seemed to be consumed by richly deserved hellflames — though now we see the monster is still breathing, still crawling among us.

A gripping, revelatory account of Lamar's wickedness is set forth in *The Wanderer: The Last American Slave Ship and the Conspiracy That Set Its Sails,* by Erik Calonius. That volume doesn't, however, cover the connection between Lamar and the racetrack — a great summary of which can be found in an article on the Southern Spaces website: "Unearthing the Weeping Time: Savannah's Ten Broeck Race Course and 1859 Slave Sale," by Kwesi DeGraft-Hanson, found here: https://southernspaces.org/2010/unearthing-weeping-time-savannahs-ten-broeck-race-course-and-1859-slave-sale/.

Chapter Two:
Flannery Knew. Flannery Got Out, What a Lucky Girl!

- My friend James Kitchens and his girlfriend Brenda Mehlhorn lived in and out of the camps for years, where I often visited them. James Kitchens called me late one night back in 2012 and asked me to come fetch him at the "Truman Marriott." A homeless man had murdered his girlfriend near the camp, and the police were making everyone pack up and flee with whatever they could carry. I picked up four folks and drove them over to a patch of woods on the Westside. At dawn, bulldozers erased that particular incarnation of the Truman encampment. Soon thereafter a new encampment was erected at the site. But this in turn was bulldozed after another murder in 2020. All the Savannah encampments are regularly destroyed by the police, yet always back they come. At last count there were thirty-nine active camps ringing the city, with thousands of residents. James and Brenda have both, recently, passed. But when they were with us, I recorded them telling some breathtakingly good one-minute

446

stories, which can be found here: thekingdomsofsavannah.com.

More on the Truman Marriott and other Savannah camps: https://www.wtoc.com/2021/03/11/i-think-its-going-get-worse-more-people-living-homeless-camps-savannah/.

- I've never visited the white supremacist camp but I've glimpsed it through the trees, near the ruins of the old mental hospital. According to legend, it's the one camp in Savannah that the police never molest. My friend Michael Chaney, who ministers to the homeless, tells me the camp is still active, at least at the time of this writing.

Chapter Three:
Mr. Kindness Opens the Door

- Sometime in the early 2000s my friend John Duncan, the eloquent and generous Savannah historian, gave me a monograph that he'd written in college. The subject was the various communities of "maroons" — people who had escaped slavery — that had existed in the swamps of South Carolina and Georgia before the Civil War. He mentioned a group of Black soldiers who had fought for the King of England during the Revolutionary War and had then refused, upon the British defeat, to return to slavery but instead built themselves a fortified village deep in the swamps of the Savannah River, where they lived peacefully for years with their families and others who had escaped slavery. This item roused my interest. At the Georgia Historical Society I found the report of the militia commander who had conquered and burned that redoubt. He was imprecise as to the exact location: "a few miles below Zubley's ferry . . . on the lower side of Bear Creek . . ." But I consulted with my brother, Bob, an archaeologist, and we pored over eighteenth-century maps and satellite photos until we found what we thought a likely site for the village. My friend Chad Faries lent his canoe. The three of us drove north and launched into Abercorn Creek from a boat ramp, assisted by a garrulous half-drunk redneck "fishing guide." We found our way to the island and went looking for the village. After a day tramping through the hot dense woods, and beating off mosquitoes and no-see-ums, we gave up. But I kept studying "the soldiers of the King." In the tomblike atmosphere of the Historical Society library, I found small jewels from the past. For example, the trial record of Lewis, one of the King's soldiers who'd been captured by the militia. He told a riveting story of the settlement, and of the betrayal of its leader, Sharper, and the battle that led to its downfall.

Once, years later, I was introduced to a charming gentleman who belonged, he said, to the family that owned that island. He said that unfortunately the place was "a real white elephant." Too hard to get easements to build upon. So it was just sitting out there, accruing back taxes. But lately, he said, he'd been approached by some crack developers who planned to turn it into a swank resort. Provided certain investments came through and the required permissions.

Another night, on the terrace of the Mansion bar, the scion of an old Savannah family told me a tale that had been passed down through generations: about a "secret island" on the river and some "escaped slaves" who'd built a "fort" there, and taken treasure off a sinking pirate ship, and buried the gold. So the legend went.

And the great historian Jane Landers discovered, while perusing the royal records of Spain, that in 1786 some Black refugees had made their way from Georgia to the Spanish fort at Saint Augustine, Florida. A man named Sharper and his wife, Nancy, and perhaps others. They petitioned the King of Spain for asylum. Their plea was granted, we know that much; then they vanish in the mist.

Timothy James Lockley's *Maroon Communities in South Carolina: A Documentary Record* brings together under one cover Lewis's trial record, the militia commander's report, newspaper accounts of the day, and letters describing the "menace" of the former "soldiers of the King." Jane Landers's *Black Society in Spanish Florida* also tells the full narrative, and adds Sharper and Nancy's petition for asylum.

• It should be emphasized that the explosion mentioned in this chapter, of the Chatham Sugar refinery, is fictional, and unrelated to an explosion that took place at the Imperial Sugar Company in 2008. The real explosion killed fourteen people with forty injured. In its aftermath, Imperial Sugar was sold off to a Dutch company. The refinery is back in operation now. The silos are clean as a whistle and the employees are all looking forward to a bright, sweet future.

- Herriat's story is fictional, stitched together from the narratives of several formerly enslaved people.

Chapter Five:
A Door Marked Nevermore, That Wasn't There Before

- "The bludgeoned brothers" was inspired by an incident that happened down the road from Savannah, in my old hometown of Brunswick, in 2009. Actually, Guy Heinze Jr., with a barrel of a shotgun, beat to death *eight* family members, including his father (eight struck me as an implausible and possibly wearying number, so I cut it back). Many theories have been bruited as to how he managed to kill so many. To me the likeliest is that he had the connivance of some of his victims along the way (during the trial it came out that this had never been a *happy* family). There used to be lots of great stories online about the case. They're disappearing. Here's one intriguing c at the time this tome is being printed: https://www.wtoc.com/story/11082463/brother-claims-accused-brunswick-murderer-is-innocent/.

ACKNOWLEDGMENTS

This strange chimera of a book, part history, part memory, and part dream, couldn't have been written without a host of friendly guides, far too many to list but here's a sampling:

Thanks to John Duncan, who generously lent me selections from his vast collection of Savannah lore, including the college paper where I first encountered the "soldiers of the King." Thanks to Jay Self, who arranged for my visit down to the otherworldly storm drains; to my cousin Alvin Neely for his perfect negronis and exquisite Turkish room; and to my cousin Harriet Speer for her deep Southern charm and hospitality.

Thanks to three denizens of the Truman Marriott: James Kitchens, Brenda Mehlhorn, and Six-Pack Billy, great raconteurs and dear friends, may they rest in peace.

Thanks to Connie Hartridge, who gave over several evenings to speak frankly about her ancestor Charley Lamar: we'll miss you, Connie.

Thanks to the eminent historian Jane Landers; to Dan Sayers, anthropologist/ historian of the Great Dismal Swamp in North Carolina; and to Dr. Paul Pressly of Savannah: all gave their time to help me understand the story of the King's soldiers within the broader context of Black resistance communities from 1600 to 1865.

Thanks to the incomparable poet Aberjhani, and to Ariel Felton and Vaughnette Goode-Walker, who told me of the mounting pushback to Savannah's ghost tourism.

Thanks to Bill Dawers, Savannah reporter and blogger, the prime source of everything Savannah.

Thanks to the Reverend Michael Chaney, who let me accompany him as he ministered to the city's encampments of unhoused people. Thanks to Caro Powell and Mimi Cay, who showed me Turners Rock. To Chad Faries, who first ferried me by canoe to Abercorn Island.

Thanks to Superior Court Justice of the Eastern District Louisa Abbot: if I've veered here from Chatham courtroom decorum, it's not your fault.

Thanks to Ginger Duncan and Joni Saxon-Giusti, who helped with all the local details. To Sheri Holman, Judy Stone, and Ursula Mackenzie, close readers and superb drinking companions.

Thanks to Alexandra Trujillo de Taylor, aka the Duchess of State, the essential Savannah hostess (no visit to our city would be complete without a stop at her superb shop, Chocolat by Adam Turoni). To Daniel Taylor, who led me through legal labyrinths of sugar-refining culpability. To Christine Turoni, ER nurse. To Tom Kohler and Clinton Edminster, who tried to enlighten me on the byzantine politics of Southern Georgia zoning. Thanks to my friend Lisa Fort and to Linette Dubois and her two train-loving boys.

Thanks to my incomparably savvy agent of thirty years, Molly Friedrich, and her smart and encouraging colleague Lucy Carson; to Marin Takikawa and Hannah Brattesani for their graciousness; and to my West Coast agent and longtime friend, Matthew Snyder. To Daniel Dirkin, for his loving creation of the map, to the map designers Jessica Anne Schwartz and Raymond Paquin, and to Syrie Moskowitz for her photographs.

Thanks to Randi Kramer; to Morgan Mitchell, the production editor who kept all the trains running and on the track; and to the whole Celadon team, who have supported the book with such constant, nurturing care and enthusiasm.

And thanks to the best editor a writer could dream of, Jamie Rabb: sharp-eyed, penetrating, somehow both down-to-earth and inspiring at the same time, the most patient wrangler of this slow and stubborn mule.

ABOUT THE AUTHOR

George Dawes Green, founder of The Moth, is an internationally celebrated author. His first novel, *The Caveman's Valentine,* won an Edgar Award and became a motion picture starring Samuel L. Jackson. *The Juror* was a *New York Times* bestseller, an international bestseller in more than twenty languages, and the basis for the movie starring Demi Moore and Alec Baldwin. *Ravens* was chosen as one of the best books of 2009 by the *Los Angeles Times, The Wall Street Journal,* London's *Daily Mail,* and many other publications. Green grew up in Georgia and now lives in Brooklyn, New York.

The employees of Thorndike Press hope you have enjoyed this Large Print book. All our Thorndike, Wheeler, and Kennebec Large Print titles are designed for easy reading, and all our books are made to last. Other Thorndike Press Large Print books are available at your library, through selected bookstores, or directly from us.

For information about titles, please call:
(800) 223-1244

or visit our website at:
gale.com/thorndike

To share your comments, please write:
Publisher
Thorndike Press
10 Water St., Suite 310
Waterville, ME 04901